BLOOD SISTERS

Also by Jane Corry

My Husband's Wife

BLOOD SISTERS

A Novel

Jane Corry

PAMELA DORMAN BOOKS
VIKING

VIKING

An imprint of Penguin Random House LLC
375 Hudson Street
New York, New York 10014
penguin.com

A Pamela Dorman Book/Viking

First published in Great Britain by Penguin Books, an imprint of
Penguin Random House UK

ISBN 9780525522188
Ebook ISBN 9780525522195

Printed in the United States of America
1   3   5   7   9   10   8   6   4   2

Set in Bell MT Std
Designed by Cassandra Garruzzo

To my warm, funny husband. Every day is different.
Also to my amazing children—as well as Millie and George,
who have changed our lives.

Acknowledgments

I used to think that if you were lucky enough to get a book accepted, it was a simple matter of it being published and then (hopefully) sold. Now I know differently. The whole process is like an intriguing plot: lots of layers that work together to form a whole. I'd therefore like to thank everyone below for playing their part in the evolution of the US edition of *Blood Sisters*:

My legendary editor, Pamela Dorman, and her assistant Jeramie Orton, whose skills have helped me adapt the text for the American market and who have also put their own special stamp on the book. I was particularly thrilled to meet Pam in person when she paid a trip to London recently.

My resourceful U.S. publicity team who have spread the word about *Blood Sisters*. As a journalist, I love talking on radio and television and really enjoy writing features about my characters and plot.

The wonderful UK Penguin team including my editor, Katy Loftus; my agent, Kate Hordern; the UK publicity department; and the sales team who sold the rights to the US.

All those prison staff who gave me advice. None of my fictional prisons is based on a real HMP, although I did work in one for three years as writer in residence.

Richard Gibbs and all the other lawyers who helped with my research. Although I have tried to be as accurate as possible, some deviations from standard court procedure have been made to preserve the plot.

Patients and staff from the many head-injury centers I visited. At times, the kind, caring professionalism reduced me to tears.

Our friends David and Jane—wonderful parents and carers—who introduced me to the wonders of the "talking machines." Although such machines exist, and are constantly being developed and improved, I have taken certain liberties with their descriptions here.

All the wonderful bloggers and Tweeters who have championed *Blood Sisters*.

My loyal readers, without whom I would not be writing this.

My friends, old and new. How lucky I am.

My family, who are my lifeblood.

Sisters everywhere. Including my own.

BLOOD SISTERS

Squeaky-clean school shoes.
Shoulder bags bobbing.
Blond plaits flapping.
Two pairs of feet. One slightly larger.
"Come on. We're going to be late."
Nearly there. Almost safe.
Pavement edge.
Another pair of feet.
No!
A scream.
Silence.
Blood seeping on the ground.
Spreading and spreading.

Part One

News just in. A murder is reported to have taken place at an open prison on the outskirts of London. No further details are available at present, but we will be bringing you an update as soon as possible. Meanwhile on Radio 2, here is the new song from Great Cynics . . .

1

September 2016

Alison

Careful. It's not the size that counts. It's the sharpness. And the angle. The blade must sing. Not scratch.

I hold the piece of blue glass up to the window light. It's the same color as the type you occasionally see in bottles lining the shelves of old-fashioned pharmacies. A nice clean cut. No sharp bits that need trimming, which is always tricky. So easy to get splinters of glass in your skin or on your clothes.

Or in your mind.

Now for the acid test. Does the glass fit the lead outline? My heart always starts to beat wildly at this stage, as though it's a matter of life or death. Silly, really, but that's how it feels. After getting this far, you don't want to get it wrong.

"Would you mind helping me with this, Mrs. Baker?"

"Actually, it's miss," I say, looking up from my demo piece. "And please, call me Alison."

A new student stands in front of me. He's substantial without being chunky—six foot one and a half, at a guess, and three inches or so taller than me.

As a child, I was teased mercilessly for being the tallest in the class. I did my best to shrink, but it didn't work. "Stand up straight," my mother would plead. She meant well, but all I wanted to do was blend in; not to be noticed—to hide my slightly overlarge nose, my thick-framed mud brown glasses and my braces. My perfectly put-together sister, on the other hand, had that gift of innate confidence that made her naturally poised.

Nowadays, I've learned there are some advantages to my height. You can carry off clothes that others can't, or put on a pound or two without it showing. Yet, every time I pass my reflection in a mirror or shop window, I am reminded to push back those offending shoulders.

"Alison?" I am jolted back to the present.

The man asking the question is—at a guess—in his early to mid-thirties like me. The more the years go by, the less I want to give out an exact figure. It makes me panic about the things I thought I'd have done by now and that somehow haven't happened.

In fact, this is the one place where maturity doesn't matter. It's the steadiness of the hand that counts. Making stained glass windows might seem like an innocuous craft, but accidents happen.

"I can't quite remember, Alison, what you said about stretching the lead."

The man's voice is deep as it slices through my thoughts. Not many men sign up for these weekly courses I run at the local college. When this particular student arrived at the first session last week, I felt an instant fluttering of unease.

It's not just the way he keeps staring. Or his intelligent questions. Or the confident manner in which he scores his glass, even though it's a beginners' class. Or his name—Clive Black, which has an authoritative abruptness. Nor is it even the way he said "Alison" just now, as though he found it intriguing rather than everyday.

It's all of these things. And something else, too, that I can't put a finger on. Over the years, I've learned to trust my instinct. And it's telling me, right now, to watch out.

Wearing my protective gloves, I pick up a thin, slightly twisted piece of lead, about a foot long. It always reminds me of a strand of silver licorice, the type my sister and I used to buy from the corner shop on the way back from school.

Swiftly, I hand Clive a pair of pliers. "Take one piece—the flat edge of the pliers needs to be on top—and pull. I'll do the same at the other end. Lean forward. That's right."

"Amazing how it doubles in length!" he says in awe.

"Incredible, isn't it?" breathes someone else as the class gathers round. I love this bit. Excitement is catching.

I pick up a different trimming knife. The funny thing is that I've been clumsy ever since childhood, yet this is the one area where I never falter.

"Next, we'll wiggle the blade from side to side and then push down," I say. "Anyone want to try?"

I address my question deliberately to a horsey-faced woman who has been in several of my courses. Once, she even offered to leave a positive review on my Facebook page and was distinctly disappointed when I confessed to not having one. "Don't you need it to publicize your work?" she'd asked incredulously.

I'd shrugged casually in an attempt to hide the real reason. "I manage without it."

Class is ending now, but the man with the deep voice—Clive—is still lurking.

In my experience, there's always a *May I ask a final question?* student who doesn't want to go. But this one is unnerving me.

"I was just wondering," he says. Then he stops for a minute, his eyes darting to the blank space on my wedding ring finger. "Are you hungry, by any chance?"

He laughs casually, as if aware he is being slightly too forward on the strength of a short acquaintance in which I am the teacher and he is the pupil. "I don't know about you," he adds, "but I didn't have time to eat anything after work before coming here."

His hand reaches into his pocket as he talks. Sweat breaks out round my neck. Then he brings out a watch and glances at it. The face appears to have a Disney cartoon on it. I'm both relieved and intrigued. But not enough to accept his invitation.

"Thanks," I say lightly, "but I'm expected back at home."

He looks disappointed. "OK. I understand."

Turning round, I tidy up the spare glass offcuts, putting one of them away for later.

On paper, Clive seems like someone my mother would approve of. Nice manners. Seemingly educated. A man of means, judging from his well-cut jacket. A good head of light brown hair, flicked back off a wide forehead.

"Maybe you're being too choosy," my mother is always saying, albeit kindly. "Sometimes, you have to take a risk in life, darling. Mr. Right can come in all shapes and forms."

Was this how she'd felt about marrying my father? I'm stung by that familiar pang of loss. If only he was still here.

Clive has gone now. All I want to do is go back to my flat in Elephant and Castle, put on some Ella Fitzgerald, knock up a tinned tuna salad, take a hot shower to wash out the day, then curl up on the sofa with a good book and try to forget that the rent is due next week.

I wash my hands carefully in the corner sink. Then, slipping on my fluffy blue mohair thrift store cardigan, I make my way downstairs, pausing at reception to hand in the classroom key. "How's it going?" asks the woman at the desk.

I put on my cheerful face. "Great, thanks. You?"

She shrugs. "Fine. I've got to rearrange the noticeboard. Someone's just dropped this off. Not sure that anyone will be interested. What do you think?"

I read the poster.

WANTED: ARTIST IN RESIDENCE FOR HMP ARCHVILLE (A MEN'S OPEN PRISON). ONE HOUR FROM CENTRAL LONDON. THREE DAYS A WEEK. TRAVEL EXPENSES PAID. COMPETITIVE REMUNERATION.
APPLICATIONS TO archville@hmps.gsi.gov.uk

My skin breaks out into goose bumps.

"You wouldn't catch me in one of those places," sniffs the receptionist. Her words bring me back to myself, and I fumble for a pen.

"You're not really interested, are you, Alison?"

I continue writing down the e-mail address. "Maybe."

"Rather you than me."

The pros and cons whirl round in my head as I make my way out into the street. Steady income. Travel costs. Enough to stop me worrying over my bank balance every month. But I've never been inside a prison before, and the thought terrifies me. My mouth is dry. My heart is thumping. I wish I'd never seen the ad.

I pass a park with teenagers smoking on the swings. One is laughing, head tossed back in a happy, carefree laugh. Just like my sister's. For her, life was a ball. Me? I was the serious one. Earnest. Even before the accident, I remember a certain mysterious heaviness in my chest. I always wanted to make things right. To do the best I could in life. The word "conscientious" featured on every one of my school reports.

But there are some things you can't make right.

"It wasn't your fault," my mother had said, time and time again. Yet, when I replay it in my mind, I keep thinking of things I could have done. And now it's too late.

I'm walking briskly through an evening market. Silk scarves flutter in the breeze. Turquoise. Pink. Primrose yellow. On the next stall, overripe tomatoes are going for 50p a bag. "You won't get cheaper, love," says the stallholder, who is wearing black fingerless gloves. I ignore him and take a left then a right. I go down a road of identical Victorian terraces with overflowing wheelie bins and beer bottles in the streets. Some homes here have curtains, while others have boarded-up windows. Mine has shutters.

There are three name stickers by three bells: my landlord's, the other tenant's and a blank—mine. I reach for my key and move into the main hall where the post is left. Nothing for me. The second key lets me into my ground-floor one-bedroom apartment. I'd have liked a room on the second floor, as it would have felt safer, but I couldn't find one at the time, and I was desperate. Now I am used to it, although I always make sure the windows are locked before I leave the house.

Shutting the door, I kick off my shoes and chuck my bag onto the secondhand beige Ikea sofa.

The yearning starts inside me. Hurry. Fast. My hands dive down for the sliver of blue in my jacket pocket like an alcoholic might reach for the bottle. To think that something so small can do such damage!

Today it's the turn of my right wrist. Far enough from the artery, but deeper than yesterday's. I gasp as the jagged edge scores my skin, and a dark thrill flashes through me followed by the pain. I need both.

But it's no good. It doesn't hurt enough. Never does.

For it's the cuts we hide inside that really do the damage. They rub and they niggle and they bruise and they bleed. And as the pain and anxiety grow in your head, they become far more dangerous than a visible open wound. Until eventually, you have to do something.

And now that time has come.

2

September 2016

Kitty

"Knit one, purl one," sang Oh Tee. "Knit one, purl one."

Knit? Purl? Who was she kidding? thought Kitty. Their stitches—Oh Tee's included—were sliding all over the place. Twisted up in woolen knots. Off the needles entirely. Or even lying on the ground in a pool of urine, courtesy of Dawn In the Room Next Door who had been incontinent and "never the same in the head" since her pushchair had collided with a lorry some thirty years earlier.

"Knit one! Purl one!"

Oh Tee's chant was getting louder.

"You're going too fast!" Kitty wanted to scream. "My good hand can't keep up."

Sometimes, the other hand thought it could work, too, but it never did. This was upsetting if she wanted to do something. But not if she didn't—like now. Occupational therapy—or Oh Tee, as the teacher gaily called it—was so boring. It wasn't just the knitting. It was the tying of the shoelaces. Left over right and right over left, or was it the other way round? So hard to remember!

Kitty was pretty sure that she used to be able to do her shoelaces herself. But when she tried to pin down her memory, it kept breaking up into tiny bits, like specks of colored dust in the sunlight.

"Recall can be affected after damage like hers." That's what she'd overheard a doctor saying to Friday Mum. "So she may not have any long-term memories."

Education classes were meant to help. She was pretending to learn her alphabet again, although she already knew it. In fact, it was good fun to give the letters new meanings. *M* was for the memory she'd bloody well gone and "lost." "Look in the wardrobe," Kitty sometimes joked. "Maybe it's there." But no one laughed, because they couldn't understand the noises that came out of her mouth. If only she could speak clearly out loud! *A* was for the accident she'd had. "What kind of accident?" she would ask the staff over and over again.

But no one ever told her. "Poor Kitty," they would say instead. "All she can do is babble."

If only they knew what was going on in her head!

J was for James. That was her surname. Or, at least, that's what it said on her bedroom door along with the list of tablets she had to be given every day. *F* was for frontal and *L* was for lobes. Kitty knew what frontal lobes were from the conversation the doctor had had with Friday Mum. They were the "part of the brain that's responsible for co-ordination and mood swings and a great deal more."

She didn't have a speech impediment, the doctor had explained to Friday Mum, as if Kitty wasn't there. Her brain just wouldn't translate her thoughts into words. "Some brain injuries make patients swear, even if they weren't habitual swearers before. Of course, as Kitty doesn't talk, it's hard for us to know exactly what's going on in her mind."

Oh Tee's voice rang out. "Put your needles away now, everyone."

The carers started tucking in wheelchair blankets and making clucking noises as though they were a brood of bloody hens. "Some of us," Kitty wanted to scream, "used to be like you once."

Not everyone, of course. Duncan with the plain round glasses had been born deprived of oxygen during birth. He could speak after a fashion but was "mentally unpredictable." Hospital notes "gone missing." Usual story. They heard it all here. Except the most important story. Like what had happened to *her.*

"Ready for lunch now, Kitty?" said the girl bending over her. She had a straight blond fringe that swung when she spoke. Her name was Barbara. Kitty kept trying it out in her head. *Bar-ber-er.*

"What are you pointing to on your picture board? Shoes? They're pretty."

They were, too. In fact, those red high heels stirred a memory at the back of her head. So much nicer than these ugly black lace-ups she had to wear now.

"What else do you like on your board, Kitty?"

Hair! That's what she would like. Blond hair like hers. Not her own dark curls.

"Ouch, Kitty. You're hurting me."

"I'll help," said one of the carers. "She's got a strong grip, that one. Let go of poor Barbara's fringe."

Kitty felt the fingers on her good hand being prized off, one by one. That was another thing about her brain. It could be happy one minute. Sad the next. Bad. Then good. Maybe she shouldn't have grabbed that girl's fringe like that. She was from the local sixth form college and wanted to be a social worker, so she was doing "voluntary work here, once a week."

Voluntary work. Fancy! She wouldn't mind doing something like that if she ever got better. In your bloody dreams, Kitty told herself.

How she loved those dreams! In them, she could skip, ride a bike, do those bloody laces up. Sometimes, she could actually sing, although she hadn't had the singing dream for a while now.

"I'm sure she's trying to tell me something."

"I used to think that when I started," said the other carer. "It's natural. But you can't always fix people. Not the ones in here. Sad, I know. Just life, I suppose. Now let's get a move on, shall we? It's fish cakes today."

"Come along now." Straight Fringe Barbara was steering the chair in a rather haphazard fashion down the corridor towards the canteen.

"Be careful," Kitty told her. "And buck up or we'll get small portions. They always do that when you're late."

"I don't know what you're saying, but it sounds like you know what you're talking about, Kitty. And that's something, isn't it?"

Nearly there now! No thanks to Straight Fringe, here, who clearly hadn't passed her wheelchair-driving test. Sometimes, it was fun to make little jokes like that even though no one else could hear them.

"Morning, Kitty!"

Now what? The supervisor was standing at the door of the canteen. Bossy Supervisor, Kitty called her. Do this. Do that.

"You look nice today, don't you?"

This old thing? Kitty glanced down at her blue jeans with an elastic waist and baggy red sweatshirt that the carer had dressed her in that morning. She shared some of her clothes with Dawn, who was also a size 18. How she hated wearing Dawn's stuff! They always smelled of pee, no matter how often they were washed. "Guess what, Kitty. I've got a surprise for you."

"I don't want any bloody surprise. I want my fish cake."

"You have a visitor!"

No way. Friday Mum came on Fridays. Today was Tuesday. *T* for Tuesday. They'd done that in Word Play this morning before the knitting. "Wouldn't you like to see who it is." Bossy Supervisor didn't add a question mark to her sentence. It was an order. "Bring her this way, would you?" The last remark was addressed to Barbara.

The first thing Kitty saw of her visitor was a pair of brown shoes. They had little holes in them, like a pattern. When you had to sit all the time, you always saw the low things first. Then you went upwards. Grey trousers. Pink and white shirt. Navy blue jacket. Silver buttons. Round, flabby face. A mouth that smiled. Eyes that didn't.

"Hello, Kitty. I'm sorry it's been so long. But you do remember me, don't you?"

Him? It was *him*? Kitty's good arm began to beat on the side of the chair. Her head knocked forward on her chest. She could taste froth on her lips.

Suddenly, the chair swiveled round and they were speeding out of the office along the corridor. Straight Fringe was helping her escape!

Just for a minute, Kitty could pretend she was running. Or riding a horse. Or jumping a wall. All these images flashed across her mind, one after the other as if she was trying them out for size.

And then they stopped. There was a loud noise. Just like the time when . . .

No. The memory had gone.

3

September 2016

Alison

———

"So, why do you want to work in a prison?" asks the man with metallic glasses. He's lean and thin with rodent-like features, a skeptical look about his face and black eyebrows that rise and fall as he speaks. Seems a bit small and wiry for a prison governor to me, but then again, he's the first one I've met.

Why *do* I want to work in a prison? Simple: I don't. This place terrifies me. Has done from the minute I stopped the car at the security gates this morning to give my name and purpose. "Alison Baker. Interview with the governor."

But, of course, I can't tell my interviewer the truth. "I feel I can contribute something," I hear myself say.

The right eyebrow rises, leaving the left behind. The effect is so disconcerting that I almost miss what he says next. "So do most artists. But why, Miss Baker, should we pick *you* instead of the many other applicants whom we are seeing this week?"

Why, indeed? Because, if it hadn't been for my art, I might have died, too, after the accident. Before that sunny summer morning, I had been what my teachers called "an academic." I could have done anything I wanted—or so they said. Alison, the bright sister. Good at maths and English, almost fluent in French. A natural scientist.

Art had always been my sister's forte. The subject for those who weren't so capable at traditional subjects. A waste of time for academics like me—at least, that's how my school had seen it when I'd declared my intention to go to art school instead of university to study history.

My mind goes back to the weeks after the accident and the funeral when my mother and I had to sort out my sister's things. On impulse, I'd opened her paint box and taken out the tube marked TURQUOISE. Her favorite color. My hand had picked up her paintbrush. It seemed to flow naturally across the page, as though she were guiding it. "I didn't realize you could paint, too," Mum had whispered. Neither had I.

But this was my secret. Not something I could share with a stranger. And certainly not a prison governor.

"I've had experience in various unusual artistic mediums," I say instead. "Like stained glass."

"We have to avoid dangerous materials." This comment comes from the other man in the room. One of the prison psychologists, according to his introduction. I only hope he can't read my mind. "I have to emphasize that many of our offenders have had severe mental problems. Some are psychopathic, although their behavior is under control with medication. None are considered to be high-risk any longer, which is why they are in an open prison. But we still have to be careful. Workshops using glass would be out of the question."

"I am also a specialist in watercolors," I continue. My hands are beginning to sweat. The walls are closing in on me. Did that man—whose name I can hardly bear to say out loud—feel that way when they first took him in? I hope so.

"Can you do portraits?"

"Yes," I say, without adding that, actually, I don't care for them. You have to get into someone's soul to make it really work. And I definitely don't want to go there.

"From a therapeutic point of view, we believe that portraits can help people take another look at themselves," the psychologist says in a gentler voice. "It's one of the reasons we want an artist in residence here."

I *had* wondered. Why should someone who's committed a crime be treated to art lessons? Surely, prisoners ought to do something deeply unpleasant while serving time.

Perhaps the governor can see the doubt on my face. "Increasing self-confidence can lower the risk of reoffending." His words carry a challenging edge, as if defending the strategy.

"I can understand that." My voice doesn't sound as though it's lying. But then again, I've had practice.

"Would you like to ask any questions, Miss Baker?"

I clear my throat nervously. "Would I hold my art sessions in the huts outside?"

"Only in the Education section. The other cabins are for admin. And some are where the men live."

"But they're locked up. Right?"

"At night." This is the psychologist again. "Prisoners are free to wander outside in the grounds during the day to go to class or work, providing they don't go out of the gates without permission. This is an open prison, as the advert said. They're often known as cells without bars. Many of our men go out to work during the day in the prison van and return by six p.m. It prepares them for life in the real world when they are released."

Sounds mad to me. "What kind of jobs do they do?"

The governor appears used to this question. "Whatever we can find them. Not everyone, as you can imagine, is keen on employing some-one who is still in prison. Charity shops can be quite flexible. Fast-food outlets, too. Local colleges sometimes allow day-release students, pro-vided they pass the risk requirements."

"How can you be certain they'll come back? Don't they try to run away?"

"That's exactly the point. It's a matter of trust. If one of our men absconds, he will be moved to a more secure prison when he is found."

When, I note. Not *if*.

I think of the brief research I've done on the Internet. "But if they're in an open prison, they're not dangerous. Right?"

His voice sounds distinctly hedgy. "Category D signifies a low risk. In other words, our prisoners here aren't considered to be a threat to society anymore. But many have committed serious crimes in the past. This is their last stopping post until release. Unless, of course, they commit another offense inside."

That's it. I want to leave. And I can tell that these men don't want me either. Not the psychologist with the deceptively gentle voice, and definitely not the governor, whose last little speech seems intended to put me off.

They need someone who is used to being in a prison. Someone who looks tough on the outside—not a skinny, round-shouldered blonde with a portfolio under her arm that she nearly keeps dropping from nerves.

I can't help thinking that my sister, with her confidence and take-charge attitude, would have been more suited for the job. What would she have made of all this? *Get out*, I can almost hear her say. *Before it's too late.*

My interviewers are rising to their feet now. "Would you like to look round, Miss Baker?"

No. I want to go home, back to the safety of my flat, and get myself ready for the class I'm running this evening at the college for people who haven't broken the law. Yet it seems as though the question is rhetorical. The door is already being opened for me and I am being led down the corridor past a man in Day-Glo orange.

"Morning, Governor."

"Morning, Mr. Evans."

Mister? But, judging from his clothes, he's a prisoner. The psychologist notices my surprise. "We believe in civility here. Staff usually address inmates in a formal manner. Bad behavior is not tolerated. Anyone breaking the rules is shipped out."

"What do you mean 'shipped out'?" I ask unsteadily. I have a vision of a small boat bobbing on the waves.

"Moved to another prison."

We're outside now: the autumn sun is making me squint. As we walk past the huts, I notice a tub of flowers outside the one nearest to me. Through the window, I spot a line of shirts hanging from the curtain rail. It seems almost homely. There's birdseed scattered on a windowsill. A kitten saunters by.

"Feral," says the governor, marking my surprise. "Started with one litter, which led to another. The men feed them." He gives me a sideways glance. "You'd be surprised at how even the most hardened criminal can be as soft as butter when it comes to animals."

We're stopping outside a cabin that appears more modern than the others. Less run-down, although the metallic steps leading up are wobbly. "This is the Education building. The successful applicant will have a studio here."

He unlocks the door. My first impression is of a sparsely furnished central room with doors leading off it. Each one is labeled: SUPPORT. READING SKILLS. MATHEMATICS. A man in a green jogging suit is sitting in a chair, bent over a book, shielding it as though he doesn't want anyone else to see.

"Morning, Mr. Jones." He emphasizes the *Mister* as if being sarcastic.

"Morning, Governor."

"Would you like to tell our visitor what you are reading?" His voice is stern.

Reluctantly, the man holds it out. White paint has been smeared over the text. Covering the pages are pencil sketches of people. A man sitting on the ground. A woman pegging out washing. A child playing on the swing.

"Are these your drawings?" I ask, intrigued.

He nods.

"This book has a library stamp in the front." The governor is looking severe. "Were you responsible for damaging it like this?"

"The librarian give it to me to use."

"Are you sure of that?"

The man's stubbly chin trembles. "Yes."

I suspect he is lying. And I'm sure the governor does, too. But these sketches are good.

"Have you always drawn?" I ask.

"No, miss. Not till I got here. But my cellmate gets on my nerves. Always talking, he is. So I started doing something to shut him out of my head."

How I know that feeling! That burning, urgent need to get away from the world. To create another where you can find peace, if only for a short time. And suddenly, I want this job. I want it very much. Because not only will it help me make things right, it might also enable me to help others.

"Thank you for your time, Miss Baker." The governor is shaking my hand on the way out. "We'll be in touch."

By the following Tuesday, I know I haven't got it. Monday, they had said. That's when they were making a final decision. I tell myself that it's just as well. Prison? Crazy idea. I stupidly crack a piece of blue glass while I am cutting it because I keep thinking about the man who was sketching his family—I just know those were his kids—and hoping he didn't get into trouble for abusing a library book. An artist needs materials. It's a basic need. Like breathing.

On Thursday morning, I am about to leave for my college watercolor class when I spot two brown envelopes on the wobbly table in the little communal hall. Both are addressed to me. One is my credit card statement. And the other has HMP stamped on the front. The first will show I am over my limit. So I start with the second.

"You've taken a job in a prison?" shrills my mother when I make my usual evening phone call. She gets nervous when I don't. Loss does that—makes you fear for your loved ones. Of course, I want to reassure her. Her voice comforts me, too. I love my mother so much that it hurts, but sometimes, it's hard to think of something new to say. Yet tonight is different.

"How can you even consider it?" she continues.

"I need the money, Mum."

"Then I'll lend it to you."

I want to hug her. "That's really kind, but you know you can't afford it."

She can't argue with that.

"But is it dangerous?"

"No. It's an open prison, where men are either nearing the end of their sentences or have committed a 'minor' crime such as stealing or petty theft. Nothing to worry about."

"Even so . . ." My mother is shaking her head now. I can picture it: she'll be sitting in her wicker conservatory chair, overlooking the garden that dips down to the sea. Later, my mother might take a walk down to the beach, making her way over the shingle and pausing every now and then to pick up a shell. Then she'll wander back and leave her offerings in the churchyard by a stone that no longer looks new. It's always the same. Rhythm is what keeps some people going.

Now I'm about to smash mine into a million little pieces.

4

September 2016

Kitty

Kitty was still bruised and shaken from the events of the day before. At least, she thought it was the day before. Her mind could be so unreliable when it came to timing.

Not that the date was important. It was what had happened that mattered. Flabby Face's visit. All Kitty knew was that he had done something that had really upset her in the past. She'd had to get away. But just as she thought she'd escaped, her wheelchair had gone out of control. "Hang on," Straight Fringe had yelled, but they'd run smack into the wall, and for a moment everything had gone fuzzy.

While Kitty was being checked by the doctor for injuries, she had listened to Bossy Supervisor in the corridor outside.

"Barbara! What on earth's going on?" she demanded.

"I was rescuing her! That man in the office quite clearly scared her."

"How do you know? She can't speak."

"It was obvious. And if you ask me, Kitty seems to understand more than we give her credit for. Otherwise, why would she have been so upset?"

"You had no right to take off like that with Kitty. We operate a calm environment here, based on routine and pattern. It makes our residents feel secure. And above all, safety has to be paramount. If you really want to work in the care industry, you need to remember that."

"I'm sorry."

"I'm afraid I'm going to have to be in touch with your sixth form head."

"*Please* give me one more chance. I need to do this for my university application."

At that point the doctor wheeled Kitty back out into the corridor. Just in time. "Don't send her away. I like her. Let her stay. She knows what I'm thinking, and her hair is pretty." Kitty's voice was loud and clear in her head. But the words were coming out differently—all jumbled up and falling over one another in their confusion.

"Come on, Kitty," said Cheery Carer. "Let's get you a nice cup of tea. What color straw shall we have tonight? Your favorite? Pink?"

Kitty shook her head. "Want Barbara to stay," she said. The girl reminded her of someone. She just couldn't remember who.

"I'm not quite sure what you mean, dear."

Don't "dear" me. Kitty began to bang the side of the chair with her good hand to make the point. "I need someone to protect me from the man with the round, flabby face and the mouth that pretended to smile."

"She's getting really worked up now." Bossy Supervisor was rooting round the medical trolley. "Time for a sedative, I think."

No!

"Hold her still," instructed Bossy Supervisor, "while I get the needle in her, can you?"

Kitty began rocking her chair back and forth.

"She'll hurt herself if she keeps doing that."

"Kitty." The soft voice was coming from Barbara, who was kneeling beside her. "Listen to this!"

The girl was taking something small and silver out of her pocket and breathing into it. The most incredible sound was coming out.

"It's a harmonica, Kitty. Do you like it?"

"She's stopped thrashing," whispered Cheery Carer. "Well done."

"Wow," said Barbara. "She's humming. Listen."

It was true. Kitty had never heard herself hum before. But when she had woken up the next morning, she'd tried it again. Now she was humming all the time. It made her body feel lighter. Happier.

But there was one thing that still troubled her: who *was* that visitor with the holey shoes? And how could you hate someone if you didn't know who they were?

5

October 2016

Alison

─────────

What do you wear on your first day to prison? Jeans? Too casual. Black trousers. Seems safe. White T-shirt?

I slip on the top. You can just barely see the outline of my bra through the fabric. This wouldn't have worried me before, but now I'm nervous. As Mum had warned me on the phone last night, I need to remember that I'm going into a prison where men have been deprived of "physical relations" for some time. "Please be careful, won't you, darling?"

Black jumper, then? Too funereal with the trousers. Maybe cream instead. A proper linen handkerchief—as an artist you never know when you might need one. And, of course, my locket. Complete with safety chain.

That's mine, says my sister's voice in my head.

I glance at the mirror. A nervous me looks back. It reminds me of the teenager I used to be. Yet my facial features bear little similarity. I no longer wear glasses: I've gotten used to my contact lenses now. My hair is fashionably spiky instead of the curtain that I used to tuck behind my ear. The nose, of course, is changed, although I don't want to think too much about that or it will bring back the memories. And I've learned to wear makeup properly thanks to a free lesson in a department store where I felt horribly exposed and rather stupid. Yet the results were worth it. "Incredible!" the girl had said, as though she had just performed a miracle.

Right now, though, my hand shakes as I apply my kohl pencil. Blast. It slips through my fingers. I wipe the smudge off the carpet before applying a touch of lip gloss. No point in making myself stand out. But at the same time, I need strength. Self-belief.

Dab of lavender behind my ear. Mum gives me a bottle every Christmas. She wore it, and so did my grandmother before her. It's a smell that takes me back to a holiday in Norfolk when Dad was still alive. Before the leukemia got him. I was only three. My memories are scant but, like many people, I find that odd ones stand out—like a big, warm hand holding mine and his voice urging me to look at the rows of pretty purple-headed flowers in the fields before us.

How I wish I knew more about him! But it upsets my mother too much to talk of him. It's why she doesn't have any photographs. Maybe if my grandparents were still alive, I would have been told more, but they all died before I was born. Death comes early, it seems, to our family. But at least I have some memories. Like the lavender.

It suddenly strikes me that it might not be sensible to smell nice when I'm going to be mixing with sex-deprived criminals. But the action had been automatic. It's what I do every morning. Too late now.

Besides, there isn't anything about it in the guidelines the prison has sent me. Nor, surprisingly, is there any advice on clothes. Instead, I am told to:

Bring identification (passport or driving license).

I take this out from my bedside nightstand, trying to ignore the lawyer's letter that nestles beside it.

Leave your mobile phone at home or in the car.
Do not have anything dangerous about your person (e.g., sharp implements).

Do not possess any illegal substances.

Do not possess alcohol.

Do not attempt to bring in anything that could be used as a bribe.

I lock my door, double-checking it, like I always do. There's only one other lodger in this house, a very quiet young accountant on the floor above, and our landlord, who keeps himself to himself. Just the way I like it.

Soon, I'm out of London, and the traffic is getting lighter. I'm passing through a small town. There are children waiting at the bus stop, wearing brown and yellow school uniforms. I slow down to twenty miles an hour, watching them carefully until I'm safely past, yet I can't help glancing in the rearview mirror to check they are all right. The children are pointing to my car. The 1972 Beetle—which my stepfather, David, gave me years ago—often attracts attention. It occurs to me that it might do the same at the prison. What if one of the prisoners takes note of my registration and somehow tracks me down? It would make sense to go by public transport, especially as this month I need new tires for my car. Yet the prison is miles from the nearest station or bus stop. A cold feeling crawls through my stomach as it begins to rain.

A small road sign—HMP ARCHVILLE—directs me left.

I turn, and the huts pop up before me. It feels so different from when I came for my interview. That was an exploration, a testing of the waters.

But now I am here. For good. Well, for three days a week over the next year. I feel claustrophobic already, and I'm not even inside.

I'm directed to the staff car park. Not the one for visitors. My throat starts to tighten. What if I hate it? What if I can't cope? Will they let me break my contract and allow me to leave? My heart is pounding in time with the rain, which is now falling more forcefully. I take my umbrella out of the boot along with a box of paints, brushes and paper.

"Can I help you carry that, miss?"

It's a young man with longish hair and stained teeth.

"Thanks." Not wanting to sound unfriendly, I add, "Have you worked here long?"

He grins. "I'm a prisoner."

Only then do I notice the orange under the black anorak.

Students are always offering to help me carry stuff at college. But this is a criminal. What if he tries to hurt me? Mum was right. I should have turned down the job, after being daft enough to apply in the first place.

"Actually, I can manage myself."

"Sure?"

I know I've offended him. But I can't help it. I don't know the rules. What if it's an offense to let him carry my things? Struggling, I follow the RECEPTION sign. There's a woman at the desk. Black uniform, like the one at the barrier. Suspicious eyes.

"It's my first day," I say, handing her my letter of appointment. "I was told to come here."

She frowns. "You're not on the list."

I feel a sense of panic combined with relief. Maybe they'll tell me to go home. "The guard at the gate knew about me."

"It's not the same. Who told you to come here?"

"The governor's secretary."

She rolls her eyes. "Before she left, I presume."

"I don't know."

There's a sigh. A mutter, too. "They don't stay long here."

It strikes me even in my panic as a rather indiscreet thing to say.

"I'll have to make a phone call."

She says this as though it's my fault. While waiting, I glance through the window. It's got bars across it, but I can still see out. There appears to be a queue of men outside. One of them looks up and winks at me. He's the one who offered to carry my equipment. I look away quickly.

"You're to go to the keys department," says the woman, slamming down the phone. Then she looks at my boxes. "What's in there?"

"Paints." I remember the guidelines. "Nothing dangerous."

She laughs. "Do you know what the men can do with that stuff? Squirt it in eyes. Blind you so they can escape."

I'm confused. "But this is an open prison. I thought they didn't do that sort of thing."

"Listen to me, love. They might call it an open prison. But it doesn't mean we don't have trouble here. Most of these men have been behind bars for years. Now they're allowed more freedom, some of them go a bit wild."

This isn't exactly what the governor had told me.

"You'll have to leave your gear here in a locker," she continues. "Don't worry. It will be safe."

"But I need it for my classes."

"Can't help that, love. Rules is rules."

As she speaks, another officer comes in. Another woman. She has large, fleshy arms with a tattoo on her wrist. A bluebird with a heart. There's a name, too, but I can't read it. It's gone fuzzy round the edges. I try not to stare.

"We need to search you before you go anywhere."

I'm led into a small side room. "Arms out."

Her hands are swift, deft.

"OK." She glances at the blue and white umbrella by my side. "But you can't take that in."

"Why not?"

"Got a spike, hasn't it. We'll put it in a locker along with those paints of yours. This way."

I follow her out of the hut. It's good to breathe fresh air again. We pass the queue of men. They're standing, I now see, by an open hatch, a bit like a stable door. "Waiting for their post," says my guide curtly.

One of the men is walking away, head down. His hands are empty.

I almost feel sorry for him.

We're going into another cabin now. There's a little flight of stairs leading up. SECURITY it says on the door. My companion reaches for the bunch of keys round her waist. She unlocks it, ushers me in and locks the door behind us.

I look around uncertainly. There's a grey carpet. A noticeboard. One brightly colored poster advises to "Watch Your Back." Another reminds me that it is my duty to inform another member of staff if I feel a prisoner is behaving in an "inappropriate manner." A third points out (unnecessarily, I would have thought), "Personal relationships between staff and prisoners are unlawful."

For a low-risk open prison, all this seems rather unnerving.

"In here, Miss Baker."

"Please," I say, "call me Alison."

I receive a stony glance in return. Once more, that feeling of apprehension crawls over me. There's another woman standing there. She has a box of black belts and pouches next to her. But she appears jollier than the one who brought me here.

"Hi! I'm Sandra. I'm going to give you your key induction chat."

Keys. I've always been anxious about everyday things since the accident. Locking up is one of them. Hence the need to constantly go back and check my own door.

"First thing is, you keep this belt on at all times. Never, ever take it off. If you voluntarily give it to a prisoner, it's a criminal offense. Always lock a door when you leave. If you find one open, you have to stay by it until someone passes and you can report it. Do not leave it unattended. Attached to the pouch is a whistle. If you get into trouble, you blow it."

"What kind of trouble?"

"Oh, you know," she says airily. "If someone attacks you. Doesn't happen often, but you need to be on your toes."

Attacks me?

"It's the mind games you really need to watch out for. There's a few men who'll try to make you feel sorry for them by telling you how they were abused as kids. They use it as an excuse for being abusers themselves."

My stomach feels sick—empty. But Sandra is rattling on. "You've got to sign in for your keys at the main office as soon as you get here and then sign them out when you leave. If you take them home, you'll be dismissed. You might even be fined, too." She made a *Wouldn't that be terrible?* face. "Got it?"

Actually, I want to say, *Would you mind running through that again?* But instead, she's giving me a form to sign, and suddenly, I have the keys to the prison! Shouldn't I have to go through a more rigorous induction before taking on a responsibility like this?

"We're a bit short-staffed today, so I can't take you to Education. I've got one of the orderlies to do it instead."

I have a mental picture of a porter pushing my sister's trolley in the hospital.

"A medical orderly?" I ask.

Sandra gives me an *Are you an idiot?* look. "Men who have proved they are trustworthy can volunteer to be orderlies. They do jobs like dishing out the post or taking visitors around the prison or cooking meals for the staff canteen. That's another thing. The food's good value if you're skint like me. I have lunch and dinner here if I can."

The door opens. "Ah, Kurt. Here you are. Thanks. Can you take Miss Baker to Education? She's the new artist in residence."

The boy with the stained teeth and long hair grins at me. I recognize him immediately as the one who offered to help me earlier. The one I'd turned away. "Follow me, miss."

There appears to be no option.

I've been to the Education hut before, of course, at my interview. But I won't find my way again through this labyrinth without Kurt. All the buildings look the same, apart from a few that have signs. My guide takes great pleasure in pointing them all out as if showing me round his own house and grounds: MUSIC ROOM. MULTIFAITH ROOM. GYM. LAUNDRY ROOM. LIBRARY.

"It's like a village," I blurt out. Kurt laughs as though I've just said something really funny.

"Yeah. A village that you can't leave."

We approach another building—THE COMPUTER CENTER.

"Are you allowed to e-mail home?" I ask.

"You're kidding!" Kurt shakes his head as if explaining something to a small child. "Not unless you want to get shipped out. Towards the end of your sentence, you can have a day out with your girl to prove you're responsible enough to come back. But I've got to wait a bit for that."

I want to ask Kurt how long he's got until his sentence is up but bite the words back. "So, what happens at the computer center?"

"We do exams and stuff so, when we come out, we've got some experience. Some of the men do qualifications in plumbing, too."

Before I can ask him more, we arrive at the Education hut. "Bet you'll have loads of students signing up for your classes, miss."

"Art's not an easy option, you know," I say, more sharply than I mean to.

"Didn't mean it that way." Kurt grins. "It's 'cos you're a woman."

I feel another uneasy shiver passing through me. "There are other female staff around here."

He's standing between me and the door. Not only are his teeth stained, but I can smell his breath. "Yeah, but they don't look as pretty as you, do they, miss?"

I don't know how to reply. It's clearly an inappropriate remark. Is he flirting with me? I don't dare to say anything, though. There's no one around if he gets angry. Why? This is a prison. Someone should be here. Looking after me. I yearn for the safety of my outside classes: my students like Clive and others like Susie and Beryl who don't represent any kind of threat.

"Come on, miss," he continues. "Aren't you going to open the door?"

I search for the right key on my black belt, remembering Sandra's brief instructions. There are three. One for the Education hut, another for the art room inside Education, and another for the staff room, in a different cabin. None has a label. I find the correct one on the third attempt.

"Lock it behind us," instructs Kurt.

I can almost hear the words at my own inquest. *The victim locked the door behind her. She willingly walked into the trap.*

But according to Sandra the key lady's instructions, I could get sacked if I don't.

I'm relieved to hear voices inside. Laughter. Mugs clinking. We're not the only ones here.

"Hello! You must be Alison. Just in time for a coffee before we start."

A jolly-looking woman with jet-black hair down to her waist pumps my hand. She has long, red, glossy nails that seem more suited to a beautician on a cosmetics counter. "I'm Angela, the Education coordinator. Good to meet you. I've never come across a real artist before."

She's appraising me as though slightly disappointed. Maybe I should have worn something more colorful than cream and black.

"Are you famous? They did tell me your name, but I have to say it didn't ring any bells."

"Afraid not."

"Never mind. We all have to take a job where we can get it, don't we? Most of us are broke, or else we wouldn't have taken a prison job. Builder's tea?"

"Do you have peppermint, by any chance?"

She snorts but in a kindly manner. "Bog-standard or nothing. If you want something fancy, you have to bring in your own, as long as you can get it past Security. I advise bringing in your own mug, too. Ours are all a bit chipped. But don't bring in anything fancy or it will get nicked."

"You don't know who's been drinking from them either," adds Kurt.

"That's true enough. Kurt here's the fussiest of us all. Now, let me tell you how this place works." Angela sits down heavily on a chair, indicating I should do the same. I can't help looking at her hair. She's of an age where many women would choose to cut it. I think back to when I chopped off mine. I was eighteen. It was soon after the accident.

"The men that come here," continues Angela, "they might be around for two weeks or two months or two years. If they want to come to Education to improve themselves, they have to go on a list. When they're accepted, they can take qualifications in maths or English. Nothing fancy like A levels or an Open University degree 'cos they're not here for long enough—although if they've already started in another prison, they can keep going, provided we've got the staff. Which we don't always have."

"Where does art fit in?"

Angela throws a *You tell me* look. "No idea. All I know is that we were told we'd got some kind of grant, so we had to have an artist. Wish some of that money could find its way into *our* budget, I can tell you."

"How many students will I have?"

"Up to you, love. You have to put up notices and walk round the place, trying to get people to come to your classes."

I think back to what Kurt had said about prisoners wanting to come and see me because I'm a woman. "Will I have a guard with me?"

"This is an open prison, love. We don't have that kind of one-to-one security. 'Sides, there's no need. There's usually someone around in Education. We haven't had any trouble since . . ."

Her voice tails off.

"Since when?" I ask urgently.

She sighs, looking at me unsurely.

"Come on, I can handle it." I make myself sound braver than I feel. "I'd rather know."

"OK." She speaks slowly and hesitantly. "Since one of the men threw boiling water mixed with sugar at someone he didn't like. Doesn't happen often, though. Only once since I've been here."

"Why sugar?"

"Sticks to the skin." She waves her words away as if they shouldn't have come out in the first place. "Now, let's show you the resources cupboard. There's some paper there you could use, although it's the cheap stuff. And felt-tips. That all right for you?"

I spend the rest of the day making posters.

WANT TO LEARN TO PAINT OR DRAW? I'M THE NEW ARTIST IN RESIDENCE. SIGN UP IN THE EDUCATION OFFICE FOR MY CLASSES.

Then I do a little drawing of an artist's easel using the faded felt-tips from the stationery cupboard. It's the best I can do under the circumstances.

On Angela's advice, I pin up my posters on the Education hut's noticeboards and then around the rest of the prison. And I do the same in the staff dining room, where Sandra is sitting with Angela. "Come over here, love, and join us!"

I'm not sure about eating food that's been cooked by prisoners.

"I've found the odd pube," says Sandra, when she sees me pick at my bowl of macaroni cheese. "Only kidding! Watch out. You've dropped your fork."

Usually, I have a solitary sandwich in the car when going from one class to another. In fact, I can't remember the last time I had lunch with friends. In fact, I don't really have any. And that suits me fine. So I'm surprised to find that it's actually rather nice to have some company over a meal that someone else has cooked for me. Angela, it turns out, has an unemployed husband at home and one son in Australia. Sandra got married last year and is "trying" for a baby. They're both remarkably open.

"What about you?"

My mouth is full as Angela speaks. It gives me time to compose a reply.

"Happily single."

The two women glance at each other.

"I've not found the right man yet," I add. That's true enough. I just don't add that I'm not looking for one. Even so, a flash of Clive's face pops into my head.

"He'll come along when you least expect him," says Sandra brightly. "I met my bloke here. One of the officers. When the guys know you're available, you'll get loads of offers. Trust me."

"Yeah," chuckles Angela. "But don't go off with one of the prisoners, will you? We had someone from Education who did that last year. Bit of all right he was. Of course, she got jailed."

I'm not sure whether to be more shocked by the last sentence or the one before.

"At it like rabbits, they were. In your room, actually."

I shiver. Another image to block out.

Luckily, the conversation moves on to something else, and the afternoon goes much faster than the morning. Before I know it, I'm signing out, having remembered to collect my precious paints.

As soon as I get in the car, I check my mobile in the glove compartment.

Missed call from Mum. She's left a message.

"Hope your first day went all right. Please ring when you get this."

Her concern reminds me of my first day of a new term at school, when she was waiting for me at home with hot buttered toast and a comforting hug. My sister had been finger painting at the time on the kitchen table and chose that moment to have one of her toddler tantrums by chucking the blue pot on the floor. I'd been furious with her back then, but now I feel a sick twinge in my stomach for not being more understanding. After all, she'd only been little.

Block it out.

I punch in Mum's number. It goes straight to voice mail. Good. It makes it easier to lie. "Everything was fine," I say brightly. "Honestly. In fact, I think I'm going to like it. Will ring when I get home."

As I drive back to my flat, I feel as if I've just stepped off a spaceship. The people walking past seem weirdly normal. A father with a pushchair; an old woman with a too-heavy shopping bag; a leggy teenager texting; a middle-aged couple holding hands. So very different from the planet I'd been on today. It was like that period immediately after the accident when I couldn't understand how everyone else could go on as if nothing had happened, when our lives had just caved in.

My heart flutters at the prospect of going in again tomorrow. But at the same time, I realize I'm almost excited. It's like being on a scary high. I've hardly thought about my life outside all day. And it's been a relief.

Yet, as I get out of the car and walk towards my front door, I have the distinct feeling I am being watched. Even though, when I turn swiftly, I can't see anyone behind me.

6

October 2016

Kitty

—————

It had been just over four weeks now since the man with the flabby face had gone, and he hadn't come back. Kitty knew it was four weeks because her period had started again the other day. They all had to have their "monthlies" ticked off on the chart. "This one's as regular as clockwork," one of the carers had remarked chirpily.

Four weeks equaled one month. It was weird, the way her brain remembered some things, although it couldn't quite pin down others. Like what it was about the flabby-faced man that had upset her so much.

Margaret, her roommate, hadn't had periods for years now. She was too old. Margaret had come here when she was a teenager. Respite care. Just for a week to give her parents a break. But they had never come back to collect her. So now a cousin paid the bills.

According to Margaret, Barbara with the straight blond fringe was coming today! The girl who reminded Kitty of someone she couldn't remember. Maybe she'd bring her harmonica again and Kitty could hum. Over the last few weeks, it had become their "thing," as one of the carers called it.

"Here she is, here she is," chanted Duncan.

That's not fair. Barbara was hers! Kitty felt a burning jealousy that reminded her of another time when there'd been someone else she had wanted all for herself. Who was it?

"Hi, everyone!"

Barbara had her hair done up in a ponytail today. If only she could have one, too, thought Kitty. Instead, her hair was hidden underneath the black helmet that was keeping her skull together.

"I've brought some of my classmates. Look! We're going to form a band. The supervisor thought you'd like it. Don't look so worried, Kitty." Barbara was squatting down next to her chair. "We'll still carry on with what we've been doing before. But it will be even better. Look, one of my friends has brought a cymbal. She and Duncan can bang it together. And this other friend of mine has brought a guitar."

"I . . . can . . . sing," butted in Margaret.

Over my dead body, thought Kitty. That woman's voice was worse than her snoring.

"Come on, Kitty. Don't sulk. Let's have a go, shall we?"

It's as though Barbara knew exactly how she was feeling. Still, that's what sisters did, didn't they? Kitty had decided that Barbara was exactly the kind of sister she would have liked, if she'd had one. Someone who played with her. Someone who liked her. Someone who stuck up for her.

They were all sitting in a circle now. The girl with the guitar had started. "She'll be coming 'round the mountain when she comes!"

Duncan was slumped in his wheelchair, a manic grin on his face and a shiny cymbal on his lap. One of the other schoolgirls was holding the stick for him.

BANG.

Duncan looked so ecstatic that it was as if he'd banged it himself.

"Bugger the mountains," he beamed.

One of the girls began giggling.

"Coming 'round the mountain . . ."

"Coming?" roared Duncan, slapping his thighs. "That's rude!"

"Nice humming," whispered Barbara encouragingly to Kitty, as if she hadn't heard the outburst.

"Bravo," said Tea Trolley Lady, who was one of Kitty's favorites, because she always gave her an extra bun if it was available.

"One more time!" laughed Smiley Carer.

"And this is the kind of community interaction I've just been talking about."

They all looked up as Bossy Supervisor walked into the room. At least those of them who were capable of doing so. A very tall, pretty blond woman stood next to a short man with round spectacles, a very thick neck and a square haircut. He was staring down at the ground as though something interesting was going on there.

"A band!" The woman's voice rang out. "That's marvelous, isn't it, Johnny?"

The man with the thick neck continued to stare at the ground. He looked about Kitty's age, although she wasn't quite sure what that was exactly. At her last birthday, she'd had one candle on her cake. They all did. "It's more democratic that way," Bossy Supervisor had said.

Something moved inside Kitty's chest. The newcomer was like her. She just knew it. For a start, she tended to watch the ground, too. It was friendlier than some people's faces. But somehow she had to get his attention.

"Hummm," she sang.

The man's head jerked up to look at her. Those thick glasses and his solemn expression reminded her of an owl from her picture book.

"Hummm," Kitty hummed again. A little higher this time.

"That's nice," he said. His speech was slow and plodding. His eyes were a lovely deep brown. They were also quite narrow—almost slits—as if he'd just woken up and was getting used to the light.

"Very pleasant." Bossy Supervisor's words were clipped. It was the first nice thing she'd said about Kitty since she had run away from the man with the flabby face.

"Would you like to try it out here, Johnny?" the blond woman was saying. "Just for a night or two to see if you enjoy it?"

Kitty couldn't remember anyone asking *her* that. "Maybe." The newcomer was staring at her as he spoke. Kitty could feel her cheeks getting hotter and hotter.

"Time to pack up now," announced Bossy Supervisor. "Thank you very much, everyone."

Johnny was looking back over his shoulder as he lumbered down the corridor with the tall blond woman. Barbara had noticed, too. "Maybe he'll be a friend for you."

"We're . . . not . . . allowed . . . boyfriends . . . here," chipped in Margaret.

"But boys can be friends," said Barbara, more sharply this time.

Kitty's skin prickled. The words reminded her of something. Something bad.

"Please don't bang your head like that. You'll hurt yourself."

But it was the only way to stop the nasty feeling that was sucking her up like a deep black cloud. Even though Kitty couldn't, for the life of her, understand why.

7

November 2016

Alison

———

WELCOME, ALISON BAKER. YOU'RE HERE AT LAST. CAN'T WAIT TO MEET YOU.

My hand is shaking as I read the note that has been left in my prison mailbox. It isn't written by hand or even typed. Instead, it is made up of letters that have been cut out individually from a magazine, presumably to hide the identity of the sender.

I stare at the words. Try to think my way around it. Could it be something innocent? But for security reasons, the rules dictate that only staff should know your surname and not the prisoners. Was it possible that someone had slipped up?

There's a knock on the door. My men have started to arrive. I stuff the note in my pocket and I open up. Ready for business. I try to put the note out of my head so I can concentrate. You need to be on the ball in prison.

"What made you come here, miss? Most of us want to get out."

The question comes from Barry, a small man with a head like a light bulb: big on top and narrow at the chin. His mug has BEST GRAN-DAD IN THE WORLD printed on the side. Everyone calls him Grandad.

Until this point, I've found his questions a diversion—even flattering—but right now I am a mess.

I glance up at the window. I know that officers walk past the art room every quarter hour. But the main office is a good ten minutes' walk from here.

"Because I want to be able to help people enjoy art as much as I do," I say briskly, rifling through the stationery cupboard in the corner. Anything to keep my hands busy.

Barry nods, apparently satisfied. I shiver, recalling Angela's latest advice. "Don't give away anything personal," she'd told me. "They can use it to get at you. Once, we had a teacher who told her class she was getting married. One of her men kept stalking her round the prison, promising her the world if she married him instead."

"That's awful!" I'd been appalled.

"She reported him to the governor, but he kept on doing it. So he got sent to another prison. Freaked her out, it did. Later it turned out that he had loads of money stashed away from his jobs, so maybe she should have waited for him after all. Don't look like that. Joking apart, you've got to be careful. The blokes here can do odd things when there are women around."

YOU'RE HERE AT LAST. CAN'T WAIT TO MEET YOU.

The words keep hammering away in my head.

Could one of my students be the culprit? I only have two. Barry and Kurt.

Yes, Kurt is here, too. Grinning at me with those stained teeth. Watching me as I bend over his sheet of paper. The thing about teaching art is that you have to get quite close physically to your students when helping them with a drawing. Not ideal in a prison situation. But Angela likes him, and I trust her.

Today we're working on cartoon cats. It's not my speciality, but Barry wants to post a picture to his grandchildren. "They love kittens," he says with a sad voice.

I try to focus on the image of him and his grandchildren instead of the note burning a hole in my pocket. I do a "cat demo" on the whiteboard with a felt pen, using circles for the body and head with straight lines for whiskers.

"Is mine better than his, miss?" asks Kurt. He's putting me on the spot, and he knows it.

"Art isn't like that," I say. "You judge each piece of work on its own merits."

"Like breaking the law?"

I try not to be spooked by his grin.

"Grandad here got off lightly, if you ask me. Want to know what he did?"

"Fuck off, Kurt."

The older man's voice comes out as a low growl. I prickle with nerves.

"Come on, Grandad. You're scaring our artist lady. Be nice now."

"Artist lady" is the tag that Kurt has recently ascribed to me. It manages to convey a mixture of amusement and sarcasm without being out-and-out offensive. I don't correct him, because I suspect this is just what he wants.

It's a relief when class has finished. Kurt leaps up to hold open the door for me. "Thank you," I say, "but you need to go first so I can lock up."

He smiles that horrible grin. "Want any help tidying up?"

Is it Kurt I should be afraid of?

"No, thank you." I breathe a sigh of relief as he finally saunters away.

At lunch, I'm desperate to confide in Angela about the note. But something—I'm not sure what—stops me.

Instead, I tell her about the class. About Grandad and my cat lesson. Try to eat my macaroni cheese without thinking too much about what might be in there.

"You mean Barry?" My new friend pauses midmouthful. Her face suddenly looks white. "He's in your group? And he's drawing cats?"

"Isn't that allowed?" My heart is suddenly hammering. What have I done?

"You weren't to know." Angela shakes her head and puts the fork down. "That man was put away for—murdering children." She shudders. "Three of them. You might have read about the case. It was in the midsixties."

"Before I was born," I say.

"Right. Silly me. Anyway, when the police caught him, they found his whole house full of cats. Beautifully cared for, they were. Then they discovered human remains in the cat food . . ."

I want to vomit. "So why does his family still keep up with him?"

"Doesn't get any visitors as far as I know."

My skin is cold. "But he's got a Best Grandad mug."

"Probably bought it himself. They can do that, you know. The men get a list of stuff they are allowed to order in."

"But why?"

"To fool us? Fool himself, maybe? Pretend that he was a nice, regular guy." Angela lowers her voice. "Listen, Alison. Lots of people here lie. Many have secrets. You'll come across some very deceptive customers. And some decent ones, too. Sometimes, it's hard to tell the difference. My advice is to make use of Kurt. He might have an odd manner, but he knows everyone here. Ask him to find you more students. And just make sure you have him in the room when Barry's there."

"What did Kurt do?" I whisper, still trembling.

Angela looks as though she's about to tell me. Then she stops and flicks back her long jet-black hair. "You're better off not knowing. I'm not easily squeamish, I can tell you. My life's been too tough for that. But if you'd seen some of the things I have in this place, you'd know that he's not the one you want to worry about."

The note, then the revelation about Barry's crime—it's all too much. I'm still wobbly as I get to college that night. Yet I also feel a sense of relief. Students who *haven't* committed a crime are exactly what I need right now. My stained glass group is already waiting for me in the classroom. The only person who isn't there is Clive. I feel a brief stab of disappointment then bury it quickly.

"Evening, Alison!" There's a chorus of excited voices. Tonight is a big event in the world of my stained glass students.

"How was your day?" asks Beryl, my horsey-faced student, brightly.

I could say I've been helping a child-killer to draw cartoon cats. But instead, I deflect the question. "How was yours?"

"Bit dull, to be honest. You know. Housework. Mucking out. Couldn't wait to get here. Left the husband with macaroni cheese in the oven."

Macaroni cheese? It takes me back to lunchtime when the others had told me about Barry, kittens and cat food. I feel sick.

"Right, everyone!" I say with a false conviviality. "Gloves on? Goggles?"

"All ready!" beams Beryl. As she speaks, there's a purr outside. I glance through the window. A sleek silver Porsche is gliding into the car park. A tall man in a green-checked Barbour is getting out. Clive.

I don't appreciate latecomers when I've started a demo. It interrupts my flow. Helping someone catch up means there's less time for those who have bothered to get here on time.

"Sorry." Clive throws me an apologetic glance as he hurries in. "Board meeting went on for longer than I thought."

I might have guessed. A director type. I don't ask my students what they do, because often they come here to escape. I am reminded of the unspoken "don't ask" rule in prison.

Focus, Alison.

"We're about to see if the glass will fit into your shapes," I say.

After my demo—I feel the old thrill of satisfaction as my piece of glass fits perfectly despite my jangling nerves—I sit down with each student in turn to help. I leave Clive to last. Partly as a punishment. And partly because he makes me feel nervous in a way I still don't understand. Even though he hasn't asked me out for dinner again, and has only been a model of politeness since.

"I really must apologize again for being late," he says in a low voice. "I took this up because I wanted something different from work, but it's hard to squeeze everything in."

"It's fine. Honestly."

Maybe I've got him wrong. He's not threatening. He just has good manners. But then our hands brush accidentally as I help to trim a sharp edge of glass. Something passes from him to me—a sizzle of danger and excitement.

"Sorry," we both blurt out at the same time.

"I've done it!" squeals Beryl. "Look, Alison."

My heart soars. Her last piece of glass fits perfectly. It's a blue tulip against a scarlet sky. "Careful," I say quickly. "We need to secure it."

Smash. Too late. The loose pieces have fallen because she didn't fasten them into the lead structures in time. I help my distraught student pick them up.

"How stupid of me!"

"It's happened to me, too," I reassure her. "We can do it again." Then I take the shattered shards out to the side room. I wrap one of them in my handkerchief for later. I can feel the need building already.

"You did a great job there," says Clive, who is the last one to leave. "I really admire the way you saved the day. In fact—"

"Thanks," I interrupt, suddenly panicking. "I've got to lock up now. See you next week."

I watch him walk out of the building towards his flashy car. Part of me—the bit that felt his hand brush mine earlier—is filled with regret that I've turned down his invitation to dinner. Yet if my sister can't enjoy life, then why should I?

Guilt makes me rush into the side room. Reach for the piece of glass. I hold it against my wrist, with both longing and loathing.

I can't wait any longer.

And I'm not just talking about the cut.

A locket.
   Still lying against warm skin.
A stranger's voice.
Floating in and out.
A siren.
Then nothing.
"Nothing will come of nothing."
I learned that somewhere.
Where?
When?
Or am I just imagining all of this?

8

November 2016

Kitty

How long had she been in this room all on her own? Hard to know. They'd definitely given her more than three meals. Cereal. Cottage pie. Omelet. She could remember a lasagna, too.

The cottage pie had made a terrible mess on the floor when she'd chucked it. It had even got into the chair spokes. The lasagna had been muckier still.

"Naughty girl," scolded Fussy Carer, getting down on her knees.

"It's your fault," Kitty said, thumping her good fist on the food tray. "I've told you before. Well, tried to. I went off meat after that program about cows."

There wasn't a television here in this room they'd put her in. Just four white walls and a mattress. No bed frame because she might hurt herself on it. Just like she'd hurt her head on the wheelchair.

"That's a right old bruise you've got there," said Fussy Carer, more gently this time. "Does it still hurt?"

Of course it bloody hurt. But because no one could understand her, she began to scream and lash out all over again.

Six more meals passed.

Someone was coming. Kitty could hear approaching footsteps in the corridor. She squeezed her good hand into a ball with fear.

"I hear you've been a good girl at last. No more meals on the floor.

Or head banging." Bossy Supervisor was addressing her as though she were a child. "If I let you go back to your old room, will you continue to behave?"

Kitty nodded her head. But instead, it came out as a shake. Left to right. Right to left.

"No?" There was a frown.

Maybe if she shook her head from side to side, it would go the other way. Sometimes, that worked. Up and down. Down and up. Thank goodness for that.

"Very well." Bossy Supervisor didn't look that convinced. "But you behave. Got it?"

Smiley Carer was waiting in her room. "We've had someone new join us since you've been away. Nice young man. I think you've seen him before. Johnny, he's called. Charming everyone, he is."

"YES, YES, YES!"

"Excited, are you? It *is* nice to have a fresh face. I agree with that."

This carer was one of the ones who pretended to know what you said. They usually got it wrong, but this time she was in the right ballpark. "Sharing with Duncan, he is. Rather him than me, I can tell you."

Smiley Carer had put her into some new clothes and was wheeling her into the day lounge. Johnny would be here! Kitty put her good hand up to the hair peeping out from under the helmet. "Do I look all right?" she asked. If only she was allowed a mirror in her room! But because of her head banging, it had been taken away. Hummm, hummm.

"Nice humming! Pleased to be back, are you? Here's Kitty, everyone!"

This was announced as if she'd just come back from holiday.

"Hello!" said Johnny. "What have they done to you?"

Kitty's cheeks began to burn. What did he mean?

Duncan cut in. "You've got a big gap in your teeth. Ugly, ugly."

"That's enough, Duncan," said the carer quickly. "It's where she hit her head on the chair. The dentist will sort it."

Kitty felt a hot tear sliding down her cheek.

"I think you look lovely," said Johnny. Then he walked over and put out his hand and actually held hers.

Kitty thought she was going to die of happiness.

"I think we'd better let go of our hands, shall we? Now, is everyone ready for Barbara? She's coming straight after lunch for some more band practice. Meanwhile, I've got some exciting news! There's going to be a concert, and we're going to invite your families."

Friday Mum was her family. At least, she thought so.

"The local paper will be there, too," she continued. "Would you like to join in, Johnny?"

"Can I sit next to Kitty?" asked Johnny.

"Oooh. Someone's got a crush!"

"Nonsense, Duncan," snapped Very Thin Carer. "You know it's strictly against the rules for residents to be overfamiliar."

But when she turned away, Johnny grabbed Kitty's hand again. It made her heart float and her knees feel all wobbly!

"Kitty," called out Smiley Carer kindly. Quickly, Johnny let go. Kitty felt a pang in her chest. "Time for the dentist. I'm afraid you'll have to miss practice."

No! She wanted to stay with Johnny.

"If you don't stop shrieking, Kitty, I'm afraid we'll have to send you back to the quiet room again."

"Don't," said Johnny. "It's not worth it. I'll still be here when you get back. And you'll look really pretty with your new teeth."

"OK," Kitty said. "I'll go to the bloody dentist. But only for you."

"I've no idea what you're saying," sighed Very Thin Carer. "But as you've stopped shrieking now, we'll accept that as an apology. Can someone help me with Kitty's chair, please?"

It wasn't easy, but Kitty managed to turn round as she left. Johnny was waving at her and—wow!—blowing her a kiss. Kitty's heart turned over. She had a boyfriend! A boyfriend was meant to look after you. She knew that from the telly.

So if the flabby-faced man with the holey shoes ever came back, Johnny would sort him out.

And then she'd never have to see him again.

9

November 2016

Alison

There have been no more notes.

Maybe, I tell myself, it was just a prank. Some prisoner with a warped sense of humor. Or possibly an officer who was winding me up.

Either way, I have put my fears to the back of my mind for self-preservation. It's not as though I haven't had practice. During the last few weeks, my classes have begun to fill up, thanks to Kurt. He's been advertising me madly. Enthusiastically running around with flyers. "My men," as I think of them, are a loyal group. They seem to take pride in coming to my classes.

How I love drawing out talent from these men around me! Talent that has possibly been lurking there for years but hasn't had the opportunity to emerge. I like to think that my father would have been proud of me. Sometimes, I even forget to cut myself in the evening. My adrenaline levels here are so high, always on the watch in case a prisoner does something, that I don't have the same urge as before. Barry and his cat cartoons continue to haunt me, though. I cannot look him in the face now. If only he'd stop coming to my class. But he's become a firm regular.

"Miss, how do I do whiskers again?" he asks me this morning. It's almost as if he knows that I know. Needling me. Wanting me to ask him how he could possibly have done something like that.

"Show you in a minute," I say curtly. "You'll have to wait your turn."

Barry looks distinctly peeved, but Kurt gives me a conspiratorial nod. "Yeah, listen to Miss Alison, old man."

"Miss" is a label that all the men give female staff, even if they're married. But Kurt's "Alison" addition shows an unwelcome familiarity.

I've purposely never mentioned my surname to my men. But I'm sure there are other ways of tracking people down. "Do you think Grandad is dangerous?" I find myself asking Kurt as he helps me clear up. (Barry has just left, claiming to be on kitchen duty, but I can tell he's in a huff because of my "wait your turn" admonition.)

"Why do you ask, miss?"

I feel as though I've been caught out. It's not considered "polite" to ask what a criminal has done. "Someone told me about Barry and . . . and his crime," I venture. "I'm just a bit scared in case . . ."

My voice runs out, but Kurt steps in. "You're worried he might kill again."

I nod.

"Could do." He scratches his chin as if in thought. "When you've been inside for as long as he has, the thought of the outside is scary—especially if there are relatives of your victims waiting to get you. He's up for parole soon, but he might not want to leave. It's possible that Grandad might do something bad here just to stay in the system and keep safe."

I bite my lip.

"Don't worry, miss." Kurt doesn't touch my arm in comfort, but he looks as though he might. "The rest of us wouldn't let no one hurt you. We like you."

Has a prisoner just offered to protect me? Have I been naive to confide in him? And—here's the scary bit—Kurt genuinely did seem to think that Grandad might still be a threat. What if he moved from children to adults? Had I been too abrupt with him in class?

The following day, I voice my fears to Angela. "Supposing I annoy someone somehow and they get one of their friends to pay me a visit at home?" I think about that feeling I had the other day, like I was being watched, but I feel too stupid to say this out loud.

She puts her head to one side, suggesting I've made a valid point. A sense of unease crawls through me. "Goes with the job, I suppose. I don't worry, because I've got my Jeff." She laughs. "One look at my old man, and any of this lot would scarper. Built like a tank, he is."

But I don't have anyone. Only the other lodger and my landlord. Angela notices my silence. "You could try putting a man's pair of boots outside your place. And keep your door on a chain. But that's just common sense, isn't it? To be honest, I've never heard of a prisoner going after a member of staff outside the prison. Only inside."

There's always a first time, I tell myself silently.

She pats me on the arm kindly. "You can't get too uptight about all this. Otherwise, we couldn't do what we do. And if anyone does try to attack you, go for their eyes. Or their balls."

"Angela! I've been wanting to catch you." A man with a clutch of earrings in his right ear plonks himself down at our table without so much as a "Do you mind?" He could pass for a prisoner, but he's staff. Works in our job center: the part of the prison responsible for finding men work on the outside. "Need to talk to you about a reference." He touches her shoulder in a rather familiar fashion. "Got this inmate who might have a chance with a hotel."

I make my excuses and wend my way back through the cabins to my "studio." This afternoon's session is on portraits. In my college classes, I use mirrors so students can copy their reflection. But in prison, this isn't allowed. So instead, they're going to draw each other. Exercises in pairs are a good way to bring people together anyway. Helps them chat. Discover common bonds. So I've been told.

I unlock the art cupboard to get scissors and paper, which I will cut into squares. Then I freeze. On the top of the pile is a roughly torn-out cutting from the prison newsletter. It shows a photograph in the "Welcome to New Staff" page. My photograph. In the middle of my face is a red drawing pin. Below, in childish-looking black felt-tip writing, are scrawled five words:

I'M GOING TO GET YOU.

Frantically, I rip up the cutting into tiny bits, pricking myself on the drawing pin. Only then does it occur to me that I should have kept it intact. But a small part of me knows I would never show it to anyone. And what does a note prove anyway? There's no indication of the writer's identity. Is it the same person who "wrote" the previous one in cut-up letters? I hadn't reported that, and I'm not going to report this one either. Something tells me that if I make a fuss, word will get round the prison, and I'll be more vulnerable than before.

Even so, I can't think straight. So I try to distract myself by cutting out my squares and then putting the scissors safely back.

Block it out, I tell myself firmly. It didn't happen.

I have six students today—including Barry—and a cocky youth. When I explain they are going to start off by sketching one another, the latter rolls his eyes. "Piece of piss."

I am constantly surprised by how childish some of these prisoners are. Was it that immaturity that got them into trouble in the first place? There are times when I feel like throwing all this in to concentrate on my local college classes and my lovely students like Beryl. She wouldn't put a drawing pin through my face.

"Begin by making dots for the nose, eyes and ears," I start to say. But then the door opens. An old man with a cane and large cauliflower ears enters. A pair of bright blue eyes fix on me. He grabs the back of the nearest chair as if needing to steady himself.

"This is Stefan. He's new." Kurt sounds nervous. Why?

"Is it OK if I join the class, miss?" The old man has a strange accent. Eastern European, I think.

He's late. I should say no. Besides, it makes for uneven numbers. It means he has to draw me. And I have to draw him. But this old man, leaning heavily on his cane, is surely too frail to be a threat. Or am I being naive?

The others take full advantage of the fact that I can't watch them and draw Stefan at the same time.

"I don't want to draw Stan, miss. His nose is too big."

"Piss off, Wayne. Your ears are small. Just like your . . ."

"Language," Kurt cuts in. "You're talking in front of a lady."

"Teacher's pet," says someone else.

Kurt smirks as though he likes this idea. Although he's ostensibly always trying to help, I'm uneasy about the way he pops up wherever I go. As for the drumming up of business, is he doing it out of the kindness of his heart or because he's expecting a favor back? Now I've made it worse by confiding in him about Barry.

Maybe I'll look up Kurt's crime when I get home. A quick Google. That's all it takes.

But if I find out he has done something awful, I know I'll find it difficult to work with him. And, although I don't want to admit it, I've come to need him.

"Fancy a cup of tea anyone?" he asks now, interrupting my thoughts.

Grandad—Barry—thumps his mug on the table. I shudder.

There's a kettle for tea and coffee in the room, even though boiling water is potentially dangerous. An open prison, I am learning, is a maze of contradictions. Criminals can make tea during class. Tea that could scald someone, especially if thrown deliberately. But they can't have sharp objects. Criminals can go out of the prison to work in those little white vans. But they must be ready to meet the same van at the allotted spot, so they get back to their cell on time.

Meanwhile, Stefan is concentrating on his drawing. He seems completely absorbed, ignoring all the noise around him. "Want to take a look?" he asks, suddenly glancing up, as though sensing my eyes on him.

I gasp. It's good. Very good. He has captured the shadowing on my face perfectly. Shadowing is notoriously tough to get right.

"Have you drawn before?" I ask.

"A long time ago. We do not have artist teachers in the prison I have just left."

Barry interrupts. "Will you put it on the wall for everyone to see? Can my cat pictures go there, too?"

Just the sound of his voice freaks me out now I know what he's done. "Let's see, shall we?"

I turn away and, as I do so, unexpectedly collide with Kurt, knocking the mug of tea from his hand. Luckily, it's not scalding hot, but it has stained my white top. Blast. I scrabble for some wet wipes that I know I have in my drawer somewhere.

Out of nowhere, there's an ear-piercing scream.

"Jesus! I've been fucking stabbed!"

For a minute, I think it's a joke. One of them messing around.

Then my blood chills.

Barry is lying, face upwards, on the ground. Howling in agony. There's a pair of scissors by his side. The same scissors I'd cut up the paper with before class started. I stumble towards him. All around me the men are jumping up.

My ears ring with shock. My skin sweats. My heart thumps so hard that it's like having a weighty pendulum in my chest. No. This can't be happening. It can't.

Barry's left eye is staring glassily at me. The right is a red pool of dark crimson blood gushing down the side of his face.

10

November 2016

Kitty

_____

The dentist fucking hurt.

"Hold her down, will you?" he kept saying to the nurse.

"I can't. Not while she's lashing out at me like this."

I'm not being difficult, Kitty wanted to say. *I'm trying to tell you that you're bruising my lip.*

If only Johnny was here. He could guess her thoughts. More or less. She also loved the fact that his own teeth weren't great either. They stuck out at strange angles and had a big, thick silver band across the top set.

"Hold her down firmer, please." The dentist's voice now had a hint of desperation in it. "Otherwise, the impression isn't going to fit."

"Can you sit still, dear?" The nurse's voice was a bit wet and wishy-washy. It reminded Kitty of Friday Mum, who hadn't visited for a few Fridays now. "Try thinking of something nice."

Not long now until she'd be sitting next to Johnny. His kiss was safely inside her pocket. She'd caught it in the air with her good hand just before leaving the home.

"Finished now. Good girl."

All the way back in the van, Kitty hoped and hoped that Johnny would be there to meet her like he'd promised. Hummm. Hummm.

"You've still got that ugly gap between your teeth." Duncan— scratching away—was hovering in the front entrance as they wheeled her in. "Thought you'd gone to the dentist to get it fixed."

"That's because they've only done the impression, stupid," Kitty said. "And while we're at it, why don't you ask them for a different cream? It might stop you tearing at your skin like that."

"Babble, babble!" Duncan threw her a pitying look. "It's all you ever do, isn't it, Kitty? By the way, you've missed band practice. It's over now."

Desperately, Kitty looked around for Johnny. Maybe in the communal lounge. Pushing the wheelchair herself with her good hand, she peeped round. Empty. Apart from Tea Trolley Lady, clearing up.

"Johnny," Kitty said urgently. "I want him."

"Back now, are you, love? Fancy an iced bun? It so happens that I've got two of them going spare! Yours and Johnny's. Went down with a temperature, he did, during that little music session. So he missed out on his afternoon snack."

Temperature? What if he got so ill that he was sent home? Or to the hospital? Kitty felt a wave of panic at the thought of the word "hospital." Why?

One thing was certain: she needed to find him. Quickly. Even if it was against all the rules.

"Going . . . to . . . Johnny's room . . . are . . . you?" Margaret's voice cut in as Kitty passed her on the corridor. "You'll get . . . caught. You . . . know . . . you're . . . not . . . allowed . . . down . . . the . . . boys' end. Hang . . . on . . . a sec . . . and . . . I'll see . . . what . . . I can . . . do . . . to help."

Bloody hell! She'd only gone and pressed the emergency button on the wall!

"Go . . . go," rasped Margaret. "I've . . . created a . . . diversion . . . for . . . you."

Quick, quick, before someone spotted her. Down this passage. Turn left. Good hand hurting. Right here. Now, which door was it?

There. *J* for Johnny. It was slightly ajar. Kitty pushed her chair in, but it got stuck.

A voice came from the bed. "Kitty? It's you!"

Poor Johnny's nose was really red. His forehead was all sweaty. "I'm so glad you came."

Really? Kitty felt a buzz of electric excitement as she maneuvered her chair right up to the edge of his bed.

"I felt terrible not meeting you when you got back as I promised. But I got a temperature almost as soon as you'd gone and now this awful headache. I often get them since the attack."

"What attack?"

"I'm guessing you're wondering what happened."

Yes!

"You know I was born with Down syndrome." His face took on a faraway look. "But there's more to it than that. One night, I was in a pub with my mates, and this thug came up to me and started teasing 'cos of the way I look. My friends told him to beat it, but then this bloke smashed his bottle of beer into my head. Never been quite the same since."

Then Johnny laughed in the way people did when something wasn't really funny.

"Poor you," said Kitty.

"I knew you'd understand." His eyes stared up at her. "How was the dentist?"

"Horrible."

"I bet it was awful. I always hate the dentist. But it will be worth it. I'll get my brace off soon. And you'll have another tooth when it's ready, I expect. Then we'll both be as good as new, won't we?"

He laughed. A properly happy laugh this time, and because his joke was really rather funny—how could she ever be as good as new?—Kitty laughed, too.

Then his face got all worried. "Don't get caught, will you?"

Yet he was still holding her hand as if he didn't want to let her go.

"Please get better soon," babbled Kitty, desperate to prolong the moment. His touch felt so nice and warm.

"Next week it's the concert. My mum and dad will be back from holiday then."

It was amazing how they could have a conversation without her actually speaking.

He let go of her hand. It felt lonely now. "I don't want to say goodbye, but we're both going to get told off if they find you here. Thanks for coming."

Then he blew her another kiss!

Kitty caught it with her good hand and put it in her pocket to add to the collection. It made her so happy that she began to hum.

"You've got such a lovely voice," said Johnny with tears in his eyes. "See you as soon as they let me get back."

"Why . . . are . . . you . . . holding . . . your . . . hand . . . over . . . your . . . pocket?" asked Margaret later, when Kitty had managed to steer herself back into their shared room without anyone noticing.

"Because it's got Johnny's kisses inside it."

"What . . . are you . . . saying? I hope it's . . . not going . . . to give you . . . nightmares again. Scream . . . and thrash . . . and mutter . . . all . . . night, you . . . do." Margaret's eyes narrowed. "It's like . . . you're trying . . . to say . . . something."

Really? But what?

"There you are." Very Thin Carer came rushing in. "I've been looking for you, you naughty girl. You're not meant to wheel yourself back to your room. It's against health and safety. Now you'd better behave or else you won't be allowed to play in the concert. Not long now. A little bird told me that you've got a special visitor coming to hear you. Isn't that exciting?"

Kitty's heart began to beat with fear. Supposing it was Flabby Face with the holey shoes again?

He wanted something. She just knew it. But what? And why did she get the feeling it was something to do with an accident? If only she could remember.

11

November 2016

Alison

I'm shaking so much that I can hardly hold two fingers against Barry's neck. I don't want to touch this child-killer's rough, mottled skin. Yet common decency means I have to check his pulse.

I took a first aid course years ago in the Scouts. But it hadn't helped my sister. Later, as part of a teaching requirement, I went on a refresher session.

Barry is still breathing, and his bloody eye is staring glassily up at me. "Get help. Quick!" My voice is hoarse.

Why are they just standing there, looking down at the ground, shifting awkwardly? One of these men has just tried to commit murder. Which one?

"Go!" I yell. Kurt tears off.

I think back to the conversation we had earlier about Barry and whether he was still a threat. "The rest of us wouldn't let no one hurt you." That's what Kurt had said.

Have I just allowed a murderer to escape?

Barry's slumped body is twitching as though an electric current is passing through. His bloodcurdling screams begin again. Piercing my ears. Making me unable to think straight.

"He's bleeding out," whimpers one of the men. Desperately, I pull my handkerchief out of my pocket and try to stem the flow. The white linen with the daisy chain border that was embroidered by my mother is soaked within seconds. There's a smear of blood on my skin. His smell is overwhelming. It makes me want to vomit. Takes me back to—

Barry's screams rise even higher. They remind me now not just of the day we lost my sister but of a farm that Mum took me to as a child. It was lovely. Until the most terrifying screams started—pigs were being slaughtered. My mother was cross with the farmer for allowing visitors at the same time. "It's the real world, lady," he'd said.

He was wrong. *This* is the real world. A world where violence happens in the blink of an eye. A world where a man is hemorrhaging to death right in front of me.

And it's all my fault.

"Do something!" I yell as his blood seeps into the carpet. "Quickly! Someone!"

12

December 2016

Kitty

It was the day of the concert. Through a stroke of luck and a bit of wheelchair barging, Kitty managed to sidle next to Johnny at breakfast.

"I like being with you," Johnny said, mopping up her dribble with his big white handkerchief. "Nod if you like it, too."

Nodding was up and down, wasn't it? But somehow, it came out side to side. Johnny's face fell.

"Don't . . . take . . . any . . . notice . . . ," said Margaret, who was sitting on the other side of Kitty. "She . . . nods . . . when she means . . . no and . . . shakes her . . . head when she means . . . yes."

Johnny's face cleared. "That's good." His hand tightened on hers. "I say the wrong thing, too, sometimes."

"Why don't you . . . come . . . to . . . our . . . room . . . again . . . tonight?" asked Margaret loudly.

"Shhh." Johnny looked around.

"Everyone's arriving now," said Duncan, who'd returned smelling much nicer. "There's my sister!"

There was an air of tense excitement. Kitty's good hand squeezed Johnny's tightly. A small woman with a mousy face came in. She stared at the group as if looking for someone. Then she waved at Duncan. "They've . . . got the same . . . long noses," giggled Margaret.

"Have you got anyone coming?" asked Johnny politely.

Margaret shook her head. "My cousin . . . doesn't . . . bother . . . with . . . me now she's . . . gone to . . . Australia . . . Goodness! . . . Who . . . is . . . that . . . woman? I . . . love . . . her . . . pearls."

"It's my mother," said Johnny casually. He said it in a way that suggested he was a bit upset. He must miss home. But if it hadn't been for his family "needing a break," he wouldn't have met Kitty. He'd told her that during the hand holding and after lights-out.

Someone else was waving now. "That's . . . Kitty's . . . mum," said Margaret knowledgeably. "She . . . hasn't . . . been . . . here . . . for . . . a . . . bit, has she? Usually . . . comes . . . on . . . a . . . Friday. All right . . . for . . . some."

Friday Mum's hair was a different color. It wasn't grey anymore. It was blond like Johnny's mother's. Kitty bit the inside of her cheek as the other guests came in. Where was her special visitor? Maybe it wasn't going to be Flabby Face at all. Maybe it was going to be someone nice! But no one else had ever come to see her apart from Friday Mum.

Straight Fringe Barbara was standing up now. She was pointing the stick in Kitty's direction. That meant she had to start humming. A solo, Barbara called it. Everyone else had to be quiet so it could be heard properly. They were all waiting. Kitty's mouth was dry with apprehension. She'd practiced so many times that she could do this in her sleep.

But now, with the audience looking expectantly at her, the hum wouldn't leave her mouth.

"I can't do it," she whispered.

"What's . . . she . . . saying?" groaned Margaret.

"Don't be nervous." Johnny took her hand. "I'm here. We can do anything together."

But the humming sound still wouldn't come out.

Everyone was staring. How awful!

Then Barbara's baton beckoned the others like a giant finger.

Duncan was going crazy on the triangle. *Bang.* Drop on floor. *Bang.* Margaret was bashing the glockenspiel with all her might. And Johnny now had to take his hand away from hers to play the guitar. Kitty sat there, silently, tears streaming down her face.

At the end, everyone got up in the audience and clapped hard. It was a standing ovation, said Barbara. Then they clapped so hard again that the others all had to do another piece that they'd been practicing, since everyone liked the first bit. This was called an On Core.

The words sounded familiar. Had she done On Cores with the girl that Barbara reminded her of? Before she'd come here? If only she could ask someone who understood what she was saying. But all this was too complicated to explain on a stupid picture board.

"That was lovely, darling." Friday Mum came up and put her arms around her afterwards.

"No, it fucking wasn't. I didn't hum like I was meant to."

"You enjoyed it, too, did you? And is this a friend?"

Mum was speaking in that voice that people used when they didn't expect a reply.

"That . . . is . . . Johnny," said Margaret, butting in. "And I'm . . . Margaret."

Friday Mum nodded. "Lovely to meet you. I'm sorry I haven't been here for a bit, Kitty. But I had to go on a couple of residential training courses."

"I . . . bet," whispered Margaret, "that's . . . why . . . we're . . . here . . . So . . . they can . . . go . . . away . . . and . . . have . . . fun."

"I beg your pardon?" Friday Mum's eyes narrowed.

"Nothing," said Margaret.

"And how long have you been here?" Friday Mum was addressing Johnny now.

"A few weeks."

They didn't like each other. Kitty could see that. Friday Mum was walking away now. She was talking, head down, to one of the members of staff. At one point, they turned to look at her and Johnny. And

suddenly, Kitty wished that Friday Mum had never come to the concert at all.

What *were* they nattering about?

"Well done, everyone," said Barbara. Her face was flushed. "You did
fantastically. Yes, Kitty. You, too, for trying. Even famous musicians
dry up sometimes. It's quite normal. Now we've got a photographer
from the local paper here. He's a very special visitor. And he wants to
take a picture of you."

So *that* was the person the carer had referred to. What a relief. It
wasn't Flabby Face after all.

"What . . . about . . . the rest . . . of us?" demanded Margaret.
"Doesn't . . . he . . . want to . . . photograph us . . . too?"

"Of course! Say 'cheese' everyone!"

Johnny put his arm around her shoulders. Kitty could have died of
happiness.

"Smile, everyone. Perfect! Great, Kitty. Now it's your turn."

"Why just her?" sniffed Duncan.

"Because I'm special!" gabbled Kitty. Hadn't someone told her that
once? The memory made her hum with happiness.

"Not that . . . bloody sound again," groaned Margaret. "Sounds
like . . . death music . . . They played that . . . at my grandmother's . . .
funeral."

Kitty's hum stopped. *Death? Funeral?* Both words rang bells.
But why?

"Please don't start head banging again, Kitty." This was Smiley
Carer. She didn't look very smiley now. "Time for a little lie-down, I
think."

No!

BANG. BANG. "Now, Kitty, you know that when you don't behave,
we have to give you something to . . ."

And after that, everything went black.

13

December 2016

Alison

———

Since the attack on Barry, my men have been subdued. And so have I. Every time I run a class, I hear his screams. See his blood seeping across the floor.

One of the tutors is ill so I've been asked to do an evening shift tonight even though I've been here all day. We're doing potato prints, but my mind can't stay still. I think back to my conversation with Angela. I'd rushed to find her as soon as the police and the governor had finished interviewing me.

Like I said before, communication is slow in prisons. Unless bad news happens—then it travels at the speed of light.

"Something awful has happened . . ." I'd begun.

Angela had reached out to touch my hand. "I heard. Well, bits of it. Not surprising, really. He was a nasty piece of work. Now, tell me exactly what went on."

So I'd told her about the scissors that I was sure I'd locked up in the cupboard.

"Are you certain?" Her face had been sympathetic. "It's easy to forget something in this place. So many rules to follow. Distractions, too."

The photograph. The red drawing pin in my face. *I'M GOING TO GET YOU.*

Had the shock made me forget to lock up properly? But I couldn't tell anyone about that, especially now.

"One of them did it when I was cleaning up the spilled tea," I'd added, in a bid to justify myself.

Angela had sucked in her breath. "Sounds like the culprit spilled tea on purpose to make you look elsewhere, love. You'd be surprised who you can trust and who you can't—including the staff."

"Really?" Then I'd whispered the thing I'd been thinking ever since it happened. "Do you think it could have been Kurt?"

She'd given me a sharp look. "Why?"

I'd flushed. "Well, he's always looking out for me."

Angela had tutted. "Watch for that. I've warned you about grooming. Remember? The men pretend to be well-behaved and encourage others to join your classes. Just when you think they're all right, they do something bad to you or ask for favors. But I still don't reckon it was Kurt. Not his style."

How did she know?

"There'll be an investigation, of course." Angela had spoken as though working out the consequences in her own head. "Who's in your group again?"

I'd listed my students' names.

She'd whistled quietly at the last. "Facial mutilation was Stan's thing. Remember that case in the nineties? Whole family in London. They . . . Never mind." She'd smiled uneasily. "Was there any friction in the class?"

Exactly what the governor had asked.

"Only a bit of bantering."

"I heard the police interviewed you, too."

"They asked me the same things the governor had. I gave them the same answers."

She'd nodded. "They're still here, apparently, questioning the men. One of the officers told me."

It had been a mistake to confide in her, I realized. Angela hadn't helped. She'd just made me more anxious, as though this had been my fault.

"You ought to eat something, love."

But I'd felt too sick.

I'd stood up then, conscious that the people at the neighboring table were looking away quickly, as if they'd been staring. "Got to get ready for the next class."

Angela's eyes had widened. "You're going to carry on working?"

"The governor said I could. Besides, I need the money."

She'd shrugged. "Like getting back on a horse again, I suppose." Her fingers had begun to drum. "Still, if you feel up to it, it's probably the best thing."

Of course I hadn't felt up to it. All I'd really wanted to do was drive home and hide under the covers. For the first time in ages, I'd craved the sharp edge of glass piercing my skin. But I had to carry on. At least, that's what I'd told myself. Not just to pay my bills. But because this was my penance.

I try to bring myself back to the potato prints. Such childish activities feel out of place now. But the men seem to be immersed in their pieces. Some of them will give them to their kids, some their nephews or nieces; some will give them to their mothers. Already, I've learned that family outside assumes huge significance for prisoners—usually more than when they were free. But even though two weeks have passed since the stabbing, they still want to talk about Barry. Speculation is reaching fever pitch.

"It's been ages, miss. How's he getting on?"

"Is he going to be blind, miss?"

"Is he still in the hospital, miss?"

I don't know the answer to any of these questions, because no one has told me. When I asked the governor's secretary, she informed me with a stony look that I would be "informed if there were any developments."

Angela, usually a fount of information, didn't know anything either. So the only thing to do was to carry on with my routine. Today, the potatoes have already been carved into shape—I did this earlier myself to avoid any more accidents. So all the men have to do is cover their potato with black paint (approved by the governor) and press it on the page.

Primary school stuff.

But I daren't take my eyes off them, and it's a relief when class is over. Swiftly, I clear up, aware that it's dark outside. Prison feels even weirder at night. More threatening.

As I'm about to lock the door and head towards the main office to sign out, a shadow approaches. I jump. Although my brain registers that it's an officer standing in front of me, my heart continues beating with fear. "The governor wants to see you," she snaps.

So late? It's seven p.m. The day ends early in prisons, and the night staff have taken over. Sounds like I'm being called in to discuss something big that can't wait. My shifts vary but it so happens that I'm due back here in the morning. Maybe Barry has died, I tell myself as I follow the woman with her crisp white shirt and black epaulets. There'll be a murder investigation. They'll blame me for not watching everything. The papers will get hold of it. Some might say it's what he deserved. Others will blame me for lack of supervision. What on earth did I think I was doing, coming here?

"Alison." The governor beckons me in as he sits down in front of me at the desk. His face is blank—it's impossible to read it.

He picks up a pen in his right hand, and there's a piece of paper in front of him. "The thing is, Alison, there's been a development."

"Is Barry all right?" I burst out.

"That depends on what you call 'all right.' He's going to survive, but, despite a few operations, they've been unable to save the sight in one eye."

Despite my relief, I find myself thinking that being partially blind is a small punishment for the lives of three children.

"I'm afraid there's something else. A member of staff has said they used the stationery cupboard shortly after you claimed you put the scissors back. They insisted it was open. There were drawing pins loose on the shelf. A real mess inside."

"I don't know about that, but I do know I locked it."

He gives me a disbelieving look. I'm so desperate to defend myself that I find myself answering back in a way I wouldn't normally do. "Who said it was open? And why didn't they say so at the time?"

The pen is moving across the report sheet. "I'm not at liberty to tell you. The point is, Alison, that we are within our rights to suspend you."

My mouth is dry. Is this it?

"But in view of the lack of corroborating evidence, I'm giving you a warning." The pen has stopped. The glasses are off. A pair of steely grey eyes stare at me. "We offered you this job, Alison, because we were impressed by your abilities as an artist and the way you handled yourself at the interview. But if anything like this happens again, we will have to let you go."

My heart is pounding as I leave. Is it fear? Or relief?

14

December 2016

Kitty

———

Johnny didn't come to Kitty's room at the usual time.

"Don't . . . get . . . upset," said Margaret. "He's . . . probably . . . gone off . . . you . . . That's . . . what . . . my . . . boyfriend . . . did in the . . . other . . . home . . . before I . . . came . . . here."

Perhaps it was because she'd messed up in the concert. More hot tears ran silently down Kitty's cheeks. Or maybe his mother had taken him home. He wouldn't be missing her one bit.

"Kitty? Are you still awake?"

Her heart leaped with relief at the sight of the square-faced man with the short, thick neck, kneeling by her bed. "You're here," she babbled.

"Did you think I wasn't coming?"

Johnny slid under the covers next to her. "I had to wait until Duncan had gone to sleep. I don't trust him. Keeps asking me where I go at night."

"Hummm, hummm," hummed Kitty in utter bliss as Johnny's warm body snuggled up again, just like the other nights. How wonderful to feel his skin against hers!

"I was so proud of you in the concert today. You were wonderful. I've always wanted a girlfriend."

Yes!

"Will you marry me, Kitty? Shall we be together forever and ever?"

Kitty's heart felt as if it was going to burst! Never had she felt anything like this before. It was as though she was flying.

No! Margaret had woken up. She was panting, just like she did when she had breathing problems. If she didn't stop making that terrible noise, they'd get found out!

"Who's..."—*gasp*—"... there? What's..."—*gasp*—"... going...on?"

"It's only me," said Johnny quickly. "Don't worry."

Margaret's gasps were getting worse. A bit like last time when she'd caused a diversion. But this sounded real.

"I think she's ill," said Johnny. His voice was sharp with panic. "We have to pull the emergency cord."

"But if we do that, the staff will come in," said Kitty.

"I reckon you agree, too."

Cord. Alarm. Footsteps flying down the corridor.

Johnny was sitting on the edge of the bed now. But his trousers were still undone.

"Do them up," hissed Kitty.

But this time he didn't seem to get what she was saying. Perhaps it was because he was too busy trying to comfort Margaret, whose lips were turning blue.

"Please wake up," begged Johnny, stroking her cheek. "Don't die."

Don't die. Kitty's skin began to crawl. She had heard those words before. Where was it?

"Don't die, Margaret." Johnny's voice got higher. Margaret's face was pale, as though the blood had left.

Kitty started shaking all over. *Don't die. Don't die.*

15

December 2016

Alison

———

If it wasn't for the governor giving me my final warning, I might have told him about the note and the photograph. But there's no way I can tell him now. He might think I was making it up to deflect attention. I need this job. Far better to lie low, keep my head down, I tell myself.

My usual nightmares have now been joined by a bloody eye staring up at me, dripping black liquid. When I woke this morning, screaming, I had to check my pajamas to make sure they weren't stained. Of course, they weren't. But I put them in the wash along with my bedsheets.

There's something else, too. According to his statement, Barry claims he hurt himself with those scissors "by accident."

"It's what they say when they're being bullied," Angela explained when I asked her about it. "Someone in that class of yours had it in for him. If he grassed, then he'd get it even worse. Trust me. I've seen it all." She gave a little sigh. "If I could find another job that paid the same, I'd be out of here like a shot."

I'm beginning to wonder if I can stick it out, too—especially when I am told that none of the other men in my group had "seen anything." The police couldn't press charges.

"What about this member of staff who said the cupboard door was open?" I asked Angela. "I don't understand why they'd lie. Or why they waited to come forward."

"Maybe it was an officer who went off shift for a bit."

"Can you help me find out?"

"Love, they all work odd hours. If you ask me, I wouldn't make any trouble. In this place, it has a habit of coming back and getting you."

Her words scare me. Meanwhile, the stabbing makes me even more aware of the lack of security.

"Can't I have a guard for my classes?" I asked the deputy governor.

But apparently, there aren't enough resources, so my only protection is the whistle on my belt. It's almost laughable. Except I'm terrified.

Now I watch my men like a hawk.

They don't trust me. And I don't trust them. At least there are no more anonymous notes. It suddenly strikes me that Barry might have been the culprit because I hadn't paid enough attention to his cat pictures. What a horrible man. Yet, if I'm right that he's the note writer—and I'm pretty sure I am—it's also a relief to know that I don't have to worry anymore.

I try to distract myself over the weekend with a day out at the Victoria and Albert. It's one of my favorite museums. The stained glass windows in the dining room alone are worth visiting. On the way home, I stop off at a charity shop to stock up on my scarf supply. But then I remember what the governor said that first day about prisoners working in places like this, and I hurry out. Nowhere feels safe anymore.

Christmas is fast approaching. This is, I am discovering, a strange time in prison. Men are edgy, desperate for their families.

On the out (as they call the outside world), there's a tangible air of excitement. My stained glass workshop students are keen to finish their panels in time to give them as presents to their nearest and dearest. Beryl's is intended for her daughter in York.

"Will it be safe to send it in the post?" she asks.

I think of all the hard work that's gone into her blue and scarlet tulip.

"Why not wait until you see her?"

She purses her lips with disappointment. "That might not be until Easter."

York isn't that far. What kind of daughter doesn't get together with her mother at this time of the year?

Yet, I don't see my mother enough either. The memories of my sister hang too heavily between us, and especially at Christmas, when families are meant to be together. I steer my mind away from thinking about that first awful December.

Clive is the only one who doesn't say who he's giving his panel to. Part of me is curious. I think of that Disney watch in his pocket. Does he have a child? Is he married? But the other part doesn't want to ask in case he sees it as a come-on. That declined invitation to dinner is an unspoken barrier between us. In another life, I might have accepted.

But this isn't another life. It's now.

In the prison class, we're making cards at the moment. I can't call them Christmas cards, because there are lots of different faiths here. So some of the men make their own for their particular festivals at other times of the year. "Diversification" is a big word in prison, I am learning. Carefully, I cut out the shapes at home with my own scissors. That way, I don't have to check the stationery cupboard lock over and over again.

"Pretty colors," says Kurt as he admires the red, silver and gold cutouts. "Can I put glitter on mine?"

Once more, I am reminded of how childish some of these grown-up murderers and rapists can be.

The cards are going on display in the main hall, near the governor's office, before they're sent home to family. So, too, are the other pictures we've been working on, including the portraits.

"Are you going to put up yours, too, miss?" asks Kurt. "The one that Stefan did of you."

I don't want to. For a start, it reminds me of the terrible scissor accident. And secondly, it brings back the mutilated photograph and the *I'M GOING TO GET YOU*. But if I refuse, then I'm depriving Stefan of the right to show his picture. So up it goes.

The week before Christmas, there's a concert with a mixture of carols and also nonreligious songs and readings. Afterwards, the governor comes up to me.

"I've had some good feedback about your work. The portrait exhibition has attracted a lot of interest." His mouth forces itself into an uneasy smile. "Not sure it's such a sensible idea to put yourself up there, mind you."

I flush. "We had uneven numbers in the class. I had to allow one of the prisoners to draw me."

His lips tighten. "Just be careful, Alison. Always keep a distance."

I try, I want to say. But he has gone, weaving in through the audience of board members and special guests. I get the feeling that, although I haven't left any more stationery cupboards unlocked, I've messed up one more time.

Right now, I can't wait to get out, even though I've agreed to come back between Christmas and New Year. "The other staff have kids," says Angela pointedly. "They need their time off. Me, I've got grandkids. In Australia. Cost me a fortune in posting presents, they do, but wouldn't be without them for the world. Just wish I could afford to visit them a bit more—or even better, go and live there. But my husband says we're too old to emigrate."

The concert is over now. "Happy Christmas, miss," says Kurt as I get ready to sign out.

Mum's house might have too many memories, but at least I'm not spending this time of the year in a cell. "Thank you, Kurt. You, too."

Aware of my hollow words, I walk down through the main hall, glancing up at my portrait as I do so.

There's something small and red written in the left-hand corner of the portrait. Something that surely wasn't there before.

SEE YOU SOON.

My mouth goes dry. I'd thought I was safe after Grandad Barry was hospitalized. But now it looks like someone else is behind these messages. Unless I have more than one stalker. I wouldn't put anything past this place. I'd love to leave, but the bills won't get paid on their own.

Goose pimples break out down my arms. Hastily, I reach into my bag for a pen and scribble out the "See you soon" before anyone else reads it and wonders what it's about. Then I walk briskly—almost running—into the office to sign out.

"Have a good one," says the officer.

It's the first time since the scissor episode that this particular woman has spoken to me.

Clearly, she thinks I'm responsible.

"Thanks," I mutter. "You, too."

As I walk towards the car, I tell myself that the *See you soon* is just a silly bit of graffiti.

When I get into the car, my mobile—safely stored in the dashboard—is flashing. I have a voice mail.

"Alison?" It's my mother. "Can you ring and tell me what time you're arriving tomorrow, please? I can't wait to see you, darling."

SEE YOU SOON.

I won't tell her about it. She'd only worry.

My phone pings in my hand, indicating an incoming e-mail. It's from the college where I run my stained glass course. A reminder for the Christmas dinner in a couple of days that I had somehow forgotten.

Not, of course, that I'm going.

Christmas has never been the same without my sister. I have a fleeting memory of wrapping mum's present together: her special perfume that we'd pooled our pocket money for. Mum had been so thrilled when she'd opened it. "My girls," she'd said. "I'm so lucky to have you."

How ironic. No wonder I can't move on.

*S*irens.
    Screaming.
Or is that the sea?
A wave hurtling towards me.
Under.
Under.
And then up again.
Screaming.
Coffee spilled on paper.
The summerhouse.
There has to be a link. Somewhere.

16

December 2016

Kitty

———

Kitty hadn't been able to move when Bossy Supervisor had seen them. She couldn't move much anyway, of course, but this was different.

Paralysis by fear.

Not just because of Bossy Supervisor's shocked, angry face. But because of the memory that had been triggered.

Don't die.

Who had said that? And when?

"Thank goodness you're here!" gasped Johnny, before Bossy Supervisor could open her mouth.

"Margaret was having breathing problems," he continued. "That's why we pulled the alarm. She got frightened and lashed out at poor Kitty. Just look at her pajama top. It's all torn."

Kitty had to hand it to Johnny. Torn pajama top? He'd been so eager just now that he'd ripped it open himself! Talk about quick thinking.

Very Thin Carer was rushing in now with an oxygen machine. That was good. Kitty didn't want Margaret to die. A new roommate might not allow Johnny's nighttime visits. Besides, she liked Margaret, even though she could be a bit weird at times.

"Would you like to explain what you are doing in the girls' wing?" snapped Bossy Supervisor.

Johnny put on his bashful look. Kitty had seen him doing this before. It was a mixture of *I'm really sorry* and *You're not going to tell me off, are you?* Very effective!

"After the concert, Margaret said I had to look after her glasses very, very carefully." He put his hand in his pocket and brought out the same pair that Kitty had seen quite clearly only a few minutes ago, next to her friend's bed. "I thought she might need them now. She likes a bit of a read in bed. That's what she's always telling us."

How wonderfully clever.

"Then you should have told one of the carers instead of bringing them here yourself."

"You're right." Johnny's voice was particularly slow and sorry now. "But I was still feeling really, really excited after the concert. I wanted to tell the girls how great they were."

There was a hint of hesitation on Bossy Supervisor's face. Kitty held her breath. Johnny might look different with those slightly slit eyes and intense way of staring. But he knew how to make people like him. Including her.

"And would you like to explain why your trousers are undone?"

Johnny looked down as if this was news to him. "Whoops! Must have forgotten to do them up after the loo." He shook his head. "I do that sometimes. Sorry."

Don't giggle, Kitty told herself sharply. It might give the game away.

"I think Margaret had breathing problems because it's so hot," he added.

Nice! He was deflecting the blame away from them.

"It *is* hot," said the carer, putting away the oxygen equipment. "I can't breathe myself. Must be the thermostat again. Perhaps you'd better get the plumber back."

"I've already left a message, but it's hard to get anyone at this time of the year." Bossy Supervisor's mouth tightened. "It looks like there's been some kind of misunderstanding. But I don't want it to leak out that a boy was found in the girls' wing."

"I'll be off, then," said Johnny quickly. "Don't leave your glasses behind again, will you, Margaret?"

This time, Kitty couldn't help it. A small giggle escaped from her mouth. Luckily, it came out as a gurgle. Johnny would be back when the fuss had died down. She just knew it. At last, she had a proper boyfriend. It was, Kitty thought with a lovely, warm feeling in her tummy, all she'd ever wanted. That and getting her memory back, of course.

Maybe if she closed her eyes and thought very, very hard, she might work out what *Don't die* meant.

But, try as she might, it wouldn't come back. And before she knew it, it was time for breakfast again.

17

Alison

———

The college where I teach stained glass is organizing a dinner in an Italian restaurant not far from Waterloo station. "You should go," said Mum when I'd stupidly mentioned it during an early evening phone call. "Honestly. You can come down to me later instead. I'm always saying you need more fun in your life. Your sister wouldn't want you to be a hermit."

Maybe she has a point. If our positions had been reversed, I know very well that she'd be out right now partying. When she was little, she played dress-up and I'd do her hair. How she'd loved that! If I stay in, I'll just think about the old times. So, against my better judgment, I decide to go to the dinner after all.

As I arrive, jazz music fills the air. Arty-looking types in pastel-colored pashminas weave in and out. There are tulip yellow tablecloths. Instantly, I know I like this place, although I now regret choosing the black trousers and roll-neck top I'd worn during my last class at Archville.

I recognize some of the tutors by sight at the big, noisy table and walk over.

"Alison!" calls out someone, waving his hand.

I stop dead. It's Clive. Sitting next to the only empty space.

He looks different. More relaxed than his college persona. His clothes are what my mother would call "smart casual": crisp pink and white shirt with dark navy jeans. He jumps up, and for a minute, I think he's going to kiss me on both cheeks. But instead, he pulls out the chair for me. I can tell that this is the sort of man who would leap out of the driver's seat and open the passenger door for you.

"They weren't sure if you were coming."

Now that I'm closer, I realize that the "relaxed" veneer is a front. In fact, his fingers are actually trembling as much as mine are as he rearranges, unnecessarily, the cutlery on the table.

I feel a sudden need to make it all right.

"You look different without your apron," I say.

I speak just as the waiter comes up to take our order. His expression is priceless. Clive and I look at each other. Clearly, the waiter doesn't realize I am referring to the pinny from the stained glass course. It makes Clive sound as though he's a bit of a girl instead! For a split second, there is silence. Then we both start to laugh at the same time until tears are running down our faces.

And after that, it's all right.

My laughter is a release. Not because of the pinny image, but because I'm no longer in that place. I'm not sure why Clive is laughing so much. The apron joke isn't that funny. Maybe it's relief, too. It's rather reassuring that he's not as confident as I'd assumed from the flashy car and the high-level job.

"Hi, Alison," says Beryl with a wave from the other end of the table. "Love the stars!"

What?

Clive reaches across and plucks something from my hair. It's sparkly red paper in a star shape. "It must have been caught in my jumper during the craft lesson," I bluster, embarrassed by his unexpectedly intimate gesture.

"You've been teaching at a school?" asks Clive, smiling.

"I've been in prison, actually."

The man opposite—whom I don't know—glances across at me nervously. Clive seems unsettled, too.

"You mean . . ."

He stops.

"I'm an artist in residence at a prison," I say hastily. I raise my voice slightly so no one else gets the wrong idea.

"What kind of prison?" Clive's eyes are now sparkling with interest. The only person who knows is my mother, and she's horrified. It's not as though I have friends anymore (my own choice), so I can't gauge what their reactions would be. "Actually, it's a prison for men."

He looks both shocked and curious. "Tell me more."

"It's an open prison for men who have either been given short sentences or are coming to the end of longer ones when they've done something serious a long time ago."

"Such as?"

Murder. Rape. Grievous bodily harm.

I could say all of these. But I don't want to. If I do, I might find myself telling this nice man everything. The stabbing, the child-killer, the strange messages I am so desperately trying to forget.

"Is it dangerous?"

A pair of scissors dances in the air before me. And that glassy stare. The blood. I can almost hear the screams.

"It could be if you're not careful," I say slowly. *Not that I've told my mother that*, I remind myself silently.

Clive's eyes hold me steadily. "I think you're very brave," he says. To my surprise, he places a hand on mine.

I'm so embarrassed that I knock over my glass of elderflower, and it spills all over him. How awful! He has to go to the gents to dry off his jeans. "No problem," he says kindly afterwards, our eyes locking again.

My other students are at the far end of the table. I should talk more to the stranger on my left, but I find that I want to know more about Clive. Despite everything, there's something that draws me to him in a way I cannot explain.

"Where do you work?" I ask, tucking into my prawn cocktail. A slightly naff choice, I know, but I've always loved it. My father used to make it sometimes, according to my mother. It was one of the few things she'd ever told me about him.

"One of my offices is nearby," he says casually, distracting me from my moment of sadness.

One of his offices?

"I own a manufacturing business in the Far East. We make paper lanterns."

He's leaning towards me in the way that people do when they're enthusiastic about something. "I love beautiful things. Especially if they're a pretty color. Always have done. It's why I signed up for your course rather than any other."

"What about family?"

The question is out of my mouth before I can take it back. But he doesn't seem to think I'm being nosy. "My mother has given up on me in the marital stakes. Says I'm too fussy."

"Mine, too!" Then, in case he thinks the previous sentence is a come-on, I add another. "Although I'm quite happy with my own company."

"I know what you mean. Anyway, work takes up most of my time. What about you? How did you get into art?"

My back starts to sweat. My mouth goes dry. I take a swig of sparkling water. "I was going to study history at university but then changed my mind and did art instead."

"Really?" He flicks back that flop of hair. "Why?"

"Last-minute change of plan."

Thankfully, he doesn't ask why.

"Now I freelance," I say swiftly. "I prefer it."

"Me, too. Couldn't bear to work for someone else now." He bats away the air as if the threat is actually physical.

Swiftly, I turn the subject to other things. We talk about art exhibitions. The Royal Academy is his favorite gallery. We both love films in translation and running along the Thames (something I haven't had time to do for ages). Neither of us mentions our family. Nor do we ask each other that question that everyone else does at this time: "What are you doing for Christmas and New Year?"

The evening goes faster than I realize.

"I wish I didn't have to leave," he says, around ten p.m., "but I have an early start. We need to check that the final orders are out for Christmas."

"I need to go, too."

"May I walk you to your car?"

Beryl's eyebrows rise as she watches us go. I'm embarrassed. But also flattered.

"So," he says, as he accompanies me to my scuffed Beetle, which, ironically, is parked just behind his shiny silver Porsche, "do you have any spaces left on your next course?"

"Just the one," I say lightly.

"I can't commit yet because of work," continues Clive. "But I'd love to do it if I can. May I confirm with the college in January?"

My euphoria is now replaced with a sickening rush of disappointment. "Of course."

Then I drive off. Telling myself that I had no right to expect anything else. It was just a Christmas college dinner. Perhaps he doesn't fancy me. After all, he didn't even ask me for my number. Would I have given it to him if he had? Yes. No. I'm not sure.

Letting myself into the flat, I head straight for my emergency box of glass bits. Quickly, I press one to the palm of my hand. A small trickle of blood starts to seep out. I feel a flash of pain combined with relief.

Just as I'm about to go further, there's a knock on the door.

It's my landlord, shifting from one maroon-slippered foot to the other as if embarrassed about troubling me. "I picked this up from the hall table by mistake," he says, handing over an envelope. "Thought I'd bring it round in person with my own card."

Luckily, I've written him a Christmas card, too. I thank him and hand it over. Then I shut the door.

I open the envelope and pull out the contents. It's a pretty, glittery scene of a young woman and man in a horse-drawn carriage from Victorian times.

Then I look inside.

HAPPY CHRISTMAS, it says.

Followed by the words *MAY ALL YOUR SINS BE FORGIVEN.*

18

Christmas Day 2016

Kitty

———

Christmas Day started with Margaret having another asthma attack. Kitty tried to pull the alarm cord, but her good arm wasn't
as good as usual, and it took a while for one of the carers to see what
was going on.

Then there was a bit of a distraction when Dawn's mother made her
annual visit—a day after she usually did, for some reason. "Don't you
recognize me, love?" she kept wailing. Everyone knew Dawn was just
trying to piss her off. Like Duncan said, "Who can blame her? We're
not fucking battery hens that people gawp at when they feel like it."

Kitty didn't want to eat lunch because she kept thinking about the
empty space at the table. Johnny's. Unlike most of them, he'd gone
home to spend Christmas with his family.

After lunch, they all dozed off in their chairs (mouths open, snore,
snore) or went to their rooms for a "little lie-down." Kitty was plonked
in front of a film where a woman in black and white spent the whole
time screaming at a man and then married him at the end.

"*So* sorry I'm late, but the traffic was terrible."

Friday Mum! There she was, walking through the door, nattering
away to Bossy Supervisor as though they were best friends.

"Don't worry. Kitty won't know any better."

"Excuse me," said Kitty. "I *am* here, you know."

"She looks a bit upset," whispered Friday Mum.

"I'm afraid we've had one or two issues."

Bossy Supervisor lowered her voice. But Kitty could hear the odd word. "Still has an attachment to the young man . . . Nothing to worry about . . . Just thought you ought to know . . ."

Then Mum came over and held her hand.

"You always loved Christmas as a child. I remember one year when you woke up to find a playhouse in the garden. Your dad and I had a terrible job putting it up the night before so you didn't see it. But it was worth it to see the magical look on your face."

Friday Mum's eyes had tears in them now.

"What happened to me?" Kitty demanded. "How did I end up here? I've heard you talking about an accident, but what kind? Was it the sea? Did I fall off a horse like Maurice fell off his bike?"

"I wish I knew what you were saying. I really do."

Friday Mum stood up. "I'm sorry. I know I've just arrived. But I can't do this. It's just too upsetting."

And then she was gone.

But another surprise came not long after that.

"You have a second visitor!" exclaimed Bossy Supervisor. "Someone's popular, aren't they? And he's bought you a present."

Johnny!

But instead, a pair of shiny, holey shoes stood in front of her.

No. NO!

"Now, now, Kitty," said Bossy Supervisor. "Let's not go through all that silly head banging again. Don't you *want* to see your father?"

Her father? Was that who he was? A vague memory was coming back now. He hadn't been so fat then. But there were parts she recognized: his deep voice, those blue eyes just like hers. And of course the presents he was always giving her. "Anything you want," she could now recall him saying. "Nothing's too good for daddy's little girl . . ."

"GO AWAY. AND TAKE YOUR BLOODY GIFT WITH YOU!"

"I'm not sure what you're saying, love, but . . ."

CRASH.

Bloody hell. She'd got herself so upset that she'd fallen out of her chair.

"Emergency," screamed Bossy Supervisor.

"Let me help."

"GET THE FUCK OUT!"

"I think it might be best if you left. Kitty seems rather upset."

You could say that again. She was pretty certain now that this man had once been responsible for someone's death. But whose? Kitty asked herself. And why?

19

Christmas Day 2016

Alison

The fever started soon after I'd got back from the college dinner. Unable to sleep, I'd forced myself to wrap up and go out again to the late-night chemist on the corner. Then I'd staggered back in the cold, heaving one foot in front of the other, desperately hoping I'd make it back to the flat.

But the medicine hasn't touched it. Right now, a pernicious ache has taken over my body like the mist outside, which is wrapping its way round the buildings as I stand at the window. Is that a shadow I can see? Or is flu making me hallucinate?

"It's doing the rounds," Angela had already warned during the days leading up to our Christmas break. "Not much you can do about it. Prisoners get ill like anyone else. In fact, I don't feel great myself. Just what I need. My husband's bloody awful at looking after anyone apart from himself, so I won't get any sympathy from him."

Fear. Flu. Call it what you will. But something scary is seeping through my bones.

I can no longer blame Grandad Barry or pretend that what's happening is a harmless prank.

Someone is after me.

MAY ALL YOUR SINS BE FORGIVEN.

No one knows where I live. I am paranoid about that. The college where I teach—and even the prison—has a PO box address listed for me. The only post I receive is from utilities. I don't have a Facebook account. I regularly change my pay-as-you-go mobile number. Naturally, I'm careful who I give it to.

So how did the card with the sparkly carriage and the London post-mark get here?

My sheets are soaked with sweat. And, despite the cold, sharp air that's coming through the open window, my entire body is burning.

Or did it begin burning during dinner with Clive? There was some-thing about him that stirred longings inside me I've only had once before. Something I don't want to think about.

Anyway, it's not right. I'm not allowed. I would be letting down my sister. Hadn't I deprived her of love? She could've been married by now. I might have been a bridesmaid. It's what sisters do . . .

These thoughts are going round my head when my mobile goes. Listlessly, I reject the call, then check the time and the caller: *11:59 a.m. Mum.*

So much time has passed! Thanks to my fever—for that's what it feels like now—I haven't even wished mum "Happy Christmas" yet! I yearn to talk to her, but I need to get my story right first.

I am going to have to leave my flat now I've been found. Find a safer place. My heart sinks at the thought. I like it here. Besides, even if I do move, what's to say I won't be found again?

One thing is clear. Mum mustn't know what's going on. She's had enough to deal with already. I start texting a message.

But then I hesitate. I don't want to say I've got flu, or she'll be round here, ministering to me. She tried to do that after the accident, and it didn't work. We were both too consumed by our grief. My sister's empty room. Her silent place at the table. Her shoes that still lay, wait-ing, for her to slip back into them.

Sorry. Am with friends

I can barely concentrate on the screen.

Speak later

Then my sweaty fingers drop the phone onto the floor, and I let the darkness take me.

20

Christmas Day 2016

Kitty

___

At the hospital, they put her arm in plaster. According to the nurse, she had fractured it. They'd also taken off her nappy and got her to pee into a bowl. And now the doctor didn't seem very happy.

"We just need to do a couple more tests, Kitty. This is a special machine called an ultrasound. It's going to look inside your tummy."

Kitty stared up at the big screen in front of her. It was a mess of lines, bobbing up and down and making funny noises. Looked like they needed a new telly. Suddenly, she remembered something else about her so-called father. Once, he'd bought her a telly for her bedroom— she was sure of it!

"Do you see that?"

The doctor's voice was different from before.

The nurse gave a strange nod.

Then there was a heavy sigh. It seemed to come from both of them. "Thank you, Kitty. Now the nurse will help you get dressed again."

"No," said Kitty, shaking her head and then nodding it just to be certain. "I rather like this gown that you've put me in. Green and white! Makes a change from the clothes I have to wear in the home. And how about bloody lunch?"

But they were wheeling her out. Back down the squeaky corridors. Into the van through the streets where people walked instead of pushing themselves in chairs. And into the home.

That's when the trouble really started.

21

January 2017

Alison

When I finally feel better, I turn on the television and watch the morning presenter wittering on. That's when I realize I've missed not only Christmas but New Year's Eve, too. They've never been the same since the accident. Even before, I'd always been conscious of a father's absence at this "family" time of year. So I'm grateful for the blurring of the last few days. All I can recall is my burning body, getting up to stagger across to the kitchen with a dry mouth to get more water and—or have I imagined this?—the sound of someone at the front door.

Now, I look down at my sweaty body and my damp sheets, which have that distinct odor of illness. I am still here. I've survived. Whoever sent those messages hasn't got me.

So far.

Of course, I tell myself as I take a warm shower and make myself get dressed despite still feeling weak, I don't *have* to go back to the prison.

Instead, I can just leave. Move flats, find a new job. Think of some story to tell Mum. But I have to be brave. For my sister's sake. As a child, she hadn't been scared of anything. "Don't be silly," she'd said once when she found me cowering in the corner of the bathroom because there was an enormous spider climbing out of the sink. Then, very gently, she had lifted it up and placed it outside the window. "See," she'd said, not unkindly. "It didn't kill me, did it?"

Reflecting on this, I search for my phone while doing up my jeans. The waist hangs loose on me after not eating for so many days. There are a few missed calls from a number I don't recognize. This freaks me out. Could it be the person who sent the card?

There are also several texts from Mum. The disappointed ones come first.

So sorry you can't make it. Hope you had a nice time with your friends.

I can tell she's curious. In truth, I don't have either the time or inclination for a social life, although I had enjoyed that college dinner with Clive . . .

Then came the worried ones.

Where are you? Please let me know you're all right.

Do all thirtysomething women feel like this about their mothers? Such a mix of guilt and fear and love?

But we are different. Mum and I had been close before. Yet the accident has given us an extra bond that no one else could understand unless they'd been through it.

When I ring, having worked out my excuse, the voice mail is on. Maybe she's out for a sherry with a neighbor who feels sorry for this woman whose own daughter can't be bothered to see her at this time of the year.

"Mum, it's me. Look, I didn't want to tell you earlier, but I haven't been well. Only flu. Can you call? I could come down next weekend, if you like. I've got to go back to the prison tomorrow."

Too late, I wish I'd said "work" instead of "prison." My mother has clearly told me that she was "not at all happy" about my new job.

Meanwhile, my stomach is rumbling. I need food. There's nothing in the fridge. I'd been planning to go shopping before I got ill. Even the eggs are out of date. But my legs have suddenly gone weak. Supposing my stalker is waiting outside the door?

"Alison!"

The voice in the communal hallway strikes fear into me before the sensible part of my brain registers who is speaking.

It's my landlord. For a minute, I almost don't recognize him. Gone are the usual rather scruffy blue jeans. Instead, he wears a pair of beige chinos and a different pair of slippers—they have Rudolph faces.

"I thought I heard the odd movement, but I haven't seen you coming in and out. Just wanted to make sure you were all right." My landlord usually keeps himself to himself. But Christmas seems to make others more solicitous, in my experience.

"I've been in bed with flu," I say.

He edges away. "Won't come near then, if you don't mind. Got the grandchildren coming round."

So he has a family. Once more, I feel desperately alone. Mum doesn't count. We're both as lonely as each other. Especially when we're together.

Then I head out into the street and make for the corner shop. Is anyone watching? I can't see an obvious candidate.

It almost makes it scarier. If I knew who was after me, at least I could prepare myself.

When I get back, I realize I'd left my mobile behind. There it is, lying on the sofa. The screen announces that I've missed a call. It's the same number I noticed before. A heavy feeling settles in my chest. Should I ring back? Yes. No.

I go to the window. A woman is walking past with her dog. A youth is cycling by. Someone out there is watching and waiting.

What would my sister do?

Get one step ahead, of course.

I can almost hear her voice.

Perhaps, instead of being scared, I need to take the initiative. I just need to think how.

22

January 2017

Alison

I've spent the last few days trying to work out my strategy and considering all the options. Who are the notes from? Maybe someone is winding me up. Hadn't Angela warned me about this? But if the notes are genuine, I'm probably safer in prison than being in the flat. At least here I'm surrounded by people, with guards only a whistle away.

Either way, I cannot give in my notice. I need the money, and there aren't that many vacancies for artists. You have to take what you can get. But I'm going to be on my guard from now on. Far more than before.

The older man with the eastern European accent, Stefan, is waiting for me today in Education, along with Kurt and some new faces. There's a banker—he's keen to tell me this, as if wanting to differentiate himself from the others. He particularly keeps his distance from Stefan, who's looking scruffier than the last time I saw him: hair unkempt and the shadow of a beard on his cheeks.

Despite my earlier determination to stand up for myself, I cannot stop shaking all through my class.

"You are ill, I think," Stefan says.

"It's nothing," I retort dismissively.

What if I find another message? By lunchtime, I have decided to ask Angela's advice. Out of everyone here, she's the one person I trust the most. I haven't seen her for the last few days—maybe I'll catch her in the canteen today.

But she's not there. Instead, there's a huddle of women from the admin office, talking quietly at a corner table. "What's going on?" I say in what I hope is an easy manner. I've never been a girl's girl. Far better on my own. In fact, Angela is the closest I've come to having a work friend. Perhaps it's because this environment is so different from anything I've come across.

"It's Angela."

No! When something bad has already happened to you in life, you are constantly on the alert for the next thing.

"Angela's been sacked."

I don't believe it.

"She's been selling mobile phones to the men."

"Come on," I say. "Is this a joke? She wouldn't do anything like that."

Not Angela who was always helping me understand prison rules.

"That's just the tip of it," adds one of the others. "She's been selling weed to the men, too. Hiding it at the back of the stationery cupboard, can you believe? That's how she was caught. She'd had a spare key made for the blokes she was passing the stuff on to. One of the officers found it during a routine search of B hut."

The stationery cupboard.

"Silly idiot," snorted someone else. "If you're going to break the law, make sure you cover your tracks."

I stay quiet. I'm trying to take it in. How could I have been so naive?

"Her husband made her do it to pay off his gambling debts," adds the first woman.

"Couldn't she have refused?" I asked.

"Why do you think she wore long sleeves all the time? He used to beat her up if she didn't do what he said. Poor woman might have put a brave face on it, but she was bloody terrified of the bastard. And now she's the one in prison."

I can barely concentrate on my afternoon workshop. I'm still reeling. No one is who they seem in this place. I've received a short note from the governor that absolves me of having left the stationery cupboard unlocked. There is no formal apology. But the inference is clear. Angela, whom I'd trusted, had allowed me to be the scapegoat for her crime. Was it possible that she had been the one who'd reported the "open" stationery cupboard? But why the delay in reporting? Perhaps she was trying to throw me off the scent. It wouldn't be the first time I'd heard of staff turning against one another in prison.

What am I doing in this terrible place?

My legs still feel weak from that wretched flu. The sooner I get home, the better. Then, just as I'm about to get into the car to set off, my phone bleeps with an e-mail from the college.

Clive. He would like to sign up for the spring-term course, but it's full. Would I mind fitting in an extra student?

I feel a flash of excitement followed by doubt and then excitement again.

That's fine, I e-mail back. Then I wonder if I've done the right thing.

Minutes after I send the reply, my phone rings. Clive? Of course not. He doesn't have my number. The screen reads *Mum*.

"Are you all right?" I ask.

I often start a phone call with Mum like this. So does she. After the accident, we both have this fear that another tragedy will befall one of us, leaving the other totally alone.

"Darling, I don't want to worry you. But something's happened."

I listen, stunned by what she is telling me. Suddenly, Clive isn't important. Nor are the men who are waiting for me. Nor is Angela, who framed me for her stationery cupboard crime—a betrayal that still hurts, even though she had a reason.

Still in the driving seat, I ring the prison switchboard to explain I have to cancel my classes tomorrow. "There's been a family emergency," I say.

23

January 2017

Kitty

———

"Kitty, would you like to come into my office now?"

Something was wrong. Bossy Supervisor was actually addressing *her*—and not one of the carers. As if she could just get up and walk!

"Johnny!" cried out Kitty as she was wheeled in.

To her relief, he lumbered up and gave her a big, warm hug. There was an "ahh" and a "Watch out for her poor arm" from Johnny's mother, who was there, too.

"I missed you," she wept.

"I've missed you," said Johnny, tenderly wiping away her tears. Then he glared at the others in the room. "We want to have our baby. You have no right to stop us."

"Baby?" babbled Kitty. Had she missed something here? "What baby?"

"You're pregnant!" said Johnny, kneeling down next to her. "Isn't that wonderful, Kitty? We're going to have a child all of our own. A real baby."

"Utterly ridiculous," sniffed a man in a suit standing next to Johnny's mother. "She can't even talk. How can she have a kid?"

"Darling, have some compassion."

Then the door opened. Flabby Face was coming towards her. The man they said was her father.

"No!" Kitty squirmed in her chair. "I don't want him here."

"Don't get upset, Kitty. We'll sort out this mess. I promise."

"Fuck off. Go away."

"Will someone stop my daughter from banging her head against the chair like that? And why hasn't anyone brushed her hair? Just because she has to wear a helmet doesn't mean you can't tidy the rest of it."

"Actually, I'd like to say something."

There was someone else in the room. A soft-voiced, tall woman who had come in behind flabby-faced man. She was younger than him. Her blond hair was very short, making her look a bit like a pixie on children's television.

For some reason, a flash of a blond plait flitted through Kitty's mind. And a school satchel.

"I'm sorry I haven't been before, Kitty. But I'm here now. And I'm going to sort it. I promise."

"Who are you?" Kitty babbled.

"Don't you recognize me, Kitty?" Those eyes were pleading. Terrified. "I'm Ali. Your sister."

24

January 2017

Alison

I study Kitty carefully as I speak. How much can she understand?

It's been so long since I last visited. Years. I've almost made it a few times. Mum nearly persuaded me to come to some concert she was in, not so long ago. But I chickened out on the day. I felt awful. They'd already told Kitty to expect a "special visitor," apparently. Shame on me. But they got round it, Mum said, by taking a picture of her for the local paper. "She liked that a lot."

My sister still has the same elfin face and the turned-up nose. But she's put on weight, and her hair is different, too. During my absence, it has grown back in another color. Brown curls now peep out from under the helmet that helps to keep her skull intact. Of course, I was there, all those years ago, when her lovely blond locks had been shaved off for surgery. Wasn't that why I'd had mine cut short, too? Not just to create a "new me," but—as far as possible—to go through the same experience, just like relatives of chemo patients who have their heads shaved in empathy.

I gulp, trying to take it all in. Dribble is coming out of her mouth as she babbles words that mean nothing to me. Yet I can see flashes of her predecessor. The way she holds my gaze as if challenging me. Those blue eyes that could worm their way into getting whatever she wanted.

It's my little sister. Or, to be more accurate, my half sister, though my mother hated it when I called her that. The thing about sisters is that you're meant to get on. Most parents expect it, even if you're chalk and cheese. But Kitty and I? We were always arguing.

As I look into her eyes, it's like looking into the past. I remember one day at the beach. Our mother had gone to the public loo. "Keep an eye on your sister, Ali." A freak wave nearly carried her off while she was paddling in the rock pools. Somehow, I'd managed to dive through the crest and catch her by the neck of her swimsuit, dragging her onto the beach and safety. "Get off me," she'd screamed furiously, apparently oblivious to the fact that I had saved her life. When my mother returned, my sister claimed I'd "hurt her." The sea was perfectly calm by then. There seemed little point in explaining what had really happened. It wasn't that my mother was unfair: she loved me dearly. But, somehow, my sister always came out on top.

Until she didn't. Brain damage, they said. Never the same again. Miracle that she survived.

Yet, ironically, Kitty has now achieved something that I have deliberately denied myself. A baby. And a man who loves her. It shouldn't be possible, but my throat swells with some of the old envy. How can my mother even think of an abortion? We'll manage somehow. We have to, even though I'm deeply apprehensive.

As for David—who no longer has a beard and has gone all jowly round his chin—I can't even look at him.

"It's out of the question for them to have the baby," my stepfather is now saying.

"Rubbish." I stand up straight. "I will help them."

I don't mean to make the offer. It's totally impractical. Yet I feel like it's the least I can do.

Sometimes over the years, I've heard my students talking about their sisters. "She's my best friend," they might say. Or, "I don't know what I'd do without her."

It always made me want to cry. But now, after all this time, perhaps I have a chance to make things right.

Because the accident was more than just an accident.

I am responsible for Kitty's injuries.

I am the one with blood on my hands.

I am the schoolgirl who killed Vanessa.

My sister's best friend.

Squeaky-clean school shoes.
    Shoulder bags bobbing.
Blond plaits flapping.
Three pairs of feet.
"Don't you dare!"
She pushes me.
I push her.
"Don't die. Don't die."
Then another memory. A fierce wave. A locket. A summerhouse.
How do they fit in?

Part Two

---

2 March 2001

My mother loves me more than anyone else.

That's what she said tonight after tucking me up in bed.

Her face cream smelled of roses.

"Don't tell anyone else," she whispered. "It's our secret."

I'm glad I don't have a real sister. It makes me more important.

It reminds me of this poem we read last term at school. One of the lines jumped out at me. It said, "Blood is thicker than water."

I felt all sick when I read that.

And then I scribbled it out with a black felt-tip.

I got a detention for "defacing a school textbook." But I didn't care.

It was worth it.

25

January 2017

Alison

Why am I here? I don't even know myself. Perhaps because nowhere is safe anymore. Home. Prison. Both are as terrifying as each other.

I think of the lawyer's letter in my bedside nightstand hidden in an old children's painting book that had belonged to Kitty. Proof that I am well and truly in a danger zone for reasons I am too scared to share with anyone.

The signing-in officer gives me my key, and I walk past the huts towards Education. Normally, I keep my wits about me, constantly on the outlook for . . . who knows.

But at this moment, all I can think about is Kitty's face. Her clever blue eyes. She remembers. I'm certain of it.

What am I going to do now? I'm still agonizing when I reach the Education Portakabin. There's a new poster on the door with rough hand-drawn letters in red crayon.

ART STUDIO INSIDE. SECOND ON LEFT.

"Like it, miss?" It's Kurt, hovering on the metal step. "I did it for you during the holiday. Where were you? Thought you was coming in."

"Flu," I say shortly, resisting the temptation to correct his "was" to "were."

He gives me a wink. "Sure. I wouldn't want to come in here myself if I was you."

"Actually, I really was ill."

His face turns sympathetic. "Are you OK now?"

Perhaps, I tell myself, this should be my New Year's resolution. To be more grateful to this man who is trying his best to assist me. Then again, that's not going to help all the people I've hurt in the past.

"Can't make your class this morning, miss," he adds as we go inside.

"Why's that?"

He follows me into the art room and begins to help me put out my wares. Sugar paper. Crayons. Safe materials.

"Have to work on the muck trucks."

These are prison-speak for food trolleys.

"Everyone's sick. That flu gets everywhere." He winks again.

Never mind, I tell myself. I can use any spare time to do some sketching of my own.

"But I've got you another student," adds Kurt proudly. "His name's Martin. Just arrived from another nick, he has. He's OK, this one. Just done his LWV course."

"What's that?"

He speaks as if I should know. "Life without violence."

Is this meant to reassure me?

As he speaks, there's a knock at the main Education door. I unlock it.

A tubby man faces me. He's bald with an angry map of red and white scars all over his face and down to his neck. I try not to stare, but I can feel my cheeks getting hot. Desperately, I concentrate on the round glasses that sit awkwardly on top of a misshapen nose. Inside, I am repulsed.

"Is this the art place?"

There's a hopeful tone in his rough voice, which leaves the *t* out of "art." I've never given a class to just one person before. But it's allowed, Angela told me at the beginning. It's an open prison after all. These men are low risk.

Low risk enough for someone to be stabbed in one of my classes.

But right now, I have a job to do. I must put my fears and that awful scene at Kitty's home out of my mind. This new student in front of me is—I sense—really interested in art. I'm right. No sooner do I give Martin permission to sit down in the studio than he picks up the crayons. He handles them lovingly, as though he's been starved of their company. I suggest that he color in the outline I've given him of a parrot. It might sound odd, but I've found that animals go down well in my classes. Grown men who have committed headline crimes appear to enjoy reverting to their childhoods. Maybe it makes them feel they have a clean slate, so to speak. My new student works, head bowed, over his sheet.

It's silent. Almost like the golden hour when I used to get up early to do work before life interrupted. Since taking on my prison job, I haven't been able to do this.

I decide to start my own picture, too, sketching the view outside the window. The other Portakabins. The fields behind. The birds that wheel in the sky overhead.

"Want to look?"

I've been so engrossed that I have almost forgotten my student was there.

But he's standing in front of me now. Holding out his picture. The parrot outline is really good. He's taken great care with the individual feathers.

"Have you done this kind of thing before?" I ask.

"Only in the last nick. But not when I was free. Never had time until I got banged up." He looks at me nervously. "Is my picture rubbish, then?"

"Not at all," I say hastily. "It shows a great eye."

Eye. The very word makes me wince. A vision of Grandad's bloody face jumps up before me. Hastily, I brush it away.

"You're not just saying it 'cos of my scars?" His eyes are narrowing. "I get that from some officers. They're sorry for me, so they say things that aren't true to make me feel good."

"No," I begin, but he interrupts.

"Some bloke did it to me in the first nick I got sent to. Sugar and boiling water. You can't get it off the skin."

I'm reminded of how Angela told me about this terrible practice when I first started the job. But now I have the results standing before me. It must have been agonizing. It's certainly not pleasant to look at.

Perhaps that's why he speaks in a jokey kind of way—to hide his embarrassment.

I don't quite know what to say. "Let's try some sketching now, shall we?"

We start by copying a photograph I've brought in. It's a daffodil. Most of my men just draw a circle with a line down for the stem. But this man has caught its bell-like shape perfectly. I can see in his face the same intensity I feel myself when drawing. Just like the expression in Kitty's before the accident.

"Brilliant," I say.

That scarred face looks up at me. "Do you think so?"

"I do."

For an instant, there's a connection between us. The type a teacher experiences when discovering a student who's a natural artist but whose talent has been boycotted for one reason or another. It's like discovering a pearl after a series of empty shells.

It's almost enough to blank out everything else that's going on. Kitty. The messages. *I'M GOING TO GET YOU.* The Christmas card. The nightmares I keep having about the accident. And, of course, Clive.

For some reason, even though everything else is terrible, I can't stop thinking about him.

The last time I felt this way was when I was eighteen. And look what happened then.

26

April 2001

Ali

___

In 2001 I was studying for my A levels—or trying to. Kitty was a constant distraction. If she and Vanessa weren't playing loud music in the bedroom, they were thundering up and down the stairs, squealing with excitement.

"I need some peace," I'd tell Mum.

But Kitty never listened to anyone, apart from Vanessa.

Vanessa reminded me of a spoiled kitten: constantly preening itself. My sister wanted to be just like her. "Twins," they called themselves. Just because their birthdays were four days apart. I often wondered whether we'd have got on better if we hadn't had a seven-year age gap. How I wished she was my friend! But for as long as I can remember, my little sister was prickly towards me. "Don't want to play with you," was one of her earliest phrases. When I tried to mother her, such as helping her to tie her laces, she'd physically push me away. "I can do it," she'd snap.

It wasn't long after the Wrights moved onto our road that Kitty spilled coffee all over my French essay.

"You shouldn't have left it on the kitchen table," she retorted.

I'd only put it there for a second while coming down to get a glass of water.

"You could at least say sorry."

"Why?" Vanessa butted in, perched on a stool at the breakfast bar as if she were part of the family, which, in a way, she was. She and Kitty had met as babies and were always in and out of each other's houses. "Like she said, it was your fault."

Then the two of them started rabbiting on about the new boy, Crispin Wright, who was, apparently, really good at art—my sister's favorite subject. "He's already got a picture accepted for the school exhibition," she cooed. You'd think from the way she spoke that he was a contemporary. In fact, he was in my year—not hers.

"Crispin's got this really floppy fringe that's so cool," simpered Vanessa.

"So cool," echoed my sister.

Didn't they realize how serious this was? "My essay counts towards my final A level mark," I yelled, grabbing a tea towel and trying to blot the pages.

"It will be all right, Ali." Mum came in to hear the tail end of our argument and handed me some paper towels in a vain attempt to soak up the coffee. But it was too late. The ink had run. My essay was totally illegible.

"They've got three cars in the drive—three—and they're building a swimming pool in the garden," squealed Kitty. "They've come from somewhere called Ealing."

Vanessa interrupted. "That's near London."

She said the word with reverence.

"I need that essay," I said, trying not to cry.

Mum was looking doubtfully at the sodden pages. "Do you have a copy?"

"NO."

I wanted to kill my sister, who was still going on about Crispin and London, oblivious to my distress about the essay. She was so spoiled. But that was her all over.

Last year, she and Vanessa had gone on a school trip to see the Houses of Parliament. How I'd have loved that—what an experience!—but they'd slipped off to Oxford Street during Prime Minister's Questions and bought a pair of jeans each with their emergency money. Not only did they frighten the teachers by disappearing like that, but they also delayed the coach back to Devon.

David and Mum actually told them off that time. Not that the girls cared. "One day," Kitty sniffed, "Vanessa and I are going to get out of this dump and find jobs in Knightsbridge. That's the best bit of London. All the magazines say so."

The sooner the better, as far as I was concerned. If only David was a bit stricter, Kitty might be better behaved. But his precious daughter— or "princess," as he was always calling her—could do no wrong in his sight. Mum just went along with it because she didn't want to upset David. She never said as much to me, but I could tell. Sometimes, when it was just the two of us together—like it used to be before she met my stepfather—she'd give me a big hug. "You know, there's always something special about a firstborn."

So she loved me best! It made me feel a whole lot better. For a time. But then Kitty would start to be horrid again, and the whole cycle would continue. Often, I thought that she and Vanessa would have made better sisters than Kitty and me.

You wouldn't think those two were only eleven, to hear them speak. Sometimes, they'd try on some of Mum's high-heeled shoes and strut around, pretending they were grown-up. Kitty's favorite was a shiny red patent pair. "I'm in love with Crispin!" I overheard my sister say to her friend when they didn't know I was listening.

"How are we going to get him to notice us?"

"I've told you." Vanessa's sharp know-it-all voice cut in. "Borrow my makeup, and put it on before you get on the bus."

"What if he fancies only one of us?"

"I don't know. But we've got to find a boyfriend soon, or we'll end up being single like Ali."

Ouch! Sometimes, I wondered how two sisters—even half sisters— with broadly similar features—blond hair and blue eyes—could turn out so differently. It wasn't just that I was tall. It was also that Kitty's nose was smaller with a pretty, turned-up bit at the end. "Roman noses like yours are a sign of intelligence," Mum would say in an attempt to comfort me. Those blue eyes? Mine were set just a tiny bit too close together. Only a fraction, but enough to give a slightly intense look. Kitty's, of course, were perfect, as if measured to scale.

I told myself that Kitty was just jealous because I was the brighter one. But, to be honest, I'd swap that in a heartbeat to look as pretty as her. And although I was fond of Robin, it was purely in a platonic sense.

Robin was my best friend. I wouldn't have minded a girl best friend, but it had never happened. Instead, this clever-looking boy had plonked himself down next to me in our first year at secondary school when I was struggling with a maths sum. "Let me help you with that," he said. Then he added, "I've seen you swimming off the west bay in the morning."

I'd seen him, too. There weren't many of us about at that time. I liked to go early on the weekends while the rest of the house was sleeping in. I swam through the year, regardless of the month, as long as the sea wasn't too rough. I loved the way the freezing waves hit me, washing away Kitty's continuing hostility and David's favoritism.

"Nothing like that brace of cold when you get in, is there?" said Robin quietly, before explaining why I needed to move the figure in the bracket to the other side of the equation.

In return, I helped him with a history essay. I was the only one in class who didn't tease him for that weird patchwork red and blue jacket he wore after school, summer and winter. Neither of us were part of the "in" crowd, or, indeed, wanted to be. Just as I got ribbed for my height, so he was taunted for his surname, Wood, which led to stupid jokes about Robin Hood, as well as his deep voice, which broke long before any other boy's in the year. Later, when we started to swim together, he proved to be a good listener to my moans and groans about my sister.

The ruined French essay was just the latest in a line of insults and spitefulness that had been going on for years. If Kitty left muddy footprints on the carpet, she blamed me. When we had to sit next to each other in the car, she'd make a fuss and say I was taking up too much room. And when she was watching one of her stupid programs on television, she always had the sound up high so I couldn't concentrate on my homework in my bedroom above.

"Turn it down," I'd complain. "I can't concentrate."

Mum did her best. But it was my stepfather who was in charge.

"Ali is far too serious," he was fond of saying.

"That's not quite fair," Mum would reply. "The two of them are just different."

How true. All I wanted was to go to university and study history. But I knew, through listening in to those conversations through my sister's door, that her eye was set on becoming a famous fashion designer. "When we get to London," my sister would say, "we'll have a flat of our own."

"And," interrupted Vanessa, "we'll go clubbing every night. We might even get to sing on the stage, too."

I didn't like Vanessa. And I don't think Mum did either. "She's rather spoiled," she confided in me once over the washing-up. "It can happen when you're an only child and don't have to share." Then she gave me a cuddle. "That's why I'm so glad you have a sister. I know Kitty might not show it, but she loves you very much, too."

Hah! I knew better.

Often I wished it was just me and Mum again. No David. No Kitty. I'd looked after Mum in those early days after Dad died. Brought her tissues when she cried. Pretended I hadn't been hungry when the cereal packet was empty.

Maybe it would have been different if my sister was . . . well, more sisterly. But instead, Kitty was constantly scratchy or downright hostile. It was like living with the school bully but never being able to swap classes.

It wasn't Mum's fault. She didn't, as she explained to me, want to "upset" David. "I'm lucky to have found another husband," I once heard her say to one of her friends.

Meanwhile, my stepfather spoiled Kitty rotten. Another pair of jeans. A locket for "being good"—Vanessa had an identical one. Violin lessons because—that's right—Vanessa had them. Ballet classes, too. Nothing was too much for his princess. Whatever Vanessa got, Kitty wanted.

And now they wanted Crispin.

27

February 2017

Alison

———

"Kitty and Johnny are going to live in the home," Mum tells me. "The supervisor is being very accommodating. I think it's because she feels guilty it happened in the first place."

I have to admit to feeling a sense of relief that I don't have to carry through with my offer to look after them—at least, not now.

"Johnny's mother wanted them to live with her," continues Mum, "but they don't have the facilities. Besides, I gather, reading between the lines, that her husband isn't so keen. Personally, I thought they should stay where they are, and so does David."

I don't want to think about that man. He's always resented me.

"What do you think?" persists Mum.

"I'm not sure," I murmur.

She squeezes my hand. "I know. It's not easy for any of us. Anyway, I thought you might like to help me find her a wedding dress."

It's what a good sister would do, isn't it?

"We'll have to choose one without her," continues Mum. "It will be easier than getting her round the shops." She gives a little sigh. "I have to say, it's not how I imagined it. But then again, life has a strange way of turning out. Doesn't it?"

———————

To my relief, David doesn't come to the wedding. "He doesn't approve," says Mum shortly.

I don't want to press her further. The less said about him the better, as far as I'm concerned. The ceremony takes place at the local register office. Most of the people around me have tears in their eyes when Kitty is wheeled in, grinning and banging her good arm, which is now out of plaster. Not me. If I did cry, it would be for another reason. One I must keep to myself.

Afterwards, there is a small reception in the home's community lounge. All the other residents have turned up. "Not missing out on free cake," I hear someone say.

There's a woman called Margaret who tells me, in between long, drawn-out gaps, that she's my sister's best friend but that she's "extremely disappointed" that Kitty doesn't have a matron of honor. I get the feeling she'd expected to fill that role.

Kitty is radiant. It's amazing what happiness can do to a face. She is actually beaming. Of course, I know why. She is queen for the day. Kitty always loved being the center of attention.

I stand to one side, observing as Kitty stuffs herself with scones, grinning with her mouth wide open to reveal a congealed mess of crumbs. Johnny has a hand on her shoulder. I wonder what will happen next. There'll be no honeymoon. Instead, they will spend the evening here with the other residents. Watching TV, perhaps. But then what?

"I'm still worried about how this is all going to work," Mum says to the supervisor as we stand there, nibbling sandwiches and making small talk while an elderly man and a young girl—both in wheelchairs—squabble loudly over the remains of the cheese straws. I don't really like this place, but it's close to Mum. Besides, Kitty's been here for years. She's used to it.

"How it's going to work?" repeats the supervisor. "What do you mean?"

"We were thinking about the physical side," I say, taking a deep breath.

There is a snort. "I think those two have already proved that this sort of thing can be achieved."

"One of the staff has just said that Kitty is still going to be in her old room with Margaret," pitches in Mum.

"There's no option at the moment, because of the layout of the building and the residents' individual requirements and financial constraints." The supervisor sighs. "This is causing us a great deal of bother, I can tell you. If it doesn't work, we'll have to look at the alternatives. We also need to take Kitty's behavior into account. She has been getting increasingly aggressive over the last few months."

Sounds like my sister is on a final warning.

"Of course, it will be a different matter when the baby is born," adds the supervisor. "We're simply not equipped to deal with that kind of situation."

"So what are we meant to do?" asks my mother with a hint of alarm in her voice.

"If I were you, I'd speak to the care providers."

Suddenly, my sister's situation seems much more complicated than we'd realized.

Meanwhile, it is time for us to go. Kitty waves us off even though it should be the other way round. "Throw your bouquet, love," urges Mum. "Use your good hand."

My sister looks at me. For a second, I swear I see the old Kitty. Smiling sarcastically. Almost hear the unspoken words. *If you think I'm going to throw it at you, you've got another think coming.* Then it passes. In its place is that happy grin again. Everyone claps as she throws the bunch of roses so high that it swoops in the air. A thorny gift. It falls directly at my feet. "You next, darling," laughs Mum delightedly.

When I get home after the wedding, I place the roses in a pretty jug I painted myself. I feel positive now. Excited, almost. My sister has a new chance to make something of her life. Maybe, with our help, it will all work out.

Then I realize I've had my phone on silent all day. Fishing it out of my bag, I find a text from the college asking me to ring one of my students. Clive Black. There are also several more missed calls from the number I don't recognize.

This is silly, I tell myself. Maybe it's just a sales scam. Forcing myself to face my fears, I call the number.

A gruff voice answers. "Hello?"

"Hello? Did you call me just now?"

"Not me, love." There's a throaty laugh. "Not unless my missus has gone all posh." There's noise in the background. Some shouting. Maybe a television.

"Well, someone rang me from this number," I say, more firmly this time.

"There's a lot of people what use this phone, love. Could be any of us."

"Is this a pub?"

There's a loud chortle. "Wish it were. This is a call phone in prison. D hut, HMP Archville, to be precise. Tell you what: you sound like a nice kind of girl. Why don't you come round and we'll give you a good time."

I slam down the phone. The area code is clear enough. I don't know why it hadn't registered before. It's *my* prison.

28

June 2001

Ali

———

SOUTHWEST SET FOR HEAT WAVE, declared the headlines.

Vanessa and Kitty had been spending hours in Kitty's bedroom, their noses pressed against the window, watching Crispin swimming laps in his gorgeous pool after school. I could just about see him from mine, too.

Sometimes, I fleetingly wondered what it would be like to swim next to him in the sea instead of Robin, whose white, gangly body was almost girl-like. Why was I drawn to Crispin, I asked myself, when he was clearly not my type? Then again, what was my type? I needed to work hard. Boys could come later. That's what Mum had always said.

Then, one Saturday afternoon, Kitty came running in, her face flushed and her long hair untied and blowing all over the place. She was closely followed by Vanessa. "Have you heard? Crispin's parents are having a party! There's going to be cocktails and a real disco. He's being allowed to ask some friends. Vanessa's mother says that most of the neighborhood is going. Are you and Mum? Can you take us, too?"

David laughed. "We're not part of their social group." He and Mum were both teachers—it was how they'd met. It had been two years after my father died, and Mum had then married David a year after that. Crispin's mother didn't work. His dad was in advertising.

"But we want to go, we want to go," chanted Kitty and Vanessa.

"You're too young, princess."

"It's not fair."

"Why don't you stay at home and finish off your Craft badge for Girl Scouts? You've still got some catching up to do, haven't you, Kitty?"

My sister pouted. "I've gone off knitting. Some of the stitches have fallen off my needles since I did it last and now it's all messed up."

"Then start again," said David.

That's when I butt in. "I've got an invitation." The words come out of my mouth before I can take them back.

"You!" They all turned to look at me.

I went beetroot. "Yes."

Kitty put her hands on her hips. "How come?"

"Crispin asked me."

It was true. He'd invited a smattering of sixth formers—including me, to my surprise. I hadn't been intending to go. Parties weren't my thing. But the jealous look on my sister's face was worth the last-minute change of mind. At last, I'd got one over on her, and, even better, she couldn't do anything about it.

If I'd known what was to come, I'd have ripped up the invitation into tiny pieces.

"Heard you were going to the party, too," said Robin casually.

We were walking back home from the bus stop. Kitty and Vanessa, as usual, were dragging along behind, sniggering and making silly comments. My sister seemed to have got it into her head that there was something between Robin and me. In fact, nothing could be further from the truth. It was actually because I *didn't* fancy him that I was able to talk so naturally. And I was sure he felt the same.

Parties certainly weren't high up on our agenda. So I was a bit surprised by the "too" part of his sentence.

I looked at him in surprise. "Are you going, then?"

"Thought I might as well." He spoke with what seemed like studied carelessness. Perhaps he was taking someone with him. Robin and I might be friends, but there were times when he kept things to himself.

"Watch out!"

For a minute, I thought Robin was talking to me. Then I realized his warning was directed at Kitty and Vanessa. They'd crept up beside us and were now about to dash across the road—despite the fact that a lorry was steaming round the corner.

I lunged forward and caught my sister's sleeve just in time. "You know you're not meant to cross without me," I said. Fear made my voice shake with anger. Mum and David would never forgive me if something happened to my sister. Hold her hand, they always said, even though she was eleven and surely able to look after herself. Usually, I managed to hang on to her. But Kitty had a mind of her own.

"We were fine," said Vanessa sulkily. "We're not babies, you know."

"It's a nasty road." Robin's voice was calm as always.

"Why don't you keep your nose out of other people's businesses."

How rude! But Vanessa was like that. She could also be very charming when she wanted. I'd seen her in action.

"Are you going to take my sister to the party?" said Kitty loudly as we stood side by side, me hanging on to her hand, waiting for the traffic to clear.

"Of course he's not," I said, flushing madly.

Robin was silent. Once we'd got to the other side and the girls had gone running off towards Vanessa's house, he cleared his throat. "Actually, I was wondering if you wanted me to pick you up on the way."

"Really? Why? I mean, I know how to get there."

I didn't mean to be so curt, but, to be honest, I'd been taken aback by his unexpected invitation.

Robin was going red now. "I just thought it might be nice to arrive with someone. It's not as though we're part of the crowd, is it?"

"I know. In fact, I don't know why he asked me."

"Or me."

Suddenly, the thought of turning up at a house full of Crispin and his friends laughing and drinking and smoking made me feel nervous. If I hadn't announced to Kitty that I was going, I'd have changed my mind and stayed at home. But she would only tease me. *Boring Ali.* I could hear the taunts now. *Gets invited to the party of the year and then pulls out.*

I wasn't going to give her that pleasure. Besides, Robin was right. It *would* be nice to have someone to arrive with.

For the first time in as long as I could remember, I actually felt good about myself.

6 June 2001

Horrible day. Ali was all bossy on the bus just because I wouldn't share my Creme Egg that Mum had put in my packed lunch.

Ali pretended she didn't care. She told me—get this—that chocolate gave you spots.

It makes me hate her more than ever.

On the bus, I heard Crispin whisper something to one of his friends. I heard him say her name.

It was like he fancied her. Ali? Honestly? She's so boring and geeky.

And now she's invited to his summer party. With any luck, she'll make a fool of herself. Dance badly. Or just sit in a corner and not say anything. Then Crispin will realize he likes me, not her.

29

March 2017

Alison

I'm so spooked out by the phone call from the prison that I put Clive out of my head for a while. Instead, I try to keep my wits about me when I'm inside.

The only thing that helps is to concentrate on my students—especially Martin and Stefan, who really do have potential. "Your classes are the best thing here, miss," the former tells me. I can't help but glow with the compliment.

Then, one Saturday, when I'm browsing at a CD stall on the Embankment, someone taps me on the shoulder.

It's Clive. In shorts and a T-shirt, soaked with sweat. I suddenly remember how he'd told me he enjoyed running alongside the river. "Alison! What a coincidence," he says. "I've been thinking of you. What are you doing tonight?" Then he gives me a disarming smile. "And before you think of an excuse, I won't take no for an answer." We go to a small Italian spot in Crouch End. The waitress clearly knows Clive. I tell myself that this is a man who must have wined and dined several women over the years—with looks like that, it's not surprising. I also tell myself that he can't possibly be interested in me. Too-tall, clumsy Alison. He's probably filling in time until his next trip.

"I wanted to explain why I couldn't come to your class." He's speaking fast, as if nervous. "I got called out to Portugal for a series of unexpected meetings. Otherwise, I'd have loved to come."

"I've been to Portugal." It pops out before I can stop myself.

"Oh, really? It's a beautiful place. They love their colors, don't they?"

My mind goes back to our last holiday before the accident. We'd gone—Mum, David, Kitty and I—to a villa near Vale do Lobo. Mum and Kitty had taken their sketch pads. Mum had also bought loads of pottery in bright colors: yellows, blues, pinks. Maybe that's why I love my different colored scarves so much. They make me think of her.

"Whoops!" I've knocked over my glass. The waiter races over to mop up the table. "I'm so sorry."

"If you don't mind me saying," says Clive, leaning towards me, "you seem rather distracted. Is everything OK?"

"My sister got married." The words burst out of my mouth before I can take them back. I've barely talked to anyone for the last few days. I'm out of practice. Now I have to brace myself for the questions. Normal, polite ones. How can I possibly answer them truthfully?

"How lovely. Was it a big wedding?"

I think back to the community lounge with its forty or so residents and the excited sixth former who played the piano.

"Medium sized." My eyes can't help filling with tears.

Immediately, I feel a hand taking mine. "Weddings can make us all feel emotional." The grip tightens.

I can't hold back now. This time a large cotton handkerchief is being pressed into my hands.

"Alison, what is it?"

So I tell him. Not everything, but enough. I explain that my sister had a "terrible road accident" years ago that left her brain damaged. And that, despite the odds, she had now fallen in love with someone in her care home and—incredibly—got pregnant.

His eyes widen as I talk. "How will they manage with a baby?"

"That's what we've all been asking. But Johnny—that's her husband—really adores her. Luckily, his mother seems very supportive."

"And your parents?"

I'd already mentioned Mum briefly in passing but not David. That would be too much. "My mother's concerned. As I am."

"You've a lot on your plate." His eyes are deep with sympathy. "And what about your prison work? How's that going?"

As he speaks, my mobile rings. "Sorry," I say, reaching into my bag. I thought I'd put it on silent. It's the same number as before. D hut.

"What's wrong?" he asks, reading my face.

"Someone's calling me from one of the prison huts," I whisper. "I don't know who. I haven't picked up again after the last time."

"Give me the phone."

I hand it over.

"Who's that?" His voice is hard. Commanding. "I don't know who you are," I hear him say, "but we know where you're ringing from. You will be found."

Then he turns it off and hands it back to me. "All I heard was breathing."

"How will we find him?" I say. "It could be any of the men there."

"Doesn't matter. It will have worried whoever it was. Hopefully, he won't do it again. You'll have to change your number." Then he frowns. "If he's rung before, why haven't you done that already?"

It's a question I've been asking myself. "It sounds silly," I falter, "but I'm beginning to feel there's no escape. This man . . . he's determined to find me."

My voice chokes, and tears blur my vision. I'm on the verge of saying something stupid, like I deserve to be caught. But I stop myself just in time.

"Not if I'm here," he says firmly. "And right now, you're having dinner with me."

He's taking my hand again. Somehow, I feel my heartbeat slowing down just a bit.

"There's something else, too," I add. Suddenly, I want to unburden myself to this man who makes me feel safe.

I tell him about the threatening notes, the Christmas card. I don't mean to, but I've got to the point that if I don't share it with someone, I'm going to go crazy. I can't confide in Mum, because it would scare her too much. But Clive has supported me with the phone call just now. I feel I can trust him. He's easy to talk to.

He listens solemnly. "Have you any idea who it is?"

I think back to the sunny morning all those years ago. Vanessa's crushed body. Kitty's new shoe on the ground.

I know your secret.

"No," I say, with a choke in my voice. "That's what makes it so terrifying."

He leans across the table. I breathe in his smell. There's the faint hint of a lemon cologne. "Listen to me, Alison," he says, releasing my hand briefly before cupping my chin and looking straight into my eyes. "I won't let anyone hurt you. You have my word."

30

June 2001

Ali

___

I deliberately didn't bother about my appearance. If I had, it would have made me too nervous. "You're going to Crispin Wright's party like that?" said Kitty, eyeing my pale blue jeans and simple white T-shirt. She rolled her eyes as though she were the older sister giving advice to a younger one. "Aren't you even going to put on proper makeup?"

"I'm wearing mascara," I said, feeling stupid.

"Panda eyes, more like. I give up." Sulkily, she went back to the sofa, where she was watching one of her mindless programs. "Honestly, that party is wasted on you."

Part of me wanted to ask her for help with my makeup. That's what sisters did, wasn't it? We could have a laugh, experimenting in front of the mirror. Then again, who am I kidding? Kitty would never help me with anything.

"Your time will come, princess," said David. I hadn't noticed him entering. Ignoring me, he carried on talking to his daughter. "Anyway, aren't you meant to be having a sleepover at Vanessa's?"

Kitty pouted. "It's not the same."

"Your neck looks a bit bare," said Mum, eyeing me up and down. She was at the kitchen table, preparing some tree sketches for her college students to do on Monday. "Don't you have a necklace, darling? Or something you could borrow?" She looked meaningfully at my sister's locket.

"It's mine. There's no way you're having this for the party," snapped my sister. "Or any other time either."

The doorbell rang. I didn't want her stupid locket anyway.

"Bye," I said, hastily heading for the door. But Kitty got there first.

"Hi, Robin." Then she turned and yelled, even though I was just behind her. "Ali! Your date is here."

Date? How embarrassing!

"Sorry about that," I murmured, slamming the door behind me.

"Sorry about what?"

"My sister."

He shrugged. "Everyone's different." Then he gently put his hand on the small of my back as we walked past a gang of boys. It was as though he was protecting me. That was strange. It was hardly like any cars were coming.

The music grew louder as we walked towards the Wrights' house. The outside was studded with loads of little fairy lights, and there were huge, fancy cars blocking the driveway. I began to feel sick. Too late, I wished I'd bothered to put on more makeup, or wear a nicer top. "We don't have to stay long if we don't want," said Robin, as if he knew just what I was thinking.

Inside, there were waitresses with glasses on trays. Wow!

"Champagne?"

"No, thanks," I said bashfully. "I don't drink." I knew it made me uncool, but whenever I'd tried alcohol, I felt sick.

"There are some nonalcoholic drinks in the back, miss. Near the conservatory."

Miss! Judging from Robin's twitching lips, he thought that was funny, too.

Together, Robin and I tried to wade through the mass of bodies. So many people. All ages, too. There were quite a few from the sixth form but also loads of adults I'd never seen before. At one point, I thought I recognized Crispin's mother, whom I'd seen a couple of times on the street.

Robin said something to me, but the music was so loud that I couldn't hear. He moved closer. I could feel his mouth touching my ear. It felt weird. "Wait there. I'll get some orange juice."

"I can go with you," I said, but he'd gone. I felt so stupid, standing there on my own. I tried to look casual, but the more I did so, the more awkward I felt. Robin was taking ages. *Hurry up,* I said silently. My palms were sweating. I felt like an idiot.

For a second, the music stopped. "Ali," said a voice. I jumped. Crispin was standing next to me. "Someone said you were here!"

I was so flummoxed I could barely reply. He spoke as though we knew each other well, even though we'd hardly exchanged a word either on the school bus or in class. That's why I'd been so amazed to get an invitation. "You look great!"

Was he joking?

"Come and dance!"

Cool Crispin Wright was actually asking *me* to dance? Kitty would go mad with jealousy if she knew!

"I can't. I'm waiting for Robin."

"Robin Hood?"

He grinned. To my shame, I gave a little laugh, too, out of nervousness. Instantly, I felt ashamed at making fun of my friend.

"He's in the summerhouse at the bottom of the garden," shouted Crispin over the music. "Asked me to tell you he was there. Got something for you, apparently."

Only Robin would retreat into a summerhouse—nursing my drink, no doubt—while a party was going on. I knew why, of course. He wanted some quiet time. In fact, he was probably already regretting joining a crowd he had always despised. I still didn't really know why he'd come along.

Crispin's hand brushed my own. Then I became aware of his fingers interlacing between mine. It felt warm. Exciting.

He was pulling me and laughing as if we were both in on a joke. "This way!"

31

March 2017

Alison

I wake in the small hours of the morning, my head whirling. Clive's hug had turned into a series of lovely long kisses that had made my entire body want to blend into his. The kind I'd dreamed of as a teenager until the party . . .

Then all of a sudden, he'd stopped. "Alison, I really like you. And there's nothing I'd like more than to ask if I can come back to your place. But some things are too precious to rush. Don't you think?"

No, I'd wanted to say. *Stay with me.* Hadn't he promised that he wouldn't let anyone hurt me?

"Ring me," he'd said. "Anytime you feel worried. See you soon."

Then he'd kissed me one more time and escorted me back to my car. When I get home, there's a text.

Miss you already. I've got some work commitments, but I'll call as soon as I know when I'm free.

All of that day—and the next—I find myself occasionally smiling to myself. Somehow, knowing Clive is there for me makes me feel better. I rather like his slightly old-fashioned approach about waiting to come to my place even though he "really likes" me. Perhaps everything will be OK after all. Maybe my fortunes are changing along with my sister's. But right now, I need to concentrate on my next class.

At the end, Stefan—my older student with the eastern European accent—stays behind.

"I help you tidy?" he asks, limping over.

Kindness can be the first step in grooming, Angela always said. Not that I should be following her advice anymore.

"Thank you, but I'll manage."

He looks affronted. I glance down at the cane. What if he uses it on me? Why is it allowed in here when you can't even bring an umbrella inside?

"I want to ask you something." He puts his head to one side quizzically. "Why you do work in place like this?"

It's not the first time I've been asked this, although I have to think for a minute to decipher his strangely worded question and accent. My answer is ready and pat. A little curt, too. "Because I love art and want to help others enjoy it."

He purses his lips questioningly. "I see." Then his eyes harden. "Be careful. This place, she is not good. You watch yourself."

His words send shivers through my blood. Does he know something? Is he trying to warn me?

I stare as he limps away. There's just time in between workshops for me to nip out to the car and check my new phone. No missed calls.

Suddenly, I feel a surge of disappointment. Yes, my stalker's calls seem to have stopped. But it's been a while now, and I've heard nothing from Clive.

Work commitments? He could still text, couldn't he?

Then again, why am I bothered? I've been stupid, I realize now, to imagine I have a chance of happiness. Even if I do find the right person, he'll leave me. As soon as he finds out what I've done.

32

June 2001

Ali

———

The summerhouse was at the bottom of the garden. Crispin was still pulling on my hand, gently leading me. A glittering cluster of fairy lights—blue, green and red—strung along the trees overhead, marked the way. The shrubbery made it darker than the part we'd just gone through. The distance from the house meant it was quieter, too.

The wooden door creaked as Crispin opened it. No one was inside. A spider scooted out from a corner. There was a smell of apples from a wooden grocery crate. I felt excited and scared all at the same time.

"Where's Robin?" I asked, looking around at the wicker sofa and matching chairs with rose-patterned cushions.

"It's just you and me, Ali." Crispin's voice had an edge of amusement to it.

"What do you mean?"

But even as I spoke, I knew. Boys like Crispin didn't go for girls like me. They were attracted to older versions of Kitty. Confident. Beautiful. Poised.

"Do you know," said Crispin, grasping my hand, "how gorgeous you are?"

Gorgeous? Me?

"That's why I wanted you here." His hand was cupping my face, and his mouth was so close to mine that I could smell his breath.

Minty—as if he'd prepared for this. "You're the only girl at school who hasn't thrown herself at me. Now why is that?"

Because you're way above me, I wanted to say. *And even though you are stunning and do something to my insides, you're not my type.* I hadn't even thought of this before. But now that we were so close, and his intentions to kiss me were—I thought—becoming clearer, I realized it was true. Crispin was too sure of himself. Too cocky. But above all, I didn't feel comfortable with him.

"Don't tell me you've got the hots for that squirt Robin."

That wasn't fair. "He's not a squirt," I said. "He's my—"

I was going to say the word "friend," but Crispin's mouth was on mine before I could finish my sentence.

I'd like to say that I pulled away, but, to my horror, my mouth responded hungrily. Often, I'd imagined what it would be like to be kissed. The nearest I'd come to it was a fumble at the school dance when I was fifteen and a boy had stuck his tongue into my mouth briefly at the end. It had made me want to be sick.

Sometimes, to be honest, I'd wondered if there was something wrong with me. But now I knew there wasn't. Everything in my body was dissolving at Crispin's touch. Even though my brain was shouting, *NO! NO!*

"Get off." I finally backed away as his hands started to undo my jeans belt.

"Face it, Ali. I can tell that, deep down, you want me, even though you pretend not to."

That wasn't true. Was it? I certainly had no intention of going this far. I knew very little about sex except that Mum had always told me it was best to wait until I'd been through university. "You don't want to get into trouble and ruin your future," she'd said on more than one occasion. "Imagine if all your hard work was wasted."

Some people might have considered this old-fashioned, but our seaside town was like that. If girls got pregnant, they married young, like one of my primary school contemporaries last year. I knew that wasn't for me. I was going to study history. Everything else could wait.

"Come on, Ali."

"I said no." I pushed his chest.

But his force was stronger than mine. Somehow, he'd undone my jeans—they were halfway down my legs. Trying to pull them up, I fell backwards. Rolling to the side, I tried to get up. But he was over me. "You want me. I can tell that from your kiss just now." He was grinning in the dusk. For a minute, there was a glimpse of doubt in his face. Then it went.

"No." I began to cry. "I didn't mean it. Let me go . . ."

After that, there were only flashes. His mouth on mine. His skin on mine. Pain. "You're hurting me!" His grunts. My whimpers. The tapping of the trees outside on the window. *Focus on that*, I remember telling myself.

The worst thing was that, otherwise, I did nothing. Just lay there. Too shocked to try and run away. Besides, he was much heavier.

When he'd finished, I came back to myself. "My mates were right," he said, standing over me and buckling up his jeans. "You're nothing special after all. Maybe I should wait until that sister of yours grows up a bit. I only wanted to find out what that Robin kid sees in you. Can't stand that swot who thinks he's so clever. At my old school, I was the one at the top of my class."

So he'd done this to get back at Robin for being my friend.

He pushed my clothes at me. "Perhaps you'd better go home now." He spat on the ground as if I was something he wanted to get rid of. "And don't try crying rape. If you do, I'll deny it."

Weeping, I pulled up my jeans, adjusted my T-shirt and ran. Robin would wonder where I was. But I could hardly tell him what had happened. Maybe it had all been my fault. I'd started off by wanting Crispin to kiss me. Somehow, I'd given him the wrong idea. Nor could I go home. How could I let Mum and David see me like this? There was only one place to hide.

I ran down the street towards the bay. Never before had I swum at night. The sea had a habit of being rough at that time—at least recently. But the sea was calm now. I ran in, fully clothed, grateful for the cold and the cleansing salt water that mixed with the tears running down my face.

"You went swimming in your clothes?" said Mum when I got home an hour or so later. She and my stepfather were sitting in the kitchen, sharing a bottle of wine. There was a tense silence between them that suggested they'd had an argument. Recently, this seemed to have been happening more and more. "At this time of night?"

"Hope you didn't go in for any of that skinny-dipping I did when I was your age," said David, offering me a glass even though he knew I didn't drink. "Still, it's nice to see you enjoying yourself for a change, Ali. You deserve it after all that studying."

I wanted to vomit. Enjoying myself? "Mind if I use the bathroom now?" I said. "Or does anyone else want it first?"

"Go ahead," said Mum. Then, as I left the room, she called out, "Take my lavender oil. David just bought it for me. It smells gorgeous."

Was it my imagination, or was she trying to overcompensate for that postargument silence I'd picked up on?

I sat in the bath for longer than I'd ever done before. But it still didn't take away the shame. Or the guilt. As soon as my results were in, I resolved, I'd get out of here. Take a leaf out of my sister's future plans. Find a job in London. As far away from this place as possible. And then go to uni.

I'd make sure I never saw Crispin again.

But then a terrible thought occurred to me. What if I was pregnant?

There was a note in my locker this morning. In her handwriting.

I can't bring myself to write down what it said.

She later swore it wasn't her.

But it had to be.

That's it.

All-out war.

33

April 2017

Alison

I check my voice messages in the prison car park. There's one from Mum: "Give me a call, Ali." But when I ring her back, she doesn't pick up.

All kinds of possibilities are whirring round my head. Kitty is ill. Kitty and her new husband have run away from the home. Kitty has suddenly got her memory back . . .

Out of all these, I'm ashamed to say, it's the last that really scares me.

What should I do now? Drive to Mum's? Go straight to the home to check on my sister? Either way, I'm in no fit state to make a long car journey to Devon in the southwest where Mum and Kitty still live. I decide to head back to my place instead and try Mum again before making a decision. Maybe take a walk to clear my head after the busy day, although the air in London is so stale and thick compared with home. For a minute, I think back to my childhood swims with Robin. How long ago they seem now.

My mobile rings just as I've got my running shoes on.

Mum.

"What's happened?" I ask.

"The supervisor called again," says Mum. "Kitty's upsetting the other residents." She gives a short, dry laugh. "You remember how she could be quite bossy before."

Oh yes. I remember. I just hadn't realized Mum had been aware, too. She'd never said anything. But I knew why. Mum had been scared of annoying David and upsetting the family life she'd created; anything rather than go back to being a single mother again.

"She's started to scream and shout when she doesn't want to do something," continues Mum.

"Like what?"

"Eating things she doesn't like, going to bed, getting dressed." Mum sounds weary. "The supervisor says she's got much worse since the pregnancy. The home can't handle her anymore."

After the accident, I'd somehow thought that Kitty might become mellower—it's how one tends to see people who have been injured. But that didn't turn out to be the case. Then again, my sister was a strong character before—so why should she be different "just" because she can't speak or remember things? That's when a scary thought strikes me: what if Kitty can remember, even though she's unable to speak? How angry that would make her!

"What about Johnny?"

"His mother says he is finding it difficult to cope with her mood swings, too."

I wondered if that might happen.

"But," adds Mum, "she's prepared to have Kitty and Johnny live with them. What do you think?"

"It could be an answer," I say slowly. Johnny's parents are well-off. They adore their son. She'll be loved, too—providing she behaves herself.

"I feel guilty about not having them with me—but the house isn't big enough, and I'm on my own. I need to work. How would I manage?"

So that's why Mum's so distressed. She needs reassurance that it's OK for my sister to move in with another family. "I think you should let her take this chance."

"Really?"

"Really." And I mean it.

"Thank you." Then she seems to remember me.

"How is the job going?"

I think of the phone calls, which have thankfully stopped since I changed my number—a decision that Clive had suggested. "Fine," I reply, crossing my fingers. "Better go now. Love you."

The call unsettles me. A jog no longer seems appealing. My fingers are itching. I haven't done this for a while, but I can't stop myself. The glass offcuts sit in the special drawer, gleaming at me. They are like rainbow icicles: some tall and thin; others short with diagonal corners; blues, reds, greens, yellows.

I select a sharp red.

The left arm. Midway between the wrist and elbow. A nick. Enough to cause pain but no serious damage.

Usually, one is enough. But tonight it does nothing for me. I make a second nick. And a third. Three spots of blood begin to trickle. Yet the satisfaction—it's hard to describe it any other way—isn't there.

I know why. The longer Kitty is as she is, the worse the pain is inside me. A mere nick will never be enough.

I need to find something bigger.

"Be careful what you wish for." That had been one of David's favorite phrases when I was growing up. I never quite understood what he meant until later.

But I was reminded of it when the governor called me into his office the next morning. The "something bigger" had clearly found me.

He gets straight to the point. "We've decided to hold a charity fundraising event. How would you feel about spending a whole night in prison?"

Is he joking?

Clearly not. The glasses have come off. He is leaning towards me intently.

"We had a writer in residence who did this a few years ago. He held an evening session for the men and then wrote about what it was like to be in a cell all night. We'd like you to do the same but with a series of sketches or paintings."

I have to admit it. An excited—if scared—sensation is crawling through me. This could have real possibilities.

"We've got a meeting of the trustees soon," continues the governor. "This would be a great opportunity to show them exactly what you are achieving here. You could include drawings from your students. Maybe hold an exhibition." His voice rises with excitement. He thumps the desk with his fist, which makes me jump. "We could call it 'Twenty-Four Hours in Archville.'"

I'm still getting my head round this. "Where will I stay?"

"In one of the huts."

"Will it be safe?"

The governor waves his arm as if physically batting my fear away. "Do you honestly think I would suggest this if it wasn't? Each room in the hut is locked at nine p.m. sharp. Doors are then unlocked at eight a.m."

My mouth is dry. My heart is pounding. Spend the night in a prison full of men? I can't even imagine what my mother would say if I told her. Which, of course, I won't.

Then I hear the words coming out of my mouth as if someone else was speaking them.

"When would you like me to do this?"

34

June 2001

Ali

I took my first exam as if I wasn't there. I tried to tell myself the shivery, scared ache inside was just that bug going around. It didn't happen, that thing with Crispin. If I repeated it enough times, it might be true. Just concentrate on A levels, my ticket out of this place.

"How did it go?" Mum would ask each time when I got back.

"Fine," I'd answer breezily before going upstairs to "revise a bit more."

"Are you feeling any better?" Mum would call up the stairs.

"Still a bit fluey."

"I'll come up with a hot drink, shall I?"

"I'm OK, thanks." Then I'd shut the door and head for the sanctuary of my desk, closing the curtains so I couldn't see the view into Crispin's back garden.

For some reason, Kitty was being nice to me. She even offered to lend me her horseshoe charm "for luck." "That's really kind of you, darling," Mum said. "Isn't it, Ali?"

"Yes," I said, rather flattered. "Thank you." Then I gave her a kiss on her cheek.

"Yuck," said my sister, wiping away my touch, but nevertheless, she looked quite pleased. Maybe, now that she was growing up, she wanted to be better friends, too. How nice that would be!

Ironically, it was Robin who was being standoffish. "I'm sorry we lost each other at the party," I'd whispered in the library the day after.

He'd brushed away my excuse.

"Actually, I was going to apologize to you. I got talking to some girl. Did you stay late?"

"No."

If only I could turn back the clock.

"Shall we have a swim tomorrow?" I ask hopefully.

He shook his head. "Sorry. I've still got too much studying to do."

It was the day before my final exam. History. After dinner, I went up to my room to do some last-minute work.

But something vital was missing. My mind flashed back to earlier when I'd found Kitty in my room, looking for a "pen to borrow."

I flew down the stairs to find her, my heart pounding. "Have you got my history notes?" I gasped.

"What would I want with that boring old stuff?" my sister asked with a smirk.

So much for me thinking she wanted to be friends.

"I don't believe you."

"Ali," said David, looking up in fury from the cooker. "Stop causing trouble."

I was almost hysterical. "But I know it was in my room earlier today."

"Then you should be a bit tidier. There are books all over your floor."

Mum got back late from work, rubbing her eyes with tiredness. She hadn't seen my notes either.

Later that night, I heard her talking to Kitty through my sister's bedroom door. "Of course I love you, darling. There's something very special about the youngest. You know that."

The next day I had to sit for my final exam without having done the extra studying I'd been banking on.

But the worst thing was knowing that I wasn't special, in my mother's eyes, after all.

There was just one consolation. That night, I woke with aching cramps. My period had arrived.

3 July 2001

We're reading this book about sisters at school. They're best friends.

But then one of them does something bad.

And the other blackmails her.

It's given me this really good idea.

I'm not sure how to do it yet.

But I will.

35

May 2017

Alison

———

What exactly do you pack for a prison sleepover? Cells are cold. The men are always complaining about that. Will there be a loo in my room, or will it be communal? Surely, they wouldn't make me share with the men? Or is that part of the experience?

My heart is beginning to pound as I put an extra warm jumper and some clean undies in a case. What have I let myself in for?

But the fear is balanced by an edgy excitement.

I barely sleep. When I do, I dream of violin cases and plaits and a voice. "Hurry up—we're late."

Then the alarm goes. Six a.m. I wake with a jolt. Today I am going into prison. And staying the night.

"In here, miss," says one of the officers. We're walking down a narrow corridor past men who don't bother to disguise their stares. The "hut" I'm staying in is more like a rambling bungalow with rooms going off at either side. There are dark stains on the walls and a musky smell in the air.

"This is your room." His voice implies *Rather you than me.*

There's a metal frame bed with a cardboard box underneath, and a chamber pot. "For your clothes, miss, the box. And the other to go to the bathroom. Though I'd recommend waiting till the morning." I shudder.

Surprisingly, a small desk sits on one side of the room next to a barred window with a pair of flimsy curtains.

"What happens now?" I ask.

"Social time." He's leaving the door open. "You can go into the lounge if you like. Play cards. Talk. Watch a bit of telly."

"On my own?"

"I've got to stay with you until you go to your pad. Governor's orders."

That's a relief.

His eyes fall on my materials. There's a curious look in his eyes. "I don't mind if you want to draw me."

I sense he'd actually like me to do this. In fact, it's a great idea. I make a quick sketch and then follow him into the lounge.

Sprawled on sofas and frayed chairs are several men. I recognize some from my classes, but instead of their usual friendly approach, they glare as if I've just wandered into a men-only club. Which I have.

"For those of you what don't know," says the officer, "this is Alison, our artist in residence. She's going to be drawing what she sees here."

"Want to come into the shower with me, pet?" A large man I haven't seen before grins at me. "You'll get some inspiration there, all right."

"In your dreams, mate," scoffs another.

Nervous sweat trickles down my back.

"None of that," snaps the officer. "Mind your manners."

Then someone turns on the television, and after that, they seem to lose interest in me. My pen skates across the page. The movement calms me down. Even though it's their free time, my keener students want to make sketches. I help them, suggesting a line here and a line there. It starts to get dark outside. I'm aware of a rumble in my stomach. Tea had been a modest affair with toast and hard scrambled egg.

Suddenly, I'm aware of the isolation here. I can't make myself a cup of tea like I might at home. I can't make a phone call—the public booth in the corridor is out of order, apparently.

I get up. "Just going outside for some fresh air."

"You can't do that," says the young man swiftly. "It's not like during the day when you can wander around."

This hadn't been explained to me.

"But it's an open prison."

He shrugs. "Only in name. More like being put in a cardboard box with the lid open. If you try to run for it, you find yourself in a proper metal box. With the lid shut."

A loud bell sounds. I jump.

"Time for bed," says the man who made the shower suggestion. "Better get a move on, miss. Or you'll get a strike."

For a minute, I think he means a whipping. "It's like a black mark," says the spotty kid. "If you get three, you lose privileges. Like not being able to ring home. Or having to take on an extra job." He grins. "I'm on toilets this week. Take a look at my nails."

They are black underneath. I want to vomit.

Already, I'm amazed at how subservient this place makes me feel, even though I'm not a prisoner myself. Then, as I make my way to my room with the officer, we pass Martin, my new, talented student, sitting on a bed with the door open. He's facing sideways, away from me, and his scars gleam in the electric light. That profile seems haughtier than usual. Maybe it's because he appears deep in thought.

"Hi," I call out.

"Hi." He starts as though I've caught him in the midst of doing something he shouldn't. Then he holds out his hand as though to shake mine. We're not allowed to have any physical contact with inmates. Surely, he knows that? But I feel bad not taking it in case it offends him. So I pretend not to notice.

If he's upset, he doesn't show it. "Welcome to our hut."

"I haven't seen you for a while."

"Yeah. Sorry. I've been on gardening duty. Really missed your classes, though."

That's nice. "Will you paint something for our exhibition? I'd appreciate it. You've got talent."

Martin looks flattered. "Thanks. Maybe I will."

The officer is waiting impatiently, his eyes indicating that I should not be on friendly terms with a prisoner. Of course, he's right.

"Have a good night," he says, showing me into my cell.

Then he shuts the door. I hear the lock clunk heavily into place. I am alone. And nervous. Grandad Barry's bloody eye keeps coming into my head. Not to mention the image of boiling water and sugar.

So I do what I always do when the old terrors and anxieties start to overtake me. I sit down and I draw. I sketch myself sitting here in a cell, looking out over the darkness outside. I put into lines the feelings in my body. Fear. Guilt. Jealousy.

There's a tapping at the window. At first, I think it's rain. But then I see it's a branch. The noise has made me edgy. Don't be daft, I tell myself. There are bars. No one can get in. Just as I cannot get out. A wave of claustrophobia hits me.

It's late now—nearly one a.m. I've been working for longer than I meant to. Time for bed. It's ridiculously narrow, even for a slight frame like mine. The pillow feels like a rock. I've heard the prisoners complain about hard pillows before and used to think they were fussing unnecessarily. Now I know what they mean.

I still cannot sleep. There's not enough noise compared with the busy prison talk and shouting during the day. At home, I love the sound of traffic outside my flat. It makes me feel that I am not alone. That there are others living equally complicated lives around me. But now, in a place that possibly contains the most complicated lives of all, it is too quiet.

It's cold, too. I get up and slip my day clothes over my pajamas. That's better. But I still cannot stop shivering.

Then there's a sound. A definite noise. The window is opening. I am sure of it. Don't be silly. The branch. It's just the branch. No. It really is opening.

I sit bolt upright in bed. My mouth dry. "Who's there?" I croak.

A shape is climbing in through the curtains.

The scream sticks in my throat.

36

July 2001

Ali

"Kitty? Are you ready?" I yelled up the stairs. "You're going to make us miss the bus."

It was the last day of school. The end-of-term concert. And I was getting a prize. Much good it would do, because I knew I'd failed my history. I don't need the results—due in August—to tell me that.

And it was all my sister's fault. That guilty look on her face had been proof enough. I should be used to her hostility by now. Her nicer attitude, just after the party, had clearly evaporated. But the missing history notes put a different perspective on things. It was payback time.

I smoothed down my school skirt, which was clinging to my tights. At least I wouldn't have to wear this anymore.

"Calm down, love," said Mum, who was rushing around, trying to get her own things ready for work. Then she gave me a squeeze, and I breathed in that lovely lavender fragrance. "I know you're feeling tense after your exams. But try to relax. Enjoy the concert. I'm really proud of you for getting a prize."

If only I could just crawl off and hide in a hole. Still, at least after today I wouldn't have to face Crispin again. For some reason, he hadn't been on the school bus recently, but we still had to share some classes, which was agony.

"Kitty!" I yelled up the stairs again. "Get a move on."

My sister finally appeared, dragging her violin case behind her.

"Is that nail polish you're wearing?" quizzed Mum.

"So what?" pouted my sister.

"It's not suitable."

"Vanessa's got some, and her parents don't mind."

"Have you made up with that friend of yours?" asked David. "Sounded like you two were having a bit of an argument the other day."

"We're good," said Kitty, pushing past us. "Anyway, it's none of your business."

My sister didn't usually speak to her father like that. What was going on?

"Don't forget your sandwiches, love."

Too late. She was storming ahead as if I was the one who had delayed her.

"Make sure you hold her hand when you cross the road," pleaded Mum, giving them to me.

As if I didn't have enough to do apart from babysitting a sister who thought she was more grown-up than I was!

"Why *did* you fall out with Vanessa?" I asked when I caught up with her. I admit it wasn't exactly out of kindness. Part of me wanted to needle her. I could tell she was bothered from the way she'd spoken to David just now.

"Keep your nose out of my life."

"I'm only trying to help."

My sister scuffed the ground with her foot. For once, she looked on the verge of tears. I felt a sudden sympathy, despite the coffee-stained French essay (which she'd shown little repentance over) and then the missing history notes. My sister never cried. This had to be bad.

"If you really want to know, someone sent Vanessa a stupid letter that said—" She stopped suddenly, as if a light had gone on in her head. "It wasn't you, was it?"

"What are you talking about?"

"It doesn't matter. You wouldn't have the nerve anyway."

Ignore her, I tell myself. Whatever I say will be wrong. By now, we'd turned out of our road and were heading down a side road that joined up with the main street, leading to school. Blast! There went the bus. Right past us.

"We'll have to walk fast if we're not going to be late," I said. Kitty's plaits were bouncing. I had my hair in plaits today, too; I hated them, but all the others in my year were doing it, as an end-of-term celebration.

That's when I noticed Vanessa coming up behind us. She'd also missed the bus.

"Hello, Ali." Vanessa wasn't usually this friendly. Normally, she treated me with contempt, as though *I* was the annoying younger sister. "How are you today?"

Something was up. I could tell from the uncomfortable way in which my sister was looking at her friend.

"Let's cross the road," said my sister suddenly.

"Wait till we get to the crossing." I tried to grab her hand, but Vanessa caught my arm first.

"Hey, Ali. I know your secret . . ."

"Shut up," Kitty butted in. "You promised not to."

"Promised not to do what?" I asked.

"You know, Kitty, I really think I ought to tell her."

"Don't bully my sister," I said fiercely.

"Shut up, Ali," retorted Kitty. "I can handle this myself." Then she glared at Vanessa. "I said I'd do it, so I will."

Vanessa gave a nasty smile. "Then what are you waiting for?"

"What's going on?" I demanded, confused. By then, we were hovering on the edge of the pavement.

My sister's eyes met mine.

"We know you got off with Crispin," she said slowly. "We saw you through the window of the summerhouse. Having sex."

37

May 2017

Alison

"You must not fear," says the voice. "I do not hurt you."

The window creaks shut. There's the sound of metal—the window bars?—falling on the floor.

A figure comes towards me, limping. *Stefan.*

"I arrive so we can talk, Ali."

Ali? I freeze. My childhood name. How does he know it?

He makes his way to the chair by the bed with the aid of his cane.

"When we first meet, I think you know me," he says, settling down and staring at me in the moonlight. "Of course, that is impossible. You were only young the last time."

The hairs on my arms stand up on end. "What do you mean?"

"Your mother, how is she?"

My eyes dart to the alarm by the door.

"Do not bother," he says softly. "It does not operate. I take it apart this morning." He appears pleased with himself. "I am good at that sort of thing. Just as I make loose some of the window bars."

"What do you want?" I edge backwards.

"I tell you already. I do not hurt you. We talk. I learn about you. I come here to get to know my daughter."

"Daughter?" My voice rasps in disbelief. What on earth is he talking about?

He puts his hand over my mouth. It's a strong hand. Much stronger than his frame suggests. "Shhh. Or they'll hear us."

Then he takes his hand away. "I want to be near you, like any father wants to be near his child."

"You think you're my father?" I stare at the old man, not sure whether to laugh or cry. "I don't have a father. He died when I was young."

Too late, I realize I've broken a basic rule. Never give out personal information about yourself.

"But his name, it is Stephen, yes?"

How does he know that?

I stiffen. *"Was.* Not is. How do you know that?"

"I know your father's name because it is *my* name, Ali." He speaks sadly but with a certain acceptance, as though it is a burden he has carried for a long time. "Stefan. Although your mother, she call me Stephen in the English style. Stephen Baker."

I can barely believe what I am hearing. "But that's not your surname on my list."

Baker is my surname, though it wasn't for a while. When Mum married David, she got me to call myself Alison Baker-James. "It makes us look more like a real family," she said. But hyphenated names made a kid stand out at my school—not a good idea. So I dropped the Baker bit to please Mum. Alison James. Kitty James. Two sisters. At least, on the surface. Later, in a bid for a new beginning after the accident, I went back to Baker.

That's what it says on my birth certificate—which I had to send the prison as part of my vetting process. Was it possible that Stefan had somehow got hold of this?

Criminals, Angela used to say, can be very clever at squeezing information out of staff.

He shrugs. "Your mother and I, we do not marry. But I take her maiden name, because it is easier for people to understand." He laughs hoarsely. "In those days, it was even more important to be English."

There's a sigh. "When they finally take me to prison, they find out my real name."

I think once more of my birth certificate. My father's name is not on it. "I was very independent in those days," my mother had said brightly when, as a teenager, I'd questioned this.

Ironically, I'd approved at the time.

But this man in front of me is clearly insane. My father is dead.

The question is, how do I get away?

"Please don't hurt me," I whimper.

Stefan's breathing fast now. "Would a father hurt his daughter? I am here, Ali, because I am desperate."

The whites of his eyes are shining madly in the moonlight streaming in through the half-open curtain. I could scream for help, but then he might use that cane. Think of something! Use emotional intelligence. Go along with it. Distract him.

"If you are really my father," I say, "why did my mother tell me you were dead?"

There's another sigh. "Lilian. She does not want you to know my shame."

He knows my mother's name.

"How dare you?" Something inside me makes me furious as well as scared. I know I shouldn't aggravate him, but I can't help it. "What right do you have to delve into my life?"

He shakes his head as if I am the one who's stepped out of line.

"And what do you mean by shame?" I thunder on.

"My own shame," he says sadly. "It is a thing that no wife or child must bear."

His hand reaches out to me. It grasps my wrist. He's going to kill me. I shouldn't have gone on the offensive. "Please," I gasp.

"Trust me," he growls. "No one will harm you when I am around." He lets go. His eyes fill with tears. "I do not mean to scare you. You look like my mother. Your grandmother, bless her soul." Here, he crosses himself. "She was tall, too. And blond."

So are many women. I'm not falling for this, despite his tears. But I must tread carefully. Buy more time until somehow I can raise the alarm. Change tack again. Pretend to be understanding. "So, why did you get arrested?" I ask in a gentler voice.

A tear is sliding down his face. He makes no move to wipe it away. "I am art student in Yugoslavia before the war." He raises his profile proudly, despite the crying. "The Bosnian Serbs, they do not like my political cartoons. They try to put me in prison, but my father, he pays all his money to captain of container ship. He takes me to the UK, but I am caught at customs and put in remand center. Then I get into fight." He pauses. "This man, he wants to kill me. So I fight back. I push him, and he falls and smashes his head. I didn't mean him to die . . ."

"You killed him?" I whisper.

He nods. "It is regretful but necessary. Then I bribe guard to help me get over wire, and I meet your mother in center for homeless. She is student but works there because she is good person." There's a fond smile. "We fall in love and make you. We go on the run for four years, but I am caught. The landlord, she is suspicious." His fists clench. "They send me to prison for murder."

My head is reeling. Clearly, he's a madman. What's going to stop him from killing me?

"Ask your mother, Ali. I see you do not believe me. Perhaps she will make you see light."

There's a hard look to his face. Yet at the same time, it manages to be sorrowful.

I need to keep him talking. Play along. "And what did you mean about coming here to get to know your daughter?" I hesitate. "It's as though you engineered our meeting."

He gives a half smile. Almost as though he is proud of himself. "After I go to prison, I try to obey your mother's request that I leave her alone. Never make contact. But it troubles me. I write to her when you were eighteen, but she never reply. Then, not long after, I read about the accident, Ali. *Your* accident and Kitty's. It was in the newspapers."

My head is buzzing. It's becoming clear now. All Stefan had to do was look up my name when I arrived at HMP Archville. He could easily have got someone on the outside to search for it on the Net. He must have discovered the accident that way. There are countless articles online.

Yet what does he want from me?

"I am glad you are not killed, Ali." His eyes are soft, warm.

"I thank the Lord you are not injured badly like your half sister."

I remind myself once more that these are all details that were in the reports at the time.

"I am in a very strict prison for many years. I do favors for other men—like giving them my food, fixing things—so that when they are released, they owe me."

He looks at me earnestly.

"The older I get, the more I need to see you, Ali. To talk to you. To explain. I try to think of a way. My sentence, it has only five more years. So I am moved to another prison." He points to the open window. "I can breathe at last. I taste fresh air whenever I want instead of piss and shit and sweat in cell. I have more freedom to find out about you."

"When is your birthday?" I ask suddenly.

He looks surprised. "Ninth of December. Why?"

I feel a flash of relief. Mum had once told me that my father had been born on the fourteenth of July, although she hadn't mentioned the year. So this man is definitely lying.

He closes his eyes for a minute as though he's very tired. Then starts talking again.

"I hear from friends that you are working here. It seems like fate. I find out that I can request transfer. I say it is because it is near the hospital for treating my illness." He grins as if pleased with himself.

With a sinking feeling, I realize he's right—I heard about this from Angela. The authorities can move prisoners for personal reasons in extreme circumstances.

"But why now, if you've been watching me all these years?"

"I tell you already." He wheezes heavily at this point. Another dramatic ploy. "I get ill. I want to know my daughter. I need to make up for lost time. And I need to protect you, too."

A shiver runs through me. "Protect me from what?"

"This is a bad place, Ali. You are in danger."

"How?"

I say it with bluster, but inside I am shaking.

"It is best you do not know. Then you say nothing when they ask you."

Then a thought strikes me. "Did you write those notes?" I ask.

"What notes?"

"Anonymous messages." My throat is dry. "They said I was being watched and that someone was out to get me."

I observe his face closely. It registers genuine surprise. "No. Not me." He shakes his head. "But it means they are after you already."

"Rubbish," I say, trying to laugh.

He picks up his cane. So I was wrong about this man! He is dangerous after all. I wince instinctively, waiting for the blow.

"I do not hurt you, Ali," he says sadly. "When I hear you are staying for the night, I think this is good chance to talk alone. I hope you tell me more about yourself and I tell you about me. But now I see you don't believe my story."

There's a pat on my shoulder. "You go, talk to your mother. She know I talk truth. Then we meet again."

"Take your hand off me."

His eyes moisten. There are real tears. "Do not you see . . ." he begins.

And then the sound of shouting breaks in. Not just one voice but several. Like men drunk after a football match. Door handles are rattling. Hard and furiously.

Stefan sighs. "They make hooch again. Alcohol, she does not agree with me," he adds. A teetotaler like me? *Coincidence*, I tell myself fiercely.

Footsteps are marching down the corridor. "Order, order!" I'm safe. Then another thought strikes me. If Stefan is found here, he might try to blame me. Say I'd asked him in. Maybe that I'd loosened those bars myself. Criminals, I am learning, will do anything to save their own skin.

"Go!" I am pushing him. "Please, just leave. It's safer for both of us."

He looks sad, but to my utter relief, he starts to move towards the window.

Then he stops. "Just one more thing." He smiles. "Your mother. Does she still smell of lavender?"

38

July 2001

Ali

M y mind was whirling as if someone had tipped me upside down and was shaking me. "What are you talking about?" I managed to say.

Vanessa was grinning.

"We were trying to crash the party. So we came in the back, over the fence. Kitty saw you—she tapped on the window to get your attention. We weren't sure if you'd seen us and wanted to make you promise you wouldn't tell. Then we realized what you were doing. And to think we all thought you were a good girl!"

My body went cold.

The tapping on the window that I'd thought was the tree in the wind. Kitty being all friendly to me afterwards—no doubt scared I was going to tell Mum that she was at the party without realizing I hadn't seen her.

"I must say, Ali." Vanessa had both hands on her hips now. "We didn't know you had it in you, did we?" She was shooting my sister a *Come on* look. "How much pocket money do you think our silence is worth, Kitty?"

My sister linked arms with Vanessa now. All chummy again. It made me glad I'd never had a girl for a best friend myself. Regretfully, I thought of Robin. Placid. Always on one level. But I'd blown that now.

"Thousands." Kitty grinned.

"Thousands? That's ridiculous."

I felt sick. Mum would be so upset. Worse, she'd be disappointed. The thought of that was too much. So, too, was the idea of my shameful secret coming out in the open. What if they told other people? Supposing Robin heard? How could my own sister do this to me?

"You can't."

Kitty's face was bright with spite. "Stop me, then."

That's the moment when I pushed her. I couldn't help it. All the anger over the years came out with it. The pain. The hurt. And now the fear. She fell over the curb and into the road.

She staggered up. "Now look what you've done." My sister's school dress had a dirty smear on it. It smelled, too.

"Dog shit. Ugh. How can I play in the concert looking like this? You cow!"

"You can't tell Mum about Crispin," I said desperately. "Anyway, if you saw me, why haven't you told Mum already?"

Vanessa butted in. "Because Kitty didn't want to get you into trouble. Said it would put you off those precious exams of yours. Instead, she had to ruin the whole evening and insist we go back home instead of staying on and having fun."

Kitty had stood up for me?

"If it hadn't been for you," spat Vanessa, "Crispin would have asked me out. I know he would. He kept looking at me on the bus."

"You?" I laughed out loud. "Don't be ridiculous. You're eleven years old! Do you honestly think he'd be interested in you?"

Vanessa's eyes went cold. "Why not? Actually, that's not the secret I was talking about. Come on, Kitty, you tell her, or I do . . ."

Not the secret she was talking about? What did she mean?

"No," said Kitty. She grabbed Vanessa's arm. "Stop. Don't say any more."

Vanessa shook her off. "Leave me alone. Why shouldn't I say? I don't owe you any loyalty. Fine kind of blood sister you are. Ali—"

There's a roaring in my ears.
    I'm back there in my head.
    The morning of the accident.
    When all our lives changed forever.

39

May 2017

Alison

————

"Sorry about the disturbance, miss," says the officer, opening my cell door. He has fresh baby skin that doesn't look as if it belongs here. "Some of the men got, well, a bit excited about your presence and began kicking up. Banging the walls between their pads. But it's sorted now."

He looks around. The window is still open. Curtain flapping. "Everything all right?"

"Fine," I manage to say. "Just needed some air."

"Hard to breathe inside, isn't it?" He glances at the window. Surely, he'll see the bars are missing. But he doesn't appear to. Weirdly, I find myself praying that Stefan is hiding in the darkness. Why do I want him to be all right?

"Let me know if you need anything, OK? Not long until morning now."

After he's locked my cell door again, I go to the window. "Are you there?" I hiss.

Nothing.

Reproaching myself for being so utterly stupid, I sit on the narrow bed and go over everything Stefan said.

I get into fight.

I didn't mean him to die.

Does she still smell of lavender?

Ninth of December.

I think about the few facts I know from Mum. Dad died when I was three. I barely remembered him apart from that scene with the lavender fields. Had he had a foreign accent then? If so, I don't remember it. Once, a few years ago, I had looked up my father online. I couldn't find anything. Then again, I'd been looking for "Stephen Baker."

This is crazy. My father is dead.

As for the lavender, it was surely a lucky guess. After all, I usually wear it myself. Maybe he presumed that a mother might share her daughter's taste—or vice versa.

Yet another part of me wonders whether it's time to ask Mum again. Even if Stefan is talking rubbish—which, of course, he is—it's stirred up the old longings to know more about my dad.

In the morning, when the loudspeaker announces that it's time to wake up and the fresh-faced officer finally unlocks my cell, I'm tempted to say what had happened. But then how would I explain why I hadn't raised the alarm when Stefan had come in during the night?

"It seems very quiet now," I say instead.

His lips tighten. "The troublemakers have been shipped out." Then he tries to make a joke as if to lighten the atmosphere. "They say the first night in prison is the worst. Just as well you're not here for longer, eh?"

It's still early—another half an hour before I officially start class—and the men are queuing up at the post hatch. You can see the ones who don't have any mail from the dejected faces, swiftly followed by overcasual whistling.

No sign of an old man with a cane.

There is just time to make my way to the car and my precious mobile in the glove compartment. An umbilical cord to the outside world. I'm beginning to see why they're such hot currency in prison. Mum picks up immediately.

"Alison? Thank heavens." Her voice is edgy. Verging on panic.

My heart misses a beat. So Stefan's got to her, too? Or was it just my sister causing trouble with the other residents?

"Kitty's in the hospital. She's bleeding."

"I'll be there as soon as I can."

Then I notice a text.

Wi-Fi is terrible out here. Hope you get this. Miss you. Meetings going on for longer than expected. Will ring as soon as am back. X

It's from Clive.

When I finally reach the ward after the long drive from London to the southwest, my mother is waiting in the visitors' area. I hold her tight. Breathe her in.

Hospitals always bring back all the old feelings after the accident. Disbelief. Terror. Guilt.

"She's OK. There was a lot of blood, but she hasn't lost the baby." Mum has a red spot on each cheek, the way she does when upset. "She's having more checks. The good news is that the baby's heartbeat seems steady."

"What caused it?"

Mum blew her nose. "They don't know. When I had a miscarriage, they said it was nature's way, but that doesn't really—"

"What?" I put a hand on her arm to stop her there. "When did you have a miscarriage?"

She shakes her head. "I didn't mean to let that slip out." Then she puts her arms around me. "Just before I had you, I lost another. A little girl." She smiles through her tears. "That's why you've always been so precious. And it's why I was so happy when I had Kitty, because I was finally able to give you the sister you deserved."

She hugs me close. "And now Kitty's having a little girl, too. Isn't that lovely?"

A girl. How I, too, would love a daughter one day. A daughter and a proper father as well.

The question is on my lips. About to come out. *Is my father* . . . But a nurse is opening the door. "Would you like to see Kitty now?"

Mum bustles along in front of me. I have to rush to keep up.

"Why aren't Johnny and his mother here?" I ask her as we walk down the corridor.

"It's not been very easy, apparently. Seems like your sister is playing up a bit." Mum sighs. "Throwing food around. Shouting at Johnny. That sort of thing. And although they've got some carers in, they're finding it quite tough. Johnny's mother will come in later, but she's having a rest at the moment."

Kitty is sitting up in bed. Her face is pale. But it jerks up at me as I come in. There's definitely a flash of recognition. A string of babble comes out, aimed directly at me.

"The nurse says that she seems to be trying to say something," says Mum. "I know the consultant said that most improvements take place in the first year. But miracles happen, don't they?"

I crouch by my sister's side, taking her hand. It's plump, sweaty. "Do you understand, Kitty?" I ask.

For a moment she really looks like she's about to say something. Then she laughs. Dribble comes out of her mouth. I get up. "Sorry, Mum," I say. "I can't deal with this."

Then I leave—conscious that I'm not just a lousy daughter. I'm a bad sister, too.

40

July 2001

Ali

The roaring in my ears was a car—Crispin's Mum's car with a learner's plate, marked by an *L* on the front, coming straight towards us.

"Get off me."

The summerhouse. The tapping trees.

I can't let Kitty tell Mum.

CRASH.

A blue school uniform in the air.

I watched, mesmerized, from the ground where I'd been thrown. Frozen.

The thud was heavy. Leaden. Final.

41

May 2017

Alison

If anyone had told me that I'd be in Clive's apartment this evening, I wouldn't have believed them.

We're sitting on a smart brown leather sofa—close but not quite touching. He'd called after the hospital visit, and his voice had made me feel instantly comforted.

"It's so good to be back," he says. "I've really missed you."

"Do your trips always last so long?"

He shrugs. "We had problems with the factories. I couldn't just rush back."

"Of course not," I say, not wanting him to think I'm pushing him. Then I explain what's been happening.

"You must be exhausted after the hospital," he says, stroking my hair. "They can be quite draining, can't they?"

"Have you had much experience?" I ask.

"No more than anyone else. The odd broken arm, that sort of thing."

I wince as his words bring back memories.

"Tell me about your sister, then," he says, gently.

"Our relationship wasn't easy before the accident," I say carefully, leaning back against a turquoise cushion with red and gold embroidery. There's a distinct oriental air about Clive's place. Maybe it's the silver and purple jars on the contemporary side table or the faint whiff

of joss sticks. That pink paper lantern light. And the soft velvet cushions, ornately brocaded with silver buttons. Intriguingly, there aren't
any photographs. I'd like to know more about his family, but something tells me not to pry too soon.

"In what way?" asks Clive. His arm is draping itself round my
shoulders now. It's sending shivers down me. Nice shivers.

"She was always arguing with me. Prickly. Hostile when there was
no need."

"That's a shame."

"Frankly, I'm not surprised that she and Johnny aren't working out."

I don't know where that came from. I didn't mean it. At least, I don't
think I did.

"It sounds as though he's more able-bodied than she is. It can't be
easy for them. Especially with a baby on the way."

"I don't know how we're going to manage. Sometimes . . . sometimes,
I feel guilty about the accident."

"Why?"

Stop right there, I tell myself.

"I . . . you know . . . keep wondering if I . . . well, if I could have done
anything that would have saved her."

"Like what?"

"I don't know."

Liar! Liar!

To my relief, he changes the subject. "Tell me," he says. "What is it
like in prison?"

I've found, since I've started this job, that everyone asks that question, from my mother to the college receptionist. The truth is that it's
hard to describe unless you're actually there to smell the air. The desperation. The resignation. The anger. "It's like another universe," I say.

"Are the men very unhappy?"

Most people—the few I have told about my job—generally ask if
they're dangerous. Clive himself did this when he first found out. But
the "unhappy" question is an intriguing one. I'm not even sure if I've

thought of it myself. "Some. But you get the feeling that others are more comfortable inside than out."

He frowns. "What do you mean?"

I consider a thick-fingered bulldog of a man in my group who has a history of escaping just before his release date so he gets another sentence. "Many don't have any family waiting for them. They're scared of coming out and finding themselves alone."

"That's sad."

Then I find myself blurting out something else. "There's even a murderer who's convinced he's my father."

Clive laughs. "You're kidding."

"No. And . . . I can't help wondering if he's right."

He frowns. "What do you mean?"

So I tell him about Stefan and the information he knows about me, ranging from my name to the lavender scent that both Mum and I wear. He shakes his head. "Criminals can find these things out. It doesn't mean anything."

His hand is stroking my thigh. Slowly, gently.

"I know." Hadn't I been telling myself exactly the same? Even so, it's reassuring to hear it from someone I respect. Respect? Or have feelings for?

He's speaking again. That rich, dark voice stirs longings inside me that I didn't know I had. Or that I once had, but thought had gone forever. "I think that when you've got as much on your plate as you have, it's easy to imagine things. You need to relax, Alison."

His fingers brush my hair back. Then his mouth comes down on mine.

Hungrily, I kiss him back. I am lost. And it feels wonderful.

When I get dressed the next morning, I spend a bit of time on my face. And I wear a smile. You have to show you're confident in prison—that you're not intimidated by anyone, not even men who claim to be your father. And, of course, it's easier to smile this morning after last night. The only dampener was that Clive had to leave early. "Another buying trip," he'd said regretfully, kissing me. "Singapore this time. I'll ring as soon as I'm back."

So this was what sex was all about. Not like that horrible night in the summerhouse—but an act of love that can be both passionate and gentle. How am I going to wait until we see each other again?

Meanwhile, I need to find out more about Stefan. It's not that I believe his wild claims, but there's something in me that's curious about this man. Maybe, I tell myself, as I drive to the prison, I could make some discreet inquiries.

"I've got someone in my class called Stefan," I mention casually to a prison officer at lunch.

"The old bloke with the cane who's been in the prison hospital? Heard he's not got long."

So he *is* ill, then? I feel a slight misgiving. "Do you know what he's in for?"

He tucks into his sausages and beans with relish. "Best not to ask, if you want my advice. Might scare you off the job."

Despite Clive telling me how "brave" I am, I'm seriously thinking of handing in my notice, even if it means I'll be broke. My share of the fees for the home is no longer so important with Kitty's new status. Johnny's parents will surely help. And I've been further spooked by Stefan's warning, which is still lingering in my head.

This is a bad place, Ali. You are in danger.

Tonight, I vow, I will have a serious discussion with Mum on the phone. I will tell her exactly what Stefan said. And when she confirms, as I know she will, that he's lying, I will go straight to the governor. This criminal might be old and disabled, but he can't be allowed to get away with this. He'd sworn he'd had nothing to do with those threatening messages. But if he'd been cunning enough to be transferred to "my" prison, he's surely capable of anything.

Or there is another option I could take. One I hardly dare to think about.

42

July 2001

Ali

___

Could that really be my sister? That crumpled shape in a pool of blood and navy blue school uniform? Violin case near her head. A polished shoe by her feet. Crawling towards it, I tenderly held it against my throbbing cheek. If my sister's shoe was all right, it surely meant that she was all right, too. Like me. The car had merely knocked me to one side. I was winded, and my nose raged with a throbbing pain, but I was still here.

There should be some warning before your life cracks into little pieces. Maybe it wasn't happening at all. Perhaps, in just a second, Kitty was going to stand up. Dab the blood off that uniform. Clean up her shoes. And say, with a cheeky grin, "Had you fooled then, didn't I, Ali? It's OK. I won't tell Mum. Your secret's safe with me."

But instead, she was just lying there. Silent.

The only consolation was that her chest was still rising and falling.

I daren't touch her in case I did more damage.

But she was alive. Thank God!

I sat on the edge of the road with tears of relief pouring down my cheeks. Life without my sister—however difficult she'd been—was unthinkable. If only we could start again right from the beginning. I'd *make* her love me. Then none of this would have happened.

As for Vanessa, I dared not look.

43

May 2017

Alison

———

There's an atmosphere in the prison the next day. I can smell it. Taste it. Something is going to happen. You sense it when you've been here a while. There are times when I can hardly believe how much has happened in the last eight months or so since I came inside. Or how I have changed.

It's chilly. I wrap my cardigan around me, a rather lovely hyacinth blue I haven't worn for a while. As I get closer to the building, I notice a man waiting outside.

My heart lifts.

Martin. Probably my most promising student. A courteous one, too. It's been a revelation to me, since starting here, that there is so much talent in prison. The music teacher says the same. She has one man who has learned to play the saxophone during his fifteen-year stint. And the writer in residence, some years ago, apparently put an ex-con in touch with his publisher. The man in question is now on the best-seller list. At times, I wonder if I might help Martin hit the head-lines, too.

"How are you doing?"

Unlike most of the other men in my group, Martin doesn't call me "miss." It's as though he knows I don't care for it.

"Fine, thanks," I say in reply to his question. "You sound as if you've got a bit of a cold."

"I don't feel great, but I didn't want to miss class." He shrugs. "It's what keeps me going."

I'm flattered. But also concerned in case I catch something. We have to be careful not to go near Kitty if we're not well, says Mum. Her injuries make her prone to infections. She is "frail," although you would not think it to see her body—growing even huger in pregnancy—taking up the entire width of the wheelchair. I have to say it for my sister: she keeps on smiling with that crooked grin. At times, her determination to go on amazes me.

"Where's everyone else?" I ask.

Martin sneezes. "Dunno. Maybe they got this virus, too."

"OK," I say, looking around. I'm sure I'll be all right with Martin. "Let's go in, shall we?"

I allow him to draw what he wants today. Free sketching, I call it. In fact, it's a bit of a cop-out. My mind won't focus for so many reasons. Kitty. Stefan. And I keep thinking of Clive, though I'm almost scared to recall the memories of our night together in case they disappear.

Concentrate, I tell myself. Get your mind back on the job. I glance at the clock on the wall. If I'm not careful, we'll run out of time.

"Need any help?" I ask Martin.

He is cupping his arm protectively round the sheet of paper I've given him. I've noticed that quite a lot of my men do that: it's almost like they're back at school and don't want anyone to see what they're writing in case it's not good enough.

I respect that. So I do a bit of doodling myself, my mind still elsewhere. Then I stare down at my page.

The clock is ticking. I stand up, pushing my chair back. It's time.

But Martin is already standing up.

"I'm a bit stuck," he says. "Can you help me?"

"Sure."

My throat tightens. Martin has drawn three figures. They are unmistakably schoolgirls. Each one wears her hair in plaits. They are crossing a road. And a car is coming towards them.

44

July 2001

Ali

———

"Are you all right?" It was a woman's voice. "What happened?"
    "My sister," I moaned. "Please help my sister."

"Ambulance." The woman had pulled out a mobile phone.

"Just past the bus stop. A schoolgirl's been hit. Badly. No, wait. Looks like two."

It was only then that I made myself glance at the body to my right. Blond plaits splayed. Violin case by her side.

Vanessa.

"And a car. No one has got out. There's a lot of smoke. Should I go see or wait here? There's a third girl, too. She's hurt her face, but she's right next to me, in shock. Stay here? Right."

"Put my jumper around you," said the woman. She had a reassuring, grandmotherly face. I'd always wanted grandparents. They might have made my sister be nicer to me.

"Please," I coughed, gagging on the blood that was running into my mouth from my nose. "Do something."

Mum wouldn't be able to cope if Kitty died. Nor would David. Nor would I.

"I'm not going to move them," continued the voice. "I don't want to make their injuries worse. Just sit tight now. Help will be here soon. Who should we contact, dear?"

"I c-can't remember . . . any numbers."

"Never mind. The police will sort it out when they arrive."

"We're going to be late for school," I blurted out. "My sister and her friend are p-playing in the concert. I'm to collect . . . collect a prize."

The woman was sitting next to me now on the pavement, holding my hand and mopping my face with a handkerchief. "It's all right, dear."

Then her voice changed. "Look at that. The driver's getting out of the car. Goodness. It's a schoolboy."

Crispin's screams were wrenching the air. "Mum," he was yelling. "Mum!"

And just at that moment, a siren began to wail in the distance.

45

May 2017

Alison

———

My heart thuds in my throat. My mind flails madly. I've found, since starting here, that men sometimes draw their crimes. "Does this picture have a particular significance for you?" I ask, barely able to get the words out.

"Significance!" He snatches the drawing and brandishes it before my eyes. "So I was right! You really don't recognize me, do you?"

"What are you talking about?"

He grabs my hand and makes my fingers trace his scars. They are slightly bumpy. The touch of his skin makes me feel sick. "It's me. Crispin. Crispin Wright." He says this with a grin that twists his entire face.

"B-But your n-name . . ." I stutter, as I try to pull my hand away.

"Think I could use 'Crispin' in a place like this? After the attack, they let me use my middle name instead. There was a geezer in a pad next to me. Didn't last five minutes, poor bloke. Meant I got a longer sentence, but it was worth it. Had to change the way I spoke, too. When you're in prison, you can't afford to stand out." He touches his scars with an index finger as if carefully stroking them. I wonder whether he realizes the irony. "It's one of the reasons they did this to me. Posh brat, they said."

His face is now very close to mine. I can smell his stale breath. "Schoolgirl killer. They didn't like that either. There's honor amongst thieves, you know. Drug dealing is cool. But mowing down a kid—that's different. And it's all your fault, Ali."

"I don't know what you're talking about."

"Oh, I think you do."

I'm terrified now.

"I've been waiting for this moment for a very long time," he spits. "Even so, I had to look twice when I turned up at that first class. Changed a bit, haven't you? Nice new nose. Different surname, too. And those long sleeves you wear to hide your scars? I've seen them ride up every now and then. Self-harming. That's what you're doing, isn't it?"

He whistles. "Sign of guilt. Anyway, when I realized you didn't recognize me, I had to make myself wait a bit. Get you on my side. Play teacher's pet."

I want to say this can't be true. But I can see glimpses of the old Crispin now behind those scars. That arrogance. The way he seemed to know exactly what I wanted. Still insecure teenage Ali, desperate for approval.

"I'm glad your sister's found a husband."

A flash of fear passes through me. "How do you know that?"

He ignores the question. "Does that mean she's all right now?"

"She'll never get better," I hiss, "after what you did."

"Ah, but I had some help, didn't I? Besides, this is my punishment. Being here." He shakes his head. "The question is, Alison, what kind of punishment will *you* get when your time comes?"

Suddenly, I feel very, very angry. If this is Crispin, it should be me who is furious with him, not the other way round. "You raped me," I hiss. "You deserve to be in prison."

He moves towards me again. "Raped? Hah! You wanted it."

A cold shiver goes through me as I remember my feelings when I first saw Clive. How he'd stirred longings inside me I'd had only once before. Something I didn't want to think about.

It's true. I *had* felt something for Crispin, for a moment. But I had said no.

"I did you a favor," he continues. "No one else wanted you. Apart from that little creep of a friend of yours. What was his name? Robin Hood. That's right."

He's coming closer. For a minute, I think he's going to strike me. I wince and stagger backwards and fall against a chair, hitting my cheek. I go light-headed. Then my scarf tightens round my neck—the primrose yellow one I'd put on that morning to complement the cardigan.

"Help," I begin to scream. "He's strangling me."

Crispin's eyes narrow above me. "Shut up!" he hisses.

"Help," I yell again.

Surely, one of the officers will hear me? The door opens and a figure stumbles in. Stefan?

"Get off her," he growls. "You will not touch her." He brandishes his cane and rushes forward.

What happens next is so fast that I can barely take it in. Stefan stumbles. There is a horrible, hollow crack as Martin grabs the old man's cane and thumps him on the head. Stefan slumps to the ground. Blood trickles onto the stained carpet tiles.

Stefan looks at me and mouths, "Please, forgive me." Then his eyes close.

"Help," I try to yell, but all that comes out is a whimper.

"Give me your key." Martin is growling.

I shouldn't do this. I know that. I try to remember what they'd told me during the key talk, but no one had given me hard practical advice on what to do if I was attacked or threatened.

"If you don't, I will kill him." This time his voice is almost soft. He holds the cane up, right over Stefan's head.

I look down and see that Stefan is still breathing. I can't let him do this. Reluctantly, I hand over the keys, and he slips them triumphantly into his pocket.

"We have to get help for Stefan," I plead. I have tears in my eyes. I fumble in my cardigan pocket, in the hope of finding an overlooked handkerchief.

"Stop that. Sit down. Pick up that pencil."

Shaking, I do as I am told.

"Now write," he says. "Tell it as it happened."

"What do you mean?"

He is still holding Stefan's cane. "Write down exactly what happened on that morning of the accident."

"But—but you know," I hiss. "You were there."

"You're right. I was. But the rest of the world wasn't. And now they're all going to know exactly what you did."

I glance down at the belt round my waist.

"And don't think of using that whistle," he says softly. "Or you're dead."

46

July 2001

Ali

___

"I want to be with my sister." I'd found my voice now, but it felt all scratchy and sore. My face was throbbing, but I furiously dismissed the pain.

"Don't you worry about her," said a man with PARAMEDIC on his badge, who was sitting with me in the back of the ambulance. He was applying something cool to my face. "Might have a broken nose here," he was murmuring. "Do you feel dizzy? Sick?"

"Yes. No. I'm not sure." The balloon of panic inside was getting bigger by the second. "But what about Vanessa? Is she OK?"

"Don't fret about her either. We've found the name of your school in your bag. Someone there will contact your folks. Now, let's take a look at that knee."

"Were they hurt?" I blurted out. "The people in the car. The Wrights."

"You knew them?"

My head was throbbing so hard that I could barely think. "I recognized the number plate."

Another voice was cutting in. "You can talk to the police about that later. Let's just concentrate on you, shall we?"

They took me to a room in the hospital. It had other beds, but they were empty. Kitty was nowhere to be seen. "I want my sister," I said tearfully.

"All in good time," said the doctor, taking my pulse.

"They've already done that in the ambulance."

"We need to check. I know this is difficult, but—"

"Ali! It's all right. We're here."

Mum's arms were around me. But not David's. He was clutching the back of a hospital chair. His face was white. He seemed smaller than this morning.

"Kitty," I whispered. "Where is she? What's happening?"

Mum sat by the side of the bed, stroking my hands. Her face was red and blotchy. "You've got to be brave, love. We all have to. Your sister has been put into what they call an induced coma. She's had some head injuries. It's the best way, apparently, to let the brain heal itself."

None of this felt real. "How bad is it?" I croak.

There was a whimper from David. "My princess," he moaned. "My little princess."

"It's quite bad." Mum's hand tightened. "Your poor nose. Does it hurt a lot?"

Of course it did, but I sensed she was distracting me. "And Vanessa?"

"The police need to interview you when you feel ready. Do you feel up to that, love?"

"Yes. Please tell me—is Vanessa hurt badly? What about Crispin?" It was all his fault. All of this. "He was yelling something about his mother."

"She wasn't wearing a seat belt. Went through the windscreen. That's what the police want to talk to you about. What exactly happened, love? Were you crossing the road?"

"We'd just . . . started to. Kitty . . . Kitty wouldn't hold my hand. And then . . . the car came straight at us. The Wrights' car with the L-plate on the front."

David's fists were clenched. "I'm going to kill that kid."

Something else wasn't right. I could feel it.

"Is Vanessa in an induced coma, too?"

Mum's eyes filled with tears. "I'm sorry, Ali-bean."

Ali-bean. The nickname Mum had used when it was just the two of us. "I'm afraid Vanessa's dead. And Crispin's mother, too."

Dead? My skin froze as her words sank into my head. That couldn't be right. Could it?

Because if it was, I had blood on my hands.

What would Mum say when she knew the truth? It would only be a matter of time now.

Because when Kitty finally came round, she'd tell everyone exactly what happened.

We were allowed to see my sister through a window in intensive care. But we couldn't go in—not yet. Instead, we just stood there. Holding hands. I was between them. Mum's hand on the left. David's on the right. Never had I felt so close to them before. It had taken Kitty's accident to do this.

Only a matter of time . . .

The monitor's bleeping got louder. It continued to shriek. It wasn't falling down to the average line.

Yes, it was.

Collectively, we breathed a sigh of relief.

Meanwhile, Kitty lay in a bed, her body covered with wires. She was wearing a kind of cap with yet more wires coming out of that. Her face and left arm were both bandaged.

Nothing mattered more than life. Why hadn't I understood that before? Not long ago, I couldn't wait to leave home to be as far from my sister as possible. And yet, here I was, praying she would survive, willing her to wake up.

The bleeping kicked into action once more. The three of us held our breaths and waited for it to subside like before. But it continued, becoming more persistent.

"What's happening?" cried out Mum.

"It's all right," snapped David, as though reassuring himself, too.

"High-frequency alert," said one of the nurses urgently.

A white coat, indicating a doctor, rushed into the room. Another attempted to usher us out, but Mum was having none of it. "What's going on?" she growled.

"There are signs of a blood clot." The white coat's face flashed pity. "We're doing what we can."

A nurse in blue and white stripes offered tea. No takers.

"Don't let our daughter die," begged David.

Die? No! She couldn't. But at the same time, I was aware of something awful rising in my chest. Something I didn't even want to acknowledge. But there it was, refusing to go away: the realization that if Kitty died, I'd be off the hook.

They managed to sort out the blood clot, though I couldn't say exactly how long it took. Time, I was beginning to understand, was a weird thing in the hospital. It seemed to pass really slowly, and then, all of a sudden, it was dark outside when you thought it was still afternoon.

"Will there be any long-lasting damage?" Mum had asked. The white coat had hesitated. There were heavy bags under his eyes. "I'm afraid it's difficult to say at this stage."

I felt relief. Hope. And fear. All at the same time.

The uncertainty was the worst part. "If we knew exactly how bad she is, we could get our heads round it," David said as we drove home. I knew what he meant. But I also wished I hadn't agreed to the suggestion about going back for clean clothes and a rest while Mum stayed with Kitty.

It was awkward, being in the car alone with David. He kept pushing me to go over the "sequence of events" again and again until I felt my head would explode. "Stop it!" I yelled finally. "I can't talk about it anymore. Don't you understand?"

Then his face had crumpled, and to my horror, he began to cry. I found myself briefly touching his hand in sympathy.

The first sight, as we opened the door, was Kitty's new turquoise trainers. Just like Vanessa's. Now they sat on the shoe rack, redundant. "She never got a chance to wear them," whispered David.

Flying up the stairs, I tore into Kitty's bedroom. Maybe she was still here! Maybe the accident had never happened. Shivering, I took in the school blouse flung on the floor. A copy of a teenage magazine with a coffee mug stain. Doodles on her desk. A poster of S Club 7 on the wall above the bed. A teddy, next to a mascara wand on the dressing table. It was all there.

Except for my sister.

Help me, Ali. I could almost hear her voice, pleading as if she was sorry for everything in the past. *Don't let me die.*

I didn't have to go to Vanessa's inquest, the hearing that would determine how she had died. Instead, said the policewoman, they would read out the statement I'd given at the time. When Mum and David came back, their eyes were red and hollow. "That poor girl," sobbed Mum. "They said she'd had multiple injuries. Just like Mrs. Wright."

"It's the trial that's important," snapped David. "But that won't happen for a while. At least the little bastard didn't get bail. That's something, I suppose."

Meanwhile, there was the funeral. "What will people think if you're not there?" Mum had said when I pleaded to stay by my sister's hospital bed instead. So I gave in. *Good girl, Alison.* If only they knew.

It seemed as if the whole school had turned up, wailing in one wave of grief after another as the coffin came in. Was it really possible that Vanessa, with her made-up face and cheeky smile, was inside that box? Her father was one of the bearers. Agony made his face unrecognizable. An only child. Her parents had nothing now.

All through the service, I wanted to stand up and shout, *Blame me!*

Afterwards, people quietly sidled up to me with well-meaning questions that failed to disguise their curiosity. "How is your sister doing?"

"Still in an induced coma," I told them, one after the other.

"At least she's alive," spat Vanessa's mother, who emerged at my side just as the last trail of mourners was leaving. "That boy deserves to hang."

"Come on, now." Vanessa's father put a burly arm around his wife. "You don't really mean that."

"I do." She was looking straight at me, her lovely violet eyes appraising me like some kind of lie detector. "I've always said I'd kill anyone who hurt my daughter. And I would."

Afterwards, I couldn't wait to get back to Kitty. "I said good-bye to Vanessa for you," I said, kneeling down at her bedside, trying to equate this strange body full of wires with my pretty, vivacious, impossible sister.

The nurses had told me to talk to her. "People in comas can still hear, you know. There's medical evidence."

Was I right, I asked myself, to tell Kitty that Vanessa was dead? But my sister would have to know if she woke up, wouldn't she? And I had to be there when she did.

47

May 2017

Alison

___

So I write. Martin—Crispin—watching every word. Every letter. I don't have to, of course. I could make up another story. But I'm tired of running. It's all getting too much.

In my usual, careful, even handwriting, I describe how my sister and I were running for school. How we'd missed the bus. How Vanessa was behind at first and then came up to join us.

Then the bombshell. How my sister and her friend said they knew my secret. Seeing me through the window of the summerhouse. Having sex with this man standing over me right now.

All the anger I've been bottling up over the years suddenly pours out. I throw the pencil down and look right at him. "How could you do such a terrible thing?"

For a minute, there's a flicker in his eyes. Remorse? Maybe. Then it's gone.

"And don't even think about calling it rape," he snaps. There's a groan from the bloody mess on the ground next to me. Stefan.

"He needs help," I plead.

"Keep on writing." He raises the cane. It falls on the desk next to my right hand. It misses my fingers by centimeters. As an artist, I'm always worried about my hands. They're my tools. One of the few ways to escape this world.

Sweat is pouring down Martin's face. Mine, too. He could kill Stefan. And me. Unless I think fast.

Shakily, I pick up the pencil again. *So I pushed my sister into the road.* "There's more," he says. "Go on."

My eyes are so wet that I can barely see my own writing now. *I pushed her in front of a car coming round the corner.* Then I fling my pencil onto the desk.

He says my sentence out loud.

Every word feels like a leaden weight. A poisoned pill.

I am exhausted. Martin's scars appear to gleam with triumph, or maybe it's just the sun streaming through the dusty window. "So you lied in court. You said you were arguing with your sister and she pulled away. But really, you pushed her, because you were scared she'd tell about us having sex. If you had told the truth, I might not be behind bars. If you hadn't pushed your sister into the road, my mother might not have *died*."

He is so close now that there is barely breathing space between us. I can see each pore in his skin.

"You killed her," he spits.

He raises the cane again. I feel strangely calm. If the accident hadn't happened, Kitty would be dancing and running and walking instead of being in a wheelchair. She might have been a famous artist or a musician. Vanessa would be alive. Her parents would still have a child.

Death will, quite frankly, be a release. I take a hankie out of my pocket and mop the sweat running down my neck.

"Leave her alone."

There's a roar. A choking noise. For a minute, I think that an officer has finally come in to see what is going on. Then I realize. It's Stefan, miraculously stumbling to his feet.

"Stay where you are, old man," hisses Martin.

But Stefan's hand appears to be reaching out for something on the dirty brown carpet tiles. A piece of glass, glinting in the sunlight. It's an offcut from my college workshop that I'd wrapped in one of my linen handkerchiefs when I'd last worn this cardigan. It must have fallen out just now when I'd mopped my neck.

It's only a small, narrow strip—which is probably why it had got through this morning's search—but still sharp.

With surprising agility, given that he'd been on the floor only just now, Stefan lunges at Martin's neck.

To my horror, Martin throws Stefan to the ground like a rag doll. But the old man staggers to his feet, snatches back his cane and whacks Martin on the head. "You do not touch my daughter. You hear?"

"I told you before. Get off."

There's a scream. High-pitched. Like an animal in pain. Then a thud.

"No." I howl. "NO."

Stefan is lying motionless. Blood spurting from his throat like a fountain. I scream, dropping to his side. Is he breathing? It's hard to know.

"He needs help," I cry.

"Too late for that." Martin grabs me, the sliver of glass still in his hand. "Your turn now," he growls. "You've had this coming for a very long time. My mother died because of you. And you are going to pay for that, the same way the bastard who did this to my face paid."

"You've killed before?" I gasp.

His eyes glint. "Merely mutilated. I wanted him to live so he had to look at himself in the mirror every morning."

I am too shocked to feel fear. All I can do is stare in horror at Stefan's throat as the blood continues to gush, spattering my trousers. Can anyone survive that?

Then there's another sound. The click of a key. The door opening. A fierce *Don't mess with me* voice from the prison officer who is running up to us.

"Let go of her. Now."

48

August 2001

Ali

___

They brought my sister out of her coma. This was it, I told myself. This was when Kitty was going to tell everyone exactly what happened.

Her eyes were open. She looked at Mum first, then me, then David.

We were all waiting. Holding our breath. Praying. Desperate.

Kitty's lips parted. I went cold. And then hot. My mouth was bone-dry, and my legs started to tremble. My sister was trying to talk. But the only thing that was coming out was a gurgle. A mishmash of incomprehensible sounds and rolling eyes.

How often had I wished that Kitty would get told off for all those cruel barbs over the years. But I'd never wanted her to end up like this.

Substantial brain damage.

Full recovery unlikely. Any improvement would probably take place in the next twelve months. But don't hold your breath.

Someone called a patient coordinator then sat us down in a small office and outlined the next set of practical steps.

Spinal ward.

Possible brain operation.

Rehab.

Likelihood of seizures due to brain injury.

Physiotherapy.

Assessment.

Occupational therapy.

Speech and language therapy.

Some people with severe head injuries become sexually promiscuous.

Many undergo complete personality changes.

Taste buds can change. She might like food she didn't care for before.

Twenty-four-hour care.

Excessive giggling or aggression or both.

Extreme difficulty in retaining information.

Or in recalling past events.

Then there were the phases that we, as Kitty's loved ones, would go through. In fact, we'd already started.

Shock.

Denial.

Deep distress.

Guilt even though the accident hadn't been their fault. (I tried to ignore that one.)

Frustration.

Depression.

Desperation (clutching at straws, hoping for a miracle cure).

Integration (trying to work out a way of living with this strange new Kitty who couldn't talk or walk).

But all this paled into insignificance in comparison with the trial. When I would have to lie. Under oath.

Squeaky-clean school shoes.
 Shoulder bags bobbing.
Blond plaits flapping.
Two pairs of feet. One slightly larger.
"Come on. We're going to be late."
Nearly there. Almost safe.
Pavement edge.
Another pair of feet.
No!
A scream.
Silence.
Blood seeping on the ground.
Spreading and spreading.
All because of a secret that I had to tell in order to protect another.
Some of it is coming back now.
But there's more.
I can feel it.

49

May 2017

Alison

The last time I saw blood like this was when Vanessa had been thrown into the air during the accident.

There is a gurgle. As if Stefan is trying to say something to me. Now, released from Martin's grasp, I crouch down by his side again. His eyes lock on mine. He gurgles again. It sounds like "Ali." And then his lids flicker and close.

"Put these cuffs on the bastard," yells an officer.

For a minute, I think he's referring to Stefan, but then I take in Martin, who is pushing against two guards attempting to hold him.

"It's all her fault," he says, jerking his head at me as the third officer finally restrains him.

Somehow, I find my voice. "I don't know what he's talking about."

"Don't believe a word that bitch says. She's the reason I'm locked up in the first place."

I don't care anymore. Suddenly, all I want is for Stefan to live, if that's still possible. Too late, I realize I should have made my mother talk about his claims earlier. To be truthful, I'd delayed it not just because of everything going on with Kitty, but because I was scared in case it was actually true. Then again, it couldn't be, could it? The birthdays didn't match up. Yet maybe there's some other connection between him and Mum.

Now, if Stefan dies, I might never know.

A team of people rushes in. I recognize the nurse from canteen chats. She gasps at the slashed throat, takes Stefan's wrist and shakes her head.

"Gone," she says.

There's a silence. The officer doesn't even swear. I'd like to say that the shock means I cannot think clearly. But I can. All too well.

"This isn't the first time she's done something bad," spits Martin. "Is it, Ali?"

Everyone stares at us. There is, I realize, nowhere to hide anymore.

"If you hadn't . . ."

I have to stop him. Before he says those words that will seal my fate.

So I scream. A scream of self-loathing that has been building up inside me for years. And that, finally, I am allowing myself to release.

When someone dies in prison, there's immediate "lockdown." Everyone has to stay in their place, and all the doors are locked—no one can go in or out. Each person must be accounted for, in case someone has used this opportunity to escape.

Then each person—be it inmate or staff—has to give a statement to the police. This can take hours.

That's what I am doing now. The nurse has found me clean clothes—"I always keep a spare set, dear, in case someone pukes on me." I've been given a cup of tea. It's very sweet. I gulp it down gratefully. Then I feel sick.

I am still feeling nauseous as the policewoman asks me what happened. So I tell her that only Martin turned up that morning. No, I say truthfully, he didn't seem to be acting oddly. Or dangerously. And no, I've no idea how Stefan got into the Education hut. I'd locked the main door behind me, just as I was meant to. And I thought I'd locked the door to my workshop, too. I wasn't sure how Stefan could just walk in.

"You're not sure?"

I nod, aware it doesn't sound good.

"Why do you think Stefan tried to defend you?"

"I don't know. Maybe he was passing by. Heard the noise." Another sob escapes me.

"Perhaps they'd fallen out about something," I add quickly. "Men do sometimes. The smallest things take on big proportions."

Then I harden my voice. Attack is the best form of defense in arguments. Hadn't my sister taught me that over the years?

"Just as well that he did," I say firmly. "None of the officers were around. All I have to defend myself is this whistle—and Martin told me that I'd be dead if I blew it."

The police officer is writing all this down. "How did Stefan get hold of a piece of glass?"

"I don't know." The lie sullies my mouth, but what else can I say?

"Did you know Stefan before you came to work here?"

"Absolutely not."

At least I can say that in all honesty.

"And did you know Martin Wright before you came here?"

Only as Crispin. So perhaps my "no" isn't quite a lie.

The police officer puts down her pen. "Are you sure, Alison?"

I nod, my fists clenched under the table.

"Because here's the thing." She's watching me very carefully. "Martin Wright—or Crispin, as he is officially called—has already given a statement. He says that you were present at the time of his offense. We've checked it out. And he's right. You *were* there. He was in the car that knocked over your sister, Kitty, and killed her friend Vanessa and Martin's mother."

I can get out of this if I choose my words well.

"Are you sure you've got the right man?" I demand. "He looks nothing like Crispin Wright. At least, I don't think he does, although I haven't seen him for over fifteen years."

The policewoman makes an unconvinced face before starting to write again. I'm aware that, as her colleague explained at the beginning, this is all being recorded.

"You are presumably familiar with prison rules." The voice has a warning edge. "Any member of staff encountering a prisoner who is known to them must report it immediately to the governor."

"I know." My voice comes out as a whisper.

"Here's the other thing, Alison. Martin says that during the class you just held, he made you write down everything that happened at the time of the crash. He says you admitted it was your fault."

"How could it have been? He was the one who was driving."

"So you *did* recognize him?"

Careful. I have to cover myself.

"Look," I say, holding out my hands in a despairing gesture, "I just thought he was some madman who knew about the accident somehow. He made me write down things that weren't true and threatened to kill me if I didn't. I thought it was safer to go along with it."

The policewoman's face is blank. Does she believe me? There's no proof. I made sure of that.

After Stefan had been knifed, I'd somehow had the presence of mind to shove my confession into my pocket. Then, when I went to change into the nurse's clothes, I'd ripped it up, stuffed it into a sanitary towel bag and put it in the ladies' pedal bin. The ease of my own deception had shocked me.

"Martin says that the deceased claimed you were his daughter."

I manage a half laugh. "First I'm accused of pretending not to recognize the man who killed a girl and brain-damaged my sister. And now I'm accused of having a father in the same prison. Doesn't that sound like a rather improbable coincidence to you?"

The policewoman is still writing, but I can see that my words have hit the mark.

"Stefan was an old man," I continue, more boldly now. "An eccentric. The officers will tell you that. I can't be held responsible for his crazy ramblings."

I feel myself getting angrier as I continue. "This is a prison full of psychopaths. Some of my students hear voices. Who knows who is telling the truth in this place? Now can I go, please? I need to visit my sister. The one who can't walk or talk, thanks to Crispin Wright, or whatever he calls himself now."

There's a flash of compassion on the policewoman's face. "Would you check and sign your statement here, please." Her voice is softer now. But her next words fill me with foreboding. "Keep your phone switched on. We may need to ask you more questions."

On the way out, I am summoned to see the governor. He comes straight to the point. I am suspended.

"As you know, staff cannot work alongside prisoners with whom there is a personal connection, either in the past or present. So we cannot allow you to work here anymore until Mr. Wright's claims are investigated. This could take some time."

"I didn't recognize him," I blurt out. "I didn't mean to deceive anyone."

The governor shakes his head. "Most people here didn't set out with that intention, Alison. But all it takes is one false step." He looks out of the window. Two men are walking side by side. They are in orange, which suggests they are part of the garden team. They could be here for so-called white-collar offenses. Or they might be rapists or pedophiles or murderers at the end of their sentences.

"Stefan," I say suddenly. "What was his offense?"

The governor's voice is crisp. Clinical. "Murder."

So, Stefan had been telling the truth. "Self-defense?" I ask. There's a hopeful tone in my voice. Just in case—and I mean just in case—he really was my father, I want there to be some excuse.

The governor's eyes narrow. "He might have seen it that way. But the victims would say different."

Victims? In the plural?

"He said . . . at the end . . . that he didn't have much time left anyway."

The governor sighed. It occurs to me that a man in his position has to hide a lot of emotion but that, every now and then, it must come out. "His cancer treatment had failed. There wasn't much more they could do."

So he *was* terminally ill. Why is it so hard to tell the truth from the lies?

"Can't you give me one more chance? You got it wrong about the stationery cupboard."

That hard look is back. "This is far more serious, although I should point out that you have made other mistakes, too, such as handing over the keys to a prisoner."

"But I had no choice! Crispin was threatening me."

"I'm afraid we only have your word for that. Then there's the fact that you failed to turn up for your classes between Christmas and New Year."

"But I had the flu. I was too ill to call in."

The governor shakes his head. "There's always an excuse, isn't there? Trust me, I've heard them all in this place."

"Just one thing," I say. "What will happen to Crispin now?"

"Been shipped out. His sentence will likely be extended after what he did to Stefan."

"And me," I butt in. "He tried to strangle me."

He bends his head in acknowledgment. "It will certainly be a long time before he's let out. Good-bye, Alison. I wish you luck."

Stunned by the speed with which things have happened, I stumble through the gates after signing out for the last time. I am carrying a cardboard box of my personal possessions. Prison officers walking past stare at me. So do prisoners on their way to tea. It strikes me that Angela must have felt like this when her crime was revealed. Once more, I marvel at how prison can distort your emotions and perspective; how it can make you root for someone who has done wrong.

I ring my mother. She is at home. "I need to see you," I say.

"Has something happened?" she asks.

"Tell you when I'm there."

And then I begin to drive. I don't turn on the radio. Because there's a tune that's singing loudly in my head. I don't know where the music came from. But the words are as clear as any well-known lyric.

Bad blood will out.

Like father, like daughter? Who knows.

Stefan didn't get away with his crimes.

But will I get away with mine?

50

August 2001

Ali

I'd never been inside a court before. It was bigger than the assembly hall at school. When I was called to the witness box, I could almost pretend I was walking up to the platform to get a prize from the head-mistress.

Except that, this time, I needed to give the performance of my life.

"In your own words, Miss James, please tell us exactly what happened," said the barrister.

I'd already given a statement to the police at the hospital after the accident. But the story was getting clearer now in my mind. I'd had time to work it out more thoroughly. Or so I hoped.

"We were late," I told the hushed court. "Kitty was being . . . difficult because she was nervous about playing in the school concert. She and her friend Vanessa had had an argument about something. I'm not sure what. Vanessa had been behind us. But then she ran up and was all friendly again."

I managed a half smile. "Best friends can be like that. Mum says it's a girl thing."

Some of the women on the jury nodded in understanding.

The air was electric. It was like that bit in a book or film where the dialogue seemed friendly but you just knew that someone was going to deliver a bombshell.

One of the jury smiled at me. Encouraged, I continued.

"Then, suddenly, Kitty decided to cross the road at a different place from usual. I tried to hold her hand, but she shook it off. Her action made me stumble into her, and we lost our balance for a minute."

I took a deep breath. It was as close to the truth as I dared go.

"She kept telling me to 'get off' and that she wasn't a baby."

I glanced at Mum. She was nodding her head solemnly, as if this made perfect sense. David looked as though he believed me, too. Kitty wasn't easy. A mind of her own. Which was far harder to read now than it had been before.

Another deep breath. "Then this car appeared. It was going fast. It had an L-plate on the front. I recognized the registration. It belonged to the Wright family. I knew them, but not very well. I'd gone to one of their parties recently. Then . . . then . . ."

I could only whisper the next bit.

"It headed straight for us."

There was a high-pitched moaning when I got to this point. Vanessa's mother.

My sister's friend was always boasting about how her mum used to be a model. She certainly looked amazing. "That woman never has a hair out of place," my mother would sometimes say with a touch of envy. But now she looked like a different woman. Those high cheekbones appeared to have sunk with grief. Her hair was scraped back. Her shoulders were slumped, and she was hanging on to her husband's arm as if she would otherwise fall to the ground.

"My daughter was the most important person in the world to me," she screamed at Crispin. "And you took her away from me."

Her poor husband wiped his eyes. "She meant everything," he moaned.

A "safety expert" was being called now. Yes, she insisted. Those girls had done nothing wrong in crossing at that point. If Crispin Wright hadn't been exceeding the speed limit—50 mph in a 30 mph area—he might have stopped sooner. Wouldn't have run into poor little Kitty and her friend Vanessa.

More moaning. From Mum and David, too. Bile flooded my mouth. Bitter. Sickly.

And then Crispin took the stand. Hollow eyed. Dark suit. Avoiding my face. "The girls were scuffling in the road, right in front of me."

"But the tire marks show you were too close to the curb."

Still nothing.

"Could you have stopped if you were going at the proper speed?"

He said nothing.

The lawyer had made his point.

When I had been cross-examined earlier by Crispin's lawyer, he had pressed me on the same issue.

"Were you scuffling in the road when the car came round the corner?"

"No. Like I said before, we lost our balance for a bit, but that was well before the car appeared. We were just waiting to cross the road." A sob broke out of my mouth. "The car was coming so fast. When she pulled away from me, Kitty . . . she didn't have a chance."

KILLER SCHOOLBOY DRIVER SENT TO PRISON, the local paper had screamed when Crispin was convicted.

Was that what I had done to him? Too late now to say something. If I did, they might put me behind bars as well.

"At least I still have you," wept Mum as she held me in her arms.

"You have Kitty, too," I sobbed.

But we both knew it wasn't true. Kitty, as we knew her, had gone.

Now I had to avenge her memory. Because that's what a loving sister would do.

51

May 2017

Alison

——————

My mother is disturbingly quiet when I tell her what happened. Not all of it, obviously. But enough.

"I still can't believe you didn't recognize Crispin," she says.

I think of the scars. His bald head. The glasses. The extra weight. "People change after fifteen years," I say. "Look at us."

It's true. Neither of us looks the same. My hair is short. My nose is different. Lines surround my eyes. I look older than a woman approaching her midthirties. That's what stress can do to you, I suppose.

Mum, meanwhile, went wafer-thin after the accident. She's one of those people who can't eat when they're upset. She still barely touches her food. Her hair went grey prematurely, although recently, she gave in to my entreaties and dyed it.

"It seems wrong to bother about my appearance when Kitty is like this," she said. "Thank goodness I still have you to look out for me."

But not if Crispin's lawyers have their way. I have to use his real name now: too many others are doing so around me. But it makes me feel sick. It unplugs all those memories of the summerhouse. The tree tapping. The smell of his skin on mine. My inability to move. That feeling of shame and self-loathing afterwards. The need to wash Crispin away in the sea.

"Was my father English?"

She gives a little start. "Why do you think otherwise?"

I notice that she's not denying it. Merely sidestepping the question. "Mum, Stefan genuinely seemed to think I was his daughter."

She makes a *So what* noise. "Just because you work with disturbed gangsters, darling, doesn't mean you have to believe them."

Then she puts her arms around me. Just as I had held her when I was little—when there were only the two of us—and she used to cry because she didn't know what would happen to us. I had held her, too, after the accident, but she'd also had David to comfort her. I was no longer needed.

"This world that you took yourself into," she continues gently. "It's not nice. You've been brave to work there. And I admire it. But I don't want you going back. We'll find another way of paying your sister's bills."

I want to tell her that it's too late. That the damage has been done. That the police might call me back any day if they find my written confession. And when it all comes out, I won't just have lost my sister as I once knew her. I will lose the sister I have been left with. And probably my mother, too.

"By the way," adds Mum. "Johnny's parents have a friend who knows an American specialist in brain injuries. Apparently, there's been an exciting development in what they call brain–computer interface research. There's a new machine that can help people share the thoughts in their head—even if they don't know they are having them—called an assistive communication device. Wouldn't it be incredible if it worked for Kitty?"

It's getting worse and worse.

That night, I toss and turn as I go over everything again and again. I don't even bother cutting myself. The desire has completely left me since Stefan's death: if it hadn't been for my spare sliver, which I'd had on me, he wouldn't have died. Something else to add to my guilt box.

I must have drifted off, because when I wake, I have an idea that seems so obvious that I can't think why it didn't occur to me before.

"Alison!" says the college receptionist when I stop in on my way back. "You don't have a class today, do you?"

"No. Just popping in to collect some of my students' paintings. I promised to mount them before the next class."

"You're so conscientious!"

I wince. "Just one other thing," I say casually. "Remember that job advert about the prison last September?"

"Yes! You took the details, didn't you?"

"That's right. I just wondered if it was e-mailed to you or posted. I know that sounds a silly question . . ."

"No," she cuts in. "I nearly mentioned it to you at the time. This man dropped it off. At first, I thought he was one of those homeless people. Looked a bit rough, if you know what I mean. But that arty lot can, can't they? Sorry—not you, of course." Her face tightens with anxiety. "Was it a scam?"

"No," I falter. "It was real. I was just curious, that was all. Do you know where he came from?"

"He didn't say anything. Sorry."

This doesn't prove anything, I tell myself. Maybe the arts trust that employed me got one of their people to drop off a poster.

Now for the next step.

It doesn't take long on the tube. Robin's offices—near Chalk Farm—are smarter than I'd thought. Finding a good lawyer is essential. I know that from my old students in prison. Many claim that theirs were "rubbish." There's only one lawyer I know personally. Mum always kept me up to date with his progress. And it was easy to find him through the Law Society website. I haven't seen him since I was eighteen, but something tells me that if I have any chance of getting through this, I need someone who understands me—not a complete stranger.

Of course, I could have made the appointment under another name and then surprised him. But I'd felt it only right to explain to the receptionist when making an appointment that Mr. Wood used to know me years ago as Ali James. Right now, my heart is thumping—not just with the fear of being prosecuted for my part in the accident but also at the prospect of seeing an old friend after all these years. Someone who, understandably, had dropped me after I'd abandoned him at the Wrights' party. Is this a big mistake?

I hover outside the building with his nameplate on it and then push open the heavy glass doors. A man is waiting. He looks at me and does a double take. I do the same. It's Robin. Yet it isn't. He is more grown-up, but there's a certain smoothness about his suit. The way his tie is knotted. So different from that red and blue jacket he used to wear. His hair is . . . well, tidy. His face is lined, but it suits him. Robin has grown into a man.

"Good to see you again, Ali."

With a jolt, I note that his voice is exactly the same. I remember suddenly how it had always been deep for his age at school—something else that he got ribbed about as well as the name and the jacket.

"It's Alison, now," I say nervously.

His hand reaches out to shake mine. As he does so, I realize that, despite our closeness all those years ago, our skin had never touched apart from the odd accidental brush.

As he takes me into his office and invites me to sit down, there is a stiff formality between us. I remind myself that this is the boy I used to swim across the bay with, early in the morning. Who shared my love of Leonard Cohen. Yet that lovely, comforting ease that had always been there between us has gone. I'd been right earlier. This is a mistake.

"How is your sister?" he asks.

My stomach sinks. I hadn't prepared myself for this question so fast. I'd selfishly been thinking about my own predicament. But then again, an old friend like Robin *would* talk about family before business. It was only polite.

"There's been very little change in her health since the accident. Although now she's pregnant and married."

His eyebrows raise. "Really?"

"It's a long story." I hesitate. "And there is some hope for her recovery. At least, there's the possibility of a new machine that might help her voice her thoughts."

"That's brilliant."

No, it's not, I want to say. The implications are terrifying. Just think what she might come out with.

But instead, I repeat one of Mum's platitudes. "Any small step is encouraging. But you also learn not to have false hopes."

"Sure."

It's then that he fiddles with a ring on his finger. A gold one. On his left hand. There's a ping inside my chest. Then I reproach myself. Naturally, a man like Robin is married. Maybe, if things had turned out differently, it could have been me. I might have had a safe life. Why don't we understand when we make rash decisions in our early youth—while praising ourselves for being spontaneous—that these choices can affect our lives forever?

"My secretary said you have a matter you wish to discuss."

So stiff. So formal. Where is the boy I used to know who was so different from everyone else? I look around his office to buy time. There are no family pictures on his desk. Just smart wooden filing cabinets. Certificates on the wall. A drinks cupboard.

"I've been working as an artist in residence at a prison," I start to say.

His eyes widen. "That's very enterprising."

If only he knew.

"Something happened recently. A man was killed."

"I'm sorry," he says. It's a sort of distant apology. The type you might make if a friend of a friend of a friend had died.

I sit forward. "There's something else. Crispin Wright was one of my students there. He's the one who killed the other man."

That's better. I can see real shock in his face now.

"He's changed. I didn't recognize him." I'm rabbiting on in my nervousness. "Now I'm suspended until, well, until the authorities have investigated the situation. Staff aren't allowed to work with inmates they know." I stop and lean closer. "Are you allowed to represent me? Given that we know each other?"

"Yes. Provided there isn't a conflict of interest."

"There isn't. As far as I can see."

Robin's eyes take on a cool intensity. It's as though he knows there's more to come. My mouth is so dry that I can barely speak. But I must. "Crispin—or Martin, as he has been calling himself—accused me of causing the crash . . ."

I stop. Preparing myself for the lie I have to tell him.

52

September 2001

Ali

K itty was out of rehab. Not much more could be done for her, apparently. She was being moved to a residential home. She still hadn't managed to speak. Slowly, I began to relax. Maybe my secret would be safe after all.

There was something else, too. David had left Mum and gone to London. I should be pleased, I told myself. How often had I wished it was just me and Mum together? But my mother was sad and lonely without him.

"Tragedies can bring couples closer," she sniffed. "Or drive them apart."

Meanwhile, we had to steel ourselves to sort out Kitty's room. "She used to hate it when I tidied up," said Mum wistfully. "Said I put it all back in the wrong order."

That's when I spied it. My history notes that had gone missing. It was sitting in a pile of books on the floor. "I knew she'd taken it!" Of course, it was too late now, but it still mattered. At least to me.

Mum rubbed her eyes. She hadn't slept properly since the accident. "No, love. That was me. I put a whole load of your books on Kitty's floor so I could go over yours with the vacuum cleaner. Thought I'd moved them back again, but I must have missed this. I'm so sorry."

I swallowed the bile in my throat. "When was this?"

"A while ago. Around the time of your exams. David had been going on about how untidy your room was." She made a little whimper. "To think I thought that was important."

I could barely speak. *I asked you if you'd seen them!* I wanted to yell. But what was the point? It couldn't bring back the past.

Yet if I'd known that my sister hadn't stolen my history notes, I wouldn't have been so angry at her. Kitty might be Kitty as she used to be. And Vanessa might still be alive . . .

I was so stunned that I could barely take in what Mum was saying. "Here—take this."

"Take what?"

"Kitty's locket." She held it out to me. "I want you to have something to remind you of your sister."

The locket that Kitty refused to lend me for the party. The cool metal was strangely soothing against my neck. It made me feel like my sister was close. Yet at the same time, I couldn't help feeling a touch of satisfaction. Kitty would be furious if she knew I was wearing her necklace.

That was when I found Kitty's paints. And later on that day, I opened a tube of turquoise and started painting. The last hand to touch this brush had been my sister's. Now my hand was slipping into its place, moving across the page almost as if my sister was guiding it. *See*, she was saying. *You can paint, too. You were just concentrating too hard on your silly books to notice.*

At first, my splashes looked like rubbish. Yet the very act of doing something that didn't tax the mind with facts and dates was therapeutic after the agony since the accident.

Keep going, said Kitty in my head. *See the way the light falls through the tree outside? Shade in the shadow. That's right. Now put some darker green round the outside of the leaf. They're not all one color, you know. They're like you and me. A mixture of contrasts. Let the colors bleed into one another. That's the joy of watercolor. You never know what's going to happen.*

It was almost as if my sister had willingly transferred her talent into my body by telepathy.

A few days later, I decided to tell Mum. I didn't want to upset her any more than she was already. But I knew this was the right thing to do. "I've made a decision about uni," I told her. "I'm not going. Not ever."

"But York agreed to defer for a year!"

"I know. But I don't want to study history anymore. It's too . . . too factual. I can't think straight now. Let's face it, Mum. None of us can. I want to do art instead."

"But that was Kitty's thing . . ."

Not anymore.

"I went to see one of the teachers at school," I continued, my hands shaking. "I took my portfolio—well, some drawings I'd done. She said it might be enough to apply for art school."

"You're sure of this?"

"Certain."

"Then maybe you're right." Mum sat down heavily at the kitchen table. "Perhaps we all need something different."

That's when the idea came. "And while we're at it, I'm not Ali anymore. I want to be known as Alison Baker from now on."

For a minute, Mum seemed as though she was about to say something. Then she closed her eyes briefly. "I understand that," she said, with a steely note to her voice. "You need to start again. Like all of us."

After our conversation, I went up into my room and opened the locket. It was just as I'd feared: a picture of Crispin—taken from the school newsletter—grinned back at me.

I ripped it up into tiny bits and flushed them down the loo.

The following day, I took Mum's kitchen scissors to the bathroom and chopped off all my hair.

To make up for the new bald Kitty.

With the help of Kitty's art teacher at school, I got a last-minute placement at a London art school. I chose not to live at college. Already, I could predict the questions from other students. (*Where do you live? Do you have family?*) Far better to use my grant to rent a small studio flat in Holloway. On my own.

London was a breath of fresh air. Away from everyone who had known me. Away from my mother's sadness. Away from the road where we had walked to school. Away from the sympathetic faces who had known Kitty and me in an earlier life. The only things I missed were my mother and the sea. And, of course, my sister.

How she would have loved this!

Don't be silly, the old Kitty seemed to say in my head when someone asked if I was going to the freshers disco. *Of course you've got to go. We would! Wouldn't we, Vanessa?*

But when a boy asked me to dance—just as the music went slow—I smelled Crispin on his skin. Heard the tapping of the trees in my head. So I'd mumbled something about "needing to leave" and ran.

Kitty wouldn't have done that. She'd have been thrilled that someone wanted to kiss her.

So, instead, I stuck with my own company. I ignored messages from people in my old life—including Robin, who got in touch every now and then to see how I was. I knew that if I was going to survive, I had to create a new identity, without ties to the past. No more Ali.

"You've got something here," said one tutor after watching me work on a very fine botanical pen-and-ink drawing. "There's a real eye for detail. Have you ever thought of doing stained glass?"

That was my epiphany—an artistic medium that Kitty had never ventured into. As soon as I began to cut into the glass, I felt something light up inside. It wasn't just my "natural skill." It was what I could do with the glass afterwards.

At first, it was an accident. It's hard *not* to cut yourself when you're making a stained glass picture. Tiny fragments are a constant hazard. "Ouch," I said when one got into my skin. The tutor showed me how to extract it with tweezers. It was nothing, I told myself, compared with the pain that Kitty had felt when the car had hit her.

Later, when I was tidying up the empty workshop, I picked up a piece of discarded glass and carefully sliced the top part of my arm. The blood was instant. So was the gratification. It wasn't a deep cut, although it did take a few bandages to stop the bleeding. After that, I was hooked.

Of course, I didn't do it every day. Only now and then, when things got particularly bad. Especially after my visits to Kitty.

At first, I would try to visit once a month or so, although not at the same time as Mum. We'd spread it out. David, apparently, "occasionally went," although Mum didn't like to talk about him. But after I qualified as a teacher and got my first job at a girls' school in the East End of London, I went much less. I tried to tell myself I was too busy, or that visiting her—if she could understand who I was—would only make her feel worse. After all, we'd never got on before the accident.

But Kitty never went away: so many of my pupils reminded me of her. There was one in particular who had the same cheeky attitude. The same blond hair. The same disregard for authority. The same talent. "I don't want to do acrylics, miss. I like watercolors."

I was softer on her than the others. Let her get away with things. I was nice to her to make up for Kitty. But the others noticed. "Teacher's pet!" So I went the other way. Became harder. The hurt on her face was too painful. Then I left. Started again at another school. But once more, another "Kitty" emerged. Dark hair this time. Like the new Kitty. The same old confident attitude. I lasted two terms that time.

When I applied for a third school, questions were asked. Why hadn't I stayed longer in my previous situations? Was I really committed?

"Maybe," said one of my old tutors whom I'd gone to for a reference, "you'd be better off teaching adults. We're looking for someone to run one of our evening groups here. Stained glass. It's one of your specialities, isn't it?"

And that's how it started. The years passed, and I became a regular tutor at different art colleges. I had a certain amount of independence that way—so much better than working for one employer. I also ran my own classes in hired rooms. I earned enough to pay my rent. And I gave the rest to Mum. It was needed for Kitty's place in the home, even after the compensation had finally been paid through the insurers.

On one of my infrequent visits, I started to tell Kitty about my art students. Suddenly, her good arm shot out and thumped me. Right under my eye. I felt the swelling immediately.

"Kitty," said one of the nurses. "That's very naughty."

No, I wanted to say. *It's all right.*

At the same time, she'd begun to babble. A stream of angry nonsense. Or so it might have seemed to anyone else. "She's really trying to say something, isn't she?" said the nurse.

Yes. She was telling me that she was jealous. That I had no right to steal her passion. *Art's* my *thing*, she might as well have said. *Not yours.*

I began to visit three times a year instead of every month. And then twice a year. And then once. Just at Christmas, when she hit me again.

After that, I stopped visiting altogether. More time passed. Months and then years marked by notches on my arms. Of watching Mum getting older and sadder, though still making her visits every Friday on her day off from the charity where she now worked. Of wondering how Crispin was doing in his northern prison.

Then the poster appeared, and Clive. My resumed visits to Kitty. Martin. The end of the road.

Is it finally time to tell the truth?

53

June 2017

Alison

———

It's our second meeting, and things have just got a lot worse.

Kitty is staring up at me from her photo in Robin's file, which is open on the desk between us.

My sister is a very different person from the little girl that we remember. And I'm terrified.

But there's no time to think. Robin is steaming ahead.

"There are several issues to deal with here. First, Crispin Wright has now launched an application for his case to be retried in the light of your written confession."

"But he's in prison. And he's going to be tried himself for attacking me and Stefan."

"That doesn't mean he can't accuse you of lying over the accident." Robin turns to the next page in the file. "Then there's the incident in the prison. Why did you take a piece of glass into the classroom?"

"It must have been in my pocket from one of my outside workshops," I say. "I didn't know it was still there. Anyway, Security should have picked it up."

Robin's expression indicates he agrees. Then he gets to the thing we've both been skirting around. "And how do you explain the discovery of your so-called written confession, in the sanitary bin of the ladies?"

Yes. They found it. I'm still reeling from the fact. Yet, what did I expect in prison? They're experts at ferreting out crime. Or at least they are sometimes.

"I . . . I'm not sure."

Robin's eyes have a wary look about them. "You wrote that you pushed Kitty into the road. Is that true?"

I get ready to deliver the lie I'd already told the policewoman. How Crispin had made me write down things that weren't true.

Yet Robin's good, kind face makes me stop. Despite my intentions a few moments ago, I feel my mind doing a U-turn. I try to pull it back. I could succeed if there was a different solicitor sitting opposite me. But this is my old friend. We go way back. I hurt him once. I owe him the truth.

"Yes," I say softly. "I did push her."

Robin shakes his head again. "Look, Ali. I see this again and again with clients. They blame themselves for accidents that happen to other people because they think, somehow, it might help. Call it an overdeveloped conscience or survivor guilt if you like. But we know Crispin was driving too fast. His car mounted the pavement. All of that has been proven beyond a doubt."

It would be so easy to let him carry on. To allow Crispin to take the whole blame.

"We were having an argument," I cut in. "Kitty kept saying . . . She kept saying that she knew my secret."

"What secret?"

This is the difficult bit.

"I can't say," I whisper.

Robin twists his wedding ring again. "I'm afraid you're going to have to. That's if we're going to have any kind of a chance in getting you off."

He's right. "Kitty saw me in the summerhouse at the Wrights' party," I blurt. "She saw me having sex with . . . with Crispin."

Robin's face looks as though someone has delivered a punch to it.

"I didn't want him to. I didn't say he could. He just went ahead and did it." The tears are pouring down my face now. "I only went to the summerhouse with him because he said you were there, waiting for me with a drink."

This last bit comes out as an anguished cry. For a minute, I think it's from Robin's mouth and not mine.

"He raped you?"

"I . . . suppose so. But I didn't see it like that at the time. I thought it must have somehow been my fault. It's only as the years have gone by and I've got older that I've realized."

"Did anyone else know about it? That it was nonconsensual sex?"

I shake my head. I can see, as I do so, the doubt in his face. "You are aware," he says slowly, "that it's very difficult to prove an historic rape."

I gulp. "Yes," I croak.

"And there are countless cases where women who claim to have been raped are torn to shreds verbally in court and discredited."

I swallow. "I'm prepared to handle that."

He is looking at me. Hard. I can see he believes me—just. At least, I think so.

"So you pushed her because you were terrified of it coming out."

I nod, unable to speak.

Silently, Robin nudges a box of tissues on the desk towards me. "I'd have killed the bastard if I'd known," he says softly.

So he does believe me. I can see Robin is hurt. We might not have been boyfriend and girlfriend, but there's a fine line between love and friendship.

And that's when I realize something else. People are wrong when they say teenage cuts are the worst. It's the middle-aged ones that hurt the most. Why? Because there's been time for both parties to contemplate the reasons and effects. For them to sink ever deeper.

Robin is writing more things down now with a fountain pen. Its nib scratches on the paper. Every word that I am saying is also being recorded. I won't be able to tear it up, as I did my forced confession.

"When I first came to see you professionally, I asked if you were allowed to represent me." I swallow. "You said you could, providing there wasn't a conflict of interest. Does it matter that you were at the party, too?"

"No," says Robin curtly. "I didn't see the . . . the alleged offense, so it's all right."

There's a deeply awkward silence. Then he speaks again. More quietly. "At the trial," says Robin, "Crispin said that you and your sister were 'scuffling around' right in front of the car. But you said you were both simply crossing the road."

I can hardly talk. But I have to.

"I lied. Like I said just now, I pushed Kitty. I was so angry with her. You know what she was like. But I didn't mean . . ."

This time he seems to believe me. Robin's face is stunned with shock, yet my shoulders feel lighter than they have for years. The relief is so great that it's as though I've lanced a boil. And then, all at once, comes a terrifying feeling of foreboding.

Robin starts to speak and then stops as though something is stuck in his throat. Then he starts again. "Did you see the car coming when you pushed her?"

My chest is so tight that I can hardly get the words out. "Yes. No. I'm not sure. It's all such a blur. But I do know I didn't want to hurt her."

He is staring into space. Then he makes a noise. It could be a groan. It might be a sigh. Either way, it doesn't sound good. "You do realize that lying to a court means you could go to prison."

Haven't I been telling myself that every day since it happened?

Robin's fingers are tapping urgently on the desk. I have a sudden memory of him doing that at school. He talks rapidly now, as though speaking to himself. "Crispin was driving too fast. But he could have argued that your pushing was a crucial factor. And this might have led to a shorter sentence if you had told the truth. But from your point of view, the fact that he raped you could be a mitigating circumstance for your untruthfulness."

I cannot face him. Instead, I stare at the certificates on the wall. But the silence when he finishes is deafening. I turn back again.

Robin is now scratching his chin, the way I remember. Running his hands through his hair, just as he had when trying to solve a mathematical problem.

"We may have a defense that could work." His voice is tight. This was my friend, I remind myself. The only person who understood me as a teenager.

"Really?" I don't know whether to feel hopeful or not. I glance away. Then back again, because there's no escape from his face. "I'm sorry. For everything."

He's about to say something. But then the phone rings. "Yes?"

The old Robin never used to bark like that.

"Tell her I'll be out in a minute." Then he gets up. "I've got to talk to someone. I'm afraid you'll need to make another appointment. There's a lot more we need to discuss."

"I'll do it when I'm home," I murmur. "When I've got my diary."

As soon as he leaves his office, I reach for my mobile. There's only one person who might just understand.

Please be in, I pray.

He picks up on the seventh ring.

"It's me," I say. "I'm sorry I haven't been able to return your calls. But I need to see you now. I'm in trouble. I'm in a lawyer's office—I got the train here—and I'm scared."

"It's all right," says Clive in that deep, reassuring voice. "Give me the address. I'll come and get you."

I'd never brought anyone back home apart from Mum. But there's nowhere else I want to go. Or anyone else I want to be with.

He doesn't ask questions. It's as if he knows I don't want to talk. Instead, he just helps my shaking body in through the door and carefully steers me to the sofa.

Then he finds the kettle without being asked and brings me a mug of coffee. "I brought some brandy with me," he said. "I know you don't drink, but you need something."

I don't argue. Instead, I sip it gratefully, the Indian sofa throw draped around my shoulders. I want him to sit next to me, but he is looking around my flat.

"Is this you?"

He picks up a picture of me next to my sister in our navy blue uniforms. It's on top of a stack of photographs that Mum had brought round on her last visit because she thought I might like them for "old times' sake." What I'd really like is to throw them out, but I can't quite bring myself to do so. Besides, what if Mum asks where they are?

"Yes," I croak. "That's me and . . . Kitty."

"You look like such a sweet, sensible schoolgirl."

"But I wasn't," I say. My words come out like a sob.

He gives an *I don't believe it* smile. "What do you mean?"

The mug of coffee is burning my hands. I think of Crispin's scarred face. "I can't say."

He walks over to me and puts an arm around me. His face is close to mine. I can breathe him in.

"I'm here if you want to tell me," he says gently. "And if you don't, that's fine, too."

So I do. I confess everything.

Then I wait for him to leave. But instead, he unbuttons my blouse. I should stop him, but I can't. Just like the last time, it feels totally natural, as though we have done this many times before in another life.

"Is this all right?" he asks gently.

I nod.

Then he makes love to me so tenderly and passionately that I think I might die.

PART THREE

54

June 2017

Kitty

———

When she'd first arrived at Johnny's home all those weeks ago, Kitty had hardly been able to believe her eyes. So many rooms! And a swimming pool, too! It reminded her of a house that she thought she'd been to once—there'd been a party. After that, her memory fizzled out.

"If there's anything you need, try to tell me on your picture board," said Johnny's mum. "And do call me Jeannie." Then she put a hand to her mouth. "I know you can't say it out loud, but maybe you can think of me like that. Now here's your bedroom. I think Johnny's there now."

There were two huge twin beds with a special hoist above hers ("so the carers and I can get you up in the morning, dear") and an en suite bathroom just for the two of them. "Come to bed," said Johnny when she wheeled herself in.

The thing inside Kitty gave a jump as if to say, *Are you joking? I don't feel like that sort of stuff anymore.* Ever since the bleeding, Kitty had been convinced this was a monster inside her and not a baby at all. How could it be anything else with kicks like that?

"I'm sure Kitty wants to rest," said Call Me Jeannie.

Kitty breathed a sigh of relief. At least someone understood.

It took a while for her to get used to the new life. "Can you believe it?" said Call Me Jeannie as she turned over a page of the calendar on the wall. "June already!"

In some ways, it was much better than the home. Food whenever she wanted it—and plenty of it. No strict bedtime routine. Telly in their bedroom. A huge one on the wall.

But in others, it was worse. Johnny always wanting to get into her bed at night—and during the day. Pawing away at her. To think she used to like this sort of lovey-dovey stuff!

"Are you happy here?" Friday Mum asked when she visited.

"It's OK," she babbled.

"I wish I knew what you were saying. That memory board isn't enough, is it?"

You could say that again! Fat lot of good that thing was. Even when Kitty managed to make her finger touch the picture she wanted, someone always interpreted it the wrong way. Or just didn't get it.

"I feel so guilty that I can't look after you myself," added Friday Mum.

Then she stared at Kitty's huge stomach. "It won't be long until you're a mother and I'm a grandmother!" Her eyes filled with tears. "It's a miracle. But I just hope we can all manage."

At least there was no Bossy Supervisor. But Johnny's father and his brothers didn't seem to want her here. "That's disgusting," one of them said—to her face!—when she slurped her way through spaghetti Bolognese over dinner.

"Shhh," said Call Me Jeannie.

Johnny just laughed.

But then came the day center.

"Johnny always used to love it," said Call Me Jeannie. "Would you like to go with him?"

No. She wanted to watch telly and see what happened to the girl who had hit the boy who had slept with her best friend. But it looked like she had no choice.

Call Me Jeannie had bought a special van that was big enough for her wheelchair. Kitty stared out through the window all the way there. So many people walking down streets as if it was perfectly easy to put one foot in front of the other. Why couldn't she do the same? What exactly had happened to her that meant she couldn't walk?

"Here we are!" sang Johnny. He was sitting on the edge of the seat, his tongue hanging out.

"You look like a dog," babbled Kitty.

Johnny smiled as though she'd said something nice. "I can't wait to introduce you to my friends."

Friends? Kitty's heart did a little flip of fear. She'd had a friend once. What was her name? Kitty could see her in her mind right now. Blond plaits. For some strange reason, she was getting a lot more of these flashes since her hospital visit.

As they went into the center, Kitty fell quiet. Everyone was coming up to Johnny. Slapping him on the back and welcoming him. "Where have you been, mate?"

Johnny looked so pleased that he forgot to introduce her. Luckily, Call Me Jeannie did it for him. "This is Kitty. She's Johnny's new wife."

One of the girls in the group, who was leaning on a cane, gave her a nasty look. "Wife?" Then she turned to Johnny. "I didn't know you'd got married."

Her husband was shifting from one foot to the other, the way he did when he felt awkward. What was going on?

"Yeah. We met at the home."

"I see." The girl was glaring at her.

Johnny had gone now. Sucked up into a wave of lads who wanted him to play pool.

The girl who'd given her a nasty look had followed them, limping on her cane and grabbing Johnny's arm when she caught up. Kitty felt a flash of jealousy. It reminded her of another time. Summer lights in the garden. Girls in the years above holding hands with boys. A tall, thin boy who she liked more than any of the others. Then the memory dissolved.

Call Me Jeannie was talking to one of the helpers in a low voice. She'd need to be quick.

Kitty put her hand on the lever of her new electric wheelchair that Johnny's family had bought her. The speed had been strictly restricted in the home. But she wasn't there anymore, was she?

"Ouch," said the girl with the cane. "You've just rammed into me."

"Good," babbled Kitty. "Keep your fucking hands off my husband."

"I'm sure she didn't mean to do it, did you?" said Johnny.

"Yes, I bloody did."

"Poor you." Johnny was actually rubbing the girl's leg. "Is that better?"

"No," yelled Kitty. "Don't do that. You're my husband. Not hers."

"She's really bruised me!"

"Stop making such a bloody fuss."

Shortly after that, they went home.

That night, when Johnny tried to crawl into bed with her, Kitty wasn't having any of it. He'd fancied that girl. She just knew it.

"I don't know if your mother mentioned it," said Call Me Jeannie a few days later, "but there's a new machine that might help you speak."

"Yeah," said Johnny. "It can read your thoughts." He slapped his thighs as if it was one huge joke.

"We're all going to see the brain specialist soon," said Call Me Jeannie. "He'll do some tests to see if you're suitable. Isn't that wonderful?"

Yes. Kitty had plenty of things she wanted to say out loud.

The worst day of the week was when they went to the day center. Thursdays. Bad things had always happened then. Kitty wasn't sure how she knew that. She just did.

"I don't want to see that bitch who has the hots for you," she'd yell, thrashing when the carer tried to lift her into the car with Call Me Jeannie.

"Don't do that, dear. You're hurting us."

In the car, she made a terrible smell.

"Ugh," said Johnny. "That's disgusting." He never used to say that in the home.

When they got there, the girl with the cane was waiting. She had long blond hair that reminded Kitty of the friend she used to have— whatever her name was.

"You're late," she said to Johnny, ignoring Kitty.

One of the center's helpers played cards with her. "Try putting this one down with your good hand," he said.

But all the time, Kitty kept looking for Johnny and the girl with the cane. Then, when the carer took her to the loo, she saw them. Standing in a corner. Johnny had his arms around the girl. The Monster inside her leaped up and down in indignation. Kitty could have cried.

When they got home, she refused to eat. Or the next day. Or the next.

Johnny didn't try to get into bed with her anymore. That night, she took off her nappy with her good hand and smeared poo all over the wall.

The social worker came to make one of her checks. "I'm not sure this is working out," Kitty heard Call Me Jeannie say.

When it was time for bath that night, she flailed around more than usual. "What's wrong, dear?" asked Friday Mum when she came to visit. "Jeannie says you don't seem very happy."

Later, Kitty listened to Call Me Jeannie and Friday Mum talking in the kitchen. They spoke as if she wasn't there. Or as if she was deaf. "I'm afraid Johnny can be very impulsive at times. Always having a crush on different girls at the day center. One of the helpers said he'd found Johnny kissing another girl the other day."

"No!" Friday Mum was clearly shocked.

"Of course, he and Kitty did get together rather fast, didn't they? If it hadn't been for the baby, well . . ."

That night, Johnny seemed sorry for everything he'd done. "Shall we have a cuddle?" he said.

CRASH!

"She's hurt me," he yelled.

Call Me Jeannie came running in, wearing a powder blue night-dress. "What's happened?" she cried.

"I didn't mean it," Kitty tried to say. "I just pushed him away and he fell on the floor. That's all."

But Johnny had to go to the hospital to have his arm put in a cast. Afterwards, Kitty refused to let the carer dress or wash her.

"Jeannie can't cope anymore," said Friday Mum when she came to visit. "Don't worry. I've persuaded the home to take you back. Johnny's parents still want to pay for the specialist, though." She wiped away a tear. "So you'll be returning next week. I think that's for the best. Don't you?

"There's something else, too, Kitty. Some rather bad news, I'm afraid. I'm not sure how much you can understand but . . . well . . . it's about your sister. She's in trouble."

Something at the back of Kitty's mind made her feel that, once upon a time, she herself hadn't been very nice. It made her feel uncomfortable.

"Your sister has been accused of something." Friday Mum was shaking when she spoke. She didn't look very well, come to think of it. Her face was very grey, and one set of fingers was twisting the other.

"She's still being interviewed by the police. A man was hurt in the prison where she works. And another man said that . . ."

Don't stop, Kitty wanted to say.

"I don't know why I'm bothering to tell you, Kitty." Friday Mum had tears streaming down her face. "It's not as though you can do anything. Except that you were the only other person who survived the accident, love. You could tell us if it's true or not."

The accident?

Kitty had a flash of plaits. New shoes. A violin. A funny smell.

And a terrible, hollow thud.

55

July 2017

Alison

————

Summer is finally here. It's hot. Couples are sitting in the local park, arms draped around each other. As I jog past, I notice a woman of about Mum's age who has hitched up her office skirt to make the most of the sun. I think of Clive and the lovely day we'd had the other weekend.

"Let's drive to Oxford and have a picnic," he'd suggested out of the blue. So we'd munched on smoked salmon and crispy salad by the river, watching the students glide by on punts. Afterwards, I'd lain on the grassy bank and put my head in his lap. "Perfect," he'd murmured, giving me lots of little butterfly kisses on my cheek that tickled me and made me giggle. Now he's away again on another buying trip. What does he get up to when he's away?

Or, more importantly, what do I?

Our defense case is building, Robin told me when I last saw him. E-mails marked URGENT are pouring into my inbox from his office address. They are always clipped, businesslike, asking me questions that might strengthen our argument. Sometimes, he rings to clarify a point, or calls me into his office for a meeting. The last one had been particularly difficult.

"Do you remember what you said when Crispin took you to the summerhouse?"

His voice is distant in the way that someone's is when they don't want to talk about something.

"Not the exact words," I say, embarrassed. "But he led me to believe that you were there."

"So he lured you on false pretenses?"

"Absolutely."

"Did you have any idea he was going to . . . to make advances?"

"No." My knees begin to shake.

"Did you want him to?"

His voice is flat. I wish we were on the phone and he couldn't see my face.

"No."

"Did you make any attempt to fight him off?"

"I tried to push his chest away, but then I gave in." This comes out as a whisper.

"I'm sorry. I didn't catch that."

"I tried, but he was so heavy, and I was in shock. I couldn't believe it was happening."

"Did you tell anyone you were raped?"

"No." My denial comes out as another groan.

"Why not?"

Do I detect a note of alarm to his voice?

"Because I felt dirty. As if it was my fault."

I wait to hear him tell me that this is exactly what it was.

"Actually, Ali, many rape victims feel exactly the same."

So he believes me!

"I'm afraid you're going to have to steel yourself for intrusive questions like this in court," he adds more kindly.

"Do you discuss cases with your wife?" I ask suddenly. Instantly, I wish I'd kept my mouth shut. Yet I can't deny I've been curious. What kind of woman has he married? When? Is she a lawyer, too? It seems odd to think of the Robin I once knew actually being a husband.

There's a brief silence. I've gone too far, I tell myself. Then he speaks. "My cases are confidential."

I feel as though I am eighteen again. Stupid. At fault. Naive.

"Besides, we are divorced."

What? I glance at his ring.

"Never got round to taking it off," he says quickly, as though it's unimportant.

So, he's not over her yet.

"A ring can be useful when dealing with overfriendly female clients," he adds.

"Does that happen?" I ask. It comes out sounding rude, as if I doubt Robin's attractiveness.

He gives a short laugh. "Women going through a divorce are vulnerable. It's easy for them to imagine there is something between them and their solicitor. One of the first things we were told at law school." His eyes face mine. Fairly and squarely. "I imagine it can be like that between prison staff and offenders."

I leave his office, feeling thoroughly confused by the different emotions flying round my own head.

Yet this is nothing compared with the latest news about Kitty. Arrangements are being made to send her back to the home. Johnny's parents can't cope with her anymore after she pushed Johnny out of bed and broke his arm.

"It was an accident," Mum keeps saying. "My Kitty isn't like that."

When I first heard, I have to confess that I felt a flash of pleasure. So Johnny's family had discovered something that I had had to live with for years! My sister is not easy. She has a mind of her own.

To clear my head after the meeting with Robin, I take a jog along the Thames. A tourist steamer goes past. A child is waving at me. I wonder what it would be like to get onto the next one and never come back. Don't try to hide, I tell myself. It's time to go back to the flat, shower and drive down to Mum's. After all, I'd promised.

She'd been really excited when—after that conversation about Kitty—I'd asked if I could come down for a few days. "Don't you have to work?"

I haven't told her yet about being suspended from the prison.

Usually I'm pretty open with Mum but I didn't want to worry her, and the more time went by, the harder it was to admit that I was unemployed. She had enough on her plate as it was. "My college art classes are over for the summer," I had explained truthfully without referring to HMP Archville. She doesn't mention it either. Mum's good at that. Ignoring what she doesn't like. Perhaps it's hereditary.

"I can't wait to see you, darling," she'd added.

"Me, too."

But she might change her mind when I get there. Because now is the time for my mother to come clean.

56

July 2017

Kitty

___

"So you're . . . back," sniffed Margaret. "They say a . . . bad . . . penny always . . . turns up."

"Don't take any notice of her," said Tea Trolley Lady. "She's missed you. We all have, dear. Welcome home."

Home? Home was a little house on her picture board with a winding path and flowers at the side. Kitty had never really thought of this place as "home" before. Instead it had been a vague idea of a house with Friday Mum and . . . someone else. Had it been the tall blonde, Half a Sister? Or was it Flabby Face—her father?

It made her head spin.

When Call Me Jeannie had taken her in, she'd told Kitty to treat their house as her home. But it wasn't. Every time she had done something, it was wrong. It wasn't her fault that the wheelchair scuffed the paint on the doorframe. Or that she dribbled. As for pushing Johnny out of bed and breaking his bones, that really had been an accident.

Now she was back in her old room with Margaret as though nothing had happened. Only the rings on her left hand showed she had got married.

"Getting . . . bigger . . . aren't you?" wheezed Margaret. "Not long . . . now . . . they say."

Not long until what? The Monster gave a big kick, as if it knew something, and her tummy gurgled.

"Hungry, are you? Nearly . . . dinner now. Tell you . . . what, you can . . . have my seconds as a . . . welcome-back treat."

Kitty thumped her knees with excitement.

She had been back for six meals—that meant two days—when she heard the rumors. "Heard your sister's in trouble." Duncan grinned. "Surprised you still see her after what she did to you."

Did to her? What were they talking about?

"Heard your mother talking to the supervisor, I did."

"Me, too," added Margaret. "And what's this . . . machine that might . . . be able to help you . . . talk? They . . . were going on about . . . that, too."

The Monster gave another massive kick. Her breasts were feeling really heavy today. And when Fussy Carer had bathed her, little drops of milk had come out of the nipples. "Your body is preparing," she said. "We need to look after you." She shook her head. "Poor darling, how are you going to manage?"

Why did everyone speak in riddles? It was all so frustrating.

Still, at least she was back in time for the next trip. That was something to look forward to. They were going to the zoo! Wouldn't that be fun?

It wasn't a long drive—just over an hour. But Margaret managed to make herself sick before they got there. Kitty knew why. She was still jealous about it being Duncan's trip.

"Where would you like to go when it's your turn to choose, Kitty?" asked Bouncy Carer, getting out the picture board. "A castle?" There was a smile. "Why do you always go for that one, ducks?"

"It's because I'm really a princess," she said. "My dad used to call me that."

Goodness! Where had that memory come from?

If her father had called her a princess, it meant he'd loved her. So why was she so upset every time she saw the flabby-faced man? Maybe he wasn't her father after all.

"I wish I knew what you were saying, Kitty." That smile was fading. "I've got a feeling you would say so much more if you could."

"Of course I bloody well would."

The first thing they did when they got to the zoo was to visit the penguins. What funny little creatures! Kitty laughed so much that a small boy turned round to stare. "Why has that lady's chair got wheels?" he said loudly.

"Shhh," said his mother.

Good question, thought Kitty. Why *did* she need a chair with wheels? She'd tried asking so many times. But right then, the Monster kicked. And with it came another memory. Something to do with cheese sandwiches and a packed lunch for school.

Afterwards, they went to look at the elephants. What would happen, wondered Kitty, if an elephant couldn't walk? It would be too big for a wheelchair, wouldn't it?

There was a lot of traffic on the main road on the way home. So, at Bouncy Carer's suggestion, they went back a different way.

"Blimey. Look at . . . that house. Like a . . . bleeding palace," said Margaret.

The Monster inside began to wriggle, as though it was excited.

The traffic was slowing down. They were coming to a pedestrian crossing. The hairs on Kitty's arm began to stand on end. She felt very cold. But hot at the same time. "Everything all right, ducks?" Bouncy Carer was looking at her closely.

No. But she didn't know why. Kitty just knew that she had to get out of this place. Fast.

"Don't hit your head on the side of the van like that, Kitty. You'll hurt yourself."

"What do you want to tell us, Kitty? Point to your picture board."

But her head hurt too much. Go away. GO AWAY!

Kitty swiped the picture board out of her hand and sent it flying across the floor of the bus. "Oi," yelled the driver. "No disturbances in the back or I'll stop."

They passed a sign. SCHOOL. STOP. Her eye began to twitch.

There were schoolkids going past. The Monster took a huge leap inside her. Suddenly, she knew without a doubt that she'd once had a navy blue blazer, too. Just like them.

Bouncy Carer was taking a keen interest. "You come from near here, don't you, ducks?"

This time, the Monster was quiet. No help there, then.

"Do you recognize anything? Use your head, Kitty. Left and right means no, remember. Up and down means yes."

"She gets it . . . wrong," sniffed Margaret. "You can't rely . . . on her."

So she did both. Just to cover all her options.

"Kitty seemed to recognize a place that we went through," reported Bouncy Carer excitedly, when they got back. "According to her notes, she used to live there."

Very Thin Carer sighed. "I don't think it helps to raise false hopes. Her in-laws are doing the same with this new research they keep going on about. The truth is that the poor woman's mind went a long time ago."

That's what they thought. But what about all those flashbacks? There had to be something there, Kitty told herself, that would explain exactly what had happened to her. All she had to do was to find it.

57

July 2017

Alison

Every time I drive down to Mum's, I marvel at the sight when I round the bend where the road leads sharply down to the coast. After miles of motorway and then narrow side roads with high hedgerows, I gasp when I see a sea of lights below, indicating the town and then the sea itself, with its glittering, sparkling waves dancing out as far as the eye can see.

I head down the steep hill, towards the lifeboat station and past the elderly couple who have sold fish for as long as I can remember. I continue along the promenade where early evening swimmers are tiptoeing gingerly into the waves. Then I snake down a side street past a cottage I'd always loved as a child with its intricate iron shell decorations on the front. And then another side road towards Mum's cottage where hollyhocks burst out of the front garden. It's much smaller than the family home round the corner where I had grown up with Kitty and David and Mum. But I prefer it. It's cozier. I look at the pictures on the mantelpiece of Kitty and me from our childhood. In one photo, we're holding hands, and she is staring up at me with a look that might be jealousy or admiration. It's hard to tell.

I have a sudden vision of the school bus one day when Vanessa refused to share part of her Creme Egg with Kitty, her so-called best friend. I'd felt upset on my sister's behalf, so I'd told Vanessa that chocolate would give her spots but she hadn't liked that. If I'd tried to like my sister's friend a bit more, would that have helped?

"Great timing," says Mum when she opens the door. Her arms envelop me. She smells of lavender. Her skin is so soft that I want to rest my own cheek against it for longer. But I have come here for a reason—something that can't be put off any longer.

"Are you hungry?" she says brightly, leading me into the kitchen. "I've made salmon pie. Your favorite. Sit down." She points to my place at the kitchen table. I always sat on the left of Mum when we were growing up. Kitty on the right.

I'd intended to ask her immediately, but now it seems churlish when she's gone to so much trouble over dinner. So we sit and talk over the meal about my work (again I try not to mention the prison as I don't want to worry her about my being sacked) and, inevitably, Kitty. "I know it can't have been easy for Jeannie, but I do think she could have tried a bit longer. Did I tell you that the home has only agreed to take her back on a trial basis?"

Before I can say no, she hadn't, Mum stops. Aware, too late, of having said "trial." The word that is hanging over us all. "How is it going?" she says tentatively.

I shrug. "Robin seems like a competent lawyer."

"Good." She nods, but I can tell her hands are nervous. They are playing with her napkin. "I mean, that man—Crispin—is clearly intent on making trouble."

I nod. Just as I haven't told Mum about being suspended, so I haven't told her the full story about my written confession. It would only worry her. I've just said that Crispin is now falsely claiming that I contributed towards the accident.

"Mum," I say, putting together my knife and fork neatly on my plate. "There's something I have to ask you."

Her face goes rigid. Part of me suddenly feels that she has been waiting all my life for this.

"It's about the man in the prison I mentioned earlier," I begin.

"Stefan. The one who said he was my father." I watch her face closely. "The man who Martin—or rather Crispin—killed."

She shudders. Then again, it might be because she's sensitive like me. Surely, no decent person likes the thought of someone being murdered, even if the victim was himself a murderer.

"He knew a lot about you," I say. Now it's my turn to twist the napkin. "He knew you wear lavender. He knew your name. He knew things about us. The—"

Mum stands up. "I told you before." Her voice is sharp. "Criminals can be very clever."

I stand, too. "How do you know, Mum?" I say. "Did you meet my paternal grandmother? The one who was tall and blond, like me? And why was my father's name never on my birth certificate? Was it because you didn't want to admit you weren't married or because you didn't dare to put down the name of someone who was on the run?"

Suddenly, she crumples. It's as if I have hit her. I catch her just in time and steer her onto a chair. She puts her head in her hands. Her body begins to shake. I shouldn't have done this, I tell myself, putting my arm around her. I ought to have let sleeping dogs lie. Haven't I already given her enough grief?

"It doesn't matter," I say urgently. "Forget I asked. Anyway, it can't really be him. This man said his birthday was on the ninth of December. When I asked you years ago, about Dad's birthday, you said it was the fourteenth of July." I stare at her pleadingly. "And I know you wouldn't lie to me."

I will her to confirm this. My father could not be a killer. It went against the lovely, warm picture I'd built up over the years. Mum looks away. She can't meet my look. My chest tightens. I wish now I'd left this well alone.

"But I did lie," she blurts out. "Not just about the date but about everything. I was frightened you might find him if I told you the truth." She looks back at me, but her eyes are scared. "You have to remember that I was so like Kitty as a young girl. Desperate to get away from home. To paint. To live in the big, wide world. I had a keen sense of right and wrong, too." She laughs hoarsely. "At art school, there was this notice asking for volunteers in a homeless center. I joined up immediately. I'd only been there a few weeks when this amazing man came in."

Mum's face is transformed. It's glowing with memories. "He was called Stefan, and he . . . I don't know . . . he just got me immediately." She flushes. "I don't mean physically, but mentally. He knew what I was thinking almost before I said it."

Like Clive, I think.

"And I felt a keen sense of injustice on his behalf. He had escaped from a country where he wasn't allowed to draw. At least, not what he wanted to."

Just what Stefan had said. I think back to the work we did together. The painting of me. Yet this doesn't mean that everything else he'd told me was true.

"He wanted to paint the scenes that were happening in his country," continues my mother. "Draw political caricatures, too. But it got him into trouble. When he came here, he had nowhere to live—at least that's what he told me originally—and the center was full. Some of us volunteers occasionally took refugees back to our own flats. I invited Stefan." She flushes. "And, well, he just stayed."

"Did you know he had broken the law and was on the run from the British authorities, too?"

She closes her eyes briefly. "Not then. Initially, he told me he was a political refugee. You've got to remember how angry we were about the situation over there. We were convinced we could do something about it. Naturally, I was shocked by what he'd done, but, well . . . love can be blind. It was only later that he told me the truth."

My throat is dry. This is where Mum will corroborate Stefan's story—or not. I place a comforting hand on her arm, but my voice is firm. "And what is the truth, Mum?"

I can see her swallowing as if it is hard for the words to come out. I have a bad feeling about this.

"His father paid for him to get out of the country in a container ship but he was caught in the UK at customs. He was taken to a remand center where he got into a fight. The other man died, and your father was helped by a guard to escape. That's when we met."

So Stefan really had been honest with me. I'm stunned and still trying to absorb this vision of my radical young mother taking in a man on the run.

"I got pregnant in the first month." She reaches out her hand. "But . . ." Her eyes fill with tears. "I had the miscarriage. Then I got pregnant again. I can't tell you how relieved we were when you were born safe and well."

"What about your art degree?"

"I gave it up."

My mother's advice during my teenage years comes back to me.

You don't want to get into trouble and ruin your future. Imagine if all your hard work was wasted.

"Did you regret it?" I now ask urgently.

Tears stream down her face. "Not at all. We adored you. Your father and I were in love. And we had four amazing years together. We moved from place to place so no one could find us. He took whatever job he could find. My parents were livid—especially when they found out I was pregnant without being married. They said it was your father or them. So I chose love."

I butt in. "Are they still alive, too? Or did you mislead me about them as well?"

She flinches at my harsh tone, but I can't help it. Part of me is angry with Mum for being so stupid. Yet part of me also sympathizes with her younger self.

"No. It's like I told you at the time. They died a few years later. It's one of my biggest regrets." She pauses to wipe her face with a sleeve.

"Then, one day, the police came." She shivers. "It was unexpected. We were so happy that we thought we were invincible."

"But weren't you scared that you were in love with a murderer?"

Her head shakes ruefully. "Stefan didn't seem like a killer." She laughs out loud as though this is a ridiculous idea. "He was kind. Loving. A wonderful father. We desperately wanted to marry, but it was too risky to apply for the papers."

I think back to my men in the prison who hadn't seemed like murderers either. One of them had gotten married halfway through his sentence.

"When he went to jail, I promised to visit. But every time I went, you cried so much."

"You took me to prison?" I have a mental flash of the babes in arms I'd seen during visiting days. I'd been one of *them*?

She nods. "It was horrible. And then . . . well . . . There was the other murder."

I freeze. "What other murder?"

My mother looks away. "Soon after your father went to prison, he got a new cellmate who had it in for him. Kept calling him names and making racist taunts. Your father was a very proud man. He would not stand for insults against anyone he loved. One morning . . ."

She stops, and I know she's going to say something awful.

"One morning," she continues falteringly, "the cellmate started up again in the showers. Your father attacked him with a razor blade."

"He didn't . . ." I begin.

"Kill him?" My mother's voice is flat now. "Yes. I'm afraid he did. Even worse, it turned out that your father had bribed a guard to get the blade, which made it look as though the murder was premeditated. So he got life."

That explained the length of Stefan's sentence! Thirty-odd years is a long time for one murder. I'd learned that much during my own time inside. But another one—especially in a prison—is a different matter.

"And that's the real reason I broke off contact with him. I could just about understand the first set of circumstances leading to his arrest. But not the second killing."

My poor mother. I reach for her hand. She grips mine back. "I began to think about your father in a different light."

"Not surprising," I murmur.

"Soon after that, I met David. He was kind. Said he'd be a father to you. And I knew you would have a better chance in life if you didn't know your father was a prisoner."

Finally, it's all beginning to make sense.

"David made me happy. I wanted you to have a proper family. I was so thrilled when Kitty was born. I didn't want you to be an only child like me."

"But Stefan said he wrote to you when I was eighteen."

She nods. "He'd just been diagnosed with cancer then—slow-burning leukemia—and it made him aware of his own mortality. He wanted to see you. Personally, I thought he had a right, but David wouldn't allow it. I made the mistake of showing him the letter."

"Had he known about Stefan before?"

"No. I'd told him you were the result of a one-night stand with someone I didn't know very well."

I think back to those arguments between Mum and David just before the time of my A levels.

"He was furious that you had a father in prison. And, well, he was jealous, too. I could tell."

"Why? You didn't feel anything for Stefan anymore, did you?"

One look at my mother's face provides the answer. "Sometimes," she says slowly, "you can't help who you fall in love with. I loved David, too, but in a different way. He could tell that. I made him promise never to tell you." She looks at me as if for confirmation.

"He didn't," I say truthfully.

"So you can see why I was so upset when you went to work in a prison," continues Mum.

"You knew Stefan was there?"

"No. But I didn't want to take any chances. When you told me about this man who claimed he was your father, I could hardly believe it. Out of all the prisons in the country, he was in that one."

"But you denied it."

"I had to. I was trying to protect you. You'd been through so much

after Kitty. How would you cope with knowing your father was a murderer?"

"I'd have liked to have known him better," I blurt out.

My mother draws me near to her. I breathe her in as I did when I
was a child. "I know," she whispers. "And I took that away from you.
I'm so sorry. Despite everything, I still can't help thinking he would
have been a good man in a different situation. Of course, he shouldn't
have killed that man while he was on remand. Or the other man in
prison. But when we are young, we do some desperate things."

Don't I know that, all too well?

And now, as the court case looms, I have to face up to what I did
myself all those years ago.

It makes me wonder.

Does bad blood run from one generation to the next?

58

August 2017

Kitty

───────

Friday Mum came to visit not long after the trip to the zoo. At least, Kitty was pretty sure it wasn't that long, although it was getting hard to tell now. She was so tired all the time. And the Monster felt as if it was going to burst her stomach. It looked like an enormous football.

"The staff tell me you have been sleeping a lot," said Friday Mum. "Babies make you tired. I was the same with you and your sister."

Sister. Kitty felt a jolt of jealousy at the word. Why could her sister walk and she couldn't? Why could Alison talk while Kitty could only babble? It wasn't fair.

"Anyway, it won't be long now," sighed Friday Mum.

Why did everyone keep saying that? What exactly were they waiting for?

"Time to go," said Bossy Supervisor, coming into the community lounge. "The bus is waiting."

Friday Mum knelt down at the side of the wheelchair. "Isn't this exciting! We've got an appointment with the doctor to see if you're suitable for this new machine." Friday Mum held her hand. "Jeannie will be there, too."

Kitty felt a leap in her chest as well as fear. "Is she still angry with me for pushing Johnny?"

Friday Mum sighed. "I'm not sure what you're saying, love, but there's something I have to tell you. If it works, this machine won't just improve your daily life. It will also allow you to tell us what happened in the accident."

But she didn't fucking know herself!

Friday Mum bit her lip. "And that might help your sister to get out of the trouble I mentioned earlier. That's . . . well . . . that's if you can remember. The thing is, Kitty, that your sister thinks she pushed you into the road on the day of the accident.

"Of course it can't be true," continued Friday Mum, taking her good hand and stroking it. "She's just upset. It's the accumulation of years of guilt because she wasn't able to save you from the car."

So it was a *road* accident, like her friend Dawn's from the home.

"All we need is for you to somehow say that your sister was innocent."

Shake your head from side to side, Kitty told herself. Why should she help someone who could walk and talk?

Bugger. There it went again. Up and down.

"They might not accept that," sniffed Friday Mum. "We know that you sometimes get your yeses muddled up with your noes. But the lawyer says that we might be able to use your picture board to show what happened. And if the new machine can help . . . well, that would be amazing."

Friday Mum's arms were around her now. "You've got to save your sister, Kitty. Or else she might go to prison."

Good, Kitty told herself as the Monster battered her insides in agreement. Because if Half a Sister Ali really had pushed her into the road, prison was exactly what she deserved.

It was a long drive to the hospital. "It's in London," said Friday Mum.

Her words brought back a memory of a place called Oxford Street— and buying jeans. There was a teacher, too, who had been cross with her, and another girl called . . . What was her name?

"I've got a good feeling about this machine," added Mum. "I can't believe your sister would have hurt you. If you can remember exactly what happened, well, that would be wonderful!"

It was always a big deal getting in and out of the van. But this time, there were lots of people in white uniforms to help her. Kitty felt like the queen on her picture board as they wheeled her through the hospital corridors. Everyone smiled at her. Especially the doctor.

"Welcome, Kitty. We're going to ask you to put on this funny hat. See those colored wires coming out of it? They'll send signals to your brain, which will tell us if you're suitable for a new technique that's being pioneered in the States." He looked questioningly at her. "Do you understand?"

"I'm not stupid," babbled Kitty, shaking her head from side to side.

"That might be a yes," said Friday Mum doubtfully. "Then again, it might be a no."

The cap was itchy. And it felt odd without the helmet. The doctors had said she would be "all right" for a short time without it, but what if her brain fell out?

"Please try to keep still," said the doctor tightly. "Could someone stop her pulling those wires out? It's a very expensive piece of equipment."

"I'm not a 'her.' I'm a 'me,'" spat Kitty.

"Don't get cross, darling." Friday Mum was beginning to sound panicky. "A lot depends on this."

"Mind if I come in?"

That sounded like Call Me Jeannie! Kitty turned round stiffly to see if Johnny was there.

No.

Part of her was pleased.

The other part was hurt.

Kitty felt Call Me Jeannie's soft hand taking one of hers. Friday Mum had the other.

Eventually, the doctor took off his headphones. "I'm afraid Kitty isn't responding to this device. But there are others we can try. There are all kinds of new developments going on at the moment, so we mustn't lose hope."

"I'm sorry, Lilian," said Call Me Jeannie softly. "I know how much this means to you."

There was a sob. "It could have meant a lot to Alison."

Alison, Alison, thought Kitty crossly. It was always Half a Sister that Friday Mum worried about. What about her? Yet, at the same time, Kitty couldn't help feeling that somehow—goodness knows why—she'd let down the girl with the blond hair who always seemed so kind to her.

"What am I going to do?" Friday Mum was really weeping now. "I'm going to lose both daughters, aren't I?"

What did she mean?

"You're probably wondering where Johnny is," said Call Me Jeannie as they wheeled her back to the van. "He's gone away for the week. The day center has organized a residential camp on Dartmoor."

Bet that girl was there, too! Kitty felt her limbs flail out in anger. "Ouch, dear. Don't do that. You'll hurt us. Kitty, I said, *don't.*"

But she couldn't stop. Even if she didn't want Johnny anymore, why should someone else have him?

By the time she got home, Kitty was hysterical. "What's going on here?" said Bossy Supervisor sharply.

Friday Mum whispered something to her.

"I'm sorry." She shook her head. "It can't be easy for her."

It was the first time Kitty had seen her look so understanding. "Let's give you something to calm you down, shall we?"

"Get off me."

But she was coming closer. For a minute, Kitty had a memory of another angry person. "You're scaring me!"

Then Bossy Supervisor reached for a needle, and everything went black.

I can remember this much. And I'm certain—don't ask me how—that there's something else here that might bring back the real truth.

Shoulder bags bobbing.

Blond plaits flapping.

Three pairs of feet.

"We're going to be late."

Summer sun. Blinding eyes.

Blue blazers. Violin case knocking knees.

A bike cycling by.

CHILDREN SLOW.

And then . . .

What?

59

September 2017

Alison

————

Good luck. Will be thinking of you.

Of all the people in the world, Clive is the one I need right now. He will know the right things to say. He will calm me down just by holding me. But his business trip has been extended. And now I must do this on my own.

Even so, I hold his text in my head for comfort as I hang on to Robin's arm. The crowds outside the court are daunting. So, too, are the photographers.

"Alison," calls out a journalist, "are you really guilty of hurting your sister and killing her friend? Did you allow Crispin to take the blame for his mother's death, too?"

"Why is there so much interest?" I gasp as we finally get inside.

Robin's face is tight. "Good PR on the other side, if you ask me. It's a so-called human-interest story. We just have to make sure that your side comes across, too."

As he speaks, we find ourselves face-to-face with Kitty and Mum. My heart lurches at the sight of my pregnant sister. Kitty is laughing and dribbling as if this is all some kind of huge joke.

Mum, on the other hand, is giving me a look I can't quite read. I think it says that she wants to believe me, but that she's not quite sure. A flutter of unease passes through me.

The barrister comes up to us. She is very tall and handsome, with golden hair—about twenty years older than me, at a guess. Robin addresses her as Lily. She is, he says, "just the woman for the job." I can only hope he is right. Apparently, she took time off to concentrate on her son, who has special needs, but now she is back. What if she isn't up to this? There hasn't been much time for us to get to know each other, because the case came up much faster than any of us anticipated.

"Time to go in, Alison," she says to me. She smiles as if trying to put me at my ease, but this makes me feel even more nervous. "Just tell the truth like you did during the bail application. The jury can usually tell if you don't."

I feel sick. My mouth is dry. The only saving grace is that the new machine has not helped Kitty. Or rather, Kitty was not suitable for that particular type of technology. So, the one person who could say exactly what happened—apart from me—is unable to speak.

The courtroom is huge, with high ceilings that make voices reverberate dramatically as if onstage. There is a great deal of oak paneling, reminding me of a large dining room in a stately home that Mum, David, Kitty and I had visited once on a day out. But that's where the similarity ends. I have to stand in a box surrounded by a glass screen.

In front of me is the judge—a woman. The jury has been sworn in. Are they friendly? Hard to tell. Several keep glancing up at me and then at Kitty. I'm still not sure if it's wise to have her here, but my barrister apparently thought it was important. She wants to stress the sisterly ties that my mother has told her about. "Alison loves Kitty," she kept saying during the preliminary meeting. "She'd do anything for her."

How simple it is to rewrite history to fit in with an idealized image. Mum still doesn't know about my confession to Robin. What will she say when she hears it from my own lips? Lily, of course, knows, but she still thinks Kitty should be here so that the jury can see what Crispin did to her. "Your actions might have contributed to the accident," she told me. "But it's still not right that you should shoulder the whole re-sponsibility."

Will the jury agree with her?

Now it's time to find out. The case has been outlined. I am accused of the manslaughter of Vanessa and of Crispin's mother and of causing grievous bodily harm to my sister.

The prosecution is calling the first witness. One Samuel Bowles.

I already knew from Robin and Lily that there had been an impor-tant later "addition to the prosecution's case," but by that time I was incapable of taking any more in. I refused—despite their entreaties—to sit through any more witness statements. Besides, the name had meant nothing to me. Kitty, seated down below with Mum, starts to roar with laughter as if she's watching one of her programs on television.

A tall, slightly stocky man with a chiseled jaw walks across the room and takes his place at the witness stand. He does not look at me. But my eyes are fixed on him.

It is Clive.

I am so shocked that I can barely take in what he is saying. The be-trayal is such that I feel as if I have been stabbed in the stomach. I have to grip the rail in front of me. For a minute, I fear I might wet myself like my sister. My breath is coming out in short, sharp gasps. The of-ficer next to me notices and gestures at the water in front of me. I want a sip, but I cannot move my arm to take it. I can only sit, stunned, and try to concentrate.

Samuel Bowles? Who is this man? And what about all the other lies he has told me? Not to mention the things I told him on the last day I saw him.

I want to run. Scream.

"Can you describe to the court how you met the accused?"

"I tracked her down at a local authority art class." He speaks clearly. His face straight ahead. Still not looking at me.

"Tracked her down?" repeats the barrister. "Why is that?"

"I was hired as a private investigator by Crispin Wright."

There is a loud gasp. From my own mouth. The jury, to a man and woman, turn to face me. Suspicion is written over each of their faces.

"At first, I just followed her."

So that explained the feeling I'd kept having that someone was trailing me near my flat.

"But then my client decided he wanted to confront her. He'd been told that he was going to be transferred to HMP Archville in the new year because of good behavior since the last episode and because he claimed the location would make it easier for a distant cousin to visit. Prison staff are meant to be aware of family issues, and in this case it worked in our favor because it was near Alison, too."

His voice drops as though he would rather not say the next bit. "It was my idea to post an advert in the college where she worked, for an artist in residence job at Archville. We also . . . well, we paid one of my contacts in the prison admin office to shred the other submissions so that Alison appeared to be the only one to have applied."

There's a gasp of disapproval from the jury that I share. So much for the governor asking why he should choose me instead of the "many other applicants" who were after the job! That was just a bluff to make it look as though they weren't desperate. As for the "contact" in admin, I'm shocked. Angela had told me about bribery in prisons, but I hadn't realized that outsiders like Clive could be involved, too.

"We hoped," he goes on, "that the guilt over the accident—as well as the need to supplement her income—would make her take the job. And it did. But we still had to wait for Mr. Wright to be moved. In the meantime, we paid someone in the prison to send her threatening notes in the internal mail and also write one on a picture."

I can scarcely believe what I am hearing.

"By then," he continues, "I'd joined her college class. It was a second tactic. My mission was to befriend her and try to extract a confession from her."

"Can you elaborate on the word 'befriend'?" says the prosecution's barrister.

"We became lovers."

I cannot gasp now. Or talk. I am beyond sound. It's not because of the jury looking at me. Or Robin. Or Lily. Or Kitty laughing. The betrayal and embarrassment are far deeper than any cut I could ever have inflicted on myself.

I slump to the ground. The judge calls for a recess to allow the defendant to "compose herself." Robin comes up and talks to me. "This," he says tightly, "is why we needed you to go through the new witness statement. When you wouldn't, we tried to exclude it on the grounds of your relationship, but our application was refused."

There are so many rules in law! Just as there are in love. And Samuel Bowles had broken the most important of all—trust.

"I should have warned you in advance," Robin said in a low voice. "I'm sorry."

"Why didn't you?" I whisper.

He looks away. "I was concerned about crossing that dividing line between being your professional advisor and your friend."

Soon, the case resumes, and Clive is being questioned again.

"Can you tell the court what the accused told you?"

"Yes. A similar story to the one she gave to my client."

"You are referring to the document that was discovered torn up in the sanitary bin at the prison?"

"I am. After an evening of . . . intimacy . . . Alison told me that she pushed her sister into the road."

My mother lets out a little cry. More of a whimper. The jury is glaring at me. Every one of them.

"But there is more to it than that." Clive's deep voice rings out. "She told me that her sister and the friend had witnessed the accused having sex with Mr. Wright at a party held in his house. Alison alleged that this had been rape but that she had nevertheless been scared of telling her mother and stepfather. However, when Kitty and Vanessa threatened to tell her parents they'd seen her having sex, she gave her sister a push into the road. So you could say that she was provoked."

He is preempting the defense that Lily had been going to use. Why? Is he trying to protect me? Crispin's face is dark, his brows knitted in anger. Clearly, he isn't happy about his investigator helping the other side.

"Please stick to the facts, Mr. Bowles. Can you tell us what else Alison told you?"

The jury is riveted. I cannot move for fear.

He looks at me with something like pity.

"She told me that Crispin Wright wasn't driving at all. It was his mother."

60

Kitty

_____

Something big was happening. Not just inside her, where the Monster was hitting out so that her body felt as if it was being stretched until it would snap. But here. In this big room where Half a Sister Ali was in a glass box high above everyone else. She had a pretty gold locket round her neck. That looked familiar. Now where had she seen it before?

Was this a game? wondered Kitty. And who was that new man over there—with handcuffs on—and horrible scars on his face? He had nice eyes, though. For a minute, Kitty was reminded of something.

I'm in love! How are we going to get him to notice us?

I've told you. Borrow my makeup, and put it on before you get on the bus.

Who was that speaking in her head?

Then Kitty stopped trying to think so hard, because everyone was talking and shouting. It was worse than at the home, where they were always arguing over which program to watch.

And now Friday Mum was crouching over her, looking all upset. "Did you really threaten to tell me about your sister and that boy? I understand if you did."

Maybe it would make it better if she shook her head. But it came out as a nod.

"Really?"

Friday Mum's face changed. Her eyes went cold. Kitty felt a nasty chill going through her. Then the tall blond woman in the long black dress came up to them. "We need to talk. The recess won't be very long." The woman knelt down next to her. "I'm Lily, the barrister for your sister. Would you like to come along with me, Kitty?"

She liked this woman, who spoke to her as if she was a real person. Not everyone did that. "But I want my turn in the bloody box," Kitty yelled as they followed Barrister Lady into a little room with Friday Mum pushing. "It's not fair." She hammered the side of the chair with her good hand to make the point.

"Stop it," said Friday Mum in a cross voice she'd never heard before.

As soon as Lily closed the door, Friday Mum burst into tears. "Why didn't Ali tell me that Crispin . . . I can't even say the word."

Lily took her hand. "Sometimes, a woman feels that a rape was her fault, even when it wasn't."

Friday Mum nodded, big tears streaming down her face. "I get that. Kitty . . . I know she wasn't always very nice to Alison. She was prickly. But I hadn't realized how bad it had got."

Lily smiled. "Children can be rather horrible to one another sometimes."

"I should have interfered more," sniffed Friday Mum. "But I didn't want to annoy David. Her father got jealous. And he adored Kitty."

Her father adored her? The flabby-faced man? But he'd done something wrong. He'd . . . For a minute then, Kitty swore she almost remembered it. But then it was gone.

The Monster launched another assault. "Fuck off," yelled Kitty.

"She's getting upset," said Friday Mum. "It's because she's picking up on this. Maybe she shouldn't come back in with us."

Lily laid a hand on Friday Mum's arm. "If you can bear it, I think she should. It might help."

"But . . ."

There was a knock on the door. A woman in uniform stood there. "Time," she said. Great! Kitty clapped her hands together. Maybe it was her turn now to go in that box. Half a Sister Ali had hogged it for long enough.

But Ali was still there. It wasn't fair! When Kitty began to shout again, Friday Mum whispered that if she wasn't quiet, she'd have to go out. Then the man with the scarred face started to talk.

"I was learning to drive. Mum used to let me practice on the way to school. But we were late that morning, and she said it would be quicker if she drove. I . . . Well, I didn't want her to."

"Why not?" said the lawyer.

Scarred Face said something so quiet that she had to strain to hear him.

"Because she'd been crying all night and was in no fit state. She and my father . . . well, they'd been having difficulties. That morning, they'd had another row on the phone—he was in London during the week. Mum was really distressed." He ran a hand over his face as if he wanted to block out the image.

"Can you tell us what happened next?"

Scarred Face was looking straight at Alison. "We were nearly there. But suddenly, there were these girls in the road in front of us. Mum didn't stand a chance. No one could have stopped in time."

"Why did you go along with Miss Baker's claim that you were driving?"

He looked down at the ground. "My mum and I were very close. I wanted to protect her like any good son—especially as my father had behaved so badly to her." He shrugged. "Dad used to say I had an over-developed conscience when it came to Mum—but she needed me. Dad wasn't . . . well, he could be pretty vile to her. Anyway . . ." His voice rose with distress here. "She was dead! Killed on the spot." His eyes filled with tears. "I wasn't going to let her memory be tarnished. I'd rather take the consequences, especially as I felt I should have been driving after that a row with Dad." He blew his nose. "If only she'd agreed."

"I also thought that I'd get off because it was the girls' fault." He gave a strange laugh. "But it didn't work out that way. At first, I just accepted my fate. I told myself I deserved it for my bad behavior over the years towards girls, and, besides, I'd lost the will to live after what happened to Mum. But the longer I stayed in prison, the angrier I got. When Dad died two years ago, I inherited some money and used it to hire a private detective. Samuel Bowles . . .

"Last September, Samuel discovered that Alison was working at a local authority art class. He also found out that HMP Archville was looking for an artist in residence. So he printed out the vacancy ad and paid someone to drop it off, hoping it would tempt Alison."

He grinned. "It was a long shot, but it worked. I'd also instructed him to get close to Alison in the college class he'd already joined."

Half a Sister was looking as though someone had hit her in the stomach.

"I was going to try and do the same when I got transferred to the prison. The good thing was that she didn't recognize me." He rubbed the side of his cheek. "I've changed. And I pretended I didn't recognize her."

"What exactly happened on the day of the assault in prison?"

"She started it!" His eyes were gleaming angrily. "I was just trying to talk to her, but she yelled out that I was strangling her. This bloke came in—Stefan. Had this thing for her, he did. He tried to hurt me, so I belted him back. It was self-defense."

"Yet later you cut Stefan's throat with the glass."

There was a furious glare. "That was self-defense, too. He'd have done the same to me if I hadn't got in first. But before that, I made Alison write down what really happened. That's when she admitted that she pushed her sister into the road."

The scary man was looking round the court. "It's the truth."

No. A very important fact was missing. Kitty knew it. What the fuck was it?

"And is it true that you raped Alison as a teenager?"

"I didn't see it as rape. I could tell she fancied me." He ran a finger over the scars on his face. "Everyone did. I looked different in those days."

"Did you rape Alison or not?"

"No. I didn't."

Something horrible was happening inside her now. Something Kitty couldn't describe. "I don't feel well," she babbled. But no one was listening. Everyone was shouting in the court. The judge was calling for silence, and Lily was now talking.

"The relationship between sisters can be a very complex one. It can be fraught with jealousy and love at the same time."

Many of the women in front of her were nodding. Kitty looked up at Half a Sister in the glass box. She had her face in her hands. The Monster gave a huge lurch inside. Suddenly, all Kitty wanted to do was get up there and hold Ali in her arms. Tell her that she was her friend. Tell her that someone here hadn't been telling the truth. She knew that. But she just couldn't remember who. Or even what the lie was.

The Monster dealt her stomach another huge blow, as if it was just as frustrated as she was. Then something really weird seemed to happen down below.

"Help," screamed Friday Mum, looking down at the pool of water. "She's going into labor!"

61

September 2017

Alison

―――――

Is Kitty all right? I'm so worried that I can't concentrate on the individual closing statements from my side and Crispin's. They're finished now, and the jury has retired to decide my future. "Would you like me to sit with you?" Robin had asked.

"No, thanks."

I couldn't look him in the eye.

So, now I'm on my own in a locked side room, where I sit and think about what's just happened.

When Clive revealed what I'd told him about Crispin not being the driver, there was a gasp like a giant wave going round the court.

I knew from the jury's faces that any sympathy about my rape had been outweighed by my lies about who was driving. Why would they believe my story about being abused if I would fib about something like who had run down my sister? Mind you, I'd always wondered why Crispin had gone along with my claim that he was driving. Part of me is touched that he took the blame for his mother's memory.

After what seems like hours but the clock tells me is thirty-seven minutes, Lily opens the door. "The jury has reached its verdict," she says.

So soon? The barrister's mouth is set as we walk back into the court. Robin touches my arm. "This could be good," he says reassuringly.

I know he's just trying to make me feel better. The jury might have instantly decided I am guilty.

In the courtroom I search for Crispin. He isn't there. Nor is Clive. Maybe it's just that I can't see them. The court is packed. Dear Lord, there are Vanessa's parents! Despite the passing of the years, I recognize the mother all right, with her high model's cheekbones. She is staring right at me. Hatred is written all over her face.

I try to concentrate on the words that are ringing round the court, but my ears are humming. It's as though I am underwater. For a minute, I am back in the past, swimming in the bay with Robin. We are taking turns to see who can stay under the water for longer. Once—I'd forgotten this until now—I'd stayed under for so long that he had dived down and brought me up again, spluttering. I was laughing. He was cross. "I thought something had happened to you."

The forewoman of the jury is standing up. She is very small. Petite, like a hummingbird in a bright red dress. The court clerk is speaking. Once more, my ears are buzzing so much that I cannot hear the exact words.

But I do hear what comes next.

"Guilty on all counts."

There is a roar around me. People are standing up. "Send the bitch to prison!" screams someone. It comes from the direction of Vanessa's parents. Robin looks as though someone has hit him with a mallet. Lily appears disappointed.

But me?

I am relieved. It is exactly what I deserve.

62

September 2017

Kitty

Loads of memories are returning now. Every time the Monster kicks, another one comes back.

How she used to love the sea! Until that time when the freak wave had nearly got her. If it hadn't been for Half a Sister Ali, she might have drowned. Her sister had rushed in and dragged her out of the water. She'd been small then. In fact, she could distinctly remember being cross, because she hadn't been able to get out on her own and had to rely on Ali saving her.

Bloody hell. Where had that come from?

"Breathe, Kitty. Breathe."

That was Friday Mum's voice. Breathe? How could she when she felt as if she was being pulled down under the water all over again. The pain was lashing at her like waves. Her body seemed to have taken on a mind of its own. What was this creature inside doing to her?

"I need to go back into court," she yelled. "I need to tell them something."

"Calm down, Kitty. It will be all right. Another breath. That's it. Good girl."

But what? What was it that she needed to say?

Plaits.

Sunshine.

A funny smell.
A secret.
A locket.
A summerhouse.
Something else. More important.
Think, Kitty tells herself. THINK!

63

September 2017

Alison

I'm allowed a short time with Robin and my barrister downstairs before they take me away.

"Where's Mum?" I ask.

"I don't know." Lily takes my hand. It strikes me that she is a different kind of barrister from the type I had imagined. This woman is kind. Compassionate. More like a friend. "Listen. I know this might seem like the end of the world right now, but we will appeal."

"No," I say sharply. "I don't want to."

"That's quite common," she says. "Some people have just had enough of the system by now, and that's understandable. But you were pushed, Alison. Mentally speaking. Don't you see that? There were mitigating circumstances. An appeal court might reduce your sentence."

I suddenly realize that I didn't take in the sentencing that followed my verdict. "How long did they give me?"

Robin's eyes are red. "Ten years. I'd hoped that the length of time since the accident might reduce the sentence, but there are some crimes like manslaughter that are punished severely no matter how long ago they happened."

"It could well be reduced for good behavior," he adds.

If not, by the time they let me out, I will be into my forties. With any luck, I won't get that far. And if I do, well, that's my punishment. I've had enough of life outside. I deserve every second behind bars.

There's a knock on the door. "Time," says a voice on the other side.

I am being taken to a holding prison.

How often have I seen the prison van arriving at HMP Archville with more prisoners to drop off? It has slit windows like narrow eyes. Yet now I can see it's different from the inside. Like a sealed box. I sit on the edge of my seat, with my wrists in handcuffs. There is no one else here apart from an officer. It feels surreal.

I am being housed here temporarily, in a holding prison, until the authorities decide where to send me. Robin thinks I will probably go to a Category C for prisoners who still represent a significant risk to society. Worse than the one I was working in.

My old student Kurt had once drawn a series of cartoons about the complicated process of arriving at jail. He'd called it "Checking In." I recall this now as they take me out of the van, my eyes blinking in the bright summer sunlight. But nothing could have really prepared me for this panic-plunge in my stomach as I take in the walls around me, topped with rolls of barbed wire. They're so high that my neck cricks.

I am marched towards the entrance. There's the sound of a key on the other side. A gruff bulldog of a man in uniform stares unflinchingly at me. I stare back. It doesn't do to show you're scared. Yet at the same time, one needs to behave with a certain respect. I know that much from my old life in prison.

The interior is more modern than the grimy exterior suggests. I am taken into a side room, where a woman officer gets me to sign a form. I don't even bother reading it. Then she holds out a plastic bag. "Personal possessions in here."

Reluctantly, I hand over my sister's locket.

I am strip-searched. Every crevice is examined. I am then handed a too-big pair of navy blue jogging bottoms and sweatshirt.

"Shoe size?"

"Six and a half."

"This isn't Russell & Bromley. Six or seven?"

I plump for seven. My feet are lost in them. But my ten-year sentence is too long for tight shoes.

Robin wants to appeal. But I won't allow it.

I am taken to my cell. It's not that different from the one I spent the night in as artist in residence. Narrow. Spartan. Except that it has bunk beds. The occupant of the lower one is lying chest down. She raises her head briefly as I come in.

"What are you in for?" she sniffs.

Maybe this question is acceptable in women's prisons. "Manslaughter, amongst other things," I say.

She makes a face. "Not good."

Then she crawls under the blanket. And I sit and wait to see what is going to happen next.

64

September 2017

Kitty

It felt like the Monster was trying to push its way out of her body. Couldn't it see there wasn't enough room?

"It's the wrong way round," said someone.

"Don't push yet, love." Friday Mum's hand gripped hers. "Think of something nice."

But all Kitty could think of was the wave that Half a Sister had rescued her from. Maybe she should have been a bit nicer.

"Take deep breaths, dear," said another voice now.

Where the fuck was Johnny? Fathers were meant to be there at times like this.

"Think we've managed to turn it now," said another voice. "Can you try and puff, love?"

Humming was better. "Hummm, hummm."

"It's all right, love. I'm here." Friday Mum stroked her hand. "You'll be all right. I promise. I won't let anyone hurt you."

I won't let anyone hurt you?

Someone had said something like that before. But it was different.

I won't let you hurt her.

That was it!

And then, suddenly, amidst a scream, Kitty remembered with startling, horrifying clarity exactly what had happened.

65

September 2017

Alison

———

It would take, they explained, a while before the paperwork could be processed for visitors. In the meantime, I am being moved to a different prison for the "foreseeable future."

It's a Cat B.

One category worse than Robin had predicted.

The girl in the lower bunk is coming, too.

"What did you do?" I ask as we sit together in the prison van. It is the old-fashioned sort—or so the officer keeps moaning—with benches down the sides rather than individual cells.

"You're not meant to ask."

I could point out that she had asked *me* about my crime earlier on. But I decide to play safe. "Sorry."

She sniffs. "Stabbed my flatmate, if you really want to know. I was using at the time and didn't know what I was doing."

So much for her earlier "Not good" when I'd said I was in for manslaughter. Clearly, her crime is pretty serious, too.

"Until recently, I worked in a prison," I volunteer.

Her face registers disgust. "You're one of the scum?"

"I was artist in residence, actually."

"Oooo," she goes in a mocking manner. Then she sniffs. "What does that mean?"

"I helped men to paint and draw."

"Why?"

I am reminded of what the governor told me all those months ago. "Art can help people come to terms with their crimes."

At first I think she is crying. But then I realize she's laughing. "What a load of bollocks." Her face tightens. "Didn't work for you, did it?"

She glances at the prison officer who is sitting opposite, her eyes steely and watchful.

"I'll give you this for free, mate. Don't make enemies." Her eyes narrow as she takes in my elfin haircut and height. "Are you a lezzer?"

"No."

"Then pretend you're bi. Did that in my last stretch. One of the girls took a fancy to me and gave me extra rations."

The journey seems to take hours. I feel sick every time the van jolts on the road. I find it hard to breathe. "Oi," says my traveling companion to the officer. "There ought to be air-conditioning in this thing. Health and safety, innit?"

The woman appears not to hear.

"I need a pee," says my companion more forcefully.

Silently, the officer hands her a pot, the type I've seen Kitty pee into in the hospital.

"Can't we bleeding well stop at a service station?"

"Not allowed."

It's one of the few sentences that the officer utters during the trip.

Eventually, the van slows down and then stops. The doors are opened. Sunlight blinds our eyes. We're being led outside. This building is older than the holding prison. It's surrounded by open fields. I nearly laughed when they told me its name. HMP Marchville. How ironic. Like my old Archville but with an *M* in front, as if one could just march out at will.

"And one more thing," calls out the girl as they take us in different directions. "Watch out for . . ."

But I can't catch it.

I am being walked now into another room, where I am searched yet again. Through a series of doors, each of which has to be locked and unlocked, as I know all too well. Down a long, wide corridor with plain walls on either side. Through another door on the right. And another. I find myself in a corridor lined with women wearing blue jogging suits standing outside their cell doors. Clearly it is part of their designated social time when they are allowed to mingle. They are looking me up and down. It's almost as though I'm in a beauty parade. With one contestant.

"Looks like we've got ourselves a new friend," says one. Her hair is matted, greasy.

She holds out her hand. Her nails are bitten to the quick. Fingers squeeze mine like a vise. "Nice to meet you, love."

Then someone calls out. "Alison? Is that you?"

I know that voice. It's Angela.

When I first started at HMP Archville, Angela used to tell me that it was quite common for both prisoners and staff to bump into their past. "After all, there are only so many prisons. Inmates get moved around. Officers, too."

It was true. I used to see newcomers greeted by old-timers with slaps on the back like grown-up classmates at a school reunion.

And now it's happening to us. Even so, she seems as surprised as I am.

"What are you doing here, love?" she's saying, her face white as though she's seen a ghost. Clearly, she hadn't expected to see me again.

Whenever I've thought of my old colleague, it's been with a mixture of anger and sadness. I'd once trusted this woman who'd allowed me to take the blame for the unlocked cupboard where she'd hidden those mobile phones and drugs. Yet now she was greeting me like a long-lost friend. And amidst all the strange faces, I can't bring myself to ignore the one that I recognize.

I give her a brief version.

"Can hardly believe it! I had you down as a good girl. Still, you probably thought the same of me, didn't you?" She claps me on the shoulder. "I didn't mean to get you in trouble. I'd hoped they'd let you off with a warning. But I was desperate, love. My Jeff . . . well, he . . ."

She left the sentence unfinished.

"I heard rumors," I said quietly.

"Whatever you heard probably wasn't as bad as it really was. The only good thing is that I'm safe in here from that son of a bitch. The worst of it is that my son in Australia is so embarrassed that he's got a mother in prison, he won't even let his kids write to me. He definitely won't be coming over anytime soon to visit."

Somehow, I'm surprised. I was constantly amazed by wives and girlfriends who had stuck by their men in HMP Archville. Even the rapists and murderers.

"Got ten years, I did. My lawyer said the courts take a dim view of prison staff that turn to the other side. What about you?"

"Same."

I say it lightly. Ten years doesn't feel real. Will I be too old to have a baby by the time I get out? Perhaps. Too old to do a lot of things.

"Bloody hell. Still, the trick is to not count the days." Angela is taking me by the arm and walking me down the corridor. "I'll introduce you to the girls. The nice ones, that is. You have to watch some of the others."

My chest flutters with apprehension.

She touches my arm in comfort. "We need to stick together."

That's when I notice the red, angry mark on her wrist. "A burn," she says quietly. "Got pushed against the hot water urn the other day. And all because I wouldn't give my biscuit to that one over there."

She indicates a large woman in overalls who is watching us, arms folded. "Just do what I say, and you'll be all right." Angela's warning words remind me of when I first met her. She hadn't looked after me then. Should I trust her now?

Yet, maybe it would be better than trusting myself.

66

September 2017

Kitty

———

The Monster, which had been so huge when it was inside her, turned out to be a tiny little baby.

"Did this really come out of me?" marveled Kitty as she stared down at the small and slithery wriggling thing they had placed on her stomach. All soft and wet and smelly.

"Baby's rooting," said the nurse. "Let me help you hold her to your breast."

It wasn't easy, even with her good hand. But Friday Mum was there to help.

"Well done, Kitty. You're a natural."

Kitty felt a stab in her chest. Baby needed her!

How it sucked at her nipple! Vigorously. Enthusiastically. Its eyes fixed rigidly on Kitty as though aware that it owed her its life.

"See," said the nurse. "She loves you!"

And Kitty's heart was filled with such love and warmth that she pushed the *I remember now* memory to one side.

Besides, what was the point if she couldn't speak? That flash of the car and the navy blue uniform rising into the air was far too complicated to explain on the picture board.

Even if she wanted to.

67

October 2017

Alison

_____

It's the absence of fresh air that gets to you here. Unlike HMP Arch-ville, you can't wander around so freely. In this prison, I feel choked by that stale indoor smell in my nostrils as I wander up and down the long corridors on my way to class or the pod or my pad. I am haunted by longing for the outside world as I stare through the window of the community lounge and see a bird flying past.

What has life come to if I don't have as much freedom as that spar-row out there?

There are no seagulls, even though we are not far from the east coast. Maybe they choose not to come here. I don't blame them. In the far distance, I can see the gentle slope of hills. Perfect for running.

"Don't even think of trying to get out," says Angela as if she's read-ing my thoughts. "A couple of girls have tried it. They're in secure units now."

Anyway, there's no point. I can't see how anyone could get out of this place. The only time we can taste fresh air is during the half-hour walk around the block. We get two turns a week. Should be more of-ten, apparently, but there are staff shortages.

I think with longing of the setup in my old prison. Only now do I really appreciate why my men had said they could finally breathe when they got to a Cat D. Here, there is no walking from one hut to another.

Instead, you are let out of the closed wing once a day to go to Education or Chapel (a large number turn to God just to get a change of view, apparently) or the gym (dodgy, because some of the other women use it to "eye up the candy," as Angela puts it).

This walk from one part of the prison to another is known as free flow. There is always an officer in charge. You are herded along like sheep. There is no respect. We do not deserve any. This is the message that is drummed into us day after day.

There's a desperation on faces like I've never seen before. Many of my new acquaintances have been separated from their children. My cellmate weeps at night, and I cry with her, remembering my lost sister. Offenses are mainly drug related. There are several "mules" here. Plus a sweet-faced woman who decapitated the boyfriend who abused her daughter. The other day in the pod, I spotted her dipping a used tampon into a mug of coffee, which she then offered to an unsuspecting mother of three, in for heroin dealing. I should have said something, but you learn to pick your friends in this place.

It's odd being an inmate instead of staff. Each of us has our own job. Mine is cleaning the loos. I have to be careful to call them "toilets." My language and accent have already been mercilessly torn to bits by some of the women. I'm lucky that I have Angela to look after me. I should feel resentful towards her, but I don't. You have to be practical here.

The darkness is the worst. That one night in HMP Archville was child's play compared with the stifling claustrophobia that now squeezes my throat after the eight p.m. lockdown. Sometimes, when the wind whips up from the hills, I fancy I hear someone tapping on the window. Stefan's ghost, perhaps?

Meanwhile, Kitty has had a little girl. Mum told me during the brief phone call that I was allowed to make when I arrived here. "Are *you* all right?" she'd added, almost as an afterthought.

Kitty's news had come first. Always Kitty.

Even when my prison phone card arrived, allowing me to make calls, I decided to ring Mum only once a month. When you're using the prison phone, there's always someone eavesdropping on your conversation. So Mum writes instead. Every week. Yet her tone is cool: she simply describes her life. Doing odd cleaning jobs in the village, because she had to give up her job to look after Kitty and the baby. Selling the odd painting. Her letters are signed with a "love" but no kiss.

And no wonder, after the court case. If it was not for me, both Kitty and Vanessa would still be here in one piece. And Crispin's mother, too.

As for Crispin, his case—or so I've read in the papers—has been reviewed. His conviction for causing death by dangerous driving was quashed because his mother had been behind the wheel. He was given eight years for perverting the course of justice by pretending to be the driver and another twenty-five for murdering Stefan. The jury hadn't bought the self-defense bit. The sixteen years he'd already served was taken off, but even so, Crispin could be out soon after me, although this doesn't take "good behavior" into account. But it won't make up for the loss of his mother. Or his father, who had died a broken man, his wife and son both torn from him.

Unlike Archville, where letters were handed out through an open window from the admin office, the post here is put into labeled cubbyholes, having gone through security. Mine is full of messages. I am trying to gather the courage to read them.

I scoop up my letters and take them back to my cell. I recognize the handwriting on most of them. Mum. Robin. I put the latter in the trash. What can they possibly say to make things better? One is internal mail. It is a visiting request form from the admin department. Someone on the outside wants to see me. I look at the name, and then I walk to the window. There's a bird out there. It has been joined by another. Together, they are pecking at something in the ground. Husband and wife? Brother and sister? Suddenly, they begin to attack each other, furiously fighting over a worm.

They must be sisters.

Slowly, I go back to my desk and tick the "yes" box.

68

October 2017

Kitty

"Kitty, love," whispered Friday Mum. "Are you awake? The baby wants feeding."

"Fuck off. I'm tired."

"It's too much for her to cope with, poor kid," whispered someone else.

"You look sleepy, love. I'm sorry to bother you, but the little one needs you."

"Shut up. Both of you." The baby, thought Kitty, through half-closed eyes, was all right when it wasn't crying. But this yelling noise was drilling through her skull.

"Don't bang your head like that on the chair, love. You'll hurt it."

Not as much as the car had hurt when it had hit her. Don't think of that now. Block it out. Sometimes, thought Kitty, it had been better when she hadn't been able to remember anything. Just after Baby had been born, she'd managed to block it out. But now it kept coming back. Not just during the day but in her nightmares, too. Last night, she'd dreamed that Vanessa was chasing Half a Sister with a violin. It seemed silly now, but in her sleep it had been terrifying.

Besides, that wasn't all. When Baby was coming out, Kitty had been certain she'd recalled everything that had happened on the day of the accident. But now, she couldn't help thinking that there was something else that had happened. Something that she couldn't quite put her finger on.

"It's no good," she heard one of the nurses say. "We'll have to give it a bottle."

Then they went away. And it was quiet again. Apart from the screaming in Kitty's head.

"Just one more thing, love."

Was this the same day or the one after or the one after that? It was hard to tell. The days seemed to merge into one. They'd bring Baby to her. Sometimes, Kitty felt like feeding it. Sometimes, she didn't. Sometimes, she wanted to hold it on her lap with her good hand and one of the nurses supporting her. And sometimes, she wanted it to go away and leave her alone.

"We need to think of a name." Friday Mum had on that forced jolly voice that pretended that everything was all right. "I've found a baby name book. Look! Do you think you could point with your good hand to the one you like best? If you can't, that's OK. We'll just think of one for you."

Suddenly, Kitty was wide awake. *A* for Amanda. *B* for Beatrice. *C* for Carol . . .

"Carol?" questioned her mother. "That's pretty."

"No, you bloody idiot. Keep turning the pages."

"I think she wants you to go on," says the nurse.

At least somebody understood.

Yes! Friday Mum had got to the *V*s. She was stabbing the page with her good hand, too, to make sure she got it.

"Vanessa? Are you sure? It won't upset you?"

Kitty shook her head. But it came out as a nod. So she nodded it. And it came out as a shake. "Touch it again if that's what you want, love."

So she did.

There was a catch in her mother's throat. "That's very sweet of you."

And then the screams began again. Not from Baby. But from inside that bloody head of hers. Still searching for that final piece. The clue that would explain everything.

69

November 2017

Alison

────────

"I wasn't sure that you'd see me," says Clive opposite me. He is attracting a good deal of attention from neighboring tables. One of the girls whose pad is next to mine has already been reprimanded by an officer for wolf-whistling at him. This is either going to give me currency on the wing or make me a target. I suspect the latter.

"I was curious." I force myself to look straight at him, even though it hurts like mad. I can still see him above me, looking down intently, the way he always did when we were making love. It had made me feel special. How ironic.

What does he think of me now? I wonder. Personally, I try not to look in the mirror too often. When I do, I see a woman whose previously elfin hairstyle has gone straggly without a decent cut. She does not wear makeup, so her blond eyelashes fade into oblivion. Yet despite this, I also glimpse an emotional weight that has been lifted. Her eyes can now meet her own in the glass because she has finally done the right thing.

"What do you want to say to me?" I have to speak loudly, because it's noisy in here. Many of my fellow inmates have got kids visiting. Some are racing around despite the officers' attempts to get them to sit at the "activity table" in the corner.

"How about sorry?"

I'm not expecting this. "I don't understand."

I want to sound hard, but the hurt is all too clear.

He reaches for my hand, but I scrape my chair back. He presses his lips together as if he's about to say something difficult. "When Crispin Wright first commissioned me to tail you, I had a personal interest."

That's when he reaches into his pocket and brings out the watch with the Disney cartoon I'd noticed when we'd first met. Back then, in the stained glass class, I'd been scared when he'd put his hand in his pocket—all part of the anxiety issues I'd been suffering from since the accident. I'd thought—yes, I know this sounds crazy—he was going to hurt me. Then when I'd seen the child's watch face, it had made me feel just a tiny bit more kindly towards him. I'd considered him merely eccentric. How wrong could I have been?

"This was my brother's. He died when he was eleven." His voice is flat, the way it is when you fight to hide emotion. "He was pushed into the road by a group of teenagers who were jostling one another to get onto the bus. It was his first day at secondary school. The first time my parents had allowed him to go on his own."

Is this another lie? "How old were you?"

"Five. I was with my mother when the police arrived." He turns away. "I'll never forget her face. The kids weren't even cautioned. It wasn't the driver's fault, but he got six years."

"I'm sorry," I say. My gut instinct is that he's telling the truth.

"My parents never got over it. They divorced shortly afterwards. And I lost my best friend. The big brother who had always been there for me. And just in case you're wondering—which you have every right to do—I'm not making it up."

Gently, reverently, he puts the watch back in his pocket. Then he turns to face me again. Square on. "When Crispin instructed me to befriend you and find out more, I wanted justice. I was convinced you were guilty, even though I had no proof. I didn't realize he'd done—that—to you."

Clearly, he can't bring himself to say the word "rape."

He rubs his face as if exhausted. "Once you'd taken the job at the prison, I did everything I could think of to tip you off balance."

"Tip me off balance?"

He looks ashamed. "It was my idea that Crispin should use his contacts to put up those messages in the prison. Crispin had had a friend in Durham who had been transferred to Archville and owed him a few favors. We thought that if we spooked you out a bit you'd be more likely to spill the beans to me once I'd cultivated our relationship. Crispin also 'buttered you up,' as he put it, to lull you into trusting him. It was a gamble in case the threats made you hand in your notice, but we hoped that your loyalty towards the 'trustworthy' students, including Crispin, would make you stay."

A voice resounds in my head. *Your classes are the best thing here, miss.*

"And it was you who posted the advert so that I took the job in the first place," I say slowly. I knew he'd said as much in court, but I wanted to check.

He nods. "I had to pretend to be surprised when you told me about it."

I shiver at the way he outlines his cold, calculated approach. Then again, hadn't I been guilty of something similar?

"This friend of Crispin's," I question. "What was his name?"

"Kurt . . ."

"Kurt?" Another name to add to the long line of people I'd trusted who were really against me.

"Actually, I was going to say Kurt's cellmate. He picked up stuff from Kurt, who was always talking about you. It was 'Alison this' and 'Alison that,' apparently. And Kurt's cellmate used the information— which days you would be working and so on—to leave threatening messages."

"What about the Christmas card?"

He rubs his chin ruefully. "I followed you home one night after the college class. Saw where you lived. During the college Christmas dinner, I paid someone to drop it round."

How cunning.

"That time I bumped into you on the Embankment . . ." he starts to say. Then he stops, as though the words are too painful.

"When you'd been running?"

"Actually, I hadn't. I'd been following you."

A cold sickness crawls through me.

"And the phone calls?" I whisper.

He bites his lip again. "You spilled your drink over me at the college Christmas party. I used the confusion to grab your phone from your bag and make a note of the number. I passed it to Kurt's cellmate in a coded letter. He was the one who rang you from D hut."

It's coming back to me now. For a minute, I'm back there.

I'm so embarrassed that I knock over my glass of elderflower, and it spills all over him. How awful! He has to go to the gents to dry off his jeans.

"But then I changed my number."

He shakes his head as if remonstrating with himself. "Remember when I left the message with the college asking them to get you to contact me?"

"But I withheld my number."

He looks down at the table. "There are ways of tracking that down if you know how."

I feel disgust. And anger. Not just with Clive but with myself. How could I have been so stupid?

"What about all your buying trips abroad?" I blurt out. "When you couldn't see me?"

A deep flush crawls up his neck. "An investigator has more than one case on at a time. I have a regular client who is in the Far East."

"Go." I scrape my chair back. "I want you to go. Now."

"Please. Wait. I haven't finished. By then, I'd got to know you." He runs his hands through his hair. "I broke one of my own rules. The more I got to know you, the more I genuinely learned to care for you."

I scrape my chair back even farther. "Yeah, right."

"No. Really." He leans forward. His face is as close to mine as my position will allow. "I couldn't believe that you would do such a thing as push your sister. Why else do you think I took you back to my place? I'd never done that before. But then—the last time, at your flat—you confessed. I was thrown. Part of me thought that Crispin deserved to be punished. But the other part . . ."

"Wanted justice for your brother."

He looks relieved. "Exactly."

"Well, you've got it," I say crisply. "What more do you want?"

"The thing is," says Clive softly, "that I can't get you out of my mind. I've never met anyone else like you. And I can't help thinking that—"

"Officer!" I raise my voice. "Can you escort this gentleman out, please? I don't want him here anymore."

Clive stands up. "You're making a mistake, Alison."

I put my hands over my ears as if I am a child again. And when I look up, he is gone. Instead, there's a roomful of eyes on me.

And a pain so deep in my chest that I can barely breathe.

70

November 2017

Kitty

———

"Look, Kitty! Your sister has sent you a card."

She was awake but pretending to be asleep. It was easier that way. All the other mothers around her in the hospital would stare or ask questions she couldn't answer. They didn't stay long. Not like her. The new ones were always the same. Looking. Whispering when people came to visit. "There's something wrong with her. But the baby seems normal. Sad, isn't it?"

"Don't you want to see the card? She made it herself." Friday Mum's voice had a bit of a wobble. "They do that sort of thing in there, apparently."

In where?

The picture showed a pink flower. Just one. Sitting in the middle of a field. It was quite pretty. Kitty traced the outline with a finger from her good hand. She used to paint once. She could remember that now. But Half a Sister hadn't. She'd been the swot. Since when did Alison get all bloody arty?

Congratulations, said the card. *Love from Alison.*

If she broke down the words into bits, she could read them in her head. Even if she couldn't speak them.

"Kitty!" Friday Mum gasped as Kitty rolled up the card into a ball with her good hand and then threw it. "That's not very nice."

Nice? Kitty began to laugh. A big dribbly laugh that made saliva run down the sides of her mouth. What did "nice" have to do with any of this?

"Kitty, love." This was Friday Mum again.

"We've got to leave the hospital soon. They've had us for as long as they can. The home hasn't got the facilities to look after the two of you." There's a sigh. "I did find another place, but it was really expensive, and the insurance didn't meet it. It was also some way off, which meant I couldn't visit every day. So Johnny's parents have kindly loaned us some money, and I've had my little cottage adapted, and you are going to come back to me with the baby. That will be nice, won't it?"

The last bit was said in a way that sounded as though Friday Mum was trying to convince herself.

"How do I fucking know?"

"I wish I knew what you were saying, love. It would be so much easier. That picture board isn't great. I thought we were getting somewhere with the cards at one point . . ."

Her voice trailed off, but Kitty knew what she was talking about. Soon after the baby name episode, the nurses had tried to help her communicate by pointing to letters on the alphabet board. Oh Tee had done the same in the home but without much success. It was all right for short words like "yes" and "no." But it took ages to get longer stuff out. And anyway, Kitty wasn't sure she wanted to. Otherwise, they might realize she'd got her memory back.

And that wouldn't be a good idea at all.

"There's something else, too." Friday Mum was speaking in the kind of voice that meant this wasn't particularly good news. "Johnny's mum wants to come and see us here before we go. She's got something to tell you." A tear rolled down her face. "I'm so sorry, Kitty. On top of what happened to your sister, we've now got this . . ."

Call Me Jeannie smelled just the same. Roses. She was in powder blue, too.

"So beautiful."

"Thank you," said Kitty, patting her hair with her good hand. Then she realized Call Me Jeannie was talking about the thing in the hospital cot.

"I would have come earlier, but I . . . well . . . Under the circumstances, I thought that . . ."

Call Me Jeannie was speaking to Friday Mum now. "I'm so sorry about all this, Lilian. I really am. Have you told her?"

"That's your job. Not mine."

"Oh dear." Call Me Jeannie gave a little shake. "Do you think I could pick up the baby first?"

"She's called Vanessa. And she's asleep."

Friday Mum sounded cross.

"Right then." Call Me Jeannie looked at her. Kitty could see her taking a deep breath. "I'm afraid that Johnny . . ."

She stopped. Suddenly, Kitty felt a terrible fear clutching her throat. Was he all right? Had someone hurt him? She had a sudden memory of someone hurting her a long time ago. And—or was this her imagination—of her hurting someone else, too. Something to do with a car . . .

Then her mother-in-law reached into her bag and brought out several sheets of paper. "My son wants a divorce."

What?

Friday Mum had her arm around her. "I'm sorry, love. But he's not worth it anyway."

"Hang on a minute, Lilian . . ."

"Well, he's not." Friday Mum's face was red. "What kind of a boy marries a girl and then dumps her—especially when she needs special care?"

"He wouldn't have married her at all if she hadn't got pregnant."

The other mothers in the ward were staring. It made Kitty feel rather special.

"I don't fucking care. If it's 'cos of that bitch in the day center I saw him snogging, she's welcome to him."

It wasn't quite true, of course. But it made her feel better to let it out.

"I'm not sure what you're saying, love," said Friday Mum. "But don't you worry. I'm going to look after the two of you now that that husband of yours has given up. As for those papers, Jeannie, I'll have to run them past our solicitor."

Call Me Jeannie had red embarrassed patches on her neck. "Of course. By the way, how is your other daughter doing? It must have been an awful shock to have finally found out what really happened."

"Actually—"

But then a white coat came in. "Mrs. James? I'm from the hospital's neurology department. There's been a development."

71

December 2017

Alison

———

The routine here is strangely soothing. I like being told what to do. It means I don't have to make decisions for myself. I find that I rather enjoy cleaning toilets because of the praise I receive. The staff say they've never seen them look so nice.

Last week, someone left feces on the floor.

I suspect it was the woman who wanted to be more than friends with me. "I'm straight," I'd explained when she tried to get in the shower with me, but she'd clearly been livid. Hence the poo.

So I carefully lifted the turd with a sheet of loo paper and gave it to Angela, who was on kitchen duties, and she put it on the woman's plate for Christmas lunch. Angela got sent to Solitary for that, but she didn't snitch. Like she said, she owed me one for the stationery cupboard. And more.

Prison life works like that. You do something for someone, they do something for you. Even if it takes years. I'm learning the rules of the game.

After Clive's visit, I earned a certain amount of kudos. Not because he's undeniably good-looking, but because I told him to leave.

The poo incident sealed this. Even though Angela hadn't given me away, the woman knew I was behind it. For once, I'm learning to stand up for myself.

No, I tell myself, as I chuck the visiting request forms. I won't see Robin. I won't appeal.

I don't even want to see Mum out of guilt. But her last letter had begged me to allow her to visit.

Eventually, I give in. It is Christmas after all.

When I am led into the visiting room, I spot her immediately waiting at one of the tables. My first thought is that she is thinner. Mum stands up to give me a warm hug—under close scrutiny from one of the women guards nearby—but I force myself to turn away. How I want to breathe her in! Yet, at the same time, I know I don't deserve it.

Instead, I sit down and appraise her. There is a certain jauntiness about her that is new.

"Your sister liked the card you sent."

Her voice is nervous after my rebuff.

I did that in our arts and crafts lesson. It's run by a well-meaning woman who draws sticks for figures. Yet I don't tell Mum that. If I say too much, I might break down.

My mother tries again. "Johnny's filing for divorce. He wants to get married to someone else."

My nails start to bite into the heel of my hand. My poor sister.

"She's living with me now. You'll have gathered that from my letters. It's lovely having a baby around."

So that explains the jauntiness.

"But your sister . . . well, she blows hot and cold with little Vanessa. I think she's out of her depth. It's hard enough for any new mum, but Kitty—well, she just doesn't know how to cope."

What does she want me to say? It's not like I can do anything to help while I'm in here.

"There's something else, too."

Mum is like that detective on TV—the one who seems to finish a conversation but then poses a killer question or statement just as he's about to leave.

"The neurologist at the hospital thinks Kitty might be suitable for a different assistive communication device from the States. It's had success with patients who didn't respond to the previous prototypes. Apparently, the person with brain damage looks at an image, and the machine comes out with a sentence that describes his or her feelings about the picture. It sounds unbelievable, but it's getting great results."

Mum's voice is becoming even more excited. "There was this teenage girl who was knocked off her bike by a van and hasn't been able to speak for years. But she looked at a picture of her parents on the screen and said that she loved them. Isn't that amazing! There are loads of stories like that—or so I'm told. In fact—"

"Who do you love best?" I hear myself say.

"What do you mean?"

"Before . . . before the accident, you always told me that I was special because I was the eldest. But one night I heard you telling Kitty that she was special because she was the youngest."

My mother's eyes are moist. Guilty. "Darling, all mothers love their children in different ways. It's true there is something special about the eldest. And the youngest, too. But that doesn't mean that I love either of you more than the other. One day, when you have children yourself, you'll realize that."

"How am I ever going to have children?" My voice rises with fury. "I'm in prison. When I get out, I'll probably be too old—and anyway, no one will want me. Not with my history."

"That's not necessarily true, love. Don't you think I blame myself, too, for letting Kitty be so spoiled? If she hadn't, you might not have . . . well . . . you know . . ." Mum looks at me pleadingly.

After she's gone, I go into the toilets and move the loose tile behind one of the loos. It's still there. I have melted down my toothbrush, thanks to a box of matches that Angela found for me. ("Don't ask how I got it, love. Just take it.") Bit by bit, I have shaped the end of the toothbrush so it is nice and sharp.

Then I cut myself. A nice clean score line. Not enough to do real damage. But enough to make my skin sing with pain.

It's the least I can do. Especially after what Mum has told me.

Because if this machine works and Kitty "talks," the real truth will be out.

72

January 2018

Kitty

The new machine was an advanced version of her picture board, apparently. Or so Dr. White had explained. "We've incorporated a screen that can show a picture of someone you know, and your brain will be able to say what you think of that person."

She laughed. "We had one little boy who—when a picture of his mum came up—said that she talked too much and that it gave him a headache! So we must all prepare ourselves for some hard truths!"

Kitty began to feel nervous. Something told her that she mustn't mention the car memory. But why?

"Sometimes," the doctor had continued, "pregnancy and birth can stimulate the brain. Your mother says you've been faster with the picture board than usual since your baby. So let's give it a go, shall we?"

They didn't have to wait long for the appointment. "Johnny's family is paying," said Friday Mum, sniffing. "Feeling guilty, as well they might."

At least it meant a whole day away from little Vanessa's screams. One of Friday Mum's neighbors was going to look after her. Ever since they'd left the hospital and moved into Friday Mum's little cottage, Kitty had been finding the baby more and more annoying. It was OK when she was asleep. But when she woke, all she did was yell. Mum kept crying, too. "I do hope Alison is all right."

Why? What was wrong with her?

When they got to the hospital, Dr. White was waiting. She talked to Kitty as if she wasn't in a wheelchair at all. "Did you have a good journey? How is your lovely little baby? Do you like living with your mother by the sea now?"

But she didn't seem to expect any answers. She talked while someone else put her in front of this really cool machine that looked like a portable TV. Perhaps they were going to watch a film.

"I know you used to play the violin," said the doctor brightly. "So I thought we'd start with this."

A picture of a violin flashed up in front of her.

Surprised, Kitty banged her good hand against her chair. She'd hated playing that thing. It was only because Vanessa had done it and she'd wanted to be the same. But who was Vanessa? And why did she have the same name as the baby?

"Violin fuck off."

Where had that voice come from? It didn't sound like her. It was all tinny and like a robot. But it said what was in her head all right.

"Kitty!" Friday Mum's voice was horrified.

But Dr. White laughed. "It's all right. We see this a lot with brain injuries. Swearing is quite common. So is the rather odd grammar. Over time, the thought-recognition software will learn Kitty's brain patterns and reproduce her thoughts more accurately." She returned her attention to her patient. "OK, Kitty, so you hated the violin. What about this?"

There was a picture of a shop with nice clothes in the window. How she wished she could wear them rather than the horrible baggy tops and trousers they put her in. "Pretty clothes. My stuff is crap."

"Kitty!" said Friday Mum again. "I mean . . . well, it's amazing to hear you talk, but you're so . . . so different."

"This can happen after brain damage." The doctor was clearly excited. "What about this little girl in the next picture, Kitty? Do you recognize her?"

"Me! It's me!" Kitty began to feel her heart racing as the tinny voice jumped out of her mouth. "School."

"You're wearing your uniform, yes. Very good. And who are you with in this picture?"

"Half a Sister."

"I'm sorry?"

"It's my other daughter," butted in Friday Mum. She gave a strange laugh. "I didn't realize Kitty thought of Alison as 'half a sister.'"

Hang on. The young Kitty was wearing something round her neck. The same thing that Alison had been wearing in court.

Kitty banged her arm on the chair. "She's stolen my locket!"

Friday Mum touched her hand. "After your accident, they said it wasn't safe for you to wear things round your neck in case they got caught up. So I gave it to Alison. I thought it would be nice for her to have something of yours."

Well, now she fucking wanted it back. "Mine! Mine!"

"The prison has it now, darling." Friday Mum sounded as though she was trying to hold back tears. "They'll return it when she's . . . if she's . . ."

Then she stopped. Dr. White gave a laugh. It sounded slightly nervous. "Amazing, isn't it, to hear what someone is really thinking? Let's get on, shall we? What about this person in the photograph? Who is she, Kitty?"

A girl with long blond hair smirked at her. She was wearing a locket round her neck. Just like hers. "Vanessa," said the voice.

"Very good. You were best friends, weren't you?"

"Yes. No. Sometimes."

Kitty had a sudden flashback. Vanessa. On the way to school on the day of the concert.

"Jealous of Ali. Wanted to be my sister. Made me spill the coffee all over Half a Sister's essay."

Dr. White glanced at Friday Mum. Kitty could suddenly feel an air of tension. "Shall I go on?"

"I suppose so. Except that she hasn't seen him for a long time. And when she does, he always seems to upset her."

Him? Who's him?

"I'd like to try, if you don't mind. There could be a reason for that. It might help unblock the rest of her memories."

And then a photograph of Flabby Face jumped up in front of a pretty little girl with blond plaits on the screen. He was holding her hand and smiling. There was an older girl, too, standing a little farther away. They were both wearing school uniforms. Kitty's arm thumped the side of her chair again. "Fuck. No. Fuck off. Take him fuck off."

"It's all right, Kitty," said Friday Mum, wrapping her arms around her.

"Can you say why you don't like your father?" said the doctor. "Did he touch you when he shouldn't have?"

"No."

"Then what did he do?"

"He told a secret. I had to keep it quiet. But then it all went wrong."

"What do you mean, Kitty?"

"Stop." Friday Mum was crying. "I don't want her to do this anymore. She's too upset. Turn it off."

It was Flabby Face's picture that did it.
 Brought it all back.
Squeaky-clean school shoes.
Shoulder bags bobbing.
Blond plaits flapping.
Three pairs of feet.
"Don't you dare!"
She pushes me.
I push her.
The earth spins.
A scream.
"Don't die. Don't die."
A silence.
Blood.
My sister Ali. Vanessa. Crispin's car.
Shit. Now I remember.
Everything. More than I remembered before.
I just can't tell.

73

Alison

———

I expect to be moved to Solitary after they find the toothbrush and the marks on my arms. But instead they bring in Sarah Holliday. She's the new psychologist. We have a couple of sessions together in what's known as the "psycho room." It's got a squashy dark purple sofa and watercolors on the wall. "Meant to make you feel safe," warns Angela. "But remember what I told you. You don't trust anyone in this place." Then she gave me a nudge. "Apart from me. I won't let you down again."

At first, Sarah and I talk about ordinary stuff. What it feels like to be in prison. The food. Whether I am sleeping. And then, one morning, she suddenly takes me by surprise.

"Why do you feel the need to hurt yourself?" she asks.

"Because of me, two people died and I nearly killed my sister."

She doesn't flinch. "It wasn't just your fault, you know. I've read the notes. The car was going too fast."

Sarah puts down her pen. "Do you hate Kitty?"

"No! I'd do anything for her. All I want is for her to love me. To be a proper sister."

The words escape through my mouth before I can take them back.

Sarah looks at me for a very long time. "That's interesting," she says. "And how would you define a proper sister?"

"She's always there for you," I say. "You're best friends. You can depend on her, whatever happens. And she'll help you when you're in trouble."

Sarah goes very quiet. "Let's hold that thought until the next session, shall we? I'll be in touch about the date."

The following week, I am put on the gardening team. I thought I'd miss the loos, but now I'm getting quite obsessive about pulling out weeds. It's therapeutic. Then I get a note through internal mail. Sarah wants to see me again. So soon?

"I'd like to talk more about your family," she says.

So I describe what it was like to be on my own with Mum, who had needed my support even though I was only little, and then how I had to get used to David coming into our lives and taking over. I explain, with a lump in my throat, how my little sister had never been friendly even from an early age, and how I constantly tried to befriend her, only to be pushed away or criticized. How did you feel when Kitty bossed you about?" she asks when I pause to wipe my eyes.

"Stupid. And embarrassed. Also angry."

"Who with?"

"David." I hesitate. "Mum, too."

"But you told me that you have a close relationship with her."

"I do. But you can love someone *and* be angry with them. It's how I felt about my sister as well."

"Do you think she felt the same way?"

I nod. "It's why it happened."

"*What* happened, Alison?"

I stand up. "I don't want to discuss this anymore."

The following week, Sarah asks me to return. I almost plead a headache, but I need to talk to someone about Stefan. Recently, for some reason, he's been troubling me in my dreams and won't go away.

"Come on in," she says when I tap on the door.

And then I stop.

My mother is sitting there. So is my barrister.

And so is Kitty.

74

February 2018

Kitty

Kitty had a bad feeling about this. Especially after that bloody machine had brought back the memories.

"We're going to visit your sister," said Friday Mum.

Little Vanessa was coming, too. Her constant yelling was doing Kitty's head in.

It took ages to get there in the special van, which Call Me Jeannie had given them. Friday Mum was a bloody awful driver. She kept shifting into the wrong gear, which made the engine stop, and then she'd have to restart the van while other drivers continued hooting from behind. Vanessa screamed most of the way from her baby seat just like Kitty knew she would. "I should have brought someone to help me," Friday Mum kept saying. "But I didn't want anyone to hear . . ."

Then she stopped, as if she'd been about to say something and then changed her mind. "You might be a bit shocked when you see your sister," she said. "I haven't told you this before, because I didn't want to upset you and because . . . well, I'm not sure how much you understand. But Alison is in a prison."

A prison? But only really bad people go there.

"Remember we went to see your sister in court?"

Of course she bloody well remembered. Half a Sister had hogged that glass box, hadn't she? Refused to share. Had worn her locket—the one she'd stolen from her.

"I don't know if you recall what I told you afterwards, but . . . well, Ali confessed to pushing you in front of the car." Friday Mum's voice was all wobbly. "So she's going to be locked up for a very long time."

Vanessa's shrieks got louder, as if she could understand

"She hasn't wanted any visitors, and . . . well . . . she doesn't actually know we're coming today. It might be a bit of a shock for her. But we're going to see if it makes a difference."

"What will?" yelled Kitty.

"Don't get upset now. Oh dear. I do hope you can help your sister, Kitty. She needs you."

Really? Something inside her stirred with love, even though she hadn't given it permission.

This place was horrible! Just look at those high walls with barbed wire on top. The prison guard at the gate looked at Kitty in her chair and then at Vanessa. Her face softened, and she waved the van through to the visitors' car park.

"They need to frisk us," Friday Mum said as they walked towards a big door. "Don't worry."

Frisked. Kitty ran the word round her head. They did that to people on telly if they thought they had drugs. "Get your fucking hands off me," she roared as one of the guards ran her hands down her body.

"Ow!"

"I'm so sorry." Friday Mum was babbling with embarrassment. "My daughter didn't mean to hit you—she just lashes out sometimes when she's scared."

On through another door with a guard next to them, and then another and another. Along one corridor. Along the next. Friday Mum was puffing as she pushed Kitty's chair with little Vanessa in the sling on her front. She was cooing now. As if this was one big game. Then into another room. There were two women there. Kitty recognized one. It was the lady from the room with the glass box.

"Hello, Kitty," she said, smiling. "Remember me? I'm Lily, your sister's lawyer."

"Hello," said the other woman.

Who the hell was she?

"Kitty, this is Sarah. She's your sister's psychologist. Do you know what that is?"

Of course she fucking knew. They were always on breakfast telly, weren't they?

"In a minute, your sister will be here." This was the Sarah woman talking. "We'd like you to have another go at your machine, if you don't mind. The hospital has kindly lent it to us for the day." The Sarah woman was leaning forward. "I know you got a bit upset the last time, but we hoped you'd give it a second try."

Kitty's body felt like ice. "I don't want to," she began.

But then the door opened and this very tall woman with limp blond hair and baggy blue trousers came in. Her eyes were on the ground. She lifted them really quickly to nod at Friday Mum and Kitty. Then she stared down at the ground again.

Could this really be Half a Sister Ali? The pretty woman whom she'd last seen in the court? She looked so . . . well, upset. Older and more tired, too.

For a minute, Kitty suddenly recalled a memory of pulling an April Fools' joke on the flabby-faced man who said he was her dad. They'd hidden his car keys. It had been fun to do it together! But then they were discovered, and Kitty had blamed Ali, who'd then got told off because she was the eldest and should have "known better."

Little Vanessa began to cry. "Not now, please," murmured Friday Mum. But Half a Sister held out her arms.

"Be very careful," whispered Friday Mum.

Everyone watched as Ali held little Vanessa in her arms, gently rocking her to and fro. The baby was staring up at Half a Sister, eyes fixed on her. She was quiet now. "I'd have liked a baby," murmured Ali.

"Perhaps you had better give her back now," said Friday Mum. She sounded nervous. Maybe she was scared that Half a Sister might drop Vanessa like she, Kitty, had almost done the other day. Just as well that Friday Mum had still been holding on.

"Kitty. Your mum says that you got upset when you used the machine before. I'd like you to tell me why, if you can."

Sarah pressed a button. A photograph of Flabby Face holding a little girl appeared on the screen. "That's you with Dad," said Friday Mum. "On the beach when you were little. Do you remember?"

Kitty thumped the chair. "No. No," she babbled.

"No. No," repeated the machine.

"Do you remember why this picture upsets you so much?" said Sarah.

Kitty began to scream. The machine made a horrible noise.

"I'm not sure about this," said Friday Mum.

Then Half a Sister leaned forward and touched her arm. Her face looked so kind. So worried. So . . . sisterly. "What happened, Kitty? You must tell us. Did he hurt you?"

Don't say anything, Kitty told herself. But the machine wouldn't listen. "Yes. Mentally, not physically. Because he told me. About your dad."

"What do you mean?" asked Lily.

"Dad was angry. Told me Ali's father not dead. In prison. Murderer. Said I should tell Ali."

Friday Mum let out a little cry. "How could he! I made him promise to keep my secret."

"And did you tell Alison?" asked the Sarah woman.

Kitty nodded her head. "No," said the machine. "It would have upset her too much. But I told Vanessa. Then she threatened to tell Ali. So I had to stop her."

The room was deathly quiet. Then Lily spoke. "How did you do that?"

"I pushed her."

There was a gasp from Friday Mum.

"Let's get this clear, Kitty? Who exactly did you push?"

"Vanessa, of course. Who else?"

75

July 2001

Kitty

———

Kitty couldn't recall a time when she hadn't known Vanessa. She'd just always been there. And—most important—she was the same age. Ali was too old to be a proper sister. It was like having an older aunt instead. (Vanessa had had an aunt.) Ali was allowed to do things that Kitty couldn't, like going to bed late. It wasn't fair. And as Kitty grew up, she began to realize that Ali was cleverer than she was. That wasn't fair either.

Vanessa was fun! Her parents let her go out on her own. She kept telling Kitty that she should "stand up for herself." When they started school, everyone else liked Vanessa, too. But it was Kitty who was her best friend. This made her feel special. But every now and then Vanessa would be friendly with another girl, and Kitty would be scared that she'd go off her.

Then, one night, when Kitty was at Vanessa's for a sleepover, they saw this program about two girls who lived next door to each other. They promised to be friends forever and ever. One of them cut her arm with a penknife and made the other do the same. Then they rubbed their arms together. "We'll be blood sisters," they told each other. "It means we'll be there for each other."

Vanessa had got really excited by this. "Why don't we do that?" she suggested.

Kitty had been scared, but she didn't want to say no in case Vanessa stopped being her friend.

"Where are you going?" asked the babysitter who was looking after them while Vanessa's parents were out.

"To get a drink," Vanessa had said quickly. "Come with me, Kitty."

She found the kitchen scissors in the cutlery drawer. "Go on," she said. "Be quick. Make a mark on your arm."

"I can't."

Vanessa's eyes had gone cold. "Then I'll ask Wendy."

No! Wendy was one of the other girls Vanessa was friendly with. It had been bad enough when Vanessa had asked Wendy over for a sleepover the other day and not Kitty.

It was only a little nick, but it hurt.

Then Vanessa did the same. She didn't even cry out.

"Now we have to rub our arms together," she said.

"What on earth are you doing?"

It was the babysitter. "Oh my God . . . put those scissors down. You've cut yourselves! Whose idea was this?"

Vanessa looked at Kitty. "Hers," she said.

Kitty swallowed. She could deny it, but if she did, Vanessa might ask Wendy to be her blood sister instead.

Luckily, the cuts weren't deep, but Vanessa's parents had still sent Kitty home that night in disgrace. "Was it really your fault?" Mum had asked.

Kitty had hung her head. "Yes."

"Well, I'm very disappointed."

The next day at school, Vanessa took her hand. "You passed the test," she whispered. "We're real blood sisters now. It means we will do anything for each other. One day I'll do something for you."

But she never did. And Kitty was always too scared not to do what Vanessa told her in case she didn't have a best friend anymore.

Then came that terrible day when Vanessa showed her the note.

I don't want to be your friend anymore, it said. *I hate you.*

The handwriting looked exactly like Kitty's.

"I didn't write this. It wasn't me," she kept saying. But Vanessa wouldn't believe her.

"You've got to prove it," she said. Her eyes had narrowed. "Otherwise, you can't be my blood sister anymore."

But how could she do that? The writing was just like hers with that loopy *f* and *y*.

"We could tell your sister that we saw her in the summerhouse," mused Vanessa. "I don't know why you haven't done that already."

Nor did Kitty, to be honest. It just felt . . . well, wrong. That picture in her head of her sister "doing it" with a boy . . . Ugh! She'd rather forget it altogether.

"No," continued Vanessa. "That's not big enough. You need to tell me a really big secret. That no one else knows."

Kitty began to feel scared then. "But I don't have one!"

"Then you'll have to find one, won't you. I'll give you until the last day of term. If you haven't come up with something, then I'll just have to be best friends with Wendy instead."

Kitty hadn't been able to eat or sleep properly after that. She couldn't think of any secrets. "Are you all right?" Mum had asked. She wasn't looking very happy either. She and Dad seemed to be arguing all the time. Then one day when Dad picked her up from Scouts (she and Vanessa had recently started), he said he had something to tell her. "You're a big girl. You deserve to know. Remember we've always told you that Ali's father had died when she was little?"

Kitty had nodded solemnly.

"Well, he's not dead at all. He's been in prison for years because he murdered someone."

A cold shiver shot through her. "Could he come and hurt us?"

"No. He's still in prison. But he wants Mum and Ali to visit him."

She had a sudden picture of a scary man behind bars like a film she and Vanessa had once seen when the babysitter was there. "Isn't that dangerous?"

"It could be." They were nearly home now. "Actually, Kitty, I think you ought to tell Ali about her dad. Just in case."

"Why doesn't Mum tell her?"

There was a sigh. "Your mum wants to wait a bit."

"Is that why you've been arguing so much?"

"The thing is," said Dad, not answering her question, "like you've just said—it might be dangerous for Ali and Mum to visit this man in prison. Besides, we don't want him in our lives, do we? We're happy the way we are."

Kitty nodded.

"But if you tell Ali about her dad and explain why you don't want her to visit him, then maybe she won't."

Kitty began to feel uneasy. "But Ali will be really sad if she knows her dad is a bad man. I would be sad if someone said that about you."

"You're a sweet kid," he said, ruffling her hair. They had pulled up in the drive now. "But you won't really mind upsetting Ali, will you? After all, it's for the best. Anyway, it's not like you're that close, is it?"

That was true, Kitty told herself. But when she got ready for bed that night, Ali put her head round the door. "How was Scouts? Did you have fun?"

Usually, Kitty would have ignored her or told her to mind her own business. But Dad's words were still whirling through her head. *Might be dangerous. Happy the way we are.*

"It was OK."

"It must be nice to have a dad to pick you up," said Ali suddenly. "I'd have liked that at your age."

"But my dad always picked you up from Scouts when you did it."

"Yes—he did. But like you said, he's your dad. Not mine."

Then this shadow seemed to pass over her face. "You know, I often wonder what life would be like if he was still here."

Kitty felt another shiver. "But then I wouldn't have been born."

She could see Ali hesitating. Wondering if that would be a good thing or not. "You're right," she said eventually. "And I'm glad you're here, Kitty, I really am. I just wish we were better friends, that's all. Anyway, I've got to get back to my revision, or I won't get anything done." She sighed. "'Nothing will come of nothing,' as Shakespeare said."

"What are you on about?"

Ali gave one of her superior smiles. "Just a quotation. See you in the morning."

She could have done it then, Kitty told herself when Ali went back to her own room. She could have destroyed her sister's life with a single sentence. *Your father is still alive, but he's in prison for murder.*

Yet she hadn't, because even though Kitty didn't want to feel sorry for Ali, she couldn't help it. Besides, if she did blab to Ali, Mum would be furious. Hadn't she told her off the other day when Kitty told her sister to "shut up" because she was talking over the television? "You really need to be a bit kinder to her," she'd said. "Ali is very good with you, you know."

Still, at least Kitty could now prove to Vanessa that she was worthy of being her blood sister.

"Really?" gasped Vanessa, when she told her about her sister's real father. "Wow, that's huge. I think she needs to know the truth."

"You can't tell her," said Kitty desperately.

"Why not?"

"It would hurt her too much."

"Why should you care?"

"I don't."

"Then that's all right, isn't it?"

But it wasn't.

"Have you told your sister yet?" Dad asked Kitty the next day.

"No."

"Well, what are you waiting for?" he snapped.

And for the first time in her life, Kitty began to feel that maybe Dad wasn't as wonderful as she'd always thought he was . . .

Kitty did everything she could to make sure that Vanessa and Ali didn't bump into each other. On the last day of term—a Thursday—she deliberately loitered upstairs so they'd be late for school. Then, with any luck, Vanessa would have already gone.

But she'd come running up behind them. Grinning as she flicked her plaits and stopping briefly to apply some lip gloss. Ready to wreck Ali's life—and get Kitty into terrible trouble with Mum.

As they walked along, Vanessa trying to hitch up her school skirt as they went in case they saw some boys, Kitty tried desperately to think of a way to stop it happening. Crispin! That was the way. She could pretend the secret was about him. Threaten to tell Mum. Pretend she was on Vanessa's side to keep her friend sweet.

Vanessa's eyes had gone all strange when Kitty had told her sister about seeing her and Crispin having sex in the summerhouse. When Ali had then pushed Kitty into the road, she had thought it would be the end of the argument.

But it wasn't enough for Vanessa. "That's not the secret I was talking about . . ."

That was when Kitty realized that she didn't like Vanessa anymore. And that, despite everything, a real sister was more important than a blood sister.

Her so-called friend Vanessa hadn't even called out when Kitty then pushed *her* to shut her up. Or if she had, it had been lost in the roar of the car that appeared almost out of nowhere. And after that, she could only remember occasional brief flashes of what had happened between then and until the baby was born.

76

February 2018

Alison

"L et's get this quite clear, Kitty," says Lily quietly. "Ali didn't lie in court when she said she pushed you. She did it because she was cross with you for threatening to tell your mother about what you saw in the summerhouse. But Ali didn't tell the court the full truth, which is that her pushing didn't hurt you. Afterwards, you got up and pushed Vanessa to stop her from telling Ali about her real dad, who was in prison. Then you really were hurt by the car that went on to kill Vanessa. Is that right?"

"Yes," says the machine.

My mind is reeling.

I replay, again and again in my mind, my own memories of those crucial moments leading up to the accident . . .

"Do you honestly think he'd be interested in you?"

Vanessa's eyes went cold. "Why not? Actually, that's not the secret I was talking about. Come on, Kitty, you tell her, or I do . . ."

"No," said Kitty. She grabbed Vanessa's arm. "Stop. Don't say any more."

Vanessa shook her off. "Leave me alone. Why shouldn't I say? I don't owe you any loyalty. Fine kind of blood sister you are."

Roaring in my ears.

Roaring all around.

Two shapes flying through the air . . .

"Alison," says Sarah gently. "Is this true? Kitty pushed Vanessa?"

For a moment I can't move. Then I nod.

"Can you tell us why you took the blame?"

I've asked myself this question over and over again since that July morning. Kitty had been horrid to me for most of my life. Even Robin—who had witnessed some of my sister's hostile behavior to me during our childhood—had questioned why I continued to be nice to her. But I just couldn't get rid of that longing inside. The need to have a sister who loved me. Who cared the way sisters are meant to care for each other. I kept thinking that one day she would grow out of it. That she would love me back. I pictured us as being best friends in the way that Vanessa and she were. I was jealous—I admit it—of Vanessa. I wanted Kitty to love me in the same way. I also knew that would make Mum happy.

But that's not the whole truth. And now it falls on me to fill in the missing piece.

"I took the blame because none of this would ever have happened if I hadn't forged a note in my sister's handwriting."

"You?" blurts out the machine.

I'm looking straight at Kitty now. It's as if there are only the two of us in the room. "You spilled coffee on my French essay. It's why I secretly pulled off your stitches from the knitting needles when you were working for the Scouts Craft badge."

"You did that?"

"Well, you shouldn't have ruined my essay."

It is as though we are arguing just as we'd done as kids. Except the machine is doing it for Kitty.

"And I thought you'd hidden my history notes, too."

Kitty is thumping her good arm on the chair so hard that Mum has to restrain it. "No, I didn't!"

"But I thought you had, you see. It was . . . well, it was just the sort of thing you would have done. It sounds childish now, but at the time, it was so real. You knew how important history was to me. I thought you wanted to destroy my chances of going to university. So I borrowed your English exercise book for an hour. I copied your handwriting and wrote a note to Vanessa, saying you didn't want to be her friend anymore. That's what I thought Vanessa was talking about when she said she knew something else. I presumed she'd found me out. I shouldn't have done it. I'm really sorry."

"OK. But why did you take the blame when I pushed Vanessa?"

Everyone is waiting. Deep breath.

"That day—you were standing up for me to Vanessa." My eyes are full of tears. "That was the first time you showed that you really cared about me. And then . . . then . . . the car came racing round the corner. You got hit. Vanessa died. And all I could think about was what Crispin had done to me. He deserved to be punished. How could I let you take the blame when you were in such a terrible state already? When I came to see you in the home, I felt so awful. So guilty. Especially as you were pregnant. What kind of life would your child have thanks to me? If I hadn't forged that note, you two might not have fallen out, and then none of this would have happened. Something inside me said I had to take the blame. I considered myself responsible for your injuries. My actions meant I had blood on my hands. They led to your best friend's death. So when it all came out, I said the truth—I pushed you. I just didn't tell them the rest of the story. That you got up and then pushed Vanessa."

Sarah leans forward, looking me in the eye. "When a shock like this happens, people can often assume responsibility for an action that had nothing to do with them. In a way, it's a bit like self-harming." She glances at my covered arms. "It makes us feel better sometimes to shoulder the blame. It might not seem logical, but it happens."

Lily nods. She looks rather distant. "I get that."

I swallow the lump in my throat. "It wasn't until I saw Kitty, lying there all crumpled up, that I realized how much I really loved my sister. Even though I didn't like her at times."

"Thanks!" chips in the machine's voice.

I almost laugh. Except it's not funny. It's true. Love is close to hate when it comes to sisters. You're as close as two humans can be. You came from the same womb. The same background. Even if you're poles apart, mentally. That's why it hurts so much when your sister is unkind. It's as though part of you is turning against yourself.

And that's why Vanessa was so jealous. She might have claimed to be a blood sister. But it's not the same thing.

Kitty, on the other hand, acted like a real sister. She's the one who wanted to shield me from the truth about my father. David might have promised not to tell me directly, but he'd made a big mistake in thinking that he could use his own daughter to tell me and get back at Mum that way. She could have done so easily—just minutes before the crash. She could have allowed Vanessa to spill the beans. But she stopped her. It's a sad tragedy that Crispin's mother was racing round the corner at the time.

"I begged her not to die," I add, recalling how I had knelt over Kitty's body.

Mum is white. "Did you really have to send yourself to prison?"

I reach out for her hand. "You'd been punished enough seeing Kitty in the state she is in." My grip tightens. I think back to my men in Archville: the ones I'd worked with quite happily until I knew what their crimes had been. "How would you have managed if you'd known that she'd pushed Vanessa in front of the car?"

Mum is silent. It's answer enough.

Sarah clears her throat. "My feeling, Alison, after getting to know you in the last few weeks, is that you might have had a breakdown after the rape, and then the accident. You've never got over the shock. It's not surprising."

I think back to that terrible time when it felt as though there was a lead weight on my chest. The grief was too deep to cry. Vanessa's death and Kitty's horrific injuries were too terrible to be true. How could the rest of the world go on around them when something like this had happened? Something I had started.

"You didn't have any counseling at the time, did you?" says Sarah softly.

I glance at Mum. "No."

"No one suggested it," she says desperately.

"Please—I'm not blaming you. Counseling wasn't so common in those days. I'm just saying that not all head injuries are obvious." She glances at Kitty. "And I think, Alison, that you are still suffering from post-traumatic stress disorder."

Could she be right?

"Take the identity of the driver. You said it was Crispin. Did you feel bad about lying?"

I hang my head. "Yes," I whisper. "Well, not at first. I did it out of anger. But when he didn't deny it, I couldn't take it back. And then over the years, I've . . . I've honestly convinced myself it was him at the wheel. It was the only way I could cope with the fact that I'd put an innocent man into prison."

Meanwhile, Lily is writing furiously. "Would you say in court," she asks Sarah, "that the rape, combined with the shock of the accident, made Alison take the blame for an accident that she did not cause?"

"I would," says Sarah. Her eyes are milky with sympathy. "If you ask me, you were the one who was pushed—mentally—over the edge."

My throat swells. My eyes blur.

"Some people," adds Sarah, "have an overactive conscience, especially if they're constantly seeking praise or have low self-esteem."

I wince. So does Mum. I can tell she's beating herself up, too.

"Hang on," Mum says in a quiet voice. "If Kitty pushed Vanessa, does that mean she could be tried for manslaughter now?"

Lily's usually steady voice now wavers slightly. "It's unlikely, given her condition, and that she was a child at the time. And there's something else that should be taken into consideration." She reaches into her bag and brings out a black book. It has a year written on it in silver loopy writing: *2001*.

"Vanessa's mother gave it to me after I went to see her recently. It's her daughter's diary."

The first page falls open. It is dated 2 March 2001.

My mother loves me more than anyone else . . .

When we finish reading, Mum and I look at each other for a long time.

"It looks," whispers Mum, "as if Vanessa was jealous of the two of you. She wanted Kitty all to herself."

My mouth is dry. "But she was also angry with Kitty for the note that said she didn't want to be her best friend anymore." My voice comes out as a cry. "It was my fault."

"No." Mum takes my hand. "It's mine for letting David spoil Kitty. For not telling you the truth about your father in the first place. I'm so sorry, my love. I was scared. I didn't want to be alone again."

I can see that.

"It must be very hard," Mum continues, "to be an only child."

How often had I wished during my childhood that I didn't have a sister. It was only when Kitty had been so terribly injured that I'd appreciated what we'd had—or rather what we could have had.

"I know Kitty wasn't easy," says Mum. "But I always hoped that when you both grew older, you'd get closer. Poor Vanessa didn't have that hope. Look at this entry."

It's dated 1 January. Just over six months before the accident.

My Christmas wish still hasn't come true—the one that I made a whole year ago when I helped Mum make the cake. I asked for a brother or a sister. It only takes nine months. I know that from biology at school. But nothing's happened.

My mother's eyes are blurred with tears. "Vanessa's mother had several miscarriages. She told me once."

I swallow the lump in my throat. "Some of the entries sound very grown-up."

"Only children often are. I always thought she acted like someone who was far older."

That was true. It just seems a shock to read these adult thoughts on the page.

But it's the final entry that really gets me.

18 July 2001

Tomorrow's the big day.
   After that, Kitty will be all mine. Like a real blood sister.
   Ali will blame her for sharing the secret with me.
   And she won't want anything to do with Kitty again.

It occurs to me, as I read this, that Vanessa and Kitty have just handed me the key to my particular prison. Yet I don't want it. I deserve to be locked up forever. Not just because of what happened that day. But for something else.

77

February 2018

Kitty

O n the way home, Kitty pretended to be asleep like baby Vanessa. But inside, her heart was going thud, thud, thud. "It was the machine's fucking fault," she kept saying to herself. Yet at the same time, she felt a whole lot better inside. It was like this big weight had been lifted from her shoulders. Almost as heavy as that huge wave that had nearly carried her off until Half a Sister had rescued her all those years ago.

But now Lily had Vanessa's diary! Vanessa would go mad if she knew that. No one was allowed to look at her diary. Not even Kitty. "No," Vanessa used to say when she was writing in it. "It's mine. *PRIVATE*. See? Can't you read?"

The funny thing was that she still loved Vanessa, even though she'd been so horrid at times. That's why she'd named the baby after her. "Love makes no sense." She'd heard someone say that on the telly. And it was true.

When they finally got back, Friday Mum took ages to get her into the house. "Stop it," she said when Kitty grabbed her arm to make her hurry up. "You'll give me another bruise. Your father should be around more. It's not fair."

Flabby Face Dad? No way. Kitty shuddered. If he hadn't told her the secret about Ali's dad, none of this would have happened. No wonder he'd upset her so much in the home. They were better off without him.

Then little Vanessa began to yell.

"Stop it," shouted Kitty. "You're hurting my ears."

But, as usual, all that came out was a loud stream of nonsense.

"Where's the carer?" Friday Mum ran her hands through her hair. "She's meant to be here by now to help put you to bed."

"How the fuck should I know?"

Maybe it was just as well they'd left the machine behind. Sometimes, Kitty almost felt ashamed of the things her mouth came out with. And her throat hurt with all the angry noise that she just couldn't stop.

"I don't know who to feed first," cried Friday Mum. "You or Vanessa."

"Me! *Me!*"

But the baby was screaming loudest. Friday Mum picked her up and held her close, right next to the wheelchair. "There, there, little one. It's all right." Then she glanced down at Kitty. "You'll just have to wait a bit, love. I'll be as quick as I can."

That wasn't bloody fair.

"Kitty!" shouted Friday Mum. "What are you doing? Let go of her. You'll break her leg."

"Then fucking well feed me first."

Her grip tightened. Vanessa was bawling so much it sounded as though she was choking.

"Stop right now!"

Why should she? It wasn't right that the baby always got more attention. Ouch!

Kitty looked down with horror at her arm. There was a bright red handprint. Friday Mum's.

"What have I done?" Friday Mum was sobbing as much as Vanessa now. "I was just trying to stop you hurting her like that. I didn't mean to hurt you, too."

Friday Mum was sitting on the floor now, rocking Vanessa back and forth and holding Kitty's good hand—the same one that had grabbed the baby. Then she reached for her phone. "I'm sorry I have to do this, love. But something's got to give. We can't go on like this."

78

June 2018

Alison

Today, I am finally being released. Lily says things have happened fast, but it has seemed incredibly slow to me. She has managed to get my conviction overturned. Kitty's testimony was taken into account, as well as my revised statement and Sarah's psychological report.

Over the last few months, Sarah has helped me to see what she calls "the bigger picture." My stepfather had low self-esteem. Bullies often do. He had resented me for being part of Mum's old life. For symbolizing the man who came before him.

"But why did David tell Kitty about Stefan?" I asked Mum. "Surely, most people would try to shield their eleven-year-old from such a terrible story."

"I think it was to get back at me out of jealousy." Mum looked wistful. "He knew your father always had a special place in my heart, despite everything. Sometimes, you can't help who you love."

Meanwhile, I can comfort myself that, awful as the accident had been, it had proved that Kitty had put me—her half sister—before her best friend and her own father who had expected her to spill the beans. Deep down, she really loved me. Just as I loved her. If only we had been allowed to grow up together into adulthood, we might now be the kind of sisters I'd always envied. We'd go shopping together. Visit Mum. Maybe push babies along, side by side. "The sister relationship is one of the most complex of all," Sarah said to me during a final session. "You might think you dislike each other, but you are bound by such strong ties that it's almost impossible to break away."

Right now, everyone has come to the door of the wing to see me off. On the way out, I spot Angela.

"I'll miss you, Alison," she says.

"I'll miss you, too," I say. It's the truth. Quite why, I don't know. You'd think I'd resent her for having got me into trouble over the stationery cupboard. But she's more than proved her friendship here. People aren't all good or bad. Besides, she didn't do it out of spite. Most of us in this place have done wrong out of desperation.

An officer takes me to the gate along with a plastic bag containing the few possessions I had when I came in. There's only one that I want.

Carefully, I take it out and fasten it round my neck.

Kitty's locket. After Mum had given it to me—and I'd destroyed the Crispin photograph—I'd felt surprisingly comforted. It had helped me imagine that if the locket wasn't damaged, then my sister was all right, too. But now I know different, thanks to Sarah. "Pretense," she says, "is a bit like alcohol. A small amount is all right. But too much can distort your vision."

Mum's car is there, waiting. Little Vanessa is strapped safely in the back. My heart gives a lurch. She has grown so much since I last saw her. Part of me wants to pick her up. The other part is too scared in case I drop her.

I still find it amazing that my sister chose to give her that name. Maybe she felt guilty, too. Or perhaps she still loves the old Vanessa despite everything.

"Darling."

Mum holds me in her arms. For a minute, it feels like it's just the two of us again, exactly as it was all those years ago.

"How is Kitty getting on?" I ask as we drive out of the gates.

My mother rubs her eyes. They are red. But her arms aren't bruised like they used to be.

"She seems quite happy in her own way. The other day, she told me—through the machine—that she had 'better food than the crap in the last place.'"

We both give a half smile.

"She also said that she got 'proper lessons' now. I see what she means. The old home had some lovely staff who helped her with her picture board. At the time, I didn't realize there was so much more that could be done. This home specializes in brain injuries rather than general disabilities. She has one-to-one help now with her hand-eye coordination. The other day, she actually used the weak arm to help tie up her own shoelaces."

"That's incredible."

So, too, is the world that's whizzing past. The world that I purposely stepped out of after the accident in order to protect my sister and mother. One where people are walking by with shopping. Unaware of prison life and all the lies that go on inside.

Mum stops at a crossroads. "But I can't help feeling guilty for not being able to cope anymore."

"It's not your fault," I say firmly.

Shortly after Kitty's confession, Mum found she simply couldn't handle the responsibility of a baby and my sister. There had been some drama, apparently, when Kitty had tugged at her baby's leg and caused bruising. Mum admitted she'd then smacked Kitty. It was enough for the authorities to sit up and take notice.

Now Kitty has been sent to a unit that offers special care. Not because of her role in Vanessa's death—as Lily said, owing to her mental condition and her age at the time of the accident, there was no case to make against her—but because she can't stop herself from lashing out in frustration.

"When can I go and visit her?" I ask, putting on my seat belt awkwardly. It's been a while since I was in a car.

"They say it's best to wait a bit. Until she settles down."

But there's something else that's wrong. I can sense it.

For a moment, I think that she's guessed the one thing I've kept back.

"What is it, Mum?"

Her eyes glance in the mirror. "There's someone here to see you."

I follow her eyes to the other side of the car park. I freeze. I would know that tall figure anywhere.

Clive.

I could have told him to leave. Just as I did when he visited me in prison.

But I didn't. Instead, I am sitting with him, a few days later, on a bench overlooking the Thames, near to where we walked on our first night together.

"I read about the appeal and had to get in touch again," he says simply.

I wait for him to continue. Silence, I have learned from Sarah, can make people say more than they mean to.

"I feel so bad about what happened. I cared for you, Alison. I really did. In fact, I still do."

I search my heart. Examine it for signs that I feel the same. But there's nothing there. For a minute, I think of my sister. She never talks about Johnny now.

"Please forgive me," he says.

The very words that my father used shortly before he died. How can I expect to be forgiven if I don't forgive others?

"Yes," I say. "I do."

He takes my hand. I wait for that thrill. That insanity I'd felt before. It doesn't come. "Could we try again?" he asks.

As he speaks, a couple walks past. The man has one of those baby carriers close to his chest. There's a mass of very blond hair poking out. He bends down and kisses the top of the child's head. I might have had a baby like that by now if I'd made different choices. Perhaps it's not too late.

"No," I say softly. "I'm sorry."

Robin is handling our case. Mum and I need to meet him to discuss our "strategy." I am both scared of seeing him and excited.

Anyway, here I am. Sitting in a restaurant not far from the bay where we used to swim when we came here on holiday.

St. Ives had been Mum's idea. "What you need," she had said softly, "is a new start. I've been thinking of moving for a while."

So here we are. In a seaside town that we have both always loved and is close to Kitty's care home. The light is perfect for painting. I've got a job at a local art college. I've even bought myself a new wet suit and swim most mornings. There's nothing like that bracing shock of cold followed by a hot shower. Even though I know the sea can turn on you. Just like life.

It was Robin's idea to come down rather than me going up to London to see him. Mum bailed at the last minute, saying she needed to stay with Vanessa rather than have a babysitter.

"You're looking good." His eyes take in my hair, which I've allowed—at Mum's suggestion—to "grow a bit." I've put on some weight and no longer look quite so scrawny.

"I feel better being here," I say. "The sea calms me down."

"I know just what you mean. I miss it." He shuffles in his seat. "And I miss . . ."

He stops.

What? I almost say. But the moment has passed. Instead, he hands me a file.

"I've gathered statements from the social worker; the baby group in the library that your mother takes Vanessa to; the local doctor and everyone else I can think of who vouches that Vanessa is thriving in your mother's care. Can you take a look?"

He pushes it towards me. Our hands fleetingly brush. I feel an unexpected flash of something. It's not what I had with Clive. Yet it's comforting. No, more than that.

For goodness' sake, I tell myself crossly. Haven't you got enough to deal with?

I glance through the notes. "There's something else," I add. "It won't just be Mum who'll be looking after Vanessa. So will I."

"Really?"

I nod. "I'm going to set up my own studio, too."

"I'm glad. It suits you here."

He pushes away his plate. The sea bream is delicious, but neither of us has an appetite. All I can think of is my sister in a place that we're not even allowed to visit yet until she "settles down."

"Vanessa belongs with us. We have to do this for my sister's sake," I say softly. "It's the one thing I can do for her."

79

July 2018

Kitty

___

B-E-L-L-A.

That was the name of the new girl who'd moved into the bedroom next to hers. Kitty knew that because it was written in pretty letters on the door. Her mother had done it with pastels. Kitty's name was just typed, like all the others here.

Bella had some gorgeous stuff in her room.

"I love your duvet cover," said Kitty, admiring the pink and blue frills.

"Thank you," said Bella slowly. "Mum made it."

Kitty had gotten a new speaking machine that Call Me Jeannie bought for her. Sometimes, this was helpful, and sometimes, it wasn't. They didn't take kindly to swearing here, and she didn't always remember to switch it off before she thought something bad. The woman who ran the meditation class said you had to breathe the good things in and breathe the cross bits out.

Bella was really calm. Maybe it was because the lorry that had crushed her head took away the angry bits. She wore a helmet like Kitty's. And she had dark hair poking out from underneath, just like her.

"You look like twins!" said Nice Carer No. 1.

"I've always wanted a sister," said Bella through her machine.

"Me, too," said Kitty, after flicking on her own.

"I thought you had one."

Kitty pondered this. "I do. But there's only half of her."

Bella held out her hand. It was all floppy and limp because of the lorry. "I could be your sister, if you like."

Kitty felt a buzz going through her. "Cool," she said through the machine. This was her favorite word now because it was Bella's, too. "I'd like that."

Her new friend reminded her of a nicer Vanessa.

That triggered another memory, too. Something about a girl called B . . . Barbara! Straight Fringe Barbara. The schoolgirl who had helped out in the home in her spare time and had got them together in a band. The one who had noticed when she'd been upset by Flabby Face Dad and had run off with her wheelchair until they'd been stopped at the end of a corridor.

It struck Kitty now that she'd liked Barbara because she'd reminded her of someone else. That was it! Her old best friend Vanessa. They'd both been nice at times but bossy at others. And they were good at music. Johnny had been in the band, too. He'd loved her until he fell in love with someone else. But now she didn't need any of them.

Because she had Bella instead.

Friday Mum and Alison came to visit the other day. They brought a kid, too. It was yelling.

"We're going to make sure we can always look after Vanessa for you," said Friday Mum.

Who was Vanessa? Kitty had a vague memory of blond plaits. Then it was gone again.

Then Half a Sister handed something to her.

"My locket!" said the machine.

"They say you can wear it if you're careful not to catch it on anything," said Friday Mum.

"I'm not a fucking baby." Then she opened it. Inside was a picture of a pretty young girl. She had plaits and a sweet smile. It reminded Kitty of someone.

"That's you when you were younger," said Half a Sister. "I put it there when you weren't . . . weren't able to wear it."

"Why?"

"Because I love you."

Kitty felt something lurch in her heart. "I love you, too."

Then Half a Sister and Friday Mum looked as though they were going to cry. But the kid got in first.

"Can you go now? That thing is hurting my head. I can't think straight."

They left soon after that. That was better! She could get on with her finger painting, and then it was fish cakes for tea. And everyone—especially the new girl next door—thought the locket was lovely.

80

September 2018

Alison

———

I'm about to start a new class. I love this feeling. That sense of excitement. Hopefulness. Not just for my students, but for me, too. This is the first stained glass workshop I have done since my sentence. It will be a test, my counselor says.

"You hold your scalpel like this," I say to the class. "Always wear gloves."

"What if we cut ourselves?" asks someone.

Her words send a chill through me. It's been ages since I hurt myself intentionally. And I plan to keep it that way. "Let me know immediately. I have a first aid kit ready."

There's a knock at the door. I bite back that wave of irritation when a student is late and I have to go over my instructions again. Still, I've only just started . . .

I open the door. Then I stop. A man is standing there, in a blue and red jacket similar to the one he used to wear as a teenager. His hair has grown a bit since I saw him two months ago. It suits him. But he still bears the same anxious expression.

"I know I haven't signed up, but the college said there was one place left." Robin's eyes hold mine. "Is that all right?"

The weeks pass. All too soon, it's the day of the custody hearing. I'm so nervous that I can hardly breathe.

"It will be all right," says Robin when I meet him at a café near the law court in London. Mum has already gone inside to settle Vanessa.

"Do you mean that?"

"We've got a strong case."

"So has Johnny's family. They've got more money."

"But you have the love."

I'm not sure how this is happening, but his hands are reaching out across the table and holding mine.

"This isn't the time or place to say it, Ali."

I almost butt in to correct him. But in a weird way, the old Alison is no more.

"I've always loved you." He looks down at his plate and then back at me. "I blame myself for that party."

My head is spinning from the first part of his sentence. "Crispin's? Why?"

"Because I got you the invitation. I wrote one of Crispin's essays for him so he'd give you one. I'd . . . I'd hoped that when we were there, I might've been able to get closer to you."

I'm confused. "But he said he'd asked me."

"He was jealous. I could tell that when I was foolish enough to confide in him. His words were . . . I'll always remember them . . . 'I thought there was more to that girl than met the eye.'"

I feel sick. "You can't blame yourself."

Robin's eyes mist over. "Exactly what I keep telling you."

We are still holding each other's hands. "After the case," he says slowly, "I think we need to talk."

"Yes," I say simply.

Together we walk towards the court where Vanessa's future will be decided. My heart is pounding again. But it is also singing.

For the first time in a long time, everything is beginning to feel right.

I am sorry for Johnny's family. Well, for his mother anyway. It is clear—even to the family judge—that it is Jeannie who really wants the baby rather than her son—their situation is rather like ours since Kitty doesn't seem to miss her daughter. Johnny is there, too, but he keeps smooching with the girl next to him, just as he used to with my sister. And his father hasn't given a very convincing display of affection towards his granddaughter. "No," he admits, "I haven't visited her."

Mum and I are awarded custody, although Johnny's family has visiting rights. At last, I have done something right for my sister. It might not make up for that terrible summer day or all those years when we squabbled as children. But it's a start.

"You can come and see Vanessa whenever you want," Mum says to Jeannie.

"Thank you."

The two women hug each other: I can tell there is genuine respect on both sides. And why not? They both know what it is like to have a special-needs child who is now an adult with all the demands that this imposes.

"Can you hold Vanessa for me, love?" says Mum as she disappears into the ladies afterwards.

I don't have a chance to say no. This is the first proper time I've had with her; nerves have always made me duck out of it before today. Now it's just my niece and me. What if she chokes? *Can* babies choke out of the blue? Supposing she yells and . . . I don't know. Has a fit or something like that? I'm not responsible enough to hold her.

Vanessa stares solemnly up at me, those blue eyes taking me in. *We'll be all right*, she seems to say. *We can learn together. I'm game. Are you?*

But would she still think that if she knew what I'd done?

81

September 2019

Kitty

———

Half a Sister had got huge. Friday Mum said she had a baby inside. The Oh Tee at this place—much younger and more patient than the last—said she'd help Kitty knit something for it. Bella was going to knit something, too.

"We need to do these things together," Bella said through her machine. Then she took a needle from Oh Tee's tray when she wasn't looking and pricked her finger. "You do the same," she said.

"Then we'll be blood sisters." Kitty felt a flash of unease. "But good ones. Not like me and Vanessa."

"Who is she?"

"A friend who was horrid to me."

"That's not nice."

"No."

Bella frowned. "What do blood sisters do?"

"They're always there for each other. You know. They do stuff together. They're like real sisters except that they aren't actually related."

"Can they knit together?" asked Bella.

"I suppose so. Why?"

"For your sister's baby, of course."

Kitty had almost forgotten about that.

"What color shall we choose?

"White," said Kitty firmly. "Mum says that does for either a girl or a boy."

"I wish I had a baby," said Bella suddenly.

"Do you?" Kitty sniffed. "I had one once. But it cried too much."

"Couldn't you stop it?"

"I tried to cuddle it, but I bruised its leg by mistake."

Bella rolled her eyes. "Then maybe I wouldn't like one after all."

Oh Tee was bustling over to them now. "Didn't you two hear the lunch bell?"

Kitty's good hand reached out for Bella's. "Fish cakes and broccoli. Come on!"

FIVE YEARS LATER

———

82

Alison

———

"Ready, everyone?" asks Robin, handing the girls their packed lunches.

It's our daughter's first day at school. She's jumping up and down with excitement because she can't wait to join her cousin. Their new shoes are shiny. The girls have matching shoulder bags. They look so grown-up!

I hadn't meant to get pregnant. But I will never forget Robin's face when I told him.

"We're going to have a baby?" he said, as if needing confirmation.

It was the "we" bit that confirmed his commitment and love for me.

We're living together now with Mum and Vanessa (whom Robin and I have adopted). The arrangement works surprisingly well. Kitty's daughter is surrounded by love. When our own daughter was born and Mum brought Vanessa in to visit, she'd torn into the maternity ward, her little face bursting with excitement. "My sister!" she'd said with a reverence that made her seem so much older.

I waited for the usual "big sister" jealousy. But it never came. Instead, Vanessa followed me around like a little hen, helping me to bathe Florence and feed her. "I'll look after her at school," she declares now. It's almost as though she was born to fill the role. One day we'll have to tell her about Kitty, who is still very happy in the unit. But not yet.

Robin is an amazing father. He's opened up a practice here but operates "family friendly" hours. At weekends, he takes the girls swimming and fishing so I have time to paint. Every now and then, he asks me to marry him. "I'm happy as we are," I say gently.

"I can't understand why you don't say yes," says my mother, who's been hoping for a white wedding.

That's simple. Marriage means total honesty.

And there's one thing Robin still doesn't know about me.

Once, I read somewhere that sometimes a secret has to be told in order to stop another from slipping out. I've told most of mine.

But I've kept just one in reserve.

A few months before I took the prison job, I'd had a letter. (The one that I'd hidden in my small bedside nightstand.) It was from the lawyer who had represented us when Crispin was originally convicted. The letter informed me that Mr. Wright was soon to be moved to an open prison. HMP Archville. A place I already lived near. Since receiving the letter, I'd been keeping my eye out for an opportunity, and when I'd spotted the job advert in the college—advertising a post in the very prison Crispin was being moved to—it seemed like the perfect opportunity. Fate playing its hand.

Yes, I did need the money. I really was broke. But I also wanted revenge. Crispin, as I later discovered, might have thought he was luring me in. Yet what he didn't realize was that I chose to go inside to follow my own agenda. That's why I had to hang on to my job until I could work out a plan.

At first, I told myself I just wanted to see him. To have my say. A prison sentence is all very well, but it doesn't allow a victim to confront the offender. I wanted to yell at him. Let out all the anger about the rape.

Besides, in my mind, he hadn't suffered enough.

Then, when I finally met Crispin in "my" prison, I realized—or so I thought—that he didn't recognize me. It occurred to me that I could pretend not to recognize him, too. So when he'd claimed never to have done art before going to prison, I went along with it—even though I knew this had been his strength at school. If he could lie, so could I. About bigger things, too.

When you work in dark places, you find that same darkness creeping into your soul, too. It's catching. You need to be on your guard—just as I was when those threatening notes arrived *before* Crispin came to my prison. I didn't know he had a hand in it. It's why I was so scared. Then, when Crispin did turn up, I felt the blackness sucking me in. That's when I formulated the final details of my plan.

What if, one day, I sent a message to all the students—apart from one—in my prison group to say that my class was cancelled due to the virus going round. This would mean that the one I had left out would still turn up: Martin. Or rather Crispin—my old enemy. If this got out, I told myself, I could always say that somehow Martin hadn't got the message and had shown up anyway, keen to do the class. That I'd taken pity on him.

This would mean we'd be alone in a room together with no witnesses. A necessary risk if I was to get my revenge.

What if I then pretended that Crispin had attacked me by claiming he had tried to strangle me with my scarf—my trademark dress signature? What if I actually tightened the scarf myself to make it look as though *he* was responsible? Then he would surely get another sentence and have to stay in for even longer.

Of course, none of this could be achieved without danger to myself. But what if—and this is the big one—I happened to be carrying a shard of glass with me, which I could use in self-defense?

It had worked almost like a dream. Yet there was one big flaw. I hadn't banked on Stefan rushing in to save me. Or on him grabbing the glass from where it had fallen. Or on Crispin killing him.

Through some awful, ironic twist of fate, I am responsible for my own father's death. Another to add to my list of crimes.

You can see why I can't tell Robin. Now my only hope is that there is some redemption in the next generation.

"Hold my hand," Vanessa says to my daughter. Her tone startles me. It sounds bossy instead of kindly. "And hurry up, or we're going to be late."

It's as though she's in charge and I'm not here at all.

Together we walk along the narrow lane. Two little girls. One taller than the other. Both with blond plaits. Both wearing the same smart navy blue uniform. Both chatting away, nineteen to the dozen.

Mum isn't your real mum, I can hear my daughter saying.

What do you mean? asks my sister's child.

Your *mum is really in a home for loonies.*

Stop it, I tell myself. Remember what Sarah told you. You can't keep imagining the worst anymore.

"Excited?" I ask them.

Vanessa nods her head. Her flute case is thumping against her legs. Florence wants lessons, too.

Then, holding hands, we stand at the traffic lights, waiting to cross the road.

Squeaky-clean school shoes.
    Shoulder bags bobbing.
Blond plaits flapping.
Two pairs of feet. One slightly larger.
"Come on. We're going to be late."
There. Safe.
For now.